Satyr's Son

LUCINDA BRANT BOOKS

'Quizzing glass and quill, into my sedan chair and away —— the 1700s rock!'

Lucinda Brant is a *New York Times*, *USA Today*, and *Audible* bestselling author of award-winning Georgian historical romances and mysteries. Her books are renowned for wit, drama and a happily ever-after. She has a degree in history and political science from the Australian National University and a post-graduate degree in education from Bond University, where she was awarded the Frank Surman Medal.

Noble Satyr, Lucinda's first novel, was awarded the $10,000 Random House/Woman's Day Romantic Fiction Prize, and she has twice been a finalist for the Romance Writers' of Australia Romantic Book of the Year. All her novels have garnered multiple awards and become worldwide bestsellers.

Lucinda lives in the middle of a koala reserve, in a writing cave that is wall-to-wall books on all aspects of the Eighteenth Century, collected over 40 years—Heaven. She loves to hear from her readers (and she'll write back!).

lucindabrant@gmail.com | lucindabrant.com

pinterest.com/lucindabrant | twitter.com/lucindabrant

facebook.com/lucindabrantbooks | youtube.com/lucindabrantauthor

A GEORGIAN HISTORICAL ROMANCE
ROXTON FAMILY SAGA BOOK FIVE

Lucinda Brant

A Sprigleaf Book
Published by Sprigleaf Pty. Ltd.

Satyr's Son: A Georgian Historical Romance.
Copyright © 2017, 2021 Lucinda Brant, all rights reserved.
Editing: Martha Stites, Cathie Maud Cabot & Rob Van De Laak.
Art & design: Sprigleaf. Model photography: GM Studio.
Cover models: Charlie Hesse and fictional male composite.
Custom jewelry: Kimberly Walters, Sign of the Gray Horse
Reproduction and historically inspired jewelry.
Lisa's Inkwell fleuron design by Sprigleaf.

Cover images: "*Schloss Pillnitz Englischer Pavillon Dresden*" by Rufus46 (Wikimedia
Commons); "*Blenheim Palace 7057958973*", (Wikimedia Commons); scene and foliage
from Royal Botanic Gardens, Kew, by Lucinda Brant (author's own photographs).

Georgian couple silhouette is a trademark belonging to Lucinda Brant.
Sprigleaf triple-leaf design is a trademark belonging to Sprigleaf Pty. Ltd.

Typeset in Adobe Garamond Pro.

Also in ebook, audiobook, and other languages.

ISBN 978-1-925614-89-3

10 9 8 7 6 5 4 3 2 1 Studio Art Perfect Bound Paperback Edition (s.iii) I

for

Karen
Lucinda P.
&
Mari

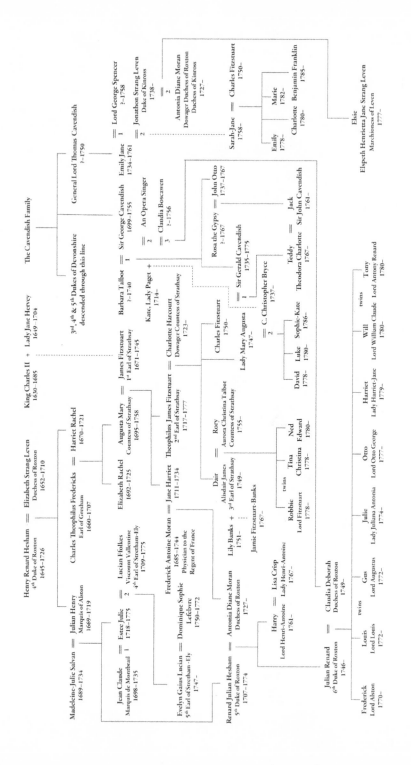

PART I

THE CITY

ONE

GERRARD STREET, LONDON, SUMMER 1786

IT WAS A SHORT WALK TO LEICESTER SQUARE FROM WARNER'S Dispensary in Gerrard Street, where Miss Lisa Crisp resided with Dr. and Mrs. Warner. She hoped the errand would see her returned before her absence was noted. It was a needless worry. She wouldn't be missed on a Wednesday afternoon. Perhaps on any other day of the week, when she assisted in the dispensary, but not on a Wednesday when she could do as she pleased. But as she was poor and friendless, she had no one to visit and nowhere to go.

This Wednesday was to prove the exception.

To the Warners, Lisa was simply there, like a piece of furniture, or the scullery maid, and thus rarely thought of at all. Perhaps this assessment was a little harsh, and more about how she felt about her situation rather than what the Warners thought of her, because the Warners were not a vindictive couple. It was just that they were unmindful of others. Dr. Warner was wholly absorbed with his medical practice, which was understandable and commendable, while Mrs. Warner was so self-absorbed that there was very little time in her day for others.

Robert Warner was an eminent physician and anatomist, and when he wasn't attending to patients at his dispensary, or making home visits to one of his wealthier more needy patients, he was shut up in the garret of his townhouse. Here was his anatomy school and laboratory, where he revealed the mysteries to be found inside the human body to fresh-faced, eager medical students during the autumn and winter months.

Mrs. Warner gave her husband as much liberty as was necessary for him to focus solely on his medical expertise. This gave her the freedom to be indolent. She never stirred from her bedchamber before noon, an hour that was very much *à la mode* with Polite Society. She read every scrap of gossip printed about these rarefied persons with all the fervor of a zealot, as if, by the very process of absorbing social minutiae about the nobility and their habits, she qualified for admittance into their select society. She did her best to ape them in every particular.

The couple frequently entertained, Mrs. Warner encouraging her husband to have guests at the table to further their—but mostly her—social ambitions. Her greatest desire, of which she made no secret, was to be addressed as 'my lady'. After all, Dr. Warner was a medical genius and deserved a baronetcy at the very least. Her husband was humbly in accord. And so with their societal ambitions aligned, suitably socially-connected individuals were regular diners at their Gerrard Street townhouse.

Lisa did not join them, when the couple dined alone, or when they had guests. She ate her dinner in the small parlor at the back of the house. For although she was not a servant but a cousin of Mrs. Warner, her indigent background and shameful past precluded her from a seat at the table among persons of an elevated sensibility.

Lisa accepted this with equanimity, as she had everything else life had thrown at her since being orphaned at nine years of age. But as she did not like eating alone, she made sure to have a good breakfast to avoid a lonely dinner; supper was routinely a cup of tea and a slice of bread on a tray in her room. If the Warners' son was still awake, she joined Nurse and helped console baby George, who was presently teething, until he fell asleep. She then spent the rest of her evening reading or writing in her diary.

Had Lisa set off to walk all the way to Portsmouth, she was certain the Warners would not have noticed her absence until the next day at the earliest, when she rose with the sun to be present at the breakfast table to provide the doctor with conversational company, should he lower his newssheet and wish to pontificate on a subject of importance to him. He never asked for her opinion. Whether a mind as vast as his thought her incapable of logical argument and thus unable to offer a response worthy of his intellect, she had no idea. Or perhaps it was because she was female, and thus her place was to listen, not to participate.

Whatever the reason, it mattered not to Lisa, who had a thirst for knowledge—her teachers had labeled her unquenchable—and thus she was content to listen to the physician with her coddled eggs, toast, and hot chocolate. And Dr. Warner had a lot to say: About the deplorable state of medical education in this country, the intractable religious opposition to the use of cadavers to advance medical knowledge, and that political bigots needed to have their eyes prised open to see that the only way forward for medical science was through scientific investigation. And that meant getting one's hands dirty with the blood and filth that was part of life. *Enlightened times called for enlightened action, not just thinking.* This phrase was oft repeated and usually signaled an end to the morning's diatribe. Dr. Warner then retreated once more between the pages of his newssheet, leaving behind a deathly silence, and Lisa to read in peace the newspapers discarded by the physician.

Lisa had been following this routine every day for two years, and while her daydreams were no different to those of any nineteen-year-old girl—falling in love, marrying, and being mistress of her own home—she was grounded enough to know such thoughts were the stuff of fairy tales, and what she could reasonably expect from life was a roof over her head, coal in the grate, and food on the table. Which was more than the vast majority of Londoners could hope for, so she was not ungrateful.

And so, as neither Dr. or Mrs. Warner would wonder at her whereabouts this fine summer's day, Lisa did not feel obliged to tell them or the household servants where she was headed. Though she did raise servant eyebrows when Cook, in conversation with the housekeeper, paused mid-sentence to watch her pass through the kitchen and leave via the servant entrance, wearing her sensible half-boots, a wide-peaked bonnet, and cotton mittens to keep the sun from turning her white skin brown.

Outside she was met in the small service area that was below street level and open to the air and noise of town, by one Becky Bannister, seamstress and haberdasher's assistant. Becky served behind the counter of her great-aunt's shop, Humphreys' Haberdashers, on the corner of Gerrard and Princes Street, and when called upon, visited clients in their homes. A well-built girl with dark hair and rosy cheeks, she bobbed a respectful curtsy and prepared to pick up the basket at her feet, eager to be off. But Lisa was not ready just yet to ascend the steps into the noise and heat of town.

Spying empty flour sacks airing atop a stack of crates, she took two and neatly placed them across the second-to-last step to save their petticoats from grime, and invited Becky to sit beside her. They needed to talk, in the shade and away from the incessant racket to be had at street level. Becky readily complied, but her smile dropped into a frown when Lisa said firmly, "Before we visit Lord Westby's residence, you had best tell me again what happened, and what it is you took."

"Miss, I done told ye," Becky explained. "I ain't took nothin'. The book fell into me work basket—"

"—and you decided to borrow it. Yes. You told me so this morning, but I need to know precisely what happened if we are to prevail upon His Lordship not to press charges against you for theft." When the girl's bottom lip quivered, Lisa smiled reassuringly and placed a hand on Becky's bare forearm. "If you say the book dropped into your basket, I believe you. Please, Becky. Tell me everything, and from the beginning. I said I would help you, and I will."

Becky sniffed and nodded, and some of her apprehension eased. Yesterday, when she had picked up her basket full of notions knowing the book was there, her only thought was that she might be able to exchange it for the shilling owed her by Peggy Markham, Lord Westby's mistress. But upon a night's reflection, her confidence in such a scheme fled, which was why, when Miss Crisp had come into the shop to purchase thread, she'd appealed to her for help.

Though this young woman was about her age, Miss Crisp possessed an innate maturity far beyond her years. And Becky had come to regard her, as had many in the area with cause to visit Warner's Dispensary, as someone to be trusted, and good in a crisis. And because Miss Crisp could read *and* write, she was the dispensary's resident amanuensis, for while the majority of Londoners prided themselves on being able to read, very few had been taught to write. So when an ailing family member was being attended to by a dispensary physician, another would sit with Miss Crisp in a designated corner of the waiting room—she with her sloping writing box, ink, and quill—and dictate to her a letter, which she then wrote for them. Often these were letters home to family in far off counties, filled with details about their new lives in the capital. Sometimes they were letters seeking employment or patronage. All were deeply personal and relied on Miss Crisp's discretion. Whatever the contents of these letters, the author always felt satisfied and better within themselves seeing Miss Crisp inscribe their words in ink.

Thus Becky knew that whatever she confided in Miss Crisp would be treated with respect and in confidence. But as much as she tried to keep the panic from her voice, it was there, just bubbling under the surface, as she recounted her visit to the Leicester Square townhouse inhabited by one Lord Westby, and where also resided his mistress, the celebrated actress of Shakespearean tragedies Mrs. Peggy Markham.

The actress had sent to Humphreys' for a selection of ribbons, hose, and garters, and so Becky was dispatched with a basket containing various boxes of the desired goods for Mrs. Markham's perusal. Her aunt pressed upon her that this time she was not to leave behind any merchandise without first getting Mrs. Markham's signature to the account.

"That's 'cause she took three ribbons, then refused to own she 'ad seen 'em, sayin' I'd made a mistake in me reckonin'," Becky explained to Lisa. "Which I never does 'cause Aunt would give m'ears a good box were I to lose coin on any of our trimmin's. So I know 'ow many ribbons I 'ad before I left the shop, and it weren't the same as when I was puttin' everythin' back into me basket!"

"And this time...?" Lisa prompted when Becky clenched her teeth in an angry huff.

"A pair o' garters. Pink silk with a pretty painted silk panel o' flowers. Worth a lot more than three ribbons, and I ain't told m'aunt them are now missin' too!"

"And Mrs. Markham refused to own she had the garters?"

"Aye. She did. I said I'd add them to the account, along with the three ribbons from the time before, and that made her mad—"

"I imagine it would," Lisa murmured.

"—and she called me a pert miss and threw up her 'ands. Said 'ow dare I question 'er word. She told me to gather me trimmin's and pointed to the door, in that dramatic way actresses 'ave about 'em. But I stood me ground."

"That was brave."

Becky glanced slyly at Lisa and confessed. "Not so brave as you think, Miss. I wanted to scramble out o' there faster than a fox in huntin' season, but me legs wouldn't work on account of 'im who was there."

Lisa frowned, trying to make sense of Becky's story. "There was someone—there was a gentleman—Lord Westby—with Mrs. Markham?"

Becky shook her head. "Not 'im. I know what 'is lordship looks like on account of 'im bein' there the first time I was. This time she was entertainin' a different gent, if you get my meanin'."

"Entertain—? Oh! Oh! I see. Are you certain?"

"I weren't born yesterday. In my line o' work I can't afford the liberty of blushes and such. I go into chambers off-limits to most. But no one takes a flea's bit o' notice of a 'aberdasher's girl, now do they? Not like I'm a visitor. Not like they got to be on their best be'avior."

"I dare say you're right... But what I meant was, are you certain it was a different gentleman and not Lord Westby?"

"As certain as I am that you are a proper lady, Miss!"

Lisa blushed. "How lovely of you to say so, Becky."

"I'm not the only one who says so. Everyone round 'ere says it. *A proper lady that Miss Crisp is*, that's what they say. Just as I can tell you with certainty that the gent who was with Mrs. Markham weren't the one and the same as the one keepin' a roof over 'er 'ead. 'E came out o' the bedchamber dressed only in his—"

"Thank you, Becky. I don't need specifics."

"—shirtsleeves, and he 'ad the book that's now in m' basket. Which is why I mention 'im. But I didn't see that right off 'cause I was starin' at 'im—No need to be coy, Miss. He was dressed," she assured Lisa, taking a peek under the brim of Lisa's straw bonnet when she dipped her head, a sudden interest in her hands in her lap. "But it weren't 'is clothes I was starin' at. It was 'is face. You'll think me feverish, but 'e's bewitchin' 'andsome."

"Oh, Becky! Bewitching? Truly?" Lisa interrupted with a giggle.

"I ain't given to exaggeratin'!"

"Of course not," Lisa replied, contrite, and pressed her lips together to stifle any further incredulous mirth.

"You'd think the same if you saw 'im. Eyes and 'air blacker than a coal pit. His nose is a bit of a beak, but y'know what they say about gents with big noses—But you wouldn't—Anyways, 'is mouth more than made up for 'is beak. Too pretty for a gent." She grinned and confessed, "I just wanted to take 'is face between me 'ands and kiss it all over!"

When Lisa gasped, Becky's brow darkened.

"Just 'cause I wanted to don't mean I ever would. I know me place, and I know a gent like that wouldn't look twice at Becky Bannister, or, for that matter, at you, Miss. For the likes of you and me, 'e might as well live on the moon. Though a girl can dream, can't she?"

"No offence taken," Lisa replied with an understanding smile. "I agree. I daydream, too. My surprise had more to do with the gentleman's description than any disapproval of your wish to kiss him. He sounds perfectly god-like, that he could very well have a place on Mount Olympus. Which is practically the moon, isn't it?"

"I don't know nothin' about Mount Oly-what's-it-called, but you're right. Mrs. Markham feels the same way, 'cause 'e only 'ad to speak for 'er to go all doe-eyed and forget I was there, 'cause his voice is worthy of a swoon just like 'is looks; rich and smooth it is, like the way hot chocolate slides down y'throat…"

"A voice like hot chocolate? Dear me, Becky, you have a lovely turn of phrase," Lisa complimented, clearing a suddenly dry throat.

"Aunt Humphreys says it's 'cause I daydream—*a lot*. But I wasn't daydreamin' in Mrs. Markham's boudoir. That gent was no phantom of me imagination! And m'knees might've gone weak and m'tongue dried out, but m'ears were still workin'. I remember what 'e said. 'E said that 'e only tolerated theatrics on a stage. And for 'er to come back to bed and finish what she'd started. 'E had an auction to *attend*." She nodded, satisfied she had relayed what the handsome gentleman had said, adding for emphasis because Miss Crisp was now staring at her with lips parted, "Auction. That's what 'e said. 'E was goin' to an *auction*."

"And he came into the room with the book that's now in your basket...?"

Becky nodded.

"'E did. I never noticed 'e 'ad it at first 'cause I was busy lookin' at 'im. But then I went back to scoopin' up the ribbons and as I was puttin' 'em away Mrs. Markham gets off 'er dressin' stool—and this is the truth, as God is m'witness—and pulls off her chemise and lets it drop to the floor. Just like that! And that's when I see me pink garters keepin' 'er stockin's up! She took 'em all right! But can you blame 'im for forgettin' about 'is book? 'E takes one look at 'er naked, and lets drop the book into m'basket while she's helpin' 'im out o' 'is breeches—"

"May I see the book, Becky?" Lisa interrupted and stuck out a hand.

She was no prude, but she did not pry into the private lives of others either. What they did behind closed doors was no one's business but their own. Her shock had more to do with the couple's lack of circumspection and disregard for their servants. No wonder gossip about members of Polite Society managed to find its way into the newssheets for her cousin Minette to pore over with her tea and cream cakes, if that is how they behaved. She did not doubt that enterprising servants managed a secondary income from passing on such salacious tidbits about their masters to the newspaper hacks.

Quickly shaking her thoughts clear of Mrs. Markham and her nameless lover, she returned to the business at hand, because the afternoon was closing in, and they were still seated on the servant step in Gerrard Street. The sooner they delivered the book to Lord Westby's townhouse, the sooner they could put this episode behind them.

The book was larger and heavier than she had anticipated, and opening it, the frontispiece told her almost everything she needed to know. It was in fact a catalog, worth the princely sum of five shillings, and contained a listing of the entire contents of the Portland Museum, once owned by the Dowager Duchess of Portland, and which now, upon her death, was being sold by auctioneers Skinner and Co. Lisa

had read reports of the month-long auction in Dr. Warner's copy of
The Gentleman's Magazine. The Dowager Duchess had been a great
patroness of Natural History, and a voracious collector of all things
associated with the science, from corals, to all manner of shells,
animals, insects, petrifications, plants, minerals, and related paraphernalia.

Flicking through the catalog's pages, she noticed annotations in the
margins beside items for sale, and returning to the frontispiece she saw
inscribed in the same elegant fist the initials H and A, separated by a
hyphen. So the catalog did not belong to Lord Westby, and perhaps
Peggy Markham's lover was this H-A? Her interest in the actress's lover
increased tenfold, for according to Becky, not only was the gentleman
handsome beyond what was expected of a mere mortal, he was
possessed of an elegantly sloping script, and from the mark-ups in the
catalog, had an interest in old snuffboxes and sea shells.

What immediately crossed Lisa's mind and made her heart beat
faster was twofold: That the owner needed the catalog to be admitted
to the auction, and as he had marked particular items not yet come up
for sale, she was confident he would most certainly be looking for his
missing catalog. Secondly, and most disturbing, as the catalog was
worth more than a shilling, its theft would be considered grand
larceny, and a guilty verdict meant a sentence of death by hanging.

None of this Becky needed to know at that precise moment, so
Lisa smiled bravely, hoping not to give away her fears, and returned the
catalog to her.

"Is there anything else you should tell me about your visit to Lord
Westby's? Or about this catalog before we head off?" When Becky
shook her head, she stood and brushed down her petticoats, adding in
a tone she hoped exuded confidence, "Good. Then when we arrive at
Lord Westby's, you had best let me do the talking."

Becky nodded and smiled, picked up her basket, put it over her
arm, and gave a huge sigh of relief.

"Thank you, Miss. I knew that if anyone can get that book back
inside without me bein' dropped into a 'ot vat o' trouble, it'd be you!"
She cocked her head in thought. "D'you think you could get 'er to put
'er mark to 'er account, too?"

"One small miracle at a time, Becky," Lisa said with false buoyancy,
and went up the steps to street level.

Lisa and Becky walked as one down Gerrard Street and up Princes Street towards the river. The racket and bustle at street level precluded conversation, so they stayed silent, the basket up front between them, and kept on the lookout for pickpockets amongst the criss-cross of pedestrians and vocal street vendors. Soon the narrow streets opened out and they were on the corner of a spacious cobbled square, fronted with rows of elegant townhouses, the grand mansion of Leicester House, once home to various members of the Royal Family and now occupied by Sir Ashton Lever's Museum of Natural History, forming the square's northern border. Central to this wide expanse was a large quadrangle of grass with gravel crosswalks and dominated by a gilt statue of the first King George. Here, within the confines of an iron fence, privileged residents took idle walks, and nursemaids supervised children in leading strings or running about in the summer sunshine with their hoops or kites. A crossing sweep worked every corner, and there was enough space for carriages, sedan chairs, riders on horseback, and pedestrians to pass one another with ease.

Once the center of Polite Society, and still home to a few aging remnants of Hanoverian royalty and their hangers-on, the square was an echo of its former glory. The city and its industry had sufficiently encroached on its elegance that several of the townhouses were now occupied by shops and manufactories, a sign of the changing times. Persons of title, wealth, and influence had moved out a decade or more earlier and gone west to a more countrified aesthetic, where the palatial squares were filled with new townhouses, healthier air, and were occupied exclusively by their own kind. Those who remained in Leicester Square, whether through lack of funds or foresight, and whose townhouses were squeezed in amongst industry, did their best to ignore their changed surroundings and their mercantile neighbors.

Lord Westby was one such resident. Heir to the Duke of Oborne, His Lordship occupied a townhouse belonging to his father, who had long since departed for the noble environs of Westminster, leaving his son to exist in a tall, narrow townhouse squashed between a carpet manufactory and the Dowager Marchioness of Fittleworth's residence. Whenever His Lordship stepped out into the square he made a habit of looking north to her abode, and never south to his mercantile neighbor.

Lisa, who had never had reason to visit Leicester Square, was fascinated by it all. In her preoccupation with the variety of pedestrians and the continual parade of carriages and sedan chairs going to and fro, she almost forgot why she was there. That was until Becky stopped in front of Lord Westby's residence.

"The servant door is back down the lane and—"

"Oh no, Becky," Lisa said, holding fast to the girl's arm. "We enter by the front door, or not at all."

Becky's eyes went wide and she swallowed. She had never entered a house by the front door, ever.

Lisa went up the shallow step and lifted the silver knocker, only for the door to be wrenched open before she could knock, as if someone had been at the window peering out into the street in anticipation of their arrival. Startled, Lisa stumbled back onto the cobbles.

A short squat man with bulging eyes and a grizzled wig appeared out of the blackness.

"You're late!" he hissed, and opened the door wider. "Come in! Come in! Quickly! Quickly!"

TWO

THE PORTER MOVED ASIDE TO LET THEM ENTER, BUT WHEN LISA and Becky just stood there, recovering from the shock of such a reception, he stomped out onto the footpath, darted behind them, and fluttered his hands low, at his bended knees, as if driving a flock of geese.

"Go in! Go in! Don't stand about! Go in!"

The girls shuffled forward, looking over their shoulders to see what the little man was up to. And once they were in the vestibule, he slammed shut the door, making them jump. They clung even tighter to one another and glanced about. But there was a decided lack of wax in the sconces, and after the bright sunlight of a summer's day outside, their sight needed time to adjust to the darkness. This was denied them when out of the gloom pounced a tall, stick-thin man with a long chin and furrowed brow. He glared down at them from a great height before looking over their heads to demand imperiously,

"Where are the others?"

"O-o-others?" Lisa stuttered, a swift look up from under her peaked bonnet.

But he hadn't addressed her. He was talking to his squat associate.

"No carriage, Mr. Packer. These two came on foot."

"No carriage? *On foot?*"

The tall, imperious personage, who Lisa decided was the butler of this establishment, rolled his eyes and sighed, as if this were the worst possible news he had ever received. He stepped to one side of the staircase, giving Lisa no time to explain, flicked a bony finger in direction of the first landing, and said in voice heavy with the worries of the

world upon his pointy shoulders, "You two will have to do—for now.
Up you go. First landing. Second door on the left. No need to knock.
Just go in."

"I beg your pardon, but there seems to be some misunder—"

"My dear girl. Don't beg my pardon. It isn't up to me or you or
your cherry-cheeked friend to wonder at the whys and wherefores, or
the how-tos, for that matter. You're here, aren't you? His lordship and
the Batoni Brotherhood don't make a habit of waiting—for anything.
Now up you go."

"Bat—Batoni Brother*hood*?"

"You're an inquisitive one, I'll say that for you!" the butler snorted,
rudely looking Lisa up and down. "Take my advice and keep your
voice bottled. You're not here for your conversation."

Lisa balked to be so familiarly addressed, and arched an eyebrow in
disapproval. "Am I not?"

"Hardly! Though to look at you—Well! You all come in different
shapes and sizes and—um—talents, don't you. So it's not for me to
say—"

"—because you're not here for your conversation, either?" Lisa
quipped, and accompanied this with a deceptively sweet smile.

"Ha! I suppose I deserved that," the butler replied good-naturedly.
"If you're quick about it, you might even get to choose your quarry,
before your friends arrive."

Lisa had no idea what he was talking about. She glanced up the
stairs, which were as ill-lit as the vestibule, and then smiled reassuringly
at Becky, who, if she had any confidence in this venture before they
entered Lord Westby's townhouse, now had none. She had lost her rosy
glow and her eyes were wary.

"Friends?"

The butler rolled his eyes again and gave a snort, a glance at Becky.
"If not friends, then your female brethren." He jerked a thumb at the
staircase. "Now up you go! Quick! Quick!"

Lisa wasn't sure what compelled her to take the course of action she
did because her first impulse was to hand over the catalog to the talk-
ative butler with the excuse she had found it in the street, then flee the
scene with Becky without divulging who they were. But something
compelled her to hold her ground—curiosity, stubbornness, impetuos-
ity, she wasn't sure which. She decided that to ascend the stairs into the
unknown without fear of the consequences might at least provide some
light relief from the ordinariness of her present and predicted future,
and prove an adventure worth taking.

It was this same adventurous—the headmistress of Blacklands

called it impetuous—streak that had seen her abscond from the school grounds to meet a friend at the Chelsea Bun House. It was the third such visit and the one reported to the headmistress, and it was her undoing. She was expelled just six months shy of her graduation. The Chelsea Bun House incident had forever tarnished her in the eyes of her school and family. But when she reflected upon her actions—and she'd had two years in which to do so—she was confident she would not have acted any differently. And with a reputation so tarnished it would never regain its luster, taking this risk would be of little consequence, surely?

But she had no wish to drag Becky into further misadventure, so she did her best to dissuade her from venturing upstairs.

"Give me the catalog, Becky," she whispered. "You may stay here while I—"

"No, Miss. I'm comin' with ye!"

"Please. I have no idea who or what we'll encounter upstairs. Very possibly an angry lord and his mistress. And as they don't know me, I may be able to persuade them to accept the catalog without further explanation. So it would be better for you to remain—"

"No, Miss. Beggin' ye pardon. I done brought y' 'ere," Becky stated stubbornly and hugged the basket closer. "We go up together, or not at all. They're me terms."

"Very well. But promise me, if I decide we need to leave—for whatever reason—we will—immediately."

When Becky nodded, Lisa untied the ribbons of her bonnet, and handed this to the butler. He held this article of feminine attire between thumb and forefinger, as if it were poisonous, and gave it to the porter. Lisa lightly patted the wisps of hair come free from her coiled braids, then smoothed her cotton mitts over her slim arms, as if steeling herself for the interview. Finally, without a second look at the butler, she nodded to Becky and they went up the stairs.

They followed the butler's directions, and at the first landing Lisa picked up a lighted taper in its holder from a corner table to light their way along the dark passage. At the second door on their left they stopped. Instinctively, Becky hung back, and Lisa gave her the taper. She did not knock to announce their presence, but opened the door and went straight in.

Not in their wildest imaginings could they have foreseen what awaited.

SEVERAL HOURS EARLIER, MEMBERS OF THE BATONI Brotherhood had gathered for their regular bi-monthly get-together, this time at the townhouse of Lord Westby, whose turn it was to play host. The Brotherhood's membership consisted of a select group of young gentlemen who had taken the Grand Tour together. Sent off by their noble parents with tutors, valets, and servants in tow, they had wandered through France, Switzerland, the Italian States, and Greece for three years. Returning home via the Mediterranean coastline and with a better appreciation of their classical education, they brought with them trunks laden with artworks, sculptures, books, finely-tailored clothing, and anything else from antiquity that took their fancy.

While abroad, these sons from Polite Society's first families made a pact that, upon their return, they would meet up once every other month to reminisce, discuss their collections of *objets d'art*, to eat a splendid supper, and drink themselves under the table. These gatherings had been going on now for just over a year, and were eagerly anticipated by all members of the Brotherhood.

But the Batoni Brotherhood was about to change forever. Sir John 'Jack' Cavendish was to be the first of the foursome to take the plunge into matrimony. While they had been well aware of the inevitability of the match—Jack had become engaged to his future bride almost immediately upon his return from the Continent—they were still in denial. The marriage had been set for early spring, only to be delayed to allow the bride's mother to sufficiently recover from the birth of her fourth child.

The delay suited the Brotherhood. No one wanted change, though they all respected Jack's wish to marry his childhood sweetheart. It was just that this get-together would be the last time they would meet as bachelors. And while everyone was determined to enjoy it for Jack's sake, there was an undercurrent of disgruntlement that this could very well be their last meeting.

Yet none of the members had voiced their concerns publicly. Lord Henri-Antoine 'Harry' Hesham, Jack's best friend, had said not a word. But that was typical of Lord Henri-Antoine, who kept his thoughts to himself, was economical with his words, and scathing in his opinions.

The other two members, Sebastian 'Seb' Lord Westby and Mr. Randal 'Bully' Knatchbull, had known Jack and Henri-Antoine since Eton. They considered Jack an affable, uncomplicated fellow, loyal to a fault—a true Trusty Trojan. Seb and Bully understood Jack. Henri-Antoine was another matter entirely. He was black to Jack's white, and always had been. He was as open with his feelings as an uncracked walnut, and about as friendly as a March gale. They had never understood him or, for that matter, the close friendship between such opposites. Jack wouldn't hear a word against Harry, even when his best friend directed his acerbic remarks at him, which was rare but occasionally happened.

Lord Westby and Randal Knatchbull were a little afraid of Lord Henri-Antoine Hesham. It was not that he would ever lift a finger in violence, raise his voice, or not help them out of a scrape. They were confident of his loyalty. It was just that, unlike with Jack, or the fellows in their extended circle of friends, they were never entirely comfortable in his company. They were uneasy being silly for its own sake, and playing a prank just for laughs became asinine under Henri-Antoine's fixed gaze. His silence spoke volumes. It made the back of their necks itch.

As for venturing an opinion on a subject which held gravitas, such as politics, religion, a point of law, or the latest play, in Henri-Antoine's presence they thought twice about blurting out the first thing that popped into their heads. It made Bully's head hurt.

Bully hated confrontation of any sort about as much as he hated formulating a counter-argument, so he held no contrary opinions and agreed with everything anyone said, which meant he agreed with no one.

And they most definitely did not offer an opinion about the French—Henri-Antoine's name was French, and so was his mama; half his blood came from the other side of the Channel. Truth told, he spoke Frenchie better than he did English and, as they discovered to their eye-rolling amazement while abroad, he was fluent in the Italian language, too.

But Lord Westby's unease with Henri-Antoine ran much deeper. Just under the surface of his conviviality there raged a seething lava flow of resentment. Westby was envious of Henri-Antoine's person, his effortless pretension, but most of all the independence his great wealth afforded him. Bully put it more bluntly:

Face facts, Seb. Harry is handsome, arrogant, and rich. You're none of those things and never will be. He dresses impeccably; you'd think his voice was coated in treacle, it turns females liquid; and his pater left him a fortune—rumor puts it at a hundred thousand pounds. Can you imagine?! One. Hundred. Thousand. Pounds. To do with as he pleases.

But you, my dear Seb, have to beg, borrow, and steal from your pater, because you're up to your eyeballs in debt, and always will be. And if that isn't enough to boil your blood, Harry can and does have any woman he fancies. He merely has to look their way and they're tripping over them-

selves to get to him first! So it's no surprise, is it, that he's bedded more women than all of the Brotherhood combined.

The only reason you've managed to keep a hold on a celebrated actress as your mistress is because you—you, Seb, not Harry—agreed to her terms. If you don't share her with Harry, she's off! You pretend you don't care. You say that in the spirit of the Brotherhood what's yours is his. But that's complete pig's pap. It's a beggarly arrangement, Seb, and you know it. You suffer it because you'd rather cut off your blind boy as let him think you care a groat. No small wonder then that you hate him. If I were in your shoes, I'd hate him too. But when all's said and done, none of it is Harry's fault, is it? And that's what's eating away at you the most.

Despite the truth in his friend's blunt assessment, Seb continued to think of himself as the injured party. And while he managed to conceal his bitter jealousy for the sake of the Brotherhood, he failed miserably when inebriated. Today, having toasted Jack's upcoming nuptials with enough fine claret to keep a ship buoyant, Seb was drunk beyond circumspection. At today's Brotherhood gathering he was determined to say what he honestly thought—consequences be damned, and Henri-Antoine along with it. Today he would end the terms set down by his mistress, and banish his rival from ever again caressing her luscious feminine curves. He would show Henri-Antoine who was master in this house, and it wasn't Henri-bloody-Antoine-bloody-high-and-mighty-bloody-Hesham.

First he needed to fortify himself with a few more glasses of claret. So it was fortuitous when at the end of that thought his butler poked his long face around the door.

"More bottles, Packer! And be quick about it. And have this mess cleared away. Room smells like Billingsgate. Can't have Harris's harlots mistaking us for a bunch of salty sea dogs—"

"—or pirates, Seb. They could mistake us for pirates."

"Pirates, Bully? Well, I wouldn't mind being mistaken for a pirate. Still. Don't want to stink like one."

"Most definitely not."

"Pirates stink of fish."

"And oysters, Bully. Fish and oysters and-and—*seaweed*."

"But if the harlots were mermaids, well! It would be a different story entirely, wouldn't it?" Bully said confidently. "I'll wager they'd like us smelling of fish then."

"How much?"

"How much what?"

"How much do you want to wager?"

"Wager?"

"A guinea says the harlots won't care that we smell of fish."

"And oysters, Seb. We smell of oysters."

"Oysters then. A guinea that—"

"A salty sea dog is a pirate," Lord Henri-Antoine cut in. "And the harlots are paid to perform regardless of your stench. Packer? Get rid of this detritus... Brandy would be appreciated."

"Yes, my lord. At once," the butler replied.

Packer said something over his shoulder, then stepped to one side to allow two footmen to clear away the silver trays piled with oyster shells, squeezed lemons, baskets of bread crumbs, stack of used plates, and clusters of empty wine bottles. And while this was being carried out, he squinted into the smoke-filled haze to locate its occupants, and found Lord Westby collapsed on a sofa, his disheveled person under a mound of maps and opened guidebooks. His master's neckcloth was unraveled, and he had an empty wine glass in one hand and in the other a smoldering cheroot.

His Lordship's three friends were in similar repose.

Mr. Knatchbull was sprawled out on the rug at Lord Westby's feet, his stubby legs spread-eagled under a low table laden with the remnants of the oyster supper. He was perusing the pages of a small book, *Harris's List of Covent Garden Ladies*, held almost at arm's length, and like his best friend, was in his shirtsleeves. He made no effort to move out of the way of the footmen and continued reading while they did their best not to step on him or spill oyster shells and lemons over him.

The other occupants were slumped in wingchairs either side of a cold fireplace. Sir John Cavendish MP, copper curls falling into his eyes, had his long legs stuck straight out before him, with his heels seemingly dug into the floorboards to stop himself sliding forwards and off the chair. While seated cross-legged opposite was the only one of the Brotherhood not in his shirtsleeves, and unlike his fellows, who had pulled their stocks free from their throats as if needing air, his cravat was still neatly wrapped about his throat. In fact, the butler was not surprised to see that this gentleman as neat in his appearance as if he had just stepped away from his valet.

Lord Henri-Antoine was always at his sartorial best on any given day, at any given hour. And while his friends' waistcoats showed evidence of the oyster feast, His Lordship's black merino breeches were without creases, and his intricately-embroidered waistcoat and frock coat pristine. He was swirling the last drop of wine in his glass, head back against the chair, with his eyes closed. Yet, it only took an injudicious remark from one of his fellows for them to realize that while his eyes were closed, his ears were very much open to the conversation. Reason Seb and Bully's guinea wager was abandoned before it was placed.

Given their steady intake of alcohol over several hours, the butler was not surprised the gentlemen looked frayed about the edges. And while they might talk up the impending arrival of a clutch of high-class whores, the smoke and empty wine bottles were a truer indication of their physical fitness for such a venture. He did not doubt their alcohol consumption meant a wild over-estimation of their sexual prowess.

What a difference three hours made. When Lord Westby had eagerly pressed a list of names and addresses on his butler and ordered the carriage be sent to collect Harris's harlots, the gentlemen had been throwing back oysters and reminiscing about their time on the Continent. There was much chortling and guffawing about a particular incident at a brothel in Padua, and with anticipatory rubbing of hands together more than a few proclamations were made of repeating that escapade here. The prospect of receiving all manner of sexual favors from the best Harris's List had to offer had Bully jumping up on the sofa, holding aloft his wig and reciting a well-known bawdy ditty. Much laughter ensued and Packer had departed the room with the list, gaze to the ceiling.

But as Packer's gaze swept the carnage of an afternoon of continual celebration, he wondered if any of the Brotherhood were capable of walking unaided, and was certain they were about to waste the sixty pounds spent to lure the whores from their places of employment to visit Lord Westby's townhouse. But it wasn't his coin, or his business to comment, so he left the gentlemen to continue breathing air thick with tobacco smoke and sent a footman to the cellar for more claret, and a bottle of brandy.

THREE

THE DOOR WAS BARELY CLOSED ON THE BUTLER'S BACK WHEN Jack lifted his chin off his chest and frowned across at his best friend. "Do you think that wise?" When Henri-Antoine made no comment he hissed loudly, "Harry?! Harry?! Do you think—"

"I'm doing my best *not* to think."

"—you should have a brandy after so many bottles of claret?"

"You've been counting."

"No! Of course not!"

At this hot denial, Henri-Antoine opened an eye. The quick flush to his best friend's cheeks exposed the fib. He stared at Jack long enough to make him aware of his disapproval, then closed his accusatory eye.

"Oh, all right! I'll admit to it," Jack confessed, folding his legs back and sitting forward, a glance over at Seb and Bully, who were now huddled together on the sofa leafing through the pages of Harris's List. Confident they were otherwise occupied, he added defensively, "You can't blame me, can you?"

"It's not your concern."

"No thanks then for watching your back?"

"You want gratitude?"

"No! Yes! No! Of course not! But perhaps you should have Michel fetched, to take you home—"

"—and ruin this splendid gathering? Michel's not here. He's at the Portland auction, buying shells."

"Was that sensible?"

"Sensible? To trust Michel with the buying of shells?"

"Haha! No! Him there; you here."

At that Henri-Antoine opened both eyes with some effort. The thud to his temple was becoming unbearable. But bear it he would, and ignore it, and hope that this time the outcome would be different. That if he could just control the warning signs, then all would be well. But it was a futile hope. Still, he'd drunk enough wine and smoked enough cheroots in the past couple of hours to believe in fairy tale outcomes. What surprised him was that he had lasted this long without the onset of a full-blown seizure. But he was determined to make it through the afternoon because it was his best friend's bachelor send-off, and that only happened once in a lifetime. Thus he made light of Jack's concern, so he would not worry, and to mask how he felt.

"I'm glad you're getting married. Time to put your worry to good use... about something, not nothing."

Jack ignored the sarcasm. "You are not nothing, Harry," he said quietly. "Never have been, never will be. You should've gone to the auction."

"I've been every day for three weeks. Seen enough shells, minerals, and dead things, to numb the most ardent collector. But Elsie will have her shells... There was one in particular... A nautilus... I hope I remembered correctly... I seem... I seem to have misplaced my catalog..."

Jack caught Henri-Antoine's grimace, and was not fooled when he made a quick recover by pretending to brush lint from the upturned cuff of his metallic-embroidered lilac silk frock coat. He knew him too well, and knew the signs to watch out for. He'd been Henri-Antoine's best friend since they were nine years old, and he'd never broken his confidence. Not that Henri-Antoine had confided in him, but Jack had been witness to the onset of his seizures several times before being ushered away by his minders.

Henri-Antoine's affliction had remained an open family secret throughout his boyhood and was treated accordingly. The old Duke of Roxton had surrounded his youngest son with physicians, nurses, attendants, and servants. And he was watched over by his parents, his brother, close family, and had never been left alone a day in his life. Any medical specialist who professed to be an expert in the treatment of the falling sickness had been consulted, from London to Constantinople. There was no known cure, but by the time Henri-Antoine had reached his teens, he had managed to convince his mother and his brother that his malady had cured itself.

It was a lie.

Jack had bought into the lie because he knew how important it was to his best friend to be thought of as just the same as every other fellow his age. Yet, it remained a mystery how he had convinced his physician to lie, too, and before his ducal parents. Henri-Antoine had even told his father he was cured, and the old Duke graciously believed him. But Jack now suspected—and he was sure Henri-Antoine did too—the old Duke had bought into the lie because he was dying, and that his young son hoped that by telling him he was cured it would somehow make his cancer go away. Henri-Antoine had loved his father so very much. The old Duke died a few weeks later. Henri-Antoine never spoke of his father again.

But the intensely private younger brother of the present Duke of Roxton still struggled with the falling sickness. Not every day, as had been the case when he was a boy, but often enough for him to employ a coterie of servants to help him maintain the charade that he was as vigorous and as healthy as any young man of five-and-twenty. Which he was, in every respect, if he ignored the malady he'd been born with.

Jack understood Henri-Antoine's need for concealment, because the falling sickness carried great social stigma for sufferers and their families. He well remembered when, as boys, hushed conversations and sidelong glances were directed at his best friend. There were whispers amongst servants about a tainted bloodline; that the old Duke was to blame, paying for past sins with his young son's affliction. When a physician had hinted at madness, he was instantly dismissed. And when a Papist priest had suggested demonic possession and the need for exorcism, he was bundled from the Duke's Parisian mansion without his feet ever touching the polished parquetry. Jack and Henri-Antoine took great delight in watching the eviction, peeking out from behind a fat column in the old Duke's library.

Jack knew the last thing Henri-Antoine wanted was for his family to be the subject of scandal or ridicule because of his affliction, and so did everything his wealth could provide to ensure his falling sickness remained a closely-guarded secret. This meant Jack surreptitiously watched for signs of the onset of a fit almost as assiduously as did his best friend's household. But when he'd had a few drinks, his anxiety increased tenfold, and he was prone to vocalizing his fears, much to Henri-Antoine's chagrin.

"It's the smoke as well as the alcohol," Jack postulated, another furtive glance over at Seb and Bully. "Neither is good for you, and when combined—"

"This concern is touching, but unnecessary."

"Let me have a window opened, get you a flask of boiled lemon water—"

"For God's sake, Jack! Don't—don't—*fuss*."

Jack sat back but was undeterred, and persistent. "It's time you confided in Roxton—"

"No."

"—because, as you rightly pointed out, once I'm married, I'll have other concerns—a wife, and hopefully in the not too distant future, children. I want children, Harry. That means I won't be around as much, and you need—"

"What I need is for you to—to…"

Henri-Antoine paused and drew in breath, willing himself to ignore the pain. He averted his face, giving Jack a view of his strong aquiline profile, and momentarily stared at the fireplace littered with the ash and discarded tips from half-a-dozen smoked India cheroots.

"What do you need me to do, Harry?" Jack whispered loudly, hoping against hope that, like him, fueled by alcohol, Henri-Antoine's guard was down and he would confide in him. It was a hollow hope, and after all these years he should have known better. "Ask. Anything. You know I'm here for you—always."

"If you think I can't function without you… think again," Henri-Antoine said with quiet menace, which was much more effective than had he shouted. But he never raised his voice. "I'm not your cast-off lover… I'm not weeping buckets because you've forsaken me. Keep your concern for those deserving of it. Live your life… with your bride and brace of brats in the Cotswolds—wherever the hell that is—and never give me another thought. My life… My life shall… shall go on perfectly well without you—Ah! The brandy!" he announced in an altogether different tone.

He tapped the table at his elbow for the footman to set down the silver tray holding decanter and glasses. He then bestirred himself to splash a generous drop of the amber fluid into each, and offered one to Jack. But when Jack hesitated to take it, Henri-Antoine peered at him. Jack's color had deepened, and through the untidy curls his eyes were glazed, mouth drawn in a thin line.

"Take it, Jack," Henri-Antoine urged softly, and with a rare smile. "I want to toast our friendship."

Jack took the glass, swallowing down the lump in his throat. But his voice was still raw with emotion. "You can be vile at times, Harry. Do you know that?"

"I've never been anything less, dear fellow. Reason you are my only friend." He raised his glass. "To Jack. Dependable. Loyal. Responsible.

Loving... Your bride is deserving of the very best, and you are the best, Jack."

Jack grinned sheepishly, losing his petulance, and the friends clinked glasses. They savored the brandy.

"Thank you, Harry. You'll always be my best friend. It's just—It's just—"

"—you've found your mate. More correctly, she found you. I am exceedingly happy for you both... I hope you are blessed with a brood."

"I wish—I wish you could be as happy as I am... That you, too, had found your soul mate."

Henri-Antoine pulled a face. "*Me*? A soul mate? And fairies are real! I grant I am excellent marriage mart material... But... what poor wretch would willingly take on the care and watering of such a pathetic creature?"

"I believe there is someone out there for you. I do," Jack said earnestly, eyes glassy again because this admission was the closest his friend had ever come to acknowledging the weakness of his affliction. "You just haven't found her—and she hasn't found you—yet!"

"Oh, don't be forlorn," Henri-Antoine said dismissively. "I'm not you. I can't imagine restricting my carnal appetite to a single female. There are too many beauties deserving of my—um—*largesse*. What is it, Bully?" he drawled, catching sight of Randal Knatchbull waving Harris's List above his head in an effort to attract attention.

"Are there six or eight nymphs coming to entertain us, Harry?"

"Eight," Henri-Antoine replied. "Jack gets first pick—"

Jack's face burned. "Not me. Not ever again."

Henri-Antoine looked at the drop of brandy in his glass, then lifted his gaze and teased Jack mercilessly.

"Indeed?" he purred. "But... I seem to recall... Yes! Those were your exact words as we stumbled up the steps into Frau Dortman's cathouse in Berne... You made the same lame protest in the vestibule of Signora Lucia's bordello in Milan. And while we were in Florence—Well! Your attempts to resist the charms of that pretty redhead were feeble at best. You—"

"Shut up, Harry!" Jack demanded hotly and shot to his feet. "If you dare say another word—"

"Your wishes are noted. So is your prudery."

"I intend to be a devoted husband, and you know it."

"I do." Henri-Antoine sighed heavily. "Regrettably, uxoriousness is a family failing." He threw back the last drops of brandy. When Jack continued to stand over him with hands clenched, he briefly closed his eyes. If Jack had one failing—no, two—it was that he was earnest to a fault, and that he rarely, if ever, appreciated Henri-Antoine's playful provocations. So he said to placate him, "I see I'm being vile again... I do beg your pardon."

"Jack? Don't tell me Harry is demanding first pick of the rose-buds?" Seb called out, happy to witness a rare altercation between the best friends. He sneered. "Are you surprised? After all, he paid for the bunch!"

Henri-Antoine waved a languid hand in Seb's direction without looking at him. "Take your pick, Westby. My treat."

"Any particular favorite?" Seb asked. "I presume you've tasted the delights of all eight of the lovelies coming here?"

"Ignoring your woeful mixing of metaphors, I would never serve a dish I hadn't tried and could recommend myself."

Seb puffed on his cheroot and blew a smoke ring towards the ceiling in direction of Henri-Antoine. "Flower or dish, it makes no difference. I'm sure they're all fragrant and delicious. Perhaps I'll try them all."

"You do that," Henri-Antoine stated flatly, and turned back to the fire and closed his eyes.

"Harry?! I say, Harry!? Is this your mark beside the Jamaican beauty of Litchfield Street?" Bully enquired, unaware Henri-Antoine had turned from the conversation because his nose was back between the pages of the little book. "Says here she treads the Cyprian stage. Says she's got white teeth and dark brown ringlets."

Henri-Antoine called out without turning around or opening his eyes.

"Miss Wilson would be well worth your time, Bully."

Randal Knatchbull's eyes widened. "Would she? Would she indeed? Thank you. I've always fancied a golden brown beauty, and it says here she—"

"But will she fancy you, Bully?" Seb interrupted with a snort of derision. "Sounds a bit exotic for your bland tastes. Best stick to the pap you know, and what they can stomach."

This cutting remark, made in an attempt to have the others laugh at Bully's expense, caused Henri-Antoine to rally and fix his derisory gaze on Lord Westby.

"Had you bothered to read Miss Wilson's excellent précis, Westby, you'd have kept your mouth shut. Now you've opened it... It behooves me to point out that her—um—*purse* requires a lover in possession of a *telum* of superior length and breadth—"

"Your *telum* I suppose?" Seb scoffed.

"Naturally. I'd not have wasted my money or insulted her talents by offering her anything less than she demands."

"Harry's in the right, Seb," Bully said, scrambling along the sofa to shove Harris's list in Lord Westby's face. "See. It's written here that Miss Wilson can contain the largest thing any gentleman can present her with but not the smallest—"

"I've no interest in a whore with a diseased purse," Seb interrupted, snatched the book and tossed it aside. "Or to know anything about—"

"Not diseased, Bully," Henri-Antoine assured his friend when Randal Knatchbull instantly looked to him for reassurance. "Seb seeks to malign the winsome Miss Wilson because he cannot meet her terms."

"Be damned if I can't!" Seb growled, jumping to his feet, cheroot stuck in the corner of his mouth. "If that's a challenge, I readily accept!"

"If you want the truth to stay buried in your breeches where it belongs, sit and be quiet."

Swaying, Seb waggled a finger in Henri-Antoine's direction. "You're a fine fellow to offer advice! You'd do well to keep yours in your breeches—"

"But that's just it, Westby," Henri-Antoine drawled, a slight twitch to his upper lip. "I do have a fine fellow. Much in demand. As Miss Wilson—and others too numerous to mention—can attest. Ask her. Though… if you know what's good for you…"

"Eh? Who are you to know what's good for *me*?"

"Seb! Seb! Don't be a complete zany," hissed Bully, grabbing at Westby's shirt sleeve and attempting to pull him back down onto the sofa. "Seb! You never win with Harry! Never!"

"Shut your porthole!" Seb snarled, and yanked his shirtsleeve free so violently that Bully lost his balance and fell sideways into the sofa cushions.

"Hey! That was a bit rough and ready, Seb!" Jack complained. "Don't leave him there. Help him up, Seb!"

But Seb ignored Jack, and Bully flailing about on the sofa cushions, attention wholly fixed on Henri-Antoine who remained cross-legged on the wingchair, unperturbed and lightly holding the brandy glass by the tips of his long fingers. His friend oozed arrogant self-assurance. And why not, when he had inherited a king's ransom from his father to live life as if he were a sultan of his own empire, employing more servants than most ducal households. He never left his house without two of their number as his constant shadow. They were downstairs now, kicking their heels.

And if Henri-Antoine's wealth and arrogance weren't enough to gnaw away at Seb's insides, it seemed that any harlot with a beating heart couldn't get enough of Harry Hesham's *fine fellow*. And that included Seb's mistress. Last night she had rejected his advances, boldly telling him, as she stretched across the bed like a satisfied feline who'd just finished a dish of cream, she was exhausted after an afternoon spent with Lord Horn. He knew to whom and what she was referring, and he had stormed out to her harsh laughter ringing in his ears.

Now, as he continued to stare at Henri-Antoine, the wonder of it was that after all these years of festering resentment, his internal organs hadn't rotted away.

"What do you know what's in my breeches, eh?" Seb finally spat out. "Over my dead nutmegs will I allow you to malign me! Stand up, Hesham! Let's settle this here and now! Jack! Bully! Furniture against the walls!"

"It's not slander if it's the truth," Henri-Antoine drawled, and without moving a muscle in response to Seb's threat. Although he was well aware his next words would goad his friend beyond tolerance, he said them anyway because Seb was a fool and needed to be verbally shaken awake to his enslavement to a second-rate actress whose best role was between the sheets. "I have it on excellent authority that I am —quite literally—twice the man you are."

"Why you-you—*whoreson*," Seb raged, face burning bright as he scrambled over the low table to get to his quarry. "I'm going to break your beak, Hesham. I'm going to mash it all over your face. Stand up! Stand up I say!"

He launched himself at Henri-Antoine as if he was jumping off a jetty to board a boat, both legs in the air, and arms swinging wide.

Jack intercepted him, stepping in front of Seb just as he landed by Henri-Antoine's chair, who remained seated and did nothing to defend himself. But he did not need to. Seb crashed into Jack and they were knocked sideways in the collision.

Jack threw his arms about Seb and tackled him to remain on the ground. They wrestled and as they grappled with each other the low table was overturned, the remaining glasses and bottles not collected up by the footmen crashing to the floor. Cheroots, maps, books, and several small paintings stacked at one end were tossed in the air and scattered across the room.

"Bully!? Bully!" Jack rasped in a thin voice, Seb's fingers twisted up in his neckcloth pressing on his windpipe. "Get—over—here! Help!"

"You get off *me*! Damn you!" Seb demanded, thrashing about because Jack now had him pinioned to the Turkey rug. "Stop playing brother's keeper! He needs a lesson! Some humility knocked into him! Dammit, Jack!"

Jack wrenched Seb's fingers free of his throat, and gulped in air. While he was coughing, Bully scrambled up off the sofa, sending that piece of furniture banging up against the window. He scuttled across the room, but far from helping either of his friends, he just stood there staring down at them with his arms folded, watching them struggle.

"You're as drunk as an emperor, Seb," Bully observed. "The felines will be here soon, and you don't want to look a crazy or they'll be too frightened to come near you."

"Get him off me, Bully! Get him off!" Seb demanded, legs kicking out wildly into thin air, Jack now sitting on his chest to keep him down.

"Sorry, Seb. Can't do that. Can't let you break Harry's nose. It's the only one he's got. Dare say he's fond of it, even if it is a beak."

Seb made a sound of disgust in his throat, and decided the only fellow who was going to help him was himself. Fuelled by a drunken fury, he realized he had more strength than he thought possible and so he gave Jack an almighty shove. It worked. Jack was thrust up and off him and with such force that he tumbled and slid on his buttocks across the polished boards.

"Now you're for it, Hesham!" Seb declared with satisfaction, up on his feet.

Having dealt with Jack, he was eager and confident he could deal with Henri-Antoine. But he took less than two steps when Bully came to life. He leapt onto Seb's back in a last minute attempt to stop him doing violence to Henri-Antoine, who still remained unmoved in the wingchair, an interested spectator to this drunken melee between friends.

Bully wrapped his legs around Seb's waist and hooked his stockinged ankles together, and with his arms about Seb's neck, stuck fast. He would not let go, no matter how many times Seb twisted this way and that. Finally, Seb grabbed Bully's wrists and yanked them apart. And while his friend was flapping about, quickly pulled his ankles free from around his waist. He then discarded Bully as if he were divesting himself of a winter cape.

Astonished to be upended with such ease, Bully forgot to drop his feet and hit the floor with a thud. He yelped with pain.

Henri-Antoine decided it was time to end this farce.

In one fluid movement he uncrossed his legs and brought himself to his full height. He was the tallest in the room. But his size was deceiving because he was slim and wiry, and with an elegant unhurried ease that tended toward the foppish. His penchant for elaborately embroidered waistcoats and frock coats in shades of purples and blues cloaked his physicality, and so his athleticism was often overlooked. But he maintained the same daily physical routine his father had insisted upon when he was a boy, all to strengthen his constitution in the hopes it would ward off, if not cure, his seizures.

These days he was pragmatic. He did not now believe he would ever be cured, and as physically fit and athletic as he was, it was all for nought when he was in the grip of *morbus caducus*. From the onset of a seizure until sometime after it abated he was as oblivious as a newborn, and just as vulnerable. And so he employed minders—his lads, as he called them—to get him to a place of safety and seclusion, and to watch over him until the seizure passed.

The thudding headache and sudden sensitivity to light should have been enough of a warning, and yet, because it was Jack's bachelor send-off, and because of his own stubborn pride, he had refused to heed the signs and continued to drink and smoke. More fool he, because now there was a drunken Seb determined to do him a physical harm. But if he left now he would surely appear a coward. Heaven forbid they should ever think him lily-livered! So instead of excusing himself, he remained, and knew he was less in control with every passing minute.

And then Seb came at him, lunged, and swung his fist. Henri-Antoine ducked and avoided contact with all the grace of a fencing master. Seb's swing went wide and connected with nothing. But such was the force behind this drunken punch that he couldn't stop himself from spinning about and over-balancing. Falling sideways into the wingchair, his shoulder became wedged between the cushion and the chair back, leaving his backside in the air.

Henri-Antoine thought this an ignominious yet fitting end to a one-sided fight that thankfully had ended before it began. Jack and Bully rushed over and peered down at Seb, who was making muffled noises into the horsehair stuffing, but no one made an effort to help him. Jack and Bully looked at Seb and then at each another, and burst out laughing. Henri-Antoine even dared to smile.

Jack finally wiped his eyes dry and nudged Randal Knatchbull.

"Come on, Bully, help me pull him out." He gave Seb's back a pat. "Don't you worry, Seb! We'll get you free!"

"Wait a minute, Jack," Bully suggested gleefully. "A rush of blood to the head might unfuddle his brain of foolishness—Oi! Harry? Are you all right?" he demanded, when Henri-Antoine closed his eyes and swayed. He nudged Jack in the ribs. "Jack! Harry's turned as white as fresh snow."

At this pronouncement Jack forgot Seb's predicament, and turned to Henri-Antoine. "Let's sit you down, Ha—"

"*Not here*," Henri-Antoine said through his teeth.

"I'll have the lads fetched."

"Do—*that*... *Mon Dieu*," Henri-Antoine muttered, willing every fiber of his being to remain in control, though he could not stop the onset of a sudden icy coldness in the palm of his left hand.

"Jack! Harry! Seb's got himself unstuck!" Bully announced with all the astonishment of one who has seen his first comet. "That was clever. Now shake hands with Harry and apologize—"

"Shake hands? *Apologize?*" Seb growled. "After he maligned me, and in my own house? He's the one that needs to—"

Henri-Antoine turned and strode away to the sounds of Seb's boisterous protests of affront that he get back here now, as Jack and Bully restrained him.

He had left it too late. He no longer had a headache. That was bad —*very bad*.

He must not panic.

He must keep his wits about him until he was in a safe place.

He must keep *thinking*.

The intense coldness had progressed to his wrist. It was as if his hand had been plunged into a pail of icy water. His tongue was tingling. Sometimes it swelled. He was never sure. All he knew was soon he wouldn't be able to talk at all, least make anyone understand what he was saying. He clamped his teeth shut.

He wouldn't call out.

He mustn't make a sound.

Not here. Not now. Not in front of others.

He had managed to make it to five-and-twenty without being a public disgrace. He wasn't about to let it happen now.

Where was Jack? He needed him to fetch the lads. Why had he sent Michel to the Portland auction? Why was the room full of bright light? He was such a fool for drinking the brandy, for not listening to Jack. Jack had been right. Dear Jack...

He staggered to the door, or did he limp? He had no idea.

He had to get away from the light. He squinted to see. The walls had begun to move.

The icy coldness had reached his shoulder. He no longer had a left arm. It felt as if it were hanging loose and useless at his side, but in truth he knew it looked very different from how it felt. The muscles contracted, forcing the elbow to bend and his arm to adhere to his side and against his chest. His hand twisted at the wrist; the fingers pulling inwards. The muscles down one side of his neck did the same, tugging his head to the left, while his mouth became slack, and he drooled.

The seizure would not last long, but for how long he had no idea because he always blacked out, always spiraled away into nothingness, and was left to the mercy of others. And while it lasted he was a distorted mess—a freak of nature—and a monstrous form of his true self. And he knew as sure as dawn followed night he would be a slave to his affliction for the rest of his days.

He saw the door. It was open. Thank God.

Now to get out of the room.

But he could not leave.

Someone blocked his path. No. Not someone. A female. A girl. Was it one of Harris's harlots? Even in his altered state he did not think so. Was it an angel? Diffuse light glowed around her hair like a halo. She had big blue eyes in a perfect oval face and she was staring at him in unblinking recognition, or was that fear? Did he know her? No! He was hallucinating. *She* was an hallucination. His befuddled, knotted, pulsating brain was confusing this girl with the Renaissance paintings he had so admired in the Italian states. Glorious Botticelli females with striking features and flowing hair.

If she were a Botticelli angel conjured by his seizure, then he reasoned he could simply walk through her. He tried to do just that and bumped up against soft feminine curves. She was flesh and blood after all. Not an ethereal being then.

She crumpled against him—fainted with fright, he did not doubt it—and he quickly threw his serviceable arm about her waist to stop her falling. She made an instant recover and pulled away. But she still blocked his escape. So he stuck his face in hers and demanded she get out of his way. What he snarled was something else entirely.

"*J'ai désespérément besoin de faire pipi!*"

Botticelli's angel instantly backed out of the room and disappeared into the blackness.

Henri-Antoine followed and promptly collapsed at her feet.

FOUR

WHEN LISA OPENED THE DOOR, BECKY AT HER BACK HOLDING aloft the single taper, she entered a drawing room filled with the haze of tobacco smoke as thick as a winter morning's fog. Her eyes instantly watered, and her nose twitched. She thought she would sneeze. There was a lot of noise, and men shouting and scuffling, and furniture being bumped about. She managed a cursory glance at the chaotic state of the room and saw a group of men over by the fireplace in the midst of an affray. She decided the best course of action was to leave the catalog on the nearest chair and flee without further explanation.

But she wasn't given the opportunity to ask Becky for her basket, least of all leave the catalog for these men to find, because one of their number turned away from his fellows and walked towards her with a purposeful stride.

Unaware she and Becky were still standing in the doorway, blocking the exit, Lisa did not think to move aside. She was staring at the man coming towards her. Not at him precisely because it was impolite to stare a stranger in the face, but at the short skirts of his waistcoat and matching close cuffed frock coat, both in lilac silk embroidered with metallic thread, and sequins on pocket flaps, cuffs, and hem. She had never seen metallic thread embroidery before nor such a soft-hued silk on a man. Faceted crystal gems covered the buckles of his polished black leather shoes, which she was sure had to be diamonds. He was the embodiment of aristocratic anecdote.

And then the resplendently-dressed gentleman was there in front of them, and Lisa had no time and nowhere to move. He lurched at her.

Becky squealed with fright, dropped her basket and fled back out into the corridor, leaving Lisa to confront him alone. Instinctively she knew Becky had deserted her, without the need to glance over her shoulder. But she did not want to. The stranger held all her attention.

She had a moment of panic, that perhaps he meant to do her a harm, but that vanished as quickly as the thought had popped into her head. She was not naturally timid, nor did she instantly think the worst of people. Assisting in the dispensary, she had encountered enough curious persons come in off the streets experiencing illness and distress to varying degrees that very little surprised her these days, about the people or what ailed them. And if she had learned anything from Dr. Warner's patients, it was that illness made no distinction between the poorest souls dressed in rags, and gentlemen such as he, dressed in fine clothes and diamonds. All were deserving of her compassion, and to be treated with dignity.

Nor did she fear him. A cursory diagnosis told her he was incapable of doing harm to anyone other than himself. He was either drunk beyond reason, taken ill, or affected by lunacy. Whatever had caused his present unhappy state he was suffering for it. Torment was writ large across his features, in the contortions in his fingers, and the straining in his neck in its fine white linen stock. He needed medical attention, something to ease his suffering, and, she realized too late, standing as a statue in the doorway was no way to be of help to him.

Yet before she could move, he walked right up to her as if she was not there at all and stepped on her foot.

This was so unexpected that she fell against him, biting her lip to stifle a cry of pain, because any sudden sound might startle him, and cause him to become agitated. Dr. Warner had cautioned his medical students when treating those who were clearly not in possession of their full faculties that any sudden movements or noise could send lunatics into an even greater frenzy.

Then the stranger startled her, grabbing her about the waist. Instantly she pulled out of his hold, and was so shocked to be manhandled that she froze. He responded by sticking his face in hers and barking out an order. She did not understand, his words were slurred and almost unintelligible. And then she had sudden revelation that he was not speaking in English, but in French and it opened wide her eyes. He said he needed to urinate, and at once. That had Lisa tripping over her own petticoats to get out of his way. Yet no sooner had she backed out into the corridor, he staggering after her, than he collapsed at her feet.

· · ·

WHEN HE HIT THE FLOOR WITH A THUD, SHE STARED DOWN AT
him, stunned. Not only by his fall, but also by the entire incident,
which was over in a matter of moments.

It took Becky rushing over and tugging at her arm to break the
spell.

"Come on, Miss!" she hissed. "Here's our chance! I'll get me basket
and we'll flee—"

Lisa pulled her arm free and dropped to her knees beside the
stranger.

"Bring the taper closer. I need to see if he's injured himself."

"Don't touch 'im, Miss! You dunno what 'es got!"

"He's unwell and needs our help," Lisa assured her, squinting up
into the glow of the candle which was just inches from her face, Becky
doing as she was asked and holding the taper over Lisa's shoulder.
"Come a little closer so I can see if he has split his head, or done
himself any other injury."

"By the looks of 'im, 'e ain't in 'is right mind!"

Becky reluctantly did as she was told, the light from the taper flickering in her trembling hand. Still, it allowed Lisa to better examine the
stranger in the soft light.

She gingerly leaned over him and gently brushed back his mop of
wavy black hair to see his face, wondering if the fall to the ground had
knocked him unconscious. But his eyes were wide open, the pupils
dilated, and he seemed to be staring without seeing. He certainly did
not react to her touch or the closeness of her, so he did not know she
was there. He trembled all over, but unlike Becky who did so from
fright, these were not gentle tremors but a series of jerky actions in his
limbs and torso, for which he seemed to have no control. The muscles
in his neck remained strained, his head pulled to one side. She wished
she could unravel his cravat—but where to start on the complicated
knot in the soft folds of linen?

He had fallen on his right side, his frock coat bunching up under
him, the skirts falling away from his black breeches. He was not at all
relaxed, which she'd have expected had he knocked himself out. His
left arm remained bent at the elbow and adhered to his chest, and his
fingers gnarled and clinging to a couple of the covered buttons of his
metallic-threaded waistcoat.

Lisa wondered from these contortions if he were in pain. Yet, he
hardly made a sound. She leaned in, beckoning Becky to bring the
light closer, to better illuminate his face. His mouth was twisted,
pulled to one side like the rest of his body, with the lips slightly parted
from which issued forth a low gurgling, but no intelligible words.

She sat back on her haunches, pondering what to do, and was distracted by the voices coming from the drawing room, where the door was still wide. At least the gentlemen were no longer shouting at one another, or disturbing the furniture.

Instinctively, she knew the last thing this gentleman would want was for his friends to see him in such a reduced and vulnerable state. No doubt that was the reason he had tried to leave the room in such a hurry. So she had Becky quietly shut the door, hoping the gentlemen were too caught up in themselves to even notice one of their number was no longer with them.

And as he continued to convulse, Lisa was reminded of young Joe, son of a local laundress, an Irishwoman, and a patient of Dr. Warner. Joe's mother was convinced her son's fits were the work of the devil, punishment for bearing a bastard. Dr. Warner told her most stridently not to be so foolish. Joe was not possessed of a demon. He suffered with the falling sickness, many children did, and it was not her fault or his. On one of Joe's many visits, Lisa had witnessed him have a fit. It had come on suddenly, without warning, his thin little body wracked with violent spasms, contorting his limbs and his face. It had ended just as abruptly, leaving Joe limp and exhausted, as if the life force had been sucked from him. She had never seen an adult have such an attack and had wrongly presumed the falling sickness a childhood ailment. Yet, here was this gentleman, a man who seemed healthy in every other particular, in much the same reduced state as poor Joe. So he was not drunk, or mad, but a fellow sufferer...

Decided, she looked up at Becky, a hand to the stranger's shoulder, hoping touch might offer reassurance that he was not alone, just as she had done with Joe—though she had no reason to believe, that just like Joe, he was aware of her presence.

"Becky, find the butler. I need a coverlet. Also a basin of warm water and a clean cloth."

Becky stared down at Lisa as if she were as mad as the gentleman writhing on the floor.

"But—Miss! That's 'im!" she hissed. "That's the gent who dun own the book. I'd not 'ave thought it, but takin' a good look at 'im now, it's true. I'd know that nose anywhere. So we can't stay 'ere'—"

Lisa hid her astonishment, saying calmly, "I will not abandon him. He needs help. And I mean to stay until—"

"Miss, how can you 'elp? Best leave 'im to whatever devil 'as possessed 'is soul. Poor sot. And we don't want to get caught up in—"

"He's ill, not mad," Lisa interrupted stridently. "Now please do as I ask and then you may leave, if that is your wish. I'll be perfectly all right. Put the catalog on the table on the landing where it will be found. Make haste, Becky. Go!"

No sooner had Becky disappeared down the passageway, to offload the book then find the butler, than the drawing room door was wrenched open. A gentleman with a head of untidy copper curls bounded out of the smoke-filled drawing room, eyes wild and searching. He did not see Lisa just inches from his feet by the wall. His gaze remained over her head, looking down the darkened corridor one way, and then the other. Lisa hoped he wouldn't notice her, that he would go off down the passageway after Becky, or return to the room. But there was something in his kind face that spoke to her—an inherent goodness—that here was a decent man, and that he was not being inquisitive for its own sake, or to be mischievous, but because he cared about the man lying beside her.

"Sir, your friend is down here with me," she said quietly.

The gentleman jumped in the air, spun about and almost tripped over his feet. This provided Lisa with a moment's levity, and then he was on his knees, leaning over his friend, who continued to writhe and twist and make unintelligible mutterings in the muted light of the candle.

"Harry? Harry? It's Jack. Jack is here," he said gently. "You're safe. There's no one else. Just us and—" He glanced at Lisa and then thought better of mentioning her presence. "I'll just go fetch the lads ..."

Yet he continued to kneel over his friend, stricken with such a mixture of distressing emotions that Lisa was compelled to offer him reassurance, even though she was unsure if this would help or hinder him in his distress.

They spoke in hushed tones.

"Sir, I've sent for a coverlet. He needs to be kept warm, and I thought it would also help—to keep him from prying eyes." When Jack nodded distractedly, she added, "Do you know how long his seizures last?"

Jack shook his head. "No..." He looked at Lisa then, a frown between his brows. "You are not alarmed by his convulsions?"

"Pardon, sir, but why would I be alarmed by another's suffering—?"

"I didn't mean—I hope you were not offended by my remark. It's just that most persons go out of their way to avoid those that are-are —*suffering.*"

"You do not. Nor do I. But I confess to being less worried, seeing that you are not at all panicked by your friend's condition. So I can presume this is not an irregular occurrence—that he suffers from such seizures often?"

"From time to time. Not often, but enough…" Jack answered evasively before confessing with a sheepish smile, "Truth is, I knew he still had attacks but I'd no notion they were still severe. I've not seen him this way since—since we were boys…"

"He's had the falling sickness since a child?"

"Yes, from birth." Jack looked at Lisa wonderingly. "You know the name of his condition? Yes, it is indeed the falling sickness."

"This is not the first attack I have witnessed."

"It isn't? Is one of your Corinthians a sufferer?"

Lisa frowned. "Corinthians?"

"Customer. Patron. Regular. It's all the same thing."

Lisa blinked at him. "It is?"

Jack baulked, realizing she had no idea what he was talking about. He swallowed hard and took a good look at her. No cosmetics. Natural hair. Clear skin. A high cut *décolletage* with a modesty fichu for good measure. Clear, confident diction. Not a hint of the coquette about her. Definitely not a prostitute. And young. If he were to hazard a further guess, not a servant either. Then who was she?

"You're not from Harris's List, are you?" he blurted out.

"Harris's List? I've no idea what that is, so that should answer your question. But I can assure you that at Warner's Dispensary where I assist, I am not panicked at all by the ill or the injured and their suffering. Nor do I have a disgust of their ailments or of-of—their bodily fluids. I would be of no use to Dr. Warner or his patients if I did. Sir, I tell you this so your mind will be at ease in leaving your friend in the care of a female stranger—me—while you fetch the-the—*lads*?"

"The lads! Yes! Thank you! I must get them. That much I can do for Harry." He scrambled to his feet and closed the drawing room door then came back and looked down at Lisa. "If any gentleman should come out of that room and find you here—"

"I shall shepherd them back inside with some excuse I will do my best to invent while you are gone."

Jack sighed his relief. "Thank you, Miss-Miss—"

"Lisa. My name is Lisa," she said firmly, not wanting to give out her surname because she should not be at Lord Westby's townhouse in the first instance, and secondly she did not want her name or Becky's attached to the missing catalog, should inquiries be made at a later date. She smiled up at him, wanting to ask his name. Instead she said, "The lads, sir…?"

· · ·

JACK FOLLOWED THE SAME ROUTE BECKY HAD TAKEN, AND PASSED a footman coming up the stairs with a coverlet, and behind him, a rosy-cheeked girl carrying a porcelain basin. He did not stop, and when he returned with two burly men, Henri-Antoine was tucked up under the coverlet. His head was propped up off the floor and resting on Lisa's thigh, and she was gently wiping his face with a damp cloth, her rosy-cheeked friend beside her, basin at the ready.

"The tremors have stopped and he's sleeping," Lisa advised Jack in a low voice when he knelt the other side of her. She glanced up at the two men who were as wide as they were tall—she wouldn't have been surprised to learn their previous employment had been lifting felled trees onto drays. "He uttered a few words that were not in English. Is your friend a Frenchman?"

"Did you have any trouble?" he asked, avoiding the question, a jerk in direction of the drawing room door.

Lisa shook her head, but she wasn't watching him. Her gaze had returned to her patient. "He became agitated when the seizures eased, and then stopped, which is when he spoke in French," she explained diffidently. "But he settled again and seemed to fall almost immediately into a deep sleep when I reassured him all was well and-and—" She paused, throat suddenly dry, and confessed, "—took to lightly stroking his hair, in the same way I did for Joe—the boy at the dispensary who has the falling sickness. He calms considerably if his hair is stroked."

"Ah. Does he? That's good to know, but what I meant was, did my friends in the drawing room bother you at all?"

"Oh! Oh! No. No, they have remained in the room." She suppressed a smile. "But that was because half-a-dozen most interesting and joyous females joined your friends not long after you went to fetch the lads. One of their number confided they were invited to help celebrate a gentleman's last weeks of freedom before his marriage—"

"Anyone would think I was being locked up!" Jack interrupted with an embarrassed huff, suddenly hot in the face. "And it wasn't my idea to invite them!"

Lisa made no comment, adding when Jack continued to look self-conscious, "They were in such high spirits they barely noticed me. And they certainly did not notice your friend because he was already under the coverlet."

Jack let out a sigh, gaze on the drawing room door. The crescendo of female laughter and chatter was audible, so, too, Seb and Bully's drunken bravado. No doubt those two were in seventh heaven to have eight high-class prostitutes all to themselves. He ignored what was going on in there for the time being, and leaned over to take another look at Henri-Antoine. He was sleeping peacefully, face turned away, head resting comfortably on the girl's petticoats, as if she were his own feather pillow.

Jack remembered that after an attack Henri-Antoine was left exhausted and dazed, and depending on its severity could sleep for upwards of four hours. When he woke he would be sluggish, irritable, and uncommunicative, sometimes for days. Nothing new in the latter, he thought with a wry smile. But the smile died thinking that what his best friend would hate more than anything else would be to wake to an unnecessary audience. He certainly would not appreciate having strangers attending on him, or knowing that he suffered from the falling sickness, even if the female washing his face and stroking his hair was out of the common way. So with that in mind, he said to Lisa, a glance at Becky,

"The lads can look after him now, Miss. That's what they're trained to do. They'll take him away from here, make him comfortable, and watch over him until he is more himself. You and your friend may go about your business. Thank you for coming to his assistance. He would be most grateful, and tell you so himself were he able."

Lisa smiled and nodded. She was not sure she believed him about his friend being grateful. He was just being polite. That his friend had minders who took care of him in such situations would suggest they were employed to prevent strangers interfering or bearing witness to an attack. She could not fault him for that, and he was fortunate indeed to have such a caring friend, and the means by which to make his situation as comfortable and as bearable as possible.

There was nothing left for her to say or do, so she carefully extracted herself from being his pillow, Jack quick to come to her assistance. She discarded the cloth she'd been using to sponge his face, dropping it into the basin, and got to her feet. Becky stood, too. And as Lisa shook the creases from her petticoats she could not resist a last look at her patient in the muted candlelight. He no longer had any muscle tightness. Gone was the strain to his neck, the clamp to the jaw, and the pull to his mouth. The handsome features with the strong nose were now in repose, the square chin nestling softly in the folds of a fine linen cravat she had dared to unknot and loosen. And the shock of black hair she had gently brushed back out of his eyes and stroked while offering him reassurance, now fell unrestrained to his shoulders. She could see that he also possessed high cheekbones, but it was at his mouth her gaze lingered longest. The lips were beautifully molded… Becky was right. It was a perfectly kissable mouth, and he was an inordinately beautiful man.

She doubted she would ever see the like of him again, wishing only that she'd had the opportunity to hear his voice when he was not agitated. She was sure he was possessed of a smooth, deep burr as Becky suggested. As to whether he sounded like hot chocolate tasted—full, velvety, and just a tiny bit sinful—that, too, she doubted she would be privileged to discover for herself.

Little could she know that she would indeed make these discoveries, and in the most surprising of ways, and within the week.

FIVE

LISA RETURNED TO GERRARD STREET TO THE UNCOMMON circumstance of the entire household being aware of her absence.

She came through the servants' entrance to the comforting aromas of cooking, the kitchen maids in the midst of a baking and cooking frenzy, with biscuits being turned out of a hot oven, several fowls rotating on the spit, and various pots on the boil. Cook was barking orders from the kitchen bench, but as soon as she saw Lisa, she quickly wiped her floured hands on her apron and pounced with the news the mistress had asked to see her, and that was an hour or more ago.

Cook warned she best have a good story to tell, adding that the mistress's mood had not improved with the arrival of Mrs. Warner's younger sister, Mrs. Cobban, even though this was Mrs. Cobban's first visit since returning from her bridal trip to Paris.

She then confided information Lisa did not need to know: The first batch of almond biscuits Mrs. Cobban so favored had burned, and the second batch were not near crisp enough. So Cook was having to resort to slicing up the seedy cake from the previous day; she didn't have time to make another. And then information that was new to Lisa: That everyone knew the secret to a good seedy cake was beating the ingredients for a good two hours or more in a warmed bowl before pouring it into a prepared tin, and then popping it in the oven.

Lisa was duly solemn and nodded at all the right intervals, and went so far as to say that as much as she loved Cook's almond biscuits, her seedy cake was the most delicious she had ever tasted. And no wonder, with such love and attention as Cook invested in its making.

Cousin Henriette—Mrs. Cobban—would not be disappointed. To which Cook grinned, then retorted she wasn't certain love was involved, but a good deal of sweat and muscle were! She then threw up her hands and bustled over to scold a kitchen maid who was not turning the spit at an even pace.

Lisa was quick to exit the kitchen, intent on going straight up to her cousin's boudoir, but was stopped before she reached the stairs by the housekeeper. Thankfully she did not repeat what Cook had told her, but asked if Lisa had examined the state of her clothes since she had returned from 'who-knew-where'?

She had not. Lisa thanked her for the warning, cheeks glowing under the woman's significant stare at the large damp stain to the front of her plain, brown linen petticoats. Lisa had been oblivious to all else while attending to her patient. Now it seemed that in her haste to wipe his face clean she had squeezed the excess water from the cloth not into the basin but down the front of her gown. She had also neglected to rearrange her mittens, which she had pushed up over her elbows, out of the way. All this she kept to herself. With another thank-you, she went up to her room and changed her petticoats, exchanged her half-boots for house slippers, and tidied her hair in the looking glass she kept in a drawer of the small desk by the window.

Mrs. Warner's much-put-upon maid answered her scratch at the door, and let it be known with a significant lift of her eyes to the ceiling that all was not harmony with the mistress. Lisa smiled at her kindly and went through to the boudoir, and there hovered in the doorway, listening, and waiting to be noticed.

Minette Warner and Henriette Cobban—the de Crespigny sisters —could not be more dissimilar had they been unrelated. Minette was dark haired, tall, and languid. Her younger sister, Henriette, a short curvy blonde, was prone to fidgeting. If they had a similarity it was to be found in the pleasing oval shape of their faces, possibly the only feature Lisa and her cousins had in common, and the sisters shared a misplaced confidence their fashion choices were the right ones.

Cousin Minette reclined on the sofa, doing her best to appear as a sultana of the Ottoman Empire in a figured silk banyan, the color of which could only be described as Oriental orange. A little turban sat atop her teased hair, and her feet were encased in silk slippers with curled toes. Her sister Henriette sat straight-backed at the end of the sofa in a *Chemise a la Reine*, the layers of diaphanous white muslin gathered under her ample bosom with a large blue sash tied in a bow, with which she fiddled, and on her feet matching blue silk mules.

Other than upbraiding her for her truancy to Lord Westby's house, of which her cousins could not have the slightest idea, Lisa racked her brain to wonder why they wished to see her. Henriette had made it plain almost from the day Lisa was orphaned, that she was unwanted. Henriette had maintained her hostility while they were at school together, when they were at home, and whenever she visited her sister's home.

Lisa was indifferent to this dislike, for the most part because she had nothing in common with Henriette, whose conversation was almost entirely about other people's lives. She was chattering now about the latest gossip sweeping Parisian salons—the trial of those involved in what had become known as the Affair of the Diamond Necklace.

Lisa had followed this sensational series of incidents involving a cardinal, a female confidence trickster, a supposed sorcerer, and a fabulous necklace made for the Queen of France, which was somehow spirited to London, when they had first appeared in *The Gentleman's Magazine*. Although she seemed to recall being more interested in news of the latest balloon ascent, and this one in Edinburgh. The thought of soaring into the skies and looking down on the world like a bird was far more exciting and fascinating—though she knew her cousins would never agree—than the machinations of a bunch of swindlers at the highest levels of French society.

"Don't loiter, Lisa. We might think you eavesdropping," Minette Warner complained, beckoning her forward with a slow wave of a lace-bordered handkerchief. She held it up for her inspection. "Aren't these little squares divine? Henriette tells me all the best people are using square handkerchiefs in Paris these days. She's bought me a dozen."

"It is lovely. And they're square because King Louis made it law—"

"Law? What law? About *handkerchiefs*?"

Lisa picked her way across the carpet strewn with opened gift boxes, careful not to step on lids, ribbons, and torn tissue paper. Thankfully the gifts were piled on a low table in front of the sofa.

"Yes. King Louis had it written into law just last year that all handkerchiefs made in France must be square," Lisa replied simply, and lightly kissed the powdered and rouged cheek Henriette presented to her. "I'm glad you're safe home, Henriette. Did you and Mr. Cobban enjoy your stay in Paris?"

"La! You are full of the most absurd knowledge," Minette said without heat, and dropped the handkerchief into its box and tossed it onto the table. "Naturally Henriette enjoyed Paris. Who doesn't?"

"We did," Cousin Henriette agreed. "Mr. Cobban is the most attentive and generous of husbands, and I've come home with a carriage load of new dresses and necessaries that will take my maid at least a week to unpack."

"But where have you been, Lisa?" Minette asked in the same languid tone. "We have been waiting to speak with you this past hour or more. And it's not as if you have anything of a pressing nature, is it? It's not one of your days at the dispensary, so the poor aren't lining up demanding you write letters for them about God-knows-what-nonsense, are they?"

"Is she still making a nuisance of herself in the dispensary?" Henriette asked, surprised, not a look at Lisa, and reverting to French, the sisters' first language.

"Oh, she's not a nuisance," Minette countered. "Dear Dr. Warner has only good things to say about our cousin's assistance. He says she is good at scenting the rooms free of miasma, which is all I care about, and for keeping the poor *orderly*." She shrugged. "Someone has to do it and it might as well be Lisa. As I just said: It's not as if she has anything else to do with her time, and it does give her something to do."

"It will have to stop," Henriette stated. "And at once. It's bad enough her fingers are ink-stained, nothing a good scrubbing with soap and a pumice won't take care of, but what if she were to get an infection handling all that filth?"

"I'd not thought of that... I dare say you are right..."

"What if the poor were to give her a hideous fever, or a rash? Mama would not be pleased."

"Would she not?" Minette wondered aloud. "I'd have thought that if Lisa were struck down with a cold or flu or something more potent, poor Mama could then breathe a sigh of relief, and refuse the invitation she has accepted on her behalf with a clear conscience."

Henriette's eyes lit up. "Oh yes! That would work in our favor!"

"But there is no point to be hopeful on that score. Lisa has never been ill a day in her life. Have you, Lisa?" Minette added loudly, reverting to English, and enunciating each word as if her cousin was incapable of understanding her. "You've never been ill a day in your life, have you?"

"No, Cousin Minette. I am blessed with good health, and good hearing."

"You see. As healthy as a milkmaid and the cow she milks," Minette Warner replied in French to her sister.

"What a shame," Henriette mused. "Declining the invitation due to ill health would solve all our problems."

"It would. But as that is not about to happen, we must do as poor Mama has asked. We owe it to her, and to our noble patroness."

"Invitation? May I know what it is, this invitation Aunt de Crespigny has accepted on my behalf?" Lisa interrupted politely, and in French, and with just a hint of a wry smile at their tactic of excluding her from a conversation they knew well enough she could understand.

The sisters turned their heads to regard Lisa with mild hostility, that she dared to intrude into their conversation and do so in French. Speaking in English to her, while they spoke in French between themselves, was just one of the many ways in which they imposed their authority on her, the poor relation, who would forever be an embarrassment and a burden on the family. Just as they deliberately kept her standing in the middle of the carpet, knowing she could not sit until given permission to do so.

That their impoverished cousin had received an invitation to attend a wedding and spend two weeks at a country estate—a wedding to which no one else in the de Crespigny family had been invited—was an unwelcome rupture to the social fabric of society and a way of life all the best people followed and to which their adherents aspired. The wedding was no ordinary wedding and the estate no ordinary country estate. The Duke of Roxton's niece was getting married, and the wedding celebrations were being held at Treat, the ancestral home of the dukes of Roxton. Such an occasion would surely be the social event of the summer, populated with the titled and wealthy of Polite Society, to be written up in all the newssheets, talked about in all the best drawing rooms, the gilt-edged card of invitation proudly displayed, propped on many a noble mantelpiece for guests to see and envy.

For Lisa to have received an invitation to such a wedding was to the sisters extraordinary, incomprehensible, and disquieting. An impoverished orphan, who knew nobody and went nowhere, did not receive invitations to such momentous occasions. It simply wasn't done. And yet, it had been done, and there was nothing either sister, or their dear mama, or the de Crespigny family, could do about it.

And while the sisters felt impotent and affronted at this startling turn of events in their cousin's life, there was something they could do to show their displeasure and reassert their superiority in this moment, before their cousin was even aware of her newfound good fortune. Which was why both sisters were uncharacteristically and petulantly interested in Lisa for the first time in their self-absorbed lives.

Minette took it upon herself to demand of Lisa to know her where-abouts of the previous hour, while Henriette was even more hostile towards her cousin than usual.

"Lisa, you seem to have forgotten that you live here because dear Dr. Warner and I have taken you in when no one else in the family would have you. And as you are not of age, I must bestir myself from time to time to ensure you live within the proper restrictions for your age and station in life. At nineteen, you are not permitted to leave the house, least of all go gallivanting about the town, without my permission. Which you did not seek, and most assuredly should have done so."

"I am sorry I did not ask your permission, Cousin Minette," Lisa replied contritely. "But I did not wish to disturb you, and I did not think—"

"You must certainly did not think!" Henriette threw at her, itching to contribute to this chastisement.

"—you would mind if I ran an errand with Becky Bannister."

"Becky—*Bannister*? Do I know this personage?"

"Yes, Cousin. Becky is the niece and haberdasher's assistant to Widow Humphreys at Humphreys' Haberdashery. She has been here several times with her trimmings and—"

Henriette goggled at her, horrified. "You were seen out in the company of a—of an—haberdasher's *assistant*?" She looked at her sister and reverted to French. "How are we to correct such social ineptitude, and in a fortnight? It is impossible! Impossible!"

"I dare say her social blindness can be attributed to the time she spends in the dispensary," Minette replied begrudgingly. "Dear Dr. Warner says that disease is the great leveler—that no matter what our social status, illness visits us all—"

"Minette! Forget the poor and your dear doctor's dictates for the moment, this is far more important," Henriette hissed. "Poor Mama's reputation—*our reputation*—is at stake. And if Lulu had lived, we wouldn't be facing this dilemma, now would we!?"

Minette sighed heavily. "There is no use making ourselves ill with sadness thinking of the past. We must deal with what is in front of us, and do the best we can."

At that, the sisters turned again and this time they looked Lisa up and down, both with the same thought: If their younger sister Louise —affectionately known as Lulu—had not died of scarlet fever, Lisa Crisp would never have been sent in Lulu's place to Blacklands boarding school for young ladies. And had Lisa not attended Blacklands, where she had mixed with girls far above her social station, who were the daughters and sisters of politicians, merchant princes, and the like, she would never have received an invitation to the society wedding of the year—an astonishing turn of events which none of the family could have anticipated.

"Sit. We have something of great importance to explain to you," Minette said in English, indicating a chair piled with emptied gift boxes and ribbons. She waited until Lisa had perched on the very edge of a cushion and placed her hands in the lap of her linen gown, before exchanging a glance with her sister—who was reaching for the last almond biscuit on the plate. "I do not know why the seedy cake has not arrived…" She looked back at Lisa and drew in a breath, as if the task ahead was going to be fatiguing in the extreme. "While Henriette was in Paris, she visited Mama—and before you ask it—Mama, Papa, and Toinette are enjoying their stay immensely. I do believe Toinette wrote you a letter. Is that so, Henriette?"

"I gave it—or did I leave it on the table? No matter. Once your girl clears everything away it will be found. It's not important. Full of childish chatter, no doubt," Henriette said dismissively of her twelve-year-old sister Toinette. "Papa spoils her beyond tolerance. He always has."

"She was so excited to be calling upon her French cousins for the first time," Lisa said with a smile. But she also remembered how fearful Toinette was about returning to England, because upon coming home, she was being sent to Blacklands for the first time.

Lisa vividly remembered her first few days at Blacklands. She had arrived at the school in the middle of term, when all the girls were known to one another and she was known to no one. Worst of all, her cousins in their grief at the passing of Lulu, had not provided her with new clothing. Her clothes were clean, but worn and patched and thoroughly unacceptable for such a school. And so she had had to wear her only gown, and scuffed half-boots, in those first few days, under the sly looks and whispered jeers of her classmates, until more suitable clothing could be made, and her Uncle de Crespigny agreed to pay the expense of outfitting her with everything necessary for a boarder at Blacklands. At least Toinette would have a better start to her school year…

"…So you must understand why it is you cannot blame Mama for withholding such letters," Minette was saying. "She thought it was for the best not to raise your expectations that anything could come of such a friendship."

Lisa nodded absently. She had not heard the first part of her cousin's sentence and so was unsure what Minette was talking about, though she sensed by their defensive posturing—their chins had most certainly lifted—that her cousins were expecting her to react in a way that required them to justify what it was their mother had done on her behalf, and without her knowledge. But she had heard Minette's mention of letters and was so surprised by it that she blurted out,

"Aunt de Crespigny has letters—letters *for me?*"

"Do open your ears and pay attention!" Henriette retorted. "How are you to go into society, to make yourself pleasant and interested in what is taking place around you, and be able to make polite conversation, if you do not listen to your betters?"

"Mama withheld the letters for your own good, and ours," Minette explained patiently. "And we—Henriette and I—agreed with her. Given the shocking nature of your expulsion from Blacklands, it was thought best that you leave those days—and any associations with the school—behind you for good."

Lisa looked from one sister to the other, and addressed both. "I do not understand. Someone from-from *Blacklands* has written to-to—*me?*"

Henriette rolled her eyes in exasperation, thinking Lisa not only socially but mentally unfit to leave her sister's house, least of all rub shoulders with her betters. Perhaps mingling with the sickly poor had affected her brain?

"We were just as surprised as you," Minette confessed, "that any girl would want to know you after you departed the school under such a dark cloud. But you only have yourself to blame for that outcome, do you not? And if you had but given up the name of the boy whom you allowed to take liberties with your person behind the Chelsea Bun House, the headmistress had been prepared to let you stay on—"

"*Liberties?*" Lisa burst out before she could stop herself, adding in a more subdued voice, "It was just a kiss. That was all it was. One kiss."

"Just a kiss? *Just a kiss?* Have you no *shame?*" Henriette breathed indignantly. "That *boy* should never have put so much as a finger on you. As for *kissing* you... Your lips are for your future husband to kiss, and no one else."

"It was one *tiny* kiss," Lisa persisted, voice barely above a whisper and cheeks burning with shame. "And it was not on the lips, but on his cheek—"

"That kiss ended your schooling, and your chances of ever marrying a good and decent man," Henriette argued.

"Blacklands was your only chance of making something of yourself," Minette said with a heavy sigh. "What a pity you could not see that at the time. But you must see, *now*, that your shameful conduct at the bun shop was not only thoughtless but also selfish."

"Yes. Yes. You are right," Lisa replied, shoulders sagging. "It was thoughtless, and it was selfish." Then she sat up and looked at one sister, and then the other, and said brightly, "But I have not lost hope that there is a gentleman out there who could love me for myself—"

"*Love you for yourself?* Don't be absurd and-and *naïve!*" Henriette blustered and gave an unladylike snort of derision. "Even if such a man existed, and he did forgive your wicked behavior, what have you got to recommend you other than your youth? Face facts: You have no dowry. You are penniless and thus have nothing to offer a prospective husband."

"But if this gentleman loved me for myself, surely my pecuniary situation would be of little consequence to him...?"

Minette and Henriette glanced at one another, pulled a face, and then Henriette burst into incredulous giggles at what she considered an outrageous expectation.

While they had been at liberty to choose their husbands, both sisters had done so with the hard-headed pragmatism that comes from making a match with a man who could offer first and foremost, financial security and a comfortable living; physical attraction and being in love were secondary considerations. And while both were pretty, they had dowries of two thousand pounds apiece, which meant they had easily found husbands. The thought that their impoverished cousin would find a man to marry who would not only provide her with a comfortable living but fall in love with her was ludicrous in the extreme. Hence Henriette's fit of incredulous amusement.

"More fool you for thinking so," Henriette announced when she was finally in control of herself. "But we are not here to listen to your daydreaming fantasies or to belabor your past thoughtless actions. What concerns us is your behavior now and in the future. To that end, you are to keep the unhappy consequences of that kiss in the forefront of your mind when you find yourself amongst persons so far above your station in life that they might as well be living on the moon, and you an unwelcome visitor!"

Lisa dared to smile at her cousin's use of the word *moon* and how her analogy closely matched what Becky had said earlier about the owner of the catalog. And now she had seen him, she agreed with her. With such striking good looks, and dressed in clothing of exquisite finery, he was almost ethereal—one of the gods of Mount Olympus, a cloud dweller, or indeed a resident of the moon. He certainly did not belong amongst the earthy, rough-and-tumble residents of the city's grimier streets. She wondered where he resided...

And as she pondered this she was distracted by a sensation in the pit of her stomach akin to nervousness. She was suddenly light-headed, and a pulse throbbed at her temple. Perhaps she was experiencing her first fever? As she had never been ill, to be suddenly overcome by such unfamiliar sensations was unsettling. Perhaps it was because she'd had more than her fair share of excitement for one day at Lord Westby's residence, and then to return to Gerrard Street to an interrogation... She just wished to go to her room and lie down, and perhaps she would fall asleep dreaming of a dark-haired gentleman with the perfect kissable mouth... Oh dear, there she went again, thinking about kissing... Her cousins would certainly be furious with her, had they the ability to read her thoughts. So she dragged herself back to the present and said politely,

"You mentioned something about letters, Cousin Minette...?"

"Indeed we did, and you shall have them, against our better judgment," Minette stated. "If it were up to the family, you would still be none the wiser to the existence of this correspondence, nor would you have known about the invitation that has been extended to you. An invitation that Mama dearly wanted to refuse on your behalf because we do not think it appropriate you attend such an illustrious occasion. But—"

"—Mama was *prevailed upon*—that is to say she was—*ordered*—by our noble patroness to give an assurance you would attend," Henriette continued, interrupting Minette when she paused on a sigh. "And so Mama's wishes were overruled and there is nothing we can do about it."

"*Prevailed upon? Ordered?*" Lisa repeated, none the wiser as to the invitation or the noble personage, who, it seemed, from the awe in her cousin's voice and the fact she could order her Aunt de Crespigny to do her bidding, was someone very important indeed.

"Are you that beetle-headed?!" Henriette snapped, exasperated, and such was her annoyance that she sat forward and glared at Lisa. "Have you never wanted to put a name to our noble patroness, she who kindly sponsored our admission to Blacklands? As the daughters of a merchant, we would never have been accepted into such an exclusive establishment without Her Grace's blessing. She took it upon herself— such is the esteem in which the Duchess of Roxton and Kinross holds Mama—to recommend us to the school. And of course the school accepted us. Who would refuse Her Grace?"

Lisa's eyes went wide with new knowledge. Why had she not connected the two? It made perfect sense. But as the family had always spoken the words "noble patroness" with quiet veneration and never put a name to the appellation, she had assumed her identity was something of a family secret. Now it seemed that secret was an open one, and she the only one in the family not to know it.

But what she did know was that her aunt adored the Duchess of Roxton and Kinross, to whom she had been chief lady-in-waiting for almost twenty years before her marriage to M'sieur de Crespigny. And with twenty years of service, she had an unlimited supply of anecdotes about her life in the service of the Duchess; though her aunt was careful never to breach the Duchess's trust, and Lisa was certain there were twice as many stories left untold as the ones she shared with her family.

When Lisa had spent her Christmas holidays at the de Crespigny house, her favorite time was suppertime, with tea and cake around the fire in the drawing room, listening to her aunt's stories of when she had lived in a palace full of servants and rooms lit with enough candles to turn night into day. Her aunt's tales were full of magnificent mansions made of marble, carriages pulled by Arabian horses, and fragrant gardens dotted with fountains and follies. There were balls under brilliantly-lit chandeliers, routs in gilded drawing rooms, masquerades attended by hundreds, and picnics by a lake. And at the center of it all, a beautiful elfin queen—the Duchess—and right behind her, Lisa's aunt, part of this fairy tale world inhabited by dukes and duchesses, kings and princes, noblemen and their ladies, and all of them dressed in sumptuous silks and glittering diamond finery.

Lisa did not doubt her aunt held a special place in the Duchess's affections. Not only had she been with her for two decades, she had helped her through the births of her noble children, the last infant born just nine years ago, and well after her aunt had left the Duchess's employ. She had been called back to be with Her Grace at the birth, to help in the nursery in those first few days, and had a privileged place at the christening. Lisa remembered this vividly because it happened around Christmastime, and her aunt was away from home for some weeks, the first Christmas the family had spent without her. But no one begrudged her attending on the Duchess; all saw it as a great honor. So Lisa understood why the Duchess would help her aunt if she asked for it, and sponsor the de Crespigny girls' admittance to an exclusive boarding school for young ladies. She also knew her aunt would do whatever the Duchess wished of her, and, astonishingly to Lisa, it seemed what the Duchess wanted was for Lisa to be given letters and to accept an invitation. Why? And she wondered why her aunt was not happy about this outcome.

"I would never do anything to jeopardize my aunt's place in the Duchess's affections," Lisa assured her cousins. "You must believe me,

Minette, Henriette. I know how much your mother treasures her years in the Duchess's service... What I do not understand is why you think I could—"

"If you *dare* say or-or do anything that might interfere or diminish the special bond between Mama and Her Grace, we will *hate* you for the rest of your days!" Henriette spat out. "Do you understand?"

Lisa nodded, taken aback by her cousin's vitriol. She looked to Minette, wondering if she felt the same.

"If you do not behave yourself, if you cause Mama the slightest aggravation, or worse, if you do something that offends Her Grace or a member of her family, we will have no option but to disown you," Minette lectured. "We do not want that to happen, or to cast you adrift, but we will. You were almost sent away after your expulsion from Blacklands, but we thought better of it, given your tender years. But Papa had no compunction about ostracizing your father. Toussaint de Crespigny was a thief and a drunk. He stole from his family, drank his inheritance away, and left you and your mother to rot in a poorhouse. The only commendable thing he ever did was change his name to Crisp."

"Our parents saved you from a poorhouse. You owe it to them—and most particularly to Mama—not to disgrace yourself before the Duchess of Roxton and Kinross and her family." Henriette adding in an enunciated hiss, "Do—you—understand?"

Lisa nodded again, more vigorously this time, sick to the pit of her stomach and trembling to be so reviled. She saw Henriette's fury and Minette's displeasure, but she could not understand why their anger was tinged with resentment and bitterness.

"I must—I must be thick-headed today because I-I still do not understand why you think—How you would think—I could cause your parents such-such distress... I have never met the Duchess, nor am I ever likely to. Please. I do not wish to-to upset anyone. Tell me—Tell me what I must do so I can—I can ease your distress."

"You cannot ease it. It is out of our hands now," Minette explained. "All we can do is what has been asked of us, then send you off. Of course we will pray each and every day you are away that you acquit yourself without incident. But you have this knack of getting yourself into trouble and thus noticed—But not this time, Lisa. Understand me?" Before Lisa could respond, Minette looked to her sister. "Give her the invitation and the letters, Henriette, and let's be done with this."

"But we won't be done, will we?" Henriette argued, the bitterness still evident in her tone, and speaking in French. "We have been tasked with clothing her. I have a couple of cast-off gowns—ones I was going to give to my maid—for daywear. They can be altered easily enough; she has no breasts or hips, so there is ample material to be trimmed. I don't have a servant girl I can spare to act as her maid. Perhaps you have—"

"Spare one of my girls? I think not."

"At least you won't need to employ a string of dancing masters or music teachers. She can sing and play the pianoforte, if requested. Blacklands taught us that much."

"Yes. She does carry herself well, and is good at languages," Minette responded, lying back against the cushions, a hand to her forehead. "All this has given me the headache, Henriette..."

"Thank God for small mercies. Imagine if she couldn't speak French?" Henriette begrudgingly mused, ignoring her sister's headache. "The shame of it. And if she remains in the background and doesn't put herself forward, there won't be any need for her to even open her mouth in any language."

Minette roused herself one last time. "*Remains in the background?* And how, pray tell, is that to be achieved when the invitation is for a stay in the country for two weeks. Two weeks, Henriette. If it were only two days we might have some hope, but a fortnight...? That is asking for trouble. Do not tell Mama I said so. She is worried sick already... Now give Lisa the invitation and be done. Dear Dr. Warner and I have guests to dinner. I must rest my poor head before I change my gown."

Henriette snatched up something off the table and waved it in Lisa's face. It was a small packet of letters, atop of which was a gilt-edged card of invitation, and all tied up into a neat bundle with a black silk ribbon.

Lisa put out her hand but Henriette wasn't ready to relinquish the bundle without revealing the nature of the invitation, and with it, one final scornful lecture.

"You have been invited to spend a fortnight at Treat. That sentence alone would send most girls—no! any other girl—into an ecstasy of excitement, but you haven't the least notion of the great honor being bestowed upon you! You—"

"Oh, but I do know, Henriette," Lisa assured her. "Treat is the ancestral home of the Dukes of Roxton. Aunt de Crespigny mentioned it many times. It is the largest privately-owned house in all of England, and has so many rooms, even those that live there can get lost if they take a wrong turn. And there is a lake, and acres and acres of white roses planted by the old Duke for—"

"Yes! Yes! We've all heard Mama's stories," Henriette interrupted dismissively. "Your task is to get through the fortnight without being noticed. A fortnight will pass like that," she said with the snap of two fingers. "Your visit to Treat is fleeting. Nothing more than a heartbeat in time. And when it is over, you will have to take your head out of the clouds and return to your life here. Never forget, Lisa: You are poor. You have nowhere else to go, and we are the only family you have. Your life is here in Gerrard Street. The best you can hope for from life is to be of some use to the beggarly poor with your scribbles and helping in the dispensary. Do you understand?"

Lisa nodded obediently, gaze on the packet of letters that was being waved in front of her. She wanted to snatch it, run up to the privacy of her room, and there tug off the ribbon and read each letter quickly, and then again as slowly as possible. Though she had not been told the identity of her correspondent, or why she had received such a startling invitation, she had begun to have an inkling. Yet she dared not hope, because she did not want the inkling to prove false. But who else would invite her to Treat? Who else did she know who had any connection to such a magical place, other than her aunt's connection to the Duchess?

And then Henriette enlightened her, confirming her inkling.

"Not all your school friends have forsaken you it seems. And the one that did not just happens to have great and powerful relatives. And they do not come any more powerful than the Duke of Roxton, who is Miss Cavendish's uncle. Imagine that? How fortunate for you! You've been invited to her wedding, and Mama has accepted on your behalf. So you'll be attending. Here's the invitation," she said, and tossed the packet into Lisa's lap. "And there are a few letters she wrote you, too. Now go away and leave us in peace."

"Teddy! Oh Teddy!" Lisa burst out breathlessly, and such was her overwhelming excitement that she rushed out of the room without a curtsy, the packet pressed to her bosom.

Teddy had written to her.

Teddy was getting married.

Teddy had invited her to the wedding.

Teddy had not forsaken her after all.

Lisa burst into tears.

SIX

Overwrought to think her best friend at Blacklands, Miss Theodora Charlotte Cavendish—known as Teddy to friends and family—had not forgotten her, Lisa was in her room, back up against the closed door, with no recollection of how she got there.

She took a moment to compose herself, to quickly wipe her cheeks dry with the back of a shaking hand, and to take a few deep breaths, packet of letters still pressed to her heaving chest. And then she could wait no longer.

Kicking off her slippers and picking up her petticoats, she scrambled up onto her bed. Here she sat, cross-legged, and with shaking fingers untied the black ribbon keeping the invitation and the collection of letters bundled together. With only a cursory glance at the invitation, she set it aside, eager to read the letters first. Seeing her name and her former address—Fournier Street, Spitalfields—written in her school friend's sloping script she gave a watery chuckle, fingers lovingly caressing those inked letters in a wonderment of recognition, that the letters were indeed from Teddy. And with recognition came remembrances of days long past...

How many hours had they spent sitting side by side, practicing in their copybooks to write in the round hand cursive script of a Blacklands schoolgirl? How many formal letters had they copied out in this script, in English and in French, again all for practice, for when the day came when they were married ladies, and had the leisure to write letters to family and friends from their wallpapered boudoirs. Teddy grumbled good-naturedly at the wasting of time over such pointless penmanship, because when she married she wouldn't be sitting in a drawing room letter-writing, but would be out riding up hill and down dale in the fresh air. Teddy's script was made all the more laborious because she wrote with her left hand, which was an extraordinary sight in itself. All girls wrote with their right hands, and those who did not had their left hand tied behind their backs so that they did. Not Teddy. She had permission to use her left hand, as long as she could copy the script as it was written and did not trail her hand in the drying ink.

Lisa had wondered aloud why Teddy was permitted to use her left hand, and Teddy told her; though she had surmised the answer. *Oh, it must be because I have powerful relatives who love me, Lisa*, she had whispered and then giggled, hunching her shoulders. But she had not said this with any degree of smugness, or a sense of superiority, just as fact. And one day she confided in Lisa just how powerful they were. One uncle was a duke, another an earl. Her closest cousin was a double duchess, and her mama was a lady, daughter of an earl. Lisa was awe struck. Teddy's relatives were not just powerful, they were from the aristocracy, and at the very apex of their class. Teddy made her promise to keep this a secret, to not mention it to the other girls. She did not want them to think any differently of her. Lisa promised and then asked why, if her relatives were nobles, she had been sent to Blacklands, and not had a governess, or been sent to a seminary for the daughters of noblemen.

Teddy had screwed up her freckled nose in thought, then shrugged, saying her mama and step-papa wanted her to be comfortable, to learn to speak French like a native—all her mama's family did—but most of all they wanted her to be happy. They thought she would be happiest at Blacklands. And Teddy was happy. Lisa marveled at her best friend's exuberance for life, her confidence, and her sunny disposition.

Though, for a short while, when she had first arrived at Blacklands, Teddy had been miserable, pining for home, and Lisa comforted her.

Lisa had already been at the school for four years, and being an orphan who spent only the Christmas holidays with her cousins, Blacklands was her home. Whereas, Teddy had never been away from her family before, and never from her mother, and this was her first stay in London. And although Blacklands was in Chelsea, on the outskirts of the fashionable streets of Westminster, so was practically the country, it was *not* the country, and never would be as far as Teddy was concerned, whose home was in far-off Gloucestershire.

Teddy told Lisa all about the beauty of the Cotswolds, the magical Puzzlewood with its fairies and travelers and woodland creatures, the big rambling house of yellow stone that she lived in with her family, and the cloth mills owned by her step-papa, who was not only a wealthy merchant, but an important squire in her corner of England. And she lived with a menagerie of animals inside the house, her step-papa's dogs, her whippet Nera, a number of cats and song birds, and outside on the farm, as well as her favorite mare, there were chickens, dairy cows, bees, and sheep known as Cotswold Lions because of their big shaggy coats.

Lisa could listen for hours to Teddy's stories of her home and her ramblings through the countryside, and did. She wished she could visit such a wondrous place. Lisa had never been further from the city than Blacklands, ever. Teddy promised that one day Lisa would indeed visit her and meet her family, which not only included her mama, her step-papa, her Granny Kate, and two little brothers, but there was also Fran, Granny Kate's companion, and Silvia and Carlo, who were from Lucca, which was somewhere in the Italian states. Lisa had never heard of such a place. Teddy assured her it existed, and that when Lisa came to stay, Silvia would make her the most delicious food she had ever tasted, and dishes made with flour and eggs called pasta. And when Teddy married Jack and took up residence at Abbeywood farm, which was just in the next vale across from her family, Lisa could come to stay for as long as she wished.

"Jack?" Lisa had asked, surprised to learn Teddy knew whom she was to marry.

They were both thirteen years old, and Lisa had not even thought of boys, least of all knew one she would one day wish to marry.

"My cousin. I'm going to marry him on my eighteenth birthday. But I promised Mama I would attend Blacklands for a few years first. That was one of the conditions," Teddy confided. "Because Mama wants me to be a lady, and to learn a little of the world, which she says will help me be a better wife to Jack."

Lisa was intrigued, and had turned her head on the pillow to look at Teddy in the moonlight that streamed in through the undraped window and across the narrow bed where they were snuggled up under the coverlet, to keep each other warm, and where they could have a whispered conversation without disturbing the night nurse.

Teddy had said this with such certainty that Lisa wondered if her marriage to Jack was an arranged union. Lisa had heard of such marriages for people who had powerful relatives. Teddy's response was to shake her head and press her lips hard together to stop herself from giggling. Lisa saw the laughter in her eyes, and smiled. She was glad Teddy wasn't being forced into a marriage. Even as a thirteen-year-old she was a romantic.

"Does Jack know you are going to marry him?"

"Naturally."

"And when did you know—know that you wanted to marry Jack?"

"When I was ten."

"*Ten*? Ten years old?"

Teddy nodded. "And I told him when I was twelve."

Lisa's eyes went very round. "When you were twelve you told him you were going to marry him? Was he surprised? What did he say?"

"He was. But he said he would marry me though it was usual for boys to do the asking. And if I was sincere, I was to ask him again when I was older. He said I might change my mind."

"Do you think you will—change your mind?"

Teddy shook her head on the pillow. "No. Never."

"How old is Jack—now?"

"He's nineteen."

So he was six years older than they were, Lisa calculated, which she thought very old indeed but did not say so.

Teddy mistook Lisa's fascination for incredulity.

"It's true. And while I'm here at Blacklands, Jack is going on a Grand Journey—no! It's not called that… Oh! He's going on the *Grand Tour*. Yes. That's what it's called. Which is what boys do when they leave Oxford—that's university. Mama says the boys go in groups and wander about old palaces and ruins, and spend a lot of their time pondering old paintings."

"Couldn't he do that here? There must be old paintings to ponder and plenty of ruins to wander about in England."

"Mama says young men need to go abroad to ponder, to see the old world. She says it's good for them, because when they come home they are no longer boys, and they will want to settle."

"Settle…?"

"Marry, silly."

"Oh! How long will he be away on this tour?"

"Mama says he'll be away for years—"

"*Years?*" Lisa was so surprised she forgot to whisper. Then added in a hiss. "But what if he forgets you while he's away?"

"Forget?" Teddy sat up on an elbow, and frowned through a tangle of hair. "He won't forget me. He's promised not to. Besides, I gave him a lock of my hair so he won't!"

"Teddy!" Lisa gasped, now also up on an elbow. "Oh, but how wonderful of you!"

Teddy grinned and nodded, and then they both quickly lay back down and snuggled in under the coverlet because there was footfall and low voices. They smiled at each other then stared up at the ceiling illuminated by moonlight, and remained still and quiet and waited. They waited a very long time for it to be quiet again, too excited to sleep. There was so much more Lisa wanted to know about Teddy's family and Jack, and the wondrous things boys could do once they had left Oxford and went abroad to ponder.

"Will you miss him while he's away?" Lisa finally asked, watching Teddy who was still staring up at the ceiling.

"I will—a little. Mama says I mustn't. That I'm not to—*fret*. That Jack being away will give me plenty of time to grow up, too. And she says I'm not to worry about him, because he's going on this tour with his best friend, Harry, and they'll keep each other company and be too preoccupied to be thinking of home."

"Their parents are not worried they are going to be away from home for so long?"

"Worried? Why would they? Mama says going on the tour is a much better use of a wealthy young man's time than spending it in gentlemen's clubs, gambling, smoking, and drinking their days away—"

"Your mama said that to you?" Lisa's eyes were very wide.

"No. Not to me. I overheard her say it to my step-papa. And he agreed with her. She also said that there was little possibility of them getting into too much trouble, when they are journeying with a-a *yeomanry of attendants*."

"What is—what is a *yeomanry of attendants*?"

"They are the persons who are part of their traveling party, so Granny Kate tells me."

"Servants who carry their belongings?"

"Oh no. Of course they do have servants with them to do such tasks as carry their trunks, and to look after the carriages and horses, and to keep them safe while traveling about. But the yeomanry are people *attending* on them while they are away. Not servants in the strictest sense, so Granny Kate says. Jack and Harry will have their own physician traveling with them, and two tutors, a major domo who looks after all the arrangements for their travel and accommodations, and of course they need their valets to dress them. Oh! And I nearly forgot, two of their school friends are also going along, too, and they'll have their own yeomanry."

Lisa's eyes could not grow any rounder. She was envious of such travel arrangements and wished she had been born male and wealthy, so she, too, could be part of such a grand adventure.

"Imagine Jack and Harry and their friends and all those men in carriages, and on horseback, riding about the countryside and through towns," Lisa whispered with excitement. "The local people would be sure to stop and stare, and their children wave and jump up and down, to see such an astonishing procession! Don't you wish you could be part of it? To visit old towns, see old paintings, and meet the people?"

Teddy shrugged and was less than enthusiastic.

"I'm happy here—not *here*—but home. When Jack comes home and we marry, we'll never leave the Cotswolds again."

"*Never?*"

"Except when Jack comes to London for Parliament. My uncle Roxton is making him a Parliamentarian when he returns from abroad, so Jack says he must spend a few months of the year in London doing whatever it is Parliamentarians do. Which is why Mama says I need to learn to be a lady, so I can be a helpmate to Jack," Teddy confided. "I don't know how I am to help him by being here at school, but I will try. Mama says if I busy myself with my schooling I won't think about Jack being away, and the time will pass very quickly. But even if I do what she says, and I try my hardest, I still can't stop thinking of my family... I miss Mama every day, and my step-papa, and—Do you have any brothers and sisters, Lisa?"

Lisa sought Teddy's hand and held it because she could see her friend was on the verge of tears.

"I don't. And both my parents are dead. I do have cousins... But they have each other... And I know if I had a mama like yours, and a family like yours, I would miss them very much too. Will you tell me about your family? I want to know *everything*. Don't leave *anything* out. I want to know *all* about them."

Teddy blinked the tears away and smiled and snuggled in, hand comfortably in Lisa's hold.

"I have two brothers. They are just babies. They are my *half*-brothers on account of Mama marrying again and starting a second family. Papa died when I was eight, and then Mama married Uncle Bryce—my step-papa. My big baby brother is named David and he's two. He has red hair just like mine. Granny Kate calls him her cheeky monkey. My little baby brother is just six months old and his name is Luke. He has black hair like my Uncle Dair, Mama's brother. But he's still too small for us to know if he'll be as cheeky as David. But he does laugh a lot and is a happy baby, so Granny Kate and I think he could very well be just as cheeky. I don't have a sister—yet. I asked Mama if her next baby could be a girl, and she said she would do her best—Lisa! I've had the best thought. You don't have any brothers or sisters, and I don't have a sister... *we* can be sisters! Would you? Would you like to have me as your sister...?"

"OH, TEDDY, I HAVE MISSED YOU SO VERY *VERY* MUCH," LISA uttered on a whispered sob, Teddy's handwriting bringing to life the vivid recollection of girlhood confidences shared with her best friend.

Such wonderful memories, such happy days... Bittersweet tears spilled on to her cheeks and her heart swelled with warmth as she briefly closed her eyes, still dazed to think that not only did she have letters from her school friend, but an invitation to her wedding, and best of all, she would soon be reunited with Teddy.

For now, she lay on her bed and read and re-read Teddy's letters, all six of them written over the two-year period since Lisa had left Blacklands. She then stared at the invitation for the longest time with the biggest smile. So Teddy was finally marrying her Jack—more correctly Sir John George Cavendish Bt.—just as she said she would, but not on her eighteenth birthday, but closer to her nineteenth, which was what her parents had wanted, so Teddy had written in her final letter. She also gave Lisa the surprising news that her Mama had finally, after all these years, given her a sister—Sophie-Kate. Teddy had written her letter to Lisa just a week after the infant's birth in the early spring. And with this welcome announcement, Teddy added a postscript that she had enlisted the help of her mother's cousin, the Duchess of Kinross, to ensure Lisa received this letter and invitation. She was determined to have her Blacklands sister at her wedding. And the Duchess had promised to do her very best to make this happen.

Lisa was in awe to think Teddy had gone to such lengths to make contact with her again. That she had also co-opted a duchess to help her verged on fantasy. But here she had that letter in her hand, and the invitation, and, finally, Teddy's other letters, too. So it was all true, and in two weeks' time she would be off to Hampshire to be reunited with Teddy, meet her family, and be part of her wedding celebrations. And she could thank the Duchess of Kinross in person for going to such lengths on her behalf.

Two weeks could not go quickly enough for Lisa. But there was still much to do between now and then, not least of which was to be fitted for gowns, shoes, and undergarments, and such fripperies as fans, pockets, and delicate lace fichus, the like of which Lisa had never had before. But that did not mean she could neglect her duties at the dispensary, so Mrs. Warner lectured on Monday morning at breakfast.

Lisa nodded mutely because she was so surprised to find her cousin up at such an hour and in the breakfast room. But there she was, and by her gown and application of cosmetics and arranged coiffure, was dressed to leave the house.

Minette Warner informed her that her parents and sister had returned from Paris, and she was off to Fournier Street for the day, to welcome them home and to give her mother an account of preparations for Lisa's stay in Hampshire. Her mother needed reassurance everything had been done that could be done to make certain Lisa was a credit to the de Crespigny family. There were no doubts she would be dressed for the various occasions during her two-week stay, the family had made certain her clothing was of a suitably high standard to be seen amongst the rarefied atmosphere of Treat. As to how she conducted herself while in such illustrious company, that was out of their control, and entirely in Lisa's hands. Did she understand?

"I do, Cousin," Lisa replied gravely and instinctively straightened her already straight back under Mrs. Warner's steady gaze.

Her cousin never missed an opportunity, since Lisa had received the invitation to Teddy's wedding, to repeat her mantra that Lisa must be on her best behavior, and never put herself forward nor get herself noticed. If she did not conduct herself with circumspection and humility, if she were singled out for any social infraction, her aunt would be mortified, and the family would never forgive her. The situation was a delicate one for everyone concerned. Nerves were frayed. Reputations and friendships balanced on a knife edge. How had it all come to this...? She wondered aloud on a sigh.

Lisa took her cousin's monologues on correct conduct and consequences in good part, and was careful to temper her enthusiasm and happiness, saying with a smile, "Please pass on my best wishes to my aunt and uncle, and to Toinette, for their safe return. And thank them on my behalf for supplying the fabrics for my gowns. And you will tell my aunt we have economized on employing a maid because Becky Bannister has agreed to accompany me to—"

"Yes. Yes. I will tell them," Minette Warner interrupted on a sigh, as if it was the most arduous task of her long day, and it not yet begun. "At least this Becky Bannister is expert with a needle, which has saved me employing my seamstress. I will grant, that was a stroke of luck— Oh! And while I'm away today, on no account are you to step outside the house. Heaven forbid something should befall you with less than a sennight until your journey, after the expense and effort we've incurred."

"Lisa will be fully occupied in the dispensary all day, dear heart, if the huddle of persons already at the door is any indication," Dr. Warner assured his wife with only one ear to the conversation, looking up over his wire rims from a letter that was consuming all his thoughts. He had left off his usual morning perusal of the newssheets.

"Good news I trust?" Mrs. Warner asked, sipping at her tea, gaze dropping to the letter in his hand.

"Good news? No. Confound it," Dr. Warner replied with uncustomary harshness. "It is not good news, my dear. It is the worst possible news!"

"Oh dear," Mrs. Warner pouted. "I do so dislike to see you so put out, Robert. It makes my head ache."

"Forgive me, my dear. But I'm afraid my mood has little chance of altering in the next little while—"

"Then it is as well I am going out for the day."

Lisa looked from Mrs. Warner, who had dropped her gaze to her teacup, to Dr. Warner, who had returned his attention to the letter, and asked in the silence, "Would you care to share your news, as disappointing as it is, sir?"

Mrs. Warner could have kicked her cousin's shin for asking, but she forced a smile, said nothing, and picked up a slice of bread smothered in jam. And as Lisa had leaned in and continued to look at him expectantly, it was all the encouragement the physician needed to vocalize his frustration. So he told them.

The letter he waved about and then dropped on top of the pile of newssheets was from the Fournier Foundation. At this, both Lisa's and Mrs. Warner's ears pricked, because Fournier Street was where the de Crespigny family home was located, and where Mrs. Warner was bound after breakfast. The very same, said her husband. The foundation's head of trustees lived in Fournier Street, an elderly physician by the name of Bailey. And it was at this Fournier Street address where the trustees met to discuss and decide on the allocation of funds, of which there was a finite amount each year.

The Foundation provided grants to those of the medical profession attending on the sick poor, and more importantly, to physicians engaged in anatomical research. There were strict criteria to meet, and if a candidate's application made it beyond the first round, the foundation's trustees visited the applicant's premises, conducted interviews with the principals, and assessed the merit of the establishment and the research being carried out. And because the money was ongoing for three years, with yearly reviews and goals to be met, every physician in London and beyond submitted a funding application. Only three dispensaries and anatomy schools were funded in any one year, and there was also the awarding of scholarships to the five most promising students of medicine in that year, who were given a stipend to assist them in completing their medical education and training without the hardship usually attendant on students. And once they passed their examinations before the Company of Surgeons, these scholarship holders agreed to be indentured for the first three years of their working life by attending on the sick poor.

"The work of this foundation is—" Lisa began and had her sentence completed by her cousin, and it was not what she was thinking at all.

"—costly."

"—is enormously worthwhile," Lisa finished, her enthusiasm causing her to interrupt her cousin. "Surely providing bright young men with the funds they need to focus on their anatomical investigations without their mind being clouded with the mundane worries of debt—whether to spend their meager allowance on books or bread—must give better focus to their studies?"

"That is very true," Dr. Warner agreed with a smile, Lisa's keen interest lifting some of the gloom from his shoulders about the letter's depressing outcome.

"This Dr. Bailey must be a very wealthy gentleman indeed," Mrs. Warner added, focused on monetary considerations. "Such scholarships and funding as required by the dispensaries must run into the hundreds of pounds, if not more than a thousand in any given year."

"Dr. Bailey is the foundation's figurehead, my dear," Dr. Warner explained. "And while it is the board of trustees which approves and allocates the funds, where those initial funds originated, and who created the Fournier Foundation, remains a mystery, to me and to my colleagues. And we are unlikely to be provided with an answer because the gentleman in question who has generously donated his largesse to this beneficial enterprise wishes to remain in the shadows. It is not even certain if Dr. Bailey knows the man's identity. But you are quite right, my dear, the foundation's charitable assistance must run into the hundreds of pounds, if not a thousand per annum."

"And you wrote to this foundation and requested funding for your endeavors," Mrs. Warner said with a bright smile.

"I did," he replied but with less enthusiasm than she was exhibiting on the expectation of a favorable outcome. "I requested monies to provide for an anatomical instructor and a morbid anatomist. The former would ease my teaching load, and the latter I could set to work making the wax models of specimens necessary for instruction. There is a new technique using various colored waxes of differing injection sizes. But it is necessary for the injection to be heated to a liquid, but not boiled, or that is likely to destroy the texture of the vessels to be filled…"

This was when the dear doctor lost the full attention of his wife, who now had only one ear to the conversation, daydreaming about the mysterious benefactor of the Fournier Foundation, wondering if he was a bachelor, married, a merchant who had made his money in any number of trade ventures, or perhaps he was a benevolent ancient nobleman with no children whose inheritance was not entailed and could be used to good purpose elsewhere other than his estate…

And because she was daydreaming, Mrs. Warner did not make immediate comment when her dear doctor revealed with a downturn to his mouth that his application had been rejected on the grounds that the foundation had met its quota for the year. It was politely suggested that Dr. Warner apply again next funding cycle, which was an entire year from now. Valuable time and opportunity to acquire unique anatomical resources—by which Lisa knew the physician was referring to human specimens—would be lost between now and then. And as this was the second application he had submitted and which had been rejected, and for the very same reason, Dr. Warner had his suspicions that his applications were not being put under the right noses.

"Do you mean Dr. Bailey's nose, sir?" Lisa asked, who had been all rapt attention while the physician described in superfluous detail the method of mixing the dyes for the purpose of injecting the different anatomical specimens.

Dr. Warner hit the side of the table with his palm, which jolted his inattentive wife from her private reveries. He smiled across at Lisa. "Precisely! That is indeed the nose I am talking about."

"Dear me, Dr. Warner! You gave me such a fright just now," Mrs. Warner complained, and to mask her inattentiveness added with a girlish pout, "I do believe it has upset my digestion."

"I do beg your pardon, my dear," the physician replied sheepishly, and pushed aside his plate of unfinished egg and toast.

"Perhaps if you were to invite Dr. Bailey to dinner, sir, you could find the opportunity to show him the dissecting room and your anatomical work?" Lisa suggested in the protracted silence between husband and wife, looking from the physician to her cousin and back again. "As a fellow medical man, he could not but be impressed by your great work, surely?"

"An excellent notion, and one I had—"

"Why indeed have we not had Dr. Bailey to dinner, Robert?" Mrs. Warner interrupted, perturbed it was left to Lisa to make such a suggestion. "I have never heard of this Fournier Foundation before today, and perhaps if we had invited the trustees earlier, you may have expected a different outcome to your application?"

"An invitation was extended to Dr. Bailey, and regretfully he declined," Dr. Warner explained patiently. "I did not wish to bother you with the disappointment, my dear—"

"You are as ever attentive to my feelings, my dear Dr. Warner," his wife said sweetly. "Surely he would not refuse a second time, not if we were to invite a few of your colleagues who might be known to Dr. Bailey and his trustees. I have always found that men are much more persuadable and malleable after a good dinner, though persuasion does not always lend itself to action—"

"Yes. Yes. Well. Well. We won't have that opportunity now," Dr. Warner blustered and coughed into his fist, cheeks bright, because Lisa was listening intently to a conversation he now considered had crossed the divide of what was polite at the breakfast table before a nineteen-year-old girl, though he had never deemed detailed discussion of medical matters in the same light. "I will do as you suggest, my dear, and issue a second invitation, and hopefully, regardless of the failure of my application, he will accept."

"He may see the dinner invitation as a gesture of goodwill? That you bear him no ill will despite the rejection of your application," Lisa suggested, quickly putting aside her mug of hot chocolate and her napkin and scraping back her chair when her cousin rose from the table. "He could not then, in good conscience, refuse the invitation."

Dr. Warner, also up on his feet, beamed at Lisa. "By Jove, that is exactly what he will see it as! That has decided me. I shall write to Dr. Bailey tonight."

Minette Warner looked at Lisa and smiled thinly. "And here was I thinking breakfast was a dull affair for you... Not so, it seems. Something to be reconsidered when you return from Hampshire. Now off you go; I wish to have a private word with Dr. Warner. And you must have a hundred and one tasks to do for the good doctor before he sees his first patient of the morning."

Lisa obediently bobbed a curtsy and departed, leaving behind a mug of hot chocolate she had been enjoying. She collected up her writing box with its quills, ink, and paper and made her way across the passageway and through to the dispensary, which occupied the front rooms of the lower level of the double-fronted townhouse. Here she deposited her writing box in her usual corner, where she offered her services as amanuensis to any who required it, took her apron off its peg, and quickly put it on over her gown. A check of the pins holding the lace cap to the crown of her head, and she bustled about performing her duties—seeing to the scent bottles and tussie mussies, that water jugs were filled, and soap, pumice, and towels provided in each of the curtained treatment cubicles—and all this accomplished without getting in the way of the medical assistants who were preparing for the first influx of patients.

And as the door to the dispensary was unlocked to admit the first patients of the day, Lisa's thoughts were all about the week after next. In a week's time she would be on her way to see Teddy, and to a place so vastly different from this that she found it difficult to imagine it at all. Just as a mere five days ago when she and Becky had set off for Leicester Square, she could hardly have imagined what would occur within the walls of Lord Westby's townhouse. That incident had slipped her mind since receiving Teddy's letters. Yet it came hurtling back to the forefront of her thoughts, when not five minutes after the dispensary opened, the crowd was made to part to allow two oversized men to enter the waiting room ahead of everyone else.

They were so out of place that Lisa blinked, and then she gave a start of recognition. They were *the lads*, the two servants sent for to assist the gentleman she had helped at Lord Westby's residence. Surely they were not flesh and blood but conjured up, for how did they know where to find her? After a quick look about the already crowded room, their gaze locked on hers, and that same spark of recognition was reflected in their eyes. There was nothing for Lisa to do but stand her ground and let them come to her.

Wide-shouldered and a good head taller than those around them, they were also healthy, upright, and mobile, which was in marked contrast to the persons shuffling in behind them. Their size and vigor might ensure everyone got out of their way, but it was their clothing that made people stare. They were dressed in suits of livery of black cloth with elaborate silver lacings and silver buttons, which was a proclamation of the wealth and importance of their master, and it gave them right-of-way to do and say as they pleased, their height and the size of their fists merely reinforcing this.

The two lads came straight up to Lisa. And when they were in front of her they did not speak, but stood aside to allow a gentleman she had failed to see because he was obscured by these tall wide blocks, to step up to her, and make her a bow. She held her breath and her heart gave the oddest little leap, hoping for a moment it might be the handsome gentleman she had assisted at Lord Westby's. And then her pulse quickened, and not in a good way, wondering if he had come in search of her and Becky over his misplaced catalog to the Portland auction. And then the gentleman removed the perfumed handkerchief he was holding up to his nose, and she breathed a sigh of relief mixed with disappointment. She did not know this man at all.

The stranger gave an imperious lift of his brows, and asked, "Are you Lisa?"

She nodded and bobbed a polite curtsy. Then added, because he continued to regard her as if he required more from her, "Lisa Crisp."

He inclined his head in thanks for this information, then said before turning on a heel and expecting her to obey,

"Follow me, Miss Crisp. My master is desirous of a word, in private, in his carriage."

SEVEN

"She—*refuses*?"

"Yes, my lord."

Lord Henri-Antoine stared at his major domo framed in the carriage window as if the man were speaking any language but one he understood, and he understood at least five. He waited for further explanation.

"Miss Crisp is unable to leave the premises."

"Unable?"

"Yes, my lord."

"Is she recently crippled?"

"Not crippled."

"Then she is not unable, she is *unwilling*."

Michel Gallet dared to smile. "I did point out that difference to her. However, she will not budge."

"Then have her carried out here."

"Kicking and screaming—"

"She's not the screaming sort."

"Is she not, my lord…?"

Henri-Antoine was not fooled by his major domo's light tone of inquiry. He set his teeth and waited for the man's smile, and his gaze, to drop.

"Apologies, my lord… What would you have me do?"

Henri-Antoine glanced over his major domo's left shoulder to the small crowd gathered on the pavement by the steps up to the entrance of Warner's Dispensary. They were a ragged lot, with dirty faces and tired expressions, their interest in the shiny black lacquered *Berlin* with its matching four grays mingled with a wariness, no doubt as to the reason why such an impressive vehicle was in this part of the city, and at this early hour, too.

He rarely ventured into this part of London—he had no need to, and when he did, it was only to visit Westby's lodgings. And he never came by carriage, but had burly chairmen in his employ take him up in his private sedan chair. His townhouse in Park Street was a mere thirty minutes west by such a conveyance, yet Warner's Dispensary here in Gerrard Street was a world away from the elegant houses, wide streets, and orderly, well-dressed pedestrians who inhabited the rarefied Westminster address where he lived. But such transportation would not do for a private word with Miss Lisa Crisp. It never entered his head that it was the four liveried postillions, the wide-shouldered lads, and most importantly his esteemed self, that were attracting more attention than his elegant town carriage.

He set his shoulders against the velvet upholstery with an annoyed sigh and had half a mind to tap the headboard with his gloved knuckle and be off. What was he doing here anyway? He was under no obligation to Miss Lisa Crisp. And if she didn't possess the good manners to come outside so he could have a civil word with her—after all he was the one who had called upon her—he need not exert himself further. He wouldn't. The act of coming here was more than enough of an acknowledgement of her good deed on his behalf.

And yet there was something—he could not put his finger on precisely *what*, but it greatly unsettled him—that made him resist giving the signal to his driver. Part of it was chivalry, instilled in him from the cradle, to do the right thing, to behave as a gentleman ought, and thank her in person. Part of it was curiosity, to want to put a face to the name Jack had given him of the girl who had come to his assistance when he had been at his most deplorable. And, if Jack were to be believed, Miss Lisa Crisp was a rare female indeed—calm, capable, cheerful, and not at all repulsed by his condition. That she worked amongst the sick poor no doubt accounted for that. Still. He wanted to see her for himself. He wanted to know if she equated to the Botticelli angel who had appeared out of his epileptic delirium as he staggered from Westby's drawing room. But most of all he wanted this feeling of disquiet and restlessness, a feeling that left him anxious for no apparent reason, to go away forthwith. And for some unfathomable reason this feeling had everything to do with the unflappable Miss Crisp.

He sat forward, his major domo still up on the carriage step at the window patiently waiting further instructions.

"I'm not going in there!" he blurted out, which said more about his troubled thoughts than his present predicament.

"A sensible decision, my lord. The place is jammed with all manner of diseased riff-raff, and the air is fetid."

"And yet Miss Crisp is in there amongst this riff-raff? Is she fetid, Michel?" he asked, hopeful of an affirmative response; it would give him the excuse he needed to leave at once.

"No, my lord. Quite the opposite. She is the spring flower blooming amongst the rotting refuse."

"Of course she is," Henri-Antoine muttered.

"Shall I try again to make her see reason...?"

Henri-Antoine nodded, a frown between his dark brows, gaze on the dispensary's front door which was being opened and closed with alarming regularity. "Do that." Adding in a complete reversal, "And you had best try your damndest, because if you can't persuade her, and she still refuses to come out, I will have to go to her."

"Is that wise, my lord? The level of miasma in such a place as a dispensary must be beyond what any healthy man can tolerate who is not used to being surrounded by illness. And for you to breathe such air would surely severely compromise your health, and thus I must counsel against putting yourself in a most dangerous situation."

There was that damned word again—*wise*—Jack, his servants, everyone around him, used it too often. If he were wise he'd not have got himself drunk, and smoked enough cheroots to burn his throat. If he were wise he'd have left Westby's drawing room well before the onset of an attack. If he were wise he wouldn't be here now, outside a London *hôtel-Dieu*.

"Then you had best be at your most persuasive," he stated, and pulled the blind on his major-domo and the crowd of curious onlookers.

MICHEL GALLET RETURNED TO THE CARRIAGE WITH THE welcome news Miss Crisp could give His Lordship a few minutes of her time. She understood his master's reluctance to breath a miasma that could very well cause him harm, but she could not come out to the carriage, of that she was adamant. She did, however, offer a solution to the dilemma. Dr. Warner had a private consulting room across the hall from the dispensary where their meeting could take place. The consulting room could be entered via a door that led onto the street, and was for the use of private patients only. M'sieur Gallet's master could come and go via this door, without coming into contact with the miasma that lingered in the dispensary.

However, she would first need to prepare herself, because Dr. Warner had rules which he himself, his medical attendants, his student physicians, and Lisa, were all required to follow when leaving the confines of the dispensary. Aprons and sleeves were to be removed, hands washed and nails scrubbed clean with soap, to remove all traces of the smell of the ill and the dying. A few drops of Warner's patented scent were then sprinkled on the skin to aid this process.

Perhaps one of the lads could wait by the private entrance, and when she was ready, Miss Crisp would unlock the consulting door and he could then inform his master?

"Such elaborate preparations, and all for a two-minute conversation," Henri-Antoine drawled, head back against the upholstery, eyes closed. He had a sudden thought and opened one eye and looked at Michel, who was still at the carriage window.

"You were careful not to mention me by name."

"I did not tell her, and she did not ask, my lord."

Lisa was standing by the desk of the consulting room, the door that opened out onto the hallway left wide, so there was a clear view of the base of the stairs that led up to the private living quarters where she lived with Dr. and Mrs. Warner. Past the staircase, further across the hall, was a closed door painted with the word *Dispensary* across the top rail. Beside this door sat Joseph, an elderly servant who had been in the physician's employ since his first marriage, and now acted as porter, when he wasn't dozing in his chair.

She had left wide the consulting room door so Joseph could see in and she could see him, because young ladies did not receive male callers who were not direct relatives or guardians, alone. Though the very idea this gentleman had come to call on her was so ludicrous as to be laughable. And although she had told one of the dispensary assistants where she would be and that she would return within the half-hour, she knew Cousin Minette would not be at all pleased she had agreed to this meeting, without Dr. Warner's knowledge or approval.

Yet she was not nervous in the same way as she had been when she and Becky had entered Lord Westby's residence, only to be mistaken for harlots. This was a different sort of nervousness. It was one of heart-pounding anticipation. She found herself worrying about her hair, and the sit of her lace cap, and the fact she was wearing a plain gown of serviceable linen, and her sensible half-boots. And it didn't matter how hard or for how long she scrubbed her hands, the ink stains from the hours spent as an amanuensis for the poor could not be scrubbed away. None of this had ever bothered her in the past. It shouldn't have bothered her now. But it did.

She felt inadequate, insignificant, ordinary. And then the door opened and none of that mattered.

First to step into the room was one of the beefy liveried lads. He took a sweeping look about him then opened the door wider to admit his master, who came in followed by the other beefy lad. This lad closed the door and stayed by it, while his twin went and stood by the open door that gave access to the hallway. Both exits were now blocked, leaving Lisa trapped with her visitor. Not that she felt trapped. Slightly unnerved by the presence of such hulks, yes, but her attention was quickly diverted from them to her visitor, who was taking a slow turn about the small room.

He stopped in front of her, close enough that all he need do to look her over was move his eyes, and without effort. He then planted the end of his walking stick to the floor by the toe of his shoe and let it lean outward, held in place by one gloved hand about its ivory handle with its diamond encrusted top. The knuckles of his right hand he put to his hip. With his chin parallel to the floor, and gaze direct, he thus presented himself, and waited, as was his right, to receive her due acknowledgment.

Lisa did not move. She could not. She was too much affected to do more than gawp at him as if he were a theater performer. Not that she had ever been to the theater or the opera, but she had read reports, and listened to her cousins talk on and on about whom they had seen in the boxes at Drury Lane, the performance of secondary importance to the illustrious personages in attendance.

Oh, but he was splendid!

He was everything she imagined he would be, if she ever had the opportunity to see him as he wished to be seen by others. Tall, lean, and angular, with a tousle of thick black hair pulled back off his face, his strong nose was just as aquiline and straight as she remembered it. And his mouth… as kissable as ever. The small horizontal crease in his square chin was a surprise and something she had not noticed when she had stroked his hair in the hopes it would soothe his suffering. It was also heavier, or perhaps that was because it now nestled in the folds of a white linen cravat tied off in a neat bow. And where he had been dressed in lilac silk at Lord Westby's, this outfit was a pale sky-blue linen, the front panels of the waistcoat delicately embroidered with a tangle of vine and flowers, with matching covered buttons. And over this he wore an expertly-tailored frock coat of the same fine linen, with a high collar, tight cuffs, and short skirts, matching embroidery to covered buttons and pocket flaps.

She supposed his tight-fitting black breeches were of summer linen, too, and that the jewels encrusted on the buckles in his black leather shoes were diamonds, but as she had already dared to linger longer than was polite on such heady masculinity presented in such sumptuous finery, she reluctantly pulled her appreciative gaze up to meet his eyes, and with an expression she hoped did not reveal her thoughts.

A pair of black orbs stared at her with unblinking directness. She suddenly found her throat unaccountably dry. Pressing her lips together she swallowed and forced herself to breathe. With that stare he could beckon forth any female he fancied, and no doubt did, frequently; show displeasure without the need to say a word, and did; and he could appraise a female from face to feet without revealing his thoughts.

And he was doing just that—*to her.*

She wondered why. Possibly he was trying to recall if he remembered her from their brief encounter in the passageway of Lord Westby's townhouse, or was it because he had never before had to bother with noticing those beneath him in consequence. And then she happened to catch the facial tick that lifted the corner of his top lip. It was an infinitesimal movement, and one perhaps he was unaware of himself. But she did not doubt its significance. His stare might not give away his thoughts, but that facial tick most certainly did. He was aware that she had just been admiring him, and it amused him.

She was so startled to be discovered that she unconsciously put a hand flat to the desk, as if needing to support herself and stop her knees from buckling. Was it suddenly hot in this room? But there was no fire in the grate, and never was, except on Tuesdays when Dr. Warner saw private patients.

And then she castigated herself for her naïvete. Receiving the admiring glances and come-hither looks of females was a matter of course for him, as natural as breathing. All part of the social transactions within his world. But she was not of his world, and he was most definitely out of his milieu in Gerrard Street. And so perhaps it amused him to find himself admired by a social inferior. So why was he here, and why did he wish to see her? The Portland catalog came to mind but if he did indeed think she and Becky had anything to do with its disappearance, then surely he would have sent the bailiffs around, not come in person to accuse her of stealing his property?

Suddenly, she realized he had spoken to her, and while she did not catch the question, she guessed it, thankful to still be leaning a hand on the desk. For if his person had made her knees unstable, his voice—that voice that was indeed as rich and as smooth as hot chocolate—was worthy of a dead faint onto a chaise longue. But as the nearest chaise was in her cousin's boudoir she remained upright and, she hoped, indifferent enough to answer him in a clear voice.

"Lisa Crisp, sir," she stated, and came away from the desk to finally find her manners and bob a curtsy, gaze respectfully lowered to the embroidered front of his waistcoat.

"I know your name, Miss Crisp. I asked for your age."

This brought her eyes up to his face, puzzled. "Why would you want to know my age, sir?"

He was taken aback she would question him. "Why would you not want to tell me?"

"I've no particular reason for withholding it from you. It's just—It's a rather mundane question—coming from you."

"Mundane? *Coming from me*? What question were you expecting me to ask?"

She smiled at his frown, and relaxed a little. Gone was the fixed stare, replaced by a look of puzzlement which made him appear far more approachable.

"I'd no particular question in mind," she responded, and unable to stop herself because she had flustered him, added teasingly, "Perhaps you'll think of one before you leave?"

"Think of one…?"

Her directness disconcerted him. He had wanted this interview to be short. He had gone to considerable trouble to find her with the limited information Jack had given him, and now he wished to thank her for her help in his hour of need, and be on his way. But the short speech of thanks that was on the tip of his tongue vanished like a popped soap bubble the moment he entered the room and saw her standing by the desk. Instead, he had asked her for her age. Why in God's name? And she had the impertinence not to tell him. He needed to regain the initiative at once, before she startled him again. He should not have been surprised when she again overthrew his intent, but he was.

"Miss Crisp, I had hoped to conduct this conversation in my carriage, so as not to attract any undue attention to either of us."

"But that must be an impossible task for you, surely?"

"Impossible? Why?"

Lisa blinked at him and such was her surprise that she took a step closer, wondering if he was being ironic. She had to ask the question.

"Are you funning with me, sir?"

Now he was not only disconcerted but uncomfortable. He set his jaw and the stare returned.

"I assure you, Miss Crisp, that I do not *fun*—with anyone."

"Do you not? Not at all?"

Irritated, he wondered if she were simple. But one look in her blue eyes and he knew she was sincere in her incredulity. He did not know whether to be annoyed or flattered.

"Tell me, Miss Crisp," he purred. "Why would I find it an impossible task not to attract attention?"

Lisa gulped. "You want me to tell you?"

"I do."

"Very well. If I must. But I do not doubt for a moment you know the answer."

"I do not. And I hope your answer, unlike my question, will not be mundane."

Lisa's blue eyes sparked and she smiled.

"Well?" he demanded when she did not give him an immediate response.

"Oh! So you truly do want me to tell you?"

When his gaze shot to the bare ceiling and then back at her and he remained silent and expectant, she lost her smile and felt the heat rise in her throat. There was nothing for it. She would have to tell him.

"Because you are exceedingly handsome, so it stands to reason you attract an audience wherever you go."

The silence stretched between them and then he nodded gravely. The only sign that he was in anyway embarrassed by her honest appraisal was the sudden color in his lean cheeks.

"So I am told. But I come from a family of exceptional beauty. I am its thorn."

Lisa gasped and then giggled, thinking his response absurd. Not that she disbelieved him, she just did not believe he could be a thorn in any family. She quickly put a hand to her mouth for her impolite response, but could not stop her shoulders from shaking.

"I beg your pardon, Miss Crisp," he drawled, affronted. "I was being perfectly candid."

Lisa nodded, quickly wiped her moist eyes dry and pressed her lips together before taking a breath and saying with a tremble, "I meant no disrespect, sir. It's just that you are no thorn, however beautiful the rest of your family members."

He threw up a gloved hand in dismissal of her frank appraisal.

"You might think so. No doubt in these heady environs, anyone with two working eyes and a straight back is considered a rose worthy of oils."

Lisa lost her smile, and her blue eyes clouded, all humor extinguished at his jibe. Perhaps he had meant it as a throwaway comment to hide his embarrassment at being complimented for his good looks. Regardless, that gave him no excuse to be so disparaging of others, and his barb stung.

"Perhaps I was wrong," she said quietly but firmly. "Perhaps you are a thorn. True beauty does not wear a mask. It shines bright from the heart—and regardless of where that heart resides on the compass point." She bobbed a curtsy. "I am glad to see you looking so well after your recent seizure, sir. Now you must excuse me. I am wanted elsewhere."

EIGHT

Lord Henri-Antoine flushed scarlet.

She had rebuked *him*, then dismissed him as if he were a lackey. A girl in a plain gown and scuffed shoes, whose fingers were ink stained, the nails short to the quick, skin rough from work, and whose family were possibly one step up from the gutter, had dared to reproach *him*, the son of a duke and a double duchess, and brother of the most powerful duke in the kingdom.

He was outraged. He clenched his teeth to stop himself vocalizing his anger. Hard gripping his walking stick and counting to five was all he could do to stop himself turning on a heel and striding from the room. But then, just as quickly, the anger cooled, emotion giving way to reason as he recalled, as he always did when a situation demanded it, his father's words of wisdom: Always control your emotions when in the public gaze. Love and laughter are reserved for the privileged few. Arrogance is a nobleman's prerogative; but a true gentleman chooses to be humble when the circumstance calls for it. Never forget you are my son; others won't.

He deserved her rebuke.

He had permitted hubris to cloud good judgment and been ill mannered. He had highlighted their disparate circumstances by making light of her surroundings and its people, and he a guest in her home. He had been ungentlemanly, his response that of a conceited jackanapes. His father would be appalled. And for all his ducal arrogance, M'sieur le Duc d'Roxton would never have said what he did in the first place. He must make amends for such a social solecism.

Jack said he owed this girl, if not his life, then the hold on his dignity. She had taken care of him, shielded him from prying eyes, soothed him, even washed his face, for God's sake... He must've been a sorry sight... And Jack said she had not flinched, or failed him. He had wanted to disbelieve Jack, though he knew he spoke the truth, thinking this girl had to be too good to be true. And then he'd discovered where she resided, and that she volunteered her time at a dispensary, and it reinforced everything Jack had told him. And there was something else, something that had occurred immediately after he had come out of his seizure, that he knew Jack had not been party to, but this girl had. It was so deeply personal he wished with every drop of blood in his veins he'd been alone, that she had not been there with him. But she had, and she knew, and there was no point wishing it was otherwise, because there was nothing he could do about that now.

That knowledge, and his distasteful display of arrogance, only strengthened his resolve to make amends. And the sooner the better. He could then return to Park Street and consign this girl, and whatever uneasiness he was experiencing because of her, to yesterday. His life would return to its daily controlled rhythm; the façade he maintained that he was seizure-free firmly back in place, no one the wiser.

But where Miss Crisp was concerned, he was soon to learn, best laid plans were destined to go awry.

"Miss Crisp—A moment, if you please," he requested in an appeasing tone.

Lisa turned back into the room. Not that she could leave even if she wanted to. The beefy servant blocked her exit and was not about to step aside to let her pass until he was given the order to do so. But she stood her ground. And so he came over to her. He made her a bow.

"Accept my humble apology for my bad manners. My comment about this place and its people was inexcusable. You are correct. I do wear a mask, and you—you have seen behind it."

"You refer to your affliction."

"I do." Adding lightly, the facial tick resurfacing, "I am still a thorn, with or without my mask. I have a prickly temperament. My family will tell you so. But what they cannot tell you is what is behind the mask, because they do not know."

Lisa took a step closer, head tilted in curiosity. "But how can they not? You have had the falling sickness since birth. So your friend confided."

Henri-Antoine's reflex was to curse Jack for his easy going confidences, throw up a hand and brush off her question. He resisted. For coming to his aid she deserved his honesty. He wanted to be open with her, and he was never open with anyone.

"I prefer not to concern my family with my condition. And so I go to great lengths to make certain, as best I can, that they not interfere, and that the world remains ignorant."

"You can be assured of my discretion, sir," Lisa told him earnestly. Adding with a wry smile, "Though I have no notion of who your family are, nor do they know me. Regardless, I would never break your confidence."

"Thank you. You did not mention the—um—incident to the doctor with whom you reside?"

"No, sir. To no one. Though I do not understand why you would not want the support of your family."

"Believe me, Miss Crisp," he drawled. "I had enough support as a child to last me a dozen lifetimes."

She smiled in understanding.

"Children like to be coddled. Men do not—That is," she confided with a bashful smile, "not directly."

"Coddled, yes. Suffocated, no," he quipped, and then her acute observation penetrated his consciousness and he looked at her keenly, a frown between his black brows. "How old did you say you were?"

Her smile widened and she lifted her chin. There was a playful light in her blue eyes. "I did not say, sir."

"This unwillingness to tell me your age is tiresome," he complained. "Though it is unnecessary for me to know your age to deduce you did not grow up here in Gerrard Street."

Her eyes went round with surprise.

"That is true. I did not. From the age of nine I attended a boarding school for young ladies in Chelsea. But how did you know?"

"A boarding school for young ladies in Chelsea?" he repeated with a detached interest that hid his surprise. "Of course you did," he muttered.

He did not like this revelation at all because it would've been much easier on his conscience to dismiss her had she not been educated and carefully nurtured in the way of girls who are expected to marry and spend their lives as wives and mothers in comfort, if not in wealth. But something told him as soon as he set eyes on her that she was no mere servant of the physician Warner. There was nothing servile or coquettish in the way she conducted herself. She had a confident air and a polite, if rather direct, approach. He doubted she knew how to flirt, and arrogantly he was glad of it. He did not like the idea of her flirting —with anyone.

He wondered why she had been sent off to a boarding school at such a young age. He knew all about boarding school. He had hated every minute of his time at Eton. Not that he had let his feelings be known because it wasn't manly to blubber at being away from his parents, and he wanted so much to be thought of as just one of the boys. His falling sickness precluded that, and forever set him apart. Yet it was only while he was at Eton that he'd considered his seizures a blessing. One too many attacks in a month, and his personal physician, who followed him everywhere, sent for his father. And M'sieur le Duc d'Roxton would arrive in state in his big black carriage with six fine horses to take him home. And all the boys and masters would be in awe of this ancient aristocrat who was king of his own dominion. And then one day his father told him he would not be returning to Eton. He and Jack would complete their education at home. It had been one of the happiest days of his life, and also one of the saddest. It was the day he had come upon his mother sobbing until she could not breathe, his father's physicians gathered around her, delivering her the news that there was no hope; M'sieur le Duc, her husband and his father, was dying...

"Sir? How did you know I did not grow up on Gerrard Street?" Lisa repeated, taking another step closer when he did not answer her immediately.

"How...?" he asked, dragging his thoughts out of the past to focus on her, which was a much more pleasant and soothing experience than reliving the painful memories of his boyhood.

She had a lovely smile and her deep blue eyes were bright and open. He doubted she had a deceitful bone in her body. A body that was too thin, with a barely-there bosom, but that did not detract from her beauty. Her pleasing oval face, slender limbs, and graceful neck, and the way she carried herself, were most attractive. And while she was not beautiful in a breathtaking sense, she was enough above the ordinary to be memorable. He wondered if she was too thin because she tended to the sick. Who could eat well, if at all, after spending the day amongst the poorest of poor wretches, with all their attendant ailments, diseases, and complaints. He was intrigued she had managed to remain healthy and so full of life, given her daily routine.

"Tell me, Miss Crisp," he demanded more harshly than he intended because he did not like the idea of such a bright young female wasting her days in a dispensary heady with miasma. "For how long have you been working in the dispensary?"

It took her a moment to respond because she had been expecting an answer to her question about not growing up on Gerrard Street. And his sudden anger surprised her.

"Two years, perhaps a little longer—"

"Two *years?*" He was flabbergasted. When she nodded he asked, "And in those two years how often have you been struck down with an illness, or been infected by these people?"

"Never. I've never—"

"*Never?* Not a cold, or a fever, or the slightest chill *ever?*"

"No, sir."

"What about smallpox, consumption, puerile fever, any contagion whatsoever?"

Lisa shook her head. "No, sir. I've never been ill a day in my life."

It was Henri-Antoine's turn to take a step closer, and he allowed his gaze to sweep over her with uncustomary openness. With her glowing unblemished skin, shiny hair, and white smile, he believed her to be the healthiest person he had ever had the privilege of meeting. Yet he was incredulous, because it was as if he could not quite believe he had come across such a rare find in this most unlikely of places.

"Fascinating."

Lisa took a step away mistaking his wonder for skepticism. "It is the truth, sir. Dr Warner will attest to it. He says I am worthy of further study."

He nodded, and before he could stop himself muttered, "You are worthy indeed, Miss Crisp."

"I am?" She still wasn't sure if she should be flattered or alarmed. And because he was regarding her in a manner she found unnerving, added to fill the silence, "Dr. Warner is never ill either. And he spends many more hours than I do, shut up with his patients, and in the garret where he has his dissecting room."

Mention of a dissecting room piqued his interest and brought him out of his abstraction.

"There is a dissecting room upstairs?"

"And an anatomy theater, and a preparation room, too."

"Dr. Warner is well equipped. Do your duties extend outside the dispensary to assist the physician in these areas as well?"

Lisa smiled as if he had said something highly amusing. "Only the medical students and teaching staff *assist* Dr. Warner. And as you are well aware, they are all men."

"But you do go up there?"

"To change out the scent fabrics and tussie mussies. Bring new candles and soap, and make certain the soiled garments are collected up for laundering. They are all part of my duties in the dispensary and upstairs as well."

He raised an eyebrow. "Dear me, what a strong constitution you have, Miss Crisp. I'm sure the stench alone must be frightful, not to mention the sight of such grisly offerings being inspected, dissected, and injected by our medical marvels. Though you must sorely test their powers of concentration as you flit amongst the cadavers with your fragrance and your flowers."

Lisa's back stiffened and she clasped her hands in front of her.

"I assure you, sir, that I take my duties very seriously. Dr. Warner is a fine physician. He is also a brilliant teacher, and his research is second to none. I do not *flit* and I would never seek to distract—"

He held up a gloved hand. "Miss Crisp, I do not doubt it. I was not casting aspersions on your dedication, or the good doctor's expertise. I was merely—how did you put it?—*funning* with you."

"Oh? Oh! Yes, I see. So you were." Her smile was shy, but her eyes held a twinkle of mischief. "A good first attempt, but you need to practice if you wish to make others smile."

Later he wasn't sure what made him say it, the shy smile or the twinkle in her blue eyes, when he spoke his thoughts, "Making others smile does not interest me. Whereas, you do…"

"I do?"

"And in answer to your previous question," he continued smoothly, waking from his trance, a glance at the pearl face of his gold pocket watch, which he had taken from a waistcoat pocket to give him time to regain his equilibrium. He then met her gaze again with no idea of the hour or the minute. "I know you did not grow up here in Gerrard Street because you do not have the same cadence as your fellows. There is little, if any, dialect in your speech. It is a learned way of speaking. From your school days, perhaps? You do it very well, and most persons would not notice. I hear it because I have an excellent linguistic ear; comes from spending my boyhood lying on a sofa, listening."

"How intriguing. I am somewhat of a linguist myself. I learned Italian at school, and French, not English, was my first language when I was a small child, which may account for my learned way of speaking in English without any dialect. My family are French emigrés. Did you learn to be fluent in the French tongue while lying on a sofa?"

She was merely responding to him by making polite conversation. That's what he told himself. But when she mentioned her first language was French, his whole manner changed. He wondered if she had told him this as a veiled reference to the deeply personal incident that had occurred when she had tended to him at Westby's residence. He hoped, but could not be certain, it was an innocent conversational remark with no further meaning. Either way, it was a timely reminder of why he had come to Warner's Dispensary in the first place: Not to exchange pleasantries or to know more than was necessary about this girl, but to thank her for coming to his aid. And having done his duty, he would leave and never think about that embarrassing incident, or her, again.

And so he ignored her question, though when he bowed to her and looked into her eyes, he could not ignore the sensation of tightness in his chest, as if his cravat was bound too tightly about his throat. He needed to end this interview and leave now, before he got caught up in something not of his own making, and which was taken wholly out of his control.

"Thank you for coming to my aid," he stated formally, and lifted his walking stick a fraction—signal of his readiness to depart, and which saw the two lads move to stand together by the entrance door. "That you were witness to the twisted tremors of my broken, ill-made self was an unfortunate circumstance which I—"

"Please, sir, you need not apologize," Lisa interrupted. "The falling sickness is not new to me, and if it will ease your mind, I have seen far worse suffering and disease here at the dispensary than perhaps you can possibly imagine."

"My dear girl, I was not about to apologize," he retorted. "Had you not trespassed into Lord Westby's residence and put yourself in harm's way, you and your friend would not have had to deal with my-my— with what was, quite frankly, none of your business. What you were doing there and at that hour, I hate to hazard a guess. Westby's servants mistook you for harlots. Ha! At least your interference in my collapse—"

Lisa gasped. "*Interference?*"

"—saved you from a state of affairs that was most certainly well beyond your purview of expertise."

"I beg your pardon, sir, but I do not understand. What did I say to anger you? What—"

"Good day, Miss Crisp... Let me out of here!" he growled at his minders as he turned on a heel, the short skirts of his frock coat swishing about his thighs, the walking stick snatched up and the diamond-studded handle pointed at the door.

Lisa went after him, but he was out the door, a servant before him, and one following up behind, and she stopped on the doorstep, a silent witness to his abrupt departure.

He crossed the short distance to his waiting carriage. The liveried postilions were keeping the crowd well back, and his major domo was on the pavement by the fold-down steps waiting for him.

"Not a word!"

Michel Gallet inclined his head and silently followed his master up into the carriage.

Lord Henri-Antoine leaned back against the padded headboard and closed his eyes. The feeling of disquiet and restlessness, the feeling that had left him anxious for no apparent reason since his seizure at Westby's, the feeling he hoped would vanish once he had met and thanked Miss Lisa Crisp, had not gone away at all. If anything, that feeling was now ten times worse. And with his eyes closed, the same vision remained in his mind's eye—that of a Botticelli beauty. Only now the beauty had a name.

NINE

HENRI-ANTOINE LOOKED UP FROM THE PAGE HE WAS READING AS a footman opened the door to the book room to admit Jack. His best friend came across the deep carpet to the fireplace and sprawled out in the chair opposite. He was frowning, and Jack rarely if ever frowned.

"Coffee?" Henri-Antoine enquired mildly, resting the open book on his silken knee and putting his coffee cup on the side table. He leaned forward to raise the silver coffee urn from its warmer. "Or do you require something stronger…?" When Jack did not immediately respond, he gave a nod to the footman. "Brandy—"

"No. No. It's too early. Coffee will be welcome," Jack replied and sat up. He raked the hair out of his eyes, but the frown lingered. "This setting-up-house business is complicated, isn't it?"

"If you want to do it well."

"There's too much choice in-in—everything. Color of paint. What wood. Type of carpet. And woe betide if you pick a color for the walls that doesn't complement the curtains. As for furniture coverings— Ugh. My head aches."

Henri-Antoine added a drop of milk and used the silver tongs to plop a small sugar lump into the coffee, precisely as Jack preferred it, gave the liquid a stir, then held out the porcelain cup on its saucer.

"So you managed to sort out the problem of the wallpaper then?" he asked, and sat back with his coffee cup, the book closed and set aside. He watched Jack gulp the brew without really tasting it. "Decision pending…?"

Jack finished the coffee without realizing he had drunk it, and holding the empty cup as if it were a tankard of ale sat forward, leaning on the padded side of the comfortable wingchair.

"Decision pending? Ha! No decision at all!" Jack replied on a huff and let his gaze wander about the book room with a new-found appreciation for interior decoration, since he'd been tasked with decorating and furnishing the townhouse he would share with Teddy once they were married. "I wish I'd paid more attention when you were setting up house," he added as his gaze lingered on the floor-to-ceiling mahogany bookcases.

The volumes that filled the shelves were bound in soft leather of different colors: Black for English titles; blue for French literature; works by Italian authors were covered in yellow; classical Greek and Roman texts bound in green; and the red leather tomes were various texts on everything from the natural histories, to pharmacopeias, to medical tracts.

And just like this room, every other room in this elegant and spacious townhouse had no expense spared by architect, interior designer, and furniture maker. Yet there was a tasteful and understated elegance to the opulence. And with an awakened understanding for the effort and difficulty in decorating and furnishing a house well, Jack saw his best friend's efforts with fresh awareness. The overall effect in this Park Street townhouse was one of harmonious simplicity and comfortable living, and all could be credited to Henri-Antoine's good taste and brilliance. He hoped his domestic efforts on his and Teddy's behalf would be half as successful.

"You have an expert eye for color and detail, Harry," Jack said on a sigh of admiration. "The upholstery on the sofas and chairs. The curtains with their tiebacks. The carpets covering the parquetry. Together they work as a whole. You've thought of everything haven't you? I'll wager you left nothing to chance and chose the paint color applied to the boiseries in your butler's pantry, and in the housekeeper's room, too."

"Thank you for the former. As for the latter, I must disappoint you. I gave my upper servants permission to choose the paint color for the wainscoting in their particular rooms. Caldwell is partial to puce. Mrs. Quigley is most happy in lilac. Not colors I would recommend you use anywhere in your house. But a happy butler and a contented housekeeper make for a harmonious household. I advise you do the same, or have Teddy do so."

Jack had a sudden thought and looked at his best friend with mild panic mixed with a dose of hopefulness.

"Perhaps you could come round to Mount Street and give me your expert opinion—on the wallpaper for the breakfast parlor, and for Teddy's sitting room. And then there's the curtains for her bedchamber—"

"Separate beds, Jack?" Henri-Antoine enquired and then instantly recanted. "Forgive me, dear fellow. Forget I said—"

"It's not what I want. And I hope it's not what she wants either. But it would be wrong of me to presume, wouldn't it?" Jack replied truthfully. "It's for her to decide. It's the gentlemanly thing to do."

"So it is," Henri-Antoine replied, hoping he sounded convincing.

If he were marrying the woman he loved, there would be no question of separate beds—ever. If he got kicked out of the marital bed, then serve him to rights, and a sleepless night on the chaise longue in his dressing room would surely be punishment enough for his infraction. His parents had never spent a night apart, least of all slept in separate beds, and it wasn't as if they weren't spoiled for choice. Treat had twenty-five guest bedchambers, not counting those for the immediate family. One of his earliest memories was being brought to his parents' apartment by his nurse, climbing the bed steps up onto the mattress all on his own—though he was sure his nurse was at his back —to his mother's applause, and then his father scooping him up and holding him high above his head, which always made him giggle. He would then snuggle in between them amongst the pillows while they had their morning hot chocolate, and he sipped the same from the spout of a monogrammed, two-handled silver mug. He must have been around three years old…

"What do you say? Harry?" Jack asked. "About coming round to Mount Street with me…?"

"Mount Street…?" Henri-Antoine repeated, giving himself a mental shake to clear his mind of childhood remembrances. It had been a very long time since he'd recalled sipping hot chocolate in his parents' bed. What had elicited that memory? Perhaps all this sentimentality was the fault of Jack's impending nuptials? "Teddy not taking an interest in furnishing her new home?"

"You've forgotten, haven't you? I told you about the agreement Teddy and I struck up about Mount Street and Abbeywood Farm."

"Remind me…" Henri-Antoine said and settled back and waited for Jack to oblige him, which he did, and without rancor.

"I'm to live at Abbeywood Farm as I find it, the way Teddy wants it, and she'll live at Mount Street as she finds it, the way I like it." Jack smiled sheepishly. "You know Teddy. Not much interest in wallpaper and fabric swatches, or paint colors for that matter. But ask her about wool yields, coppice felling for firewood, and cider rations for the hay cutters at harvest time, and she's your man. Which is just as well because one of us has to be able to talk farm management with the steward. I'm just thankful her step-papa was open to teaching her about her ancestral estate."

"*Your* ancestral estate, Jack," Henri-Antoine stated quietly. "Never forget that when you inherited the title on the death of Teddy's father, you also inherited Abbeywood. It matters not that she grew up there. Just as I have no claim to my boyhood home, and rightly so as a second son. Treat belongs to Roxton for his lifetime and then it will belong to Freddy. Abbeywood is yours until it passes to your son, which, God willing, Teddy will give you. What is unusual in your case, but not unheard of in our circles, is that you are marrying your predecessor's daughter, who also happens to be your first cousin. All parties and both families can celebrate a most satisfactory union, and Teddy need never vacate her home, which is the fulfillment of her greatest wish."

Jack stared into his coffee cup, realized it was empty, and set it aside on the silver tray holding the coffee things. He took a moment to adjust its placement, all to gather his thoughts and to assuage his annoyance. He finally met Henri-Antoine's gaze with a lop-sided smile.

"Do you remember when you counseled me against marrying Teddy—"

"Jack, my homily on your ancestral estate wasn't a veiled attempt to have you cry off at the eleventh hour. Far from it. You and Teddy are made for each other, and I saw the error of my ways a long time ago. And have I not told you this—numerous times?"

"But that first time, do you remember you questioned not that I was in love with Teddy, but whether she was in love with me. You said her great love was Abbeywood. That I would always come second to her love for the estate. You said that if I married her, I had to be prepared to accept that. But what you—"

"I remember, and I regret saying it. My only concern was, and has always been, your happiness. We've been best friends since we were nine. No one means more to me beyond my family than you, Jack. Naturally I want Teddy to be happy too. I want you both to be happy, together."

"I do know it. And I—we—appreciate your support greatly. I doubt I could be entirely happily married to Teddy if you were against the match. But what you do not seem to fathom, or I've failed to convince you, is that I am perfectly at ease coming a close second to Abbeywood in Teddy's affections. Please! Hear me out," Jack added gruffly, which was as angry as he ever got, when Henri-Antoine went to interject. "And I am comfortable because there is room in Teddy's heart for both Abbeywood and me. Truth is, coming second is a close-run thing, because if you throw the Cotswolds into the mix, then there's three of us squeezed in there. But Teddy's heart is large, and she wouldn't be her without Abbeywood. And I do so want her to be her, if that makes sense. And the Cotswolds is in her blood, not mine. I suspect she'd never leave Gloucestershire if she had her way. I'm just glad she's agreed to come to London with me when Parliament sits. And that may not always be so, particularly when the children come along. She wants them to grow up on the estate. Not here in London. I agree. And whether she leaves them behind to join me here during sittings, or stays with them, that's something to talk about when the time comes."

"Dear me. How civil and conciliatory. Roxton will make a Parliamentarian of you yet. And Teddy is indeed fortunate to be marrying such an understanding and amenable fellow."

"Ha! She's not having it all her own way. Which is what I most want you to grasp about Teddy and me. It is only fair I'm understanding about her love for Abbeywood, because my first love has and always will be my music. Teddy knows this and accepts it. She is perfectly content to allow me to spend my time composing and playing my viola and pianoforte, here in London when I'm not busy with my parliamentary duties, or in the wilds of the Cotswolds, while she spends her days on all matters farming-related, whether it's with the steward, or with her parents in the next vale, or she gads about the countryside where she is happiest. She knows my heart is large like hers, large enough to accommodate her and our children, and my music. So you see, you are not to worry about me—or Teddy—or our marriage."

Henri-Antoine frowned and pulled a face at this confessional.

"That is all very grown up. I am an infant by comparison." He regarded Jack keenly. "And you are both happy with this pact? For that is what it is, isn't it—a pact." When Jack nodded and grinned, he threw up a hand. "Very well. Then so shall I be. Though," he added irritably, because Jack was still grinning, "I have no idea why you're staring at me like a beaming Bedlam inmate, as if I've failed to see there is some humor in all of this—Have I failed?"

"No. Not failed. It's just… It's just—I'm not like you, Harry."

"Like me?" Henri-Antoine sat up with a frown. "Thank God for that. You're most definitely not like me. I wouldn't get along with me at all. Though I still do not see what there is to grin about—"

"I'm not as smart or as wise or as clever as you. Never have been.

Never will be. Nor will I ever be your equal in sartorial elegance, in a ballroom, or in sword play. As for your reputation with females, I most definitely do not possess your sangfroid—"

"Spare me my blushes," Henri-Antoine muttered with a roll of his eyes.

"But I do excel in music, and in knowing you better than anyone alive—"

"True on both counts."

"Possibly better than you know yourself—"

"Rot!"

"You would not be happy with such a pact. You accept it because you want Teddy and me to be happy, but you do not really understand it, which is why I'm grinning. Because it amuses me that it is the musician who is the practical one when it comes to matters of the heart, while you, who profess not to be the marrying kind, are the unabashed romantic."

Henri-Antoine glared at Jack, shocked. He went white. "Don't be idiotic!" And because Jack continued to look at him in an odd sort of way, he uncrossed his legs and got out of the wingchair to stir the coals in the grate with a poker.

Jack joined him there, folding his arms and leaning a shoulder against the mantel.

"You want us to be happy, but that is what I want for you too," Jack told him quietly. "You can try and convince yourself and others you don't believe in a soul mate—"

"We had this conversation at Westby's only last week..." Henri-Antoine replied without taking his eyes from the glowing coals.

"We were both drunk then, and we're not now.... And I won't bother you with this again—"

"That's something at least."

"—but I believe there is someone out there for you, and that she will be the great love of your life because that is what you need, Harry. And it is what you deserve. And because you are a romantic I know that when you *fall in love* you'll well and truly *fall*, as if off a cliff. And when that happens, don't fight it; embrace it. There! Enough said. And I give you my word I won't say it again."

Henri-Antoine turned to face Jack.

"You know what I believe, Jack? That impending marriage has clogged your brain with romantic pap." When Jack laughed and shook his head, Henri-Antoine favored him with one of his rare smiles and gave his shoulder an affectionate pat. "Thank you. You are the kindest man I know. But your brain is still mush. Let us return to more immediate concerns: Choosing the wallpaper for Mount Street."

Jack's eyes lit up and he sighed his relief. "Would you? It shouldn't take up more than an hour of your time."

"An hour?" Henri-Antoine pulled a face. "Don't be preposterous. If you want the house to be perfect for your bride, then you had best set aside half a day to show me what you've already chosen, and the other half for me to correct those choices."

"If you say so."

"But I'll only do it if you give me your word not to tell Teddy I had a hand in any of it. Your bride must think readying the nest was all your work."

"Done. Though there is one thing I need to confess I could not keep from her—Teddy knows Mount Street is your wedding gift to us."

"Jack! You gave me your word."

"No, I did not. I refused. You thought threatening to call me out if I told her would be enough for me to agree to your terms. Not so, my friend. I told you I know you better than you know yourself. For one thing you would never call me out, and for the other, being a romantic, you want Teddy and me to have our happily ever after. Which would not be possible if you called me out and killed me. Which you would because you are a far superior swordsman.

"Besides," Jack continued on a shrug of finality. "I had no choice but to tell her. I could never afford to lease a house in Mount Street, and could only dream of owning such a dwelling at such an address. Teddy knows this. We will have a comfortable life at Abbeywood. The income from the farm and her dowry will mean we won't want for anything. But we aren't wealthy on the same scale as you. You can cater to your every extravagant whim, but we still need to think about where we spend our coin. So imagine if I'd brought her to a spacious town-house in Mount Street, painted, papered, and furnished in the latest style, just a five-minute walk from here, and presented it to her as our London home? She'd rightly refuse to enter it because she would justifiably be concerned I had grossly over-stepped our finances and put us in debt."

"You are both so practical it's irksome," Henri-Antoine drawled without heat.

"Yes. We must be."

"I hope Teddy accepted the wedding gift without needing persuasion?"

"She did, saying your gift was over-generous and a grand romantic gesture, and that if it had come from anyone else, she would have refused it. But because it is from you, she will thank you with a kiss when next she sees you. And if you order me not to tell her, she will inform everyone at the wedding breakfast you have gifted us an urn, or a shell, or something so inferior in quality that you'll be labeled a miser. So you had best let her thank you with a kiss, is my advice."

"Tell Teddy I will accept her kiss, despite her threat of blackmail, but that my gift was for purely selfish reasons. I don't want you moving too far away."

"Ha! That's what she said to me."

"Did she? Well she's right. Though I hope you assured her I will not bother you unless you wish to be bothered…?"

"You couldn't bother us if you tried, Harry," Jack said, suddenly so emotionally overwhelmed he felt tears in his eyes. He wondered why, after everything that had just been said between them, he should fall all to pieces now. He quickly turned away, wiping a hand across his face, then poured himself another cup of coffee. "Would tomorrow be soon enough to visit Mount Street with me?" he asked on what he hoped was a light note.

"It will have to wait until the day after," Henri-Antoine replied, and resumed his seat with an outward flick of his frock coat skirts. When Jack held up the coffee pot, he shook his head. "The Fournier Foundation trustees meet tomorrow."

Jack was surprised. "We do? I thought all funding applications had been vetted. Those lucky few medical establishments worthy of inspection are scheduled for the start of the autumn teaching year, aren't they?"

"That was what was decided, but it seems Bailey has received a special request from the Foundation's patron that cannot be ignored."

Jack sipped at his coffee. It was lukewarm at best.

"Ah. Well, in that case, we had best honor it. What is it?"

Henri-Antoine opened the pages of *Thucydides' History of the Peloponnesian War* which he had been reading when Jack came into the room, and removed a letter he was using as a place holder. This he handed to Jack. It was from Dr. Bailey, the foundation's director.

"Bailey and the trustees are invited to dinner and to tour the facilities of Warner's Dispensary in Gerrard Street."

Jack looked up from perusing the short missive.

"Warner's Dispensary? But didn't we put aside Dr. Warner's submission… Can't remember why—"

"I'm not surprised. There were over a dozen submissions. He was asked to submit again next cycle."

Jack gave a start. He hastily set down his coffee cup.

"Harry! Warner's Dispensary. Gerrard Street. I *knew* there was something about that girl! Not the girl precisely, but when she mentioned Warner's Dispensary, a cog turned in here," he said and tapped his head. "But I couldn't place where I'd heard of it before. And to be honest, I was more concerned about you and—Were you as surprised at the coincidence that we're off to inspect the very dispensary where your ministering angel toils?"

"Yes. Had I received Bailey's letter sooner, I could've saved myself the effort and thanked her tomorrow."

"So you did pay her a call?"

"Several days ago."

"And...?" Jack prompted when Henri-Antoine was not forthcoming.

Henri-Antoine looked at his friend without expression. "And what?"

"Did you see her? Did you thank her? What did you make of her?"

"To the first two questions: Yes. To the third: You can decide that for yourself tomorrow."

"I will. But what I asked is what *you* made of her."

Henri-Antoine shrugged. "I cannot answer you."

Jack stared at him, then threw a hand up in dismissal. "Very well. Have it your way. I know when not to press you when it comes to females—"

"I cannot answer you because I do not know what to make of Miss Crisp," Henri-Antoine enunciated coldly, and with more emotion than he intended.

And he spoke the truth. He did not know. In fact, he did not want to think of Miss Crisp at all. She stirred within him emotions that were best left unexplored, and responses that were uncharacteristic and unwanted. Both left him confused and annoyed and uneasy.

He had stormed out of the dispensary in a most ungentlemanly manner, determined that was an end to his obligation to Miss Crisp, and he need never think of her again. And yet, by some whim of lunacy, when the carriage set to, he had peered out the window and at the precise moment it slowly passed her by, so that the vision of her framed in the doorway was now burned into his brain. He saw her whenever he closed his eyes: Slender arms at right angles and hands clasped under her neat bosom. Her feet together, the scuffed toes of her half-boots just peeking out from under the hem of her plain gown. The curl of hair that had come loose from its pins tucked behind an ear out of the way and tickling her white throat. And the confusion writ large on her lovely face. But all that was minor detail compared with what came next. Her blue eyes sparked with recognition seeing him looking out of his carriage. She smiled and it lit up her whole face. She glowed. Dear God but she was lovely. He had wished at that moment those blue eyes and that smile were for him and him alone. And his wish was granted. Locked in the moment, it did not occur to him that she was looking directly at him, but she was.

What was his response? He did not give a curt nod in acknowledgement and then slowly pull the blind. Which would have been the polite thing to do, and the only response he need give her. No. He had not done that. He had reacted in a most uncharacteristic and cowardly manner. He threw himself back against the upholstery, back into the shadows of the carriage interior, back where she could not see him. Heart racing and face hot, he felt as if he'd been caught out committing a heinous act; he felt peculiar and ridiculous. He forgot to breathe.

He reasoned it was not his fault, and that he owed her nothing.

She was not his concern. To calm himself he said this over and over again. There was nothing he could do to help her, not that she had asked for or wanted his help. She seemed to take pride in her efforts to help the sick poor. Yet she made him feel as if he should do something, anything, to make her situation better. She had been educated, and had all the hallmarks of a female who had a right to expect to live a life far from the one she was living now, down amongst the diseased and downtrodden. Why? Why did he feel this way? All because she had helped him? Or was there another reason? One he had no wish to acknowledge or explore. He told himself he would not be drawn in to something from which he was very certain he could not extricate himself without great personal and emotional cost. What was she to him anyway? She was not his responsibility.

And yet every night since that cowardly action of hiding himself away in the shadows of his carriage, he saw her, and wished he did not. So he was going to do something about it; something for himself. Something utterly self-centered he was certain would expunge Miss Lisa Crisp from his mind's eye and pull his life back from the precipice of uncertainty. Something that would return his life to its natural order, where his preeminent position in society as son of a duke was never questioned, so that when next he saw Miss Lisa Crisp, as he knew he would when the Fournier Foundation trustees visited Warner's Dispensary, he would see her as she appeared to others: A girl of no particular family, so far beneath him on the social ladder that he need not acknowledge her at all.

. . .

"You're not staying in tonight?" Jack enquired to break Henri-Antoine out of his brooding silence.

He noticed his best friend had changed out of the frock coat and waistcoat he'd been wearing when they had dined earlier that day, for an ensemble of black silk smothered in an embroidery of silver thread and sapphire spangles. It was an outfit to be worn in the public gaze, and under a blaze of candles he would look magnificent.

"What?"

Jack's mild enquiry worked, and broke Henri-Antoine's preoccupation, and it was only then that he realized he was up out of his chair and had his gold pocket watch in his hand and was looking at its pearl face. He had no idea of the time.

"You're going out?" Jack asked again.

"I have a prior engagement at the Opera. Mrs. Markham has something I want—"

"I wish you'd find another preoccupation, and so does Seb," Jack complained.

"Allow me to finish… Mrs. Markham has something I want *returned to me*. My Portland catalog somehow ended up in her possession—"

"I can think of how that happened," Jack murmured, unimpressed.

"—and she will only return it if I take a box at the Opera. If it will make you sleep better tonight, know that this will be the last occasion I intend to be seen in her company, in public or private. Seb's clownish antics the other night were enough for me to realize that regardless of my efforts for him to face facts, he does care for her."

"Of course he cares for Peggy Markham. I've told you on numerous occasions. He's in love with her."

"More fool him. But I do see that now—"

"Do you also see why he reacted the way he did to your goading?" Jack stuck in.

Henri-Antoine stared at him.

"Spare me the moral outrage. You know me well enough that I would never come between a couple in love. Seb may be in love with Peggy. But she is not in love with him. Removing myself from her orbit won't change that. But Seb, for all his bitter envy, is still a friend, and I do not wish to hurt him. She'll do that on her own."

There was a knock on the door and at Henri-Antoine's nod, the footman opened it to admit one of his lads—his shadows—who followed him everywhere whenever he stepped outside his house.

"The carriage is ready, my lord."

"Two minutes." Henri-Antoine looked to Jack who was still

sprawled out in the chair by the fire. "I return in the morning. Possibly after breakfast. Don't panic. Michel knows where to find me, and I'll be home in time for Kyte to dress me for the visit to Gerrard Street."

"Michel not going with you?"

"Not tonight. No one below a baronet is permitted through the doors of this particular bagnio."

Jack's brows lifted in surprise. He knew to which Turkish bath Henri-Antoine alluded. It was the most exclusive in London, and the most expensive. But blue blood wasn't enough to gain a gentleman admittance. He had to be a direct descendant of a nobleman, possess a line of credit worthy of a sultan, and, it was rumored, his member had to be just as impressive.

"You're off to Burke's." It wasn't a question.

"I am."

"And the lads? How are they to keep an eye on you there?"

"Not an eye. Never an eye, Jack."

"You know what I mean."

Henri-Antoine sighed wearily. "You worry too much about the mundane, dear fellow."

"But if you need them?"

"They'll be around—"

"—lurking in passageways, an ear to the thin walls?" Jack huffed. "Needs must, I suppose."

Henri-Antoine remained passive, though the facial tick resurfaced. "A pity you wouldn't allow me to sponsor you. Then you'd know there are no internal walls at Burke's. Colonnades. Hot and cold plunge pools. Assignation alcoves aplenty." He teased his friend. "You're welcome to come along… For old time's sake…?"

"Lord no! I've got nothing to hide, but I don't possess enough arrogance to strut about in a place with more town bulls than Smithfield markets. But you do. Though I doubt you'll find what you're looking for in a place like Burke's."

Henri-Antoine turned in the doorway, frowning. "Meaning?"

Jack shrugged.

"To be perfectly frank, I'm not sure. But I wish I could find it for you."

"There are times, Jack Cavendish, when I find you unfathomable. *Bonne nuit, mon cher ami.*"

Jack followed him to the first landing and there remained, while downstairs in the wide entrance hall his best friend was buckled into his sword and sash, tugged on his soft leather gloves, and was handed his diamond-topped walking stick. Watching him with a sentimental smile, Jack was reminded of the old Duke of Roxton, Henri-Antoine's father, and whom he resembled greatly. In profile he was indeed the image of the ancient aristocrat. The portraits, the marble busts, and the impressive funerary statue in the Roxton mausoleum of M'sieur le Duc d'Roxton all attested to it. So did Jack's memory of the old Duke. As boys they would peer down between the railings as the Duke and Duchess prepared to leave for the theater or the opera, or for some ball or other. The Duke always austere and commanding, the Duchess a whirlwind of sparkles and light.

He wondered if being the living embodiment of such an aloof and powerful aristocrat, not only in form but in manner, had placed an unnecessary onus on his best friend, made all the more burdensome because he suffered from the falling sickness. And while he was eagerly anticipating this next stage in his life to be shared with Teddy, there was no denying he would miss Henri-Antoine's company dreadfully. They had been inseparable for sixteen years, which was more than half their lives. And they had always been there for each other. He hardly remembered a time before Henri-Antoine, and he found it difficult to imagine life without him.

But with Teddy, and with the family they would eventually have, he would forge a new chapter in his life, and be content. Henri-Antoine had yet to find his soul mate, and it worried Jack that he might never do so. Or perhaps, like the old Duke, he would find her too late in life, and then die before his time, before his family were ready to let him go. M'sieur le Duc's death had a profound effect on everyone, and Henri-Antoine never fully recovered from the loss of his father, of that Jack was convinced.

Jack did not want his best friend to live his life alone, to battle his affliction without the love and support of a family, or spend his time in the emotional wasteland of places such as Burke's. Henri-Antoine had a right to follow his own path, but it was where that path was leading him that greatly worried Jack.

He watched Henri-Antoine go out onto the street without looking back, step up into his carriage, the lads, as habitual and as unseen as his shadow, hopping up in beside him and closing the door. And he stayed leaning on the balustrade, staring down in the void for a long time after the porter had come back into the vestibule and the butler had disappeared into the bowels of the servant wing. He then went off to his apartment with the silent prayer that the life path Henri-Antoine was presently treading would lead him to the edge of a cliff, and there, on the precipice, he would meet a girl, and they would take a leap off that cliff together.

TEN

THE WARNER HOUSEHOLD HAD BEEN IN TURMOIL SINCE THE arrival of a letter from the Fournier Foundation informing Dr. Warner that the trustees wished to schedule a visit to his dispensary and anatomy school before the end of the week. The director, Dr. Bailey, wrote it was an unusual step and short notice, but if Dr. Warner hoped to be considered in the present funding cycle, then the visit needed to be conducted almost at once. No special arrangements were necessary. The only stipulation was that the visit be conducted on a day the dispensary was closed to the sick poor, and this was deliberate. Without patients, the trustees would have the ease of movement required to inspect the facilities, and uninterrupted time to conduct interviews with Dr. Warner and his staff.

Dr. Warner sent a reply within the hour, agreeing to all the terms stipulated. He voiced his regret to his wife that the trustees would not have the opportunity to see how efficiently the dispensary was managed, but conceded that without patients, the consulting rooms could be scrubbed of noxious odors and perfumed, thus reducing the likelihood of the trustees breathing the odorous air of the sick poor, and becoming ill themselves. His wife agreed, adding that it was surely a good sign the trustees wanted the time to interview the dear doctor, for he could not fail to impress them with his knowledge, and plans for the future; providing them with a leisurely dinner could only help.

And so the maids were set to dusting, scrubbing, polishing, and perfuming every surface in both the dispensary and the living quarters, from floorboards to the silver soup tureen, while Mrs. Warner and the housekeeper devised a menu of several courses fit for such distinguished guests. Cook sent her subordinates out to market at dawn to procure the freshest produce, and on the night before the visit there was a great deal of baking, basting, and roasting.

As these domestic arrangements continued apace, the physician and his medical staff set to organizing the anatomy theater and the preparation rooms. Various specimens, medical instruments, and scientific apparatus used in his student lectures were set out for display. Also a number of his research log books and patient case studies were opened and ready for the trustees' perusal. All of this Dr. Warner hoped would provide enough material to impress the visitors.

The good doctor and his wife were also keenly aware of making a favorable impression at dinner, and to this end, the couple were fastidious in dressing for the occasion.

"I'm still at a loss to know how I am to address these *other* gentlemen, Robert," Minette Warner complained as she took one last critical look at herself in the looking glass. She plucked at the lace at her elbows to even out the folds. "The director Dr. Bailey and two of the trustees are medical men, and you say they are identified in the letter...?"

"They are indeed. Dr. Willan is a physician at the Fever Hospital, and Dr. Blizard is a consultant surgeon at the London Hospital. Both are not known to me personally, being a decade behind me in their careers, but I am well acquainted with Willan's work at the Carey Street Dispensary."

"But the other gentlemen, the ones who are not medical men. Dr. Bailey's letter says the identities of the three remaining trustees shall remain anonymous for the duration of their visit, even when they sit down to dine with us. But how then am I to address them, Robert? It is most irregular and unsettling not to know the social standing of the men at my own table."

"Most irregular, dear heart," Dr. Warner agreed. "But if I wish their consideration we must abide by their rules of inspection. Dr. Bailey included these regulations with his brief note." From his frock coat pocket he produced the letter and unfolded it. "We are to address those trustees who remain nameless to us as 'sir' with no further appellation required. Nor are we to enquire into their names, their occupations, or their station in life. They are here first and foremost to inspect and assess the medical merit of my work. That Dr. Bailey and the trustees have agreed to remain to dinner is an honor indeed. Though I'm afraid that dinner will be a dull affair for you, my dear," he added with what he hoped was a look of disappointment. "There will be little or no opportunity to take the conversation in any direction other than the one they wish to take it in. I must follow their lead. I would not blame you if you did not wish to join us—"

"Not join you?" Minette Warner was affronted. "But—Robert... When have I not presided over a dinner at my own table? When have I not supported you in all your endeavors—"

"Dear heart, I know that, and you are a wonderful helpmate to me. It's just that upon this occasion the diners are not known to us, and they may not be the most convivial company. Indeed I find myself rather nervous at the prospect of entertaining gentlemen whose names and reputations remain a closely-guarded secret. But I at least can talk with them on a medical level—"

"You cannot know that for certain, Robert. Are these nameless gentlemen medical men? If they are, surely they would've revealed themselves, in the same way as Drs. Willan and Blizard?"

She turned from her looking glass reflection with a self-satisfied smile that she had done all she could to be at her fashionable best. Her sunflower-yellow silk gown a la polonaise was in the latest style, and lavishly trimmed at bodice and elbow with small cornflower-blue bows. The silk ribbons threaded through her upswept hair, and her cornflower-blue silk shoes complemented the outfit perfectly. Such was her confidence in her preparations and her outfit that she was convinced that any gentleman seated at her table would be beguiled, and perhaps the conversation might stray from the medical to allow her to contribute.

"I suspect the anonymous gentlemen are not medical men at all," Minette Warner said, stating her wishful thinking aloud as she collected her fan from the dressing table. "Which is more reason for me to take my usual place at our table, to do my very best to appear most interested in anything they say—for you, dear Robert."

Dr. Warner quickly folded the letter, smiled away any misgivings he had that his young wife would find the run of conversation unfathomable, and kissed her temple. "Thank you, dear heart. That is all I can ask of you."

The couple went downstairs to await their guests in the comfort of the drawing room, nervous, but confident in their own minds they were as prepared as they would ever be for the visit of the trustees of the Fournier Foundation. And while the household continued to be busy around them, from the kitchen to the nursery, the only person not tasked to provide assistance in any capacity was Lisa. She had been ordered by her cousin to remain in her room for the duration, and not to come out until told to do so, or unless the house was burning down around her ears. So it came as a shock to the couple, and most particularly to Mrs. Warner, when upon their arrival, and just after introductions were made, one of the trustees asked the whereabouts of Miss Crisp.

LISA TOOK HER COUSIN'S DIRECTIVE AS SHE DID EVERYTHING ELSE within the Warner household, placidly and with good grace. Besides, there was no reason for her to be present; what could she offer the trustees? And Becky Bannister was making minor adjustments to the length, fit, and fall of the gowns, petticoats, corsets, and jackets she was taking with her on her visit into Hampshire. These clothes would then be packed in the traveling trunk which lay open against the wall. It would then to be taken downstairs to the hall after the visitors had left, in readiness for the journey. Becky's small trunk was already stowed in a corner of the scullery, along with her coat and hat, as she was spending the night on a cot in Lisa's room.

Both girls were to be woken in the small hours of the night and taken by hackney to the bustling Bell Savage Inn in Ludgate Hill. Here stagecoaches, wagons, and diligences departed for the southern counties at all hours of the day and night, and every day of the week except Sundays. Lisa and Becky were taking the stagecoach that departed for Alston in Hampshire at four in the morning. Traveling the London to Portsmouth road, with plenty of stops along the way to set down and pick up passengers making their way to Southampton on the coast, there would be a change of horses and time for refreshment at Guildford, and then the stagecoach would head towards Winchester.

Lisa and Becky would be set down at the Swan Inn in the town of Alston's High Street. Here they would be taken up by a privately-hired carriage, which should be awaiting them upon their arrival, for the final five-mile journey cross country to the ducal estate of Treat. All in all, a journey of almost forty miles. They were not likely to reach their final destination until late afternoon, having spent the better part of thirteen hours traveling.

Becky's enthusiasm was not diminished at the prospect of being shut up in a stagecoach with a bunch of strangers, to be bumped along for hours on end. Never in her wildest imaginings had she ever thought she would venture into the country, and so to travel a distance of forty miles from London was to her the greatest adventure of her young life. She had spent her twenty years in and around Gerrard Street, and the closest she had ever been to persons of rank was her visit to Lord Westby's townhouse to wait on the nobleman's mistress. To think she was accompanying Lisa as her personal maid to the wedding of a duke's niece was the stuff of dreams.

Lisa was happy to have Becky's company. For although she knew she was to see Teddy at the end of the journey, having someone she knew to travel with, and to be with her at Treat, in surroundings that were as foreign to her as they were to Becky, was comforting. And far better than had her cousin hired a stranger to act as her maid. Not only was Becky a happy soul, she was no-nonsense, and an expert seamstress. It was Becky, her great-aunt, and two seamstresses employed by Widow Humphreys who had done wonders with refashioning the four cast-off gowns given to Lisa by her cousins. They not only managed to create outfits that complemented Lisa's slender frame, but with the excess material made her matching mitts, and had the cordwainer cover two pairs of shoes.

The fabric supplied by her aunt and uncle remained untouched. This pleased Lisa because she considered the brocade silk too heavy a weight for the summer, and the silver thread embroidery far too grand for her. Saving this costly fabric pleased Minette Warner so much that she agreed to advance Becky half her salary, the other half to be paid upon return from Hampshire. From this coin Becky was able to repay her great aunt for the loss of the ribbons and garters stolen by Mrs. Markham. Which put Widow Humphreys in a better mood at bearing the loss of Becky's services for the fortnight she was absent from the shop.

"I've not seen you look prettier, Miss," Becky announced proudly as she got up off her knees and stepped back to inspect the line of the hem of Lisa's newly-fashioned Indienne cotton robe à l'anglaise. She had pinned and then sewn a small section of hem that had been missed in the rush to get Lisa's gowns ready in time. "A proper fittin' dress is what you needed, and in a pretty floral pattern, and now I reckon you'd turn the head of a duke, make no mistake."

Lisa blushed and bobbed a curtsy. "Why, thank you. All credit to your expert needle, Becky. I would not have thought it possible to salvage enough fabric from such worn gowns, and then turn them into something that would fit me, least of all look *à la mode*."

Becky grinned at such praise. "There ain't much of you to fit, is there? So not much yardage was needed."

"That is very true," Lisa agreed with a smile, smoothing her hands over the snug-fitting bodice and down over her slim hips.

She tried to look over her shoulder to where the material was tightly gathered into a v-shape in the small of her narrow back, and wished she had access to a looking glass to see for herself how the gown fitted. She certainly felt prettier for wearing such delicate and colorful fabrics, which were a welcome change from her serviceable linen gowns in dull browns and blues. She just hoped these outfits were suitable for her stay at Treat. But as she could not do anything about their suitability, she wasted no more time on needless worry. Teddy's relatives would have to take her as they found her, and she would do her best to remain in the background, which hopefully would mean no one would notice her or the clothes she was wearing.

"It's just as well, ain't it," Becky continued running a critical eye over the gown and the fabric, and determined to say her piece about the backhanded generosity of Lisa's cousins. "If you ask me, those gowns had seen better days, and weren't fit to be worn by the scullery, least of all you—"

"I did not ask you," Lisa replied with the same smile. "And I am most grateful, to them for any offering of clothing, and to you and Mrs. Humphreys for what you have done for me. Never forget that though I live in this house, I am poorer than Tina. At least the scullery is paid for her services."

Becky was about to speak when a knock on the door surprised them both, and a maid entered to inform Lisa she was wanted in the drawing room. The girl was asked to repeat this summons because of the specific instructions from her cousin to remain in her room.

"Madam wasn't the one who asked for you, Miss," said the maid. "It was one of the gentlemen whose come to look over the master's medical rooms."

"One of the members of the Fournier Foundation?" Lisa was mystified as to why she would be called to speak to one of the trustees.

"Aye, Miss. For they all came together. But when the others went through to the dispensary, this gent stayed behind. He did not give his name. Just asked for you, Miss. He be a fine looking gent with—"

"Thank you, Ann. I did not ask for your opinion of him, or his description," Lisa said, and turned away to say to Becky, "Make haste. I must change out of this gown and—"

"No, Miss," Becky said firmly. "You should go down to the drawin' room as you are. 'Bout time you got used to wearin' pretty things. And as you'll be in these clothes for the next two weeks, it's right to start wearin' 'em now, with this visitor."

"So shall I tell him—" asked the maid Ann, who still hovered in the doorway, and was cut off.

"No need. I will come straight away."

And so it was that Lisa silently entered the drawing room, self-conscious in her newly-fashioned cotton gown, a lace-edged fichu tucked at her *décolletage*, and a small lace-edged cap pinned to the crown of her head. If there was anything amiss with her attire, it was her footwear. Not in anticipation of going outdoors, and having packed her new shoes in the traveling trunk, she only had her half-boots to hand, and they were beside the bed ready for the journey. She still wore her leather house mules on her stockinged feet, which, had she chanced to look down, were rather out of place paired with her cotton gown.

But her apprehension made her oblivious to her footwear, and, in fact, to how she presented in her new gown, for she was deep in thought wondering why she had been summoned by a member of the Fournier Foundation. Was something out of place in the dispensary that required her to explain herself? Perhaps it was the scent boxes, or had she not distributed enough tussie mussies to ward off the odors? But surely every surface had been scrubbed until it was odor free...? She hoped she had not caused Dr. Warner any embarrassment... Perhaps her worry was needless and they merely wished to ask her questions of a general nature...?

She was across the room before she realized it was occupied and she was not alone. But it was not the sense that there was someone else there, it was being addressed that brought her up short. She was so surprised, not so much to find herself spoken to, her private reverie cut short, but by the voice itself. She knew at once to whom it belonged. She was so happy he had returned to Gerrard Street—when he had stormed away she hardly expected to see him again—that it never occurred to her to make a pretense of being anything else. She turned to him with a beaming smile.

Henri-Antoine smiled back. He could not help himself.

Her unaffected delight was his undoing.

HALF AN HOUR EARLIER, IN THOSE FEW MINUTES BEFORE HE stepped out of his carriage to join the rest of the trustees who were milling about on the pavement outside Warner's Dispensary, Henri-Antoine had hesitated, wondering what he was doing here once again. But he knew the answer, and he had brought it on himself. But returning here made him doubt himself, and he never doubted himself about anything.

Why had he orchestrated this meeting when he should have left well enough alone—in plain terms, he should have left Miss Crisp alone. Dr. Warner would have submitted another application in due course, and perhaps the foundation would have given his third submission their full attention, and they would have found themselves here anyway. But those submissions and those visits would have been a good six to eight months in the future.

So he had interfered. And Bailey was always obliging. He had to make certain the inspection happened before he and Jack quit London for Treat. He would be absent from town for a month, perhaps two. *What difference would two months make?* he wondered. Miss Crisp would still be here. Where else had she to go? The question was not would she still be here, it was why did he care? And that bothered him enough to make him doubt himself.

"Shall we join them, my lord?" Michel Gallet asked into the heavy silence, a glance at Sir John, whose gaze remained on Lord Henri-Antoine.

"Give us a minute, Michel," Jack said quietly, and waited until the major domo had alighted and the carriage door closed before speaking. "I heard you come in last night."

"Did you…?"

"I was still up. In the music room. I've had this composition stuck in my head for weeks, and had to get it out and write it down, and play it, before we head off to Treat." When Henri-Antoine made no comment, Jack added, hoping he sounded blithe, "What with everything that's going on down there—the pre-wedding celebrations, cricket match, fireworks display, the wedding day, the ball that evening—and the place crawling with family and friends, and too many children to count, there'll be precious little time for my musical scribbles, will there? I doubt I'll get a chance to pick up the viola. Not that I mind. It's just I had to get this composition written down—"

"And did you—get it written down?"

"I did… It was about three in the morning when I heard you come in."

"Was it? You were recently at Toulmin and Gale's, weren't you?"

The question threw Jack.

"The shop on New Bond Street that sells travel goods and the like? There's a stationer's next door. I bought a new quill. And Bully wanted a travel box for his brother."

"I suppose my ink and paper must come from somewhere," Henri-Antoine mused. "Michel would know… Toulmin and Gale have a most excellent window display, which I noticed on my way to the Opera… I had an illuminating discussion with the proprietor—about travel inkwells. There's a new type of stopper which prevents the ink from leaking—ingenious..."

Jack eyed the parcel tied up with black ribbon on the seat beside Henri-Antoine. It was about the size of a large book and about as thick. But he did not think it was a book. He wondered if whatever was inside the wrapping had been purchased from Toulmin and Gale.

"Is that what's in that package—an inkwell?"

Henri-Antoine looked at Jack. "Hardly." He lightly brushed the sleeve of his cream linen frock coat, commenting, "I did not make it to the Opera."

"You played truant with Mrs. M?" Jack couldn't have been happier, but he gave a low whistle and shook his head. "Now that was a public break if ever there was one."

"There was nothing to break. Still. No doubt there will be a small struggle to retrieve my Portland catalog, but I have every confidence in Michel."

"Ha! What incentive did you give him? Mrs. M is known for her temper tantrums and she won't be pleased with you when you send Michel in your stead. Hairbrushes will fly."

"I'm giving him leave to visit his twin while we're in Hampshire."

Jack frowned, confused. "His brother is in Hampshire. Michel's brother Marc is your mother's major domo."

"Yes. It's worked out rather neatly."

Jack gave a bark of laughter then said as casually as he could, when Henri-Antoine picked up the package, "And did you make it to Burke's, or did you spend the entire evening talking about inkwells?"

"I did—make it to Burke's. And that answers your second question." He lightly tapped the carriage door with his walking stick. "Let's not keep our esteemed colleagues waiting. I'm sure they are thinking more about the dinner afterwards than the fascinating specimens in jars that await us in Warner's garret. So the sooner the tour is over, the sooner we can get down to business."

The carriage door opened and a footman held it wide. Another unfolded the steps. One of the lads appeared in the doorframe and Henri-Antoine gave him the package. He then took a moment, sensing Jack was displeased with him. A glance over his shoulder and he knew he was right. Jack was no longer smiling.

"It disappoints you I went to Burke's." He held his best friend's gaze, his thoughts his own, adding softly, "It may give you some comfort to know I disappoint myself. Often."

"And the package...?"

"Ah. That is my first order of business, not yours."

. . .

HENRI-ANTOINE PLACED THE PACKAGE ON THE SOFA, ONLY TO move it to the low table, and then back again in the short interval while he waited for Miss Crisp to arrive. The trustees had gone off to tour the vacant dispensary where Dr. Warner's medical associates waited to show them around. Mrs. Warner wanted to stay behind and await the gentlemen in the comfort of her drawing room. Henri-Antoine guessed from her manner, her dress, and her liberal use of cosmetics that she had rarely if ever been inside her husband's dispensary. A look to his major domo, and Michel knew what he wanted. Mrs. Warner was soon engaged in conversation. So engrossed did she become in whatever topic Michel had broached with her, that she went out of the room with him, following behind the trustees, the door closed, and Henri-Antoine was left alone with the package and its placement.

When Lisa came into the room the package was back on the low table, and Henri-Antoine was standing by the window looking out on the street and the crowd that had gathered, but which was now dispersing as his town carriage moved off, to return when he sent for it.

He turned as the door opened and watched Lisa cross the room with a purposeful but light tread, elbows in at her sides and hands clasped under her bosom in that way she must have been taught at boarding school and which was so ingrained it was habitual. He liked it, and he liked the way she carried herself. What surprised him was the effect she had on him dressed in a simple gown of Indienne cotton. But he gave himself no time to ruminate on this by addressing her so she knew where he was in the room, because she seemed not to have noticed it was occupied.

And when she turned at the sound of his voice and smiled at him, he, for the first time in his life, felt his face split into a grin of its own accord. He was helpless to do anything about it, and felt utterly foolish. Only lunatics grinned. Sane people—*he*—did not. He was always in control of himself and his emotions because there were times— those times when he was victim to his affliction—when he had no control at all. And yet—and this was new to him, too—for the first time in his life, he did not care.

"Oh!? Hello." She bobbed a curtsy of welcome. "Is your visit a coincidence, or are you truly a trustee of the Fournier Foundation?"

"I am—*truly*—a trustee."

As he seemed incapable of moving away from the window, and his walking stick was planted in the floor, she came over to him.

"Oh!? You are?" She was so surprised she blurted this out, then immediately apologized. "Forgive me. I don't know why I should be astonished. Of course you could be. Only, it seemed it was a coincidence—"

"—because you hoped I was here to see you?"

She smiled and blushed but she was not backward. "Yes. How did you guess?"

That made him laugh. God! What was wrong with him? First he was grinning and now he was laughing out loud. The newness of this experience made him suddenly light-headed.

Lisa's blush deepened. He had a lovely white smile when he laughed. And it made her want to throw her arms around his neck and kiss him. She of course did not. She kept her elbows in at her sides and her hands together, dropped her chin and turned away to go over to the arrangement of sofa and chairs. She indicated the sofa, saying in what she hoped was an easiness of manner, when she was anything but calm, "Would you care to sit? Would you like me to ring for tea? Would you—"

"—like to tell me how it is you are a trustee of the Fournier Foundation? That is what you want to know, is it not, Miss Crisp?" he replied, coming to join her. He flicked out the skirts of his frock coat and sat at one end of the sofa, one foot slightly forward, and with his walking stick between his knees. He then indicated the rest of the sofa. "Please. Sit. And I will tell you."

She sat facing him. But not at the furthest end of the seat cushions but halfway along, so that they were in close proximity. Not close enough for her to appear forward, but not so far away that she would come across as a frigid miss. She then put her hands in her lap and waited.

"*Si vous êtes d'accord, je souhaiterais vous parler dans ma langue maternelle.*"

She had swift intake of breath and her blue eyes widened. "French is your first language, too?"

She should not have been surprised, but she was. It opened a Pandora's box of questions none of which she asked. Instead she smiled and replied in French.

"I wish very much for us to speak in French. Though you will have to forgive me because I am only permitted to speak English here in the house. So while I will understand what you say to me, I am out of practice with my speaking."

"*Tout ce dont vous avez besoin, c'est d'entraînement et de confiance en vous. J'espère que plus nous converserons, plus vous trouverez cela facile. D'accord?"*

She nodded and smiled but did not immediately reply. Not because she did not understand or because she could not answer, but because she needed a moment to compose herself. Listening and watching him as the French language rolled off his tongue with honeyed ease filled her with sensations she did not understand nor could she articulate them in any meaningful way had she been asked to do so. All she wanted to do was lie back on the cushions and close her eyes, and let him talk on and on so that his words washed over her, covering her in a warm coverlet of exquisite conversation. A word came to mind about this feeling—euphoria.

"That is very true: The more I speak in French, the more confident I will become in speaking it... *with you*," she said, repeating back what he had said to her, her euphoria twisting itself inside out into foolishness. She clasped her fingers a little too tightly, as if this would stop her from descending further into some sort of ridiculous stupor. "What is it you wish to ask me? Oh! No! But you first," she added with a light laugh at her own slip. She leaned in a little. "You offered to tell me how it is you are a trustee of the Fournier Foundation..."

He unconsciously mimicked her action and leaned in to her and said, "I see that it pleases you I am."

She did not dissemble but was also filled with a mix of emotions: Surprised that he saw the pleasure writ large on her face; relieved he thought that pleasure derived from a mutual interest in the advancement of medical knowledge; and guilty that she was not thinking about the foundation at all, but was selfishly absorbed in how he made her feel.

"It does, sir. I am not surprised you have an interest in medicine, as anyone with your affliction must. Any investigations that unlock the secrets and wonders of the human body must give you, and others, some hope that one day physicians may be able to offer effective treatment, if not a cure."

"There will not be a cure for the falling sickness in my lifetime, Miss Crisp."

"Which makes your involvement in the foundation all the more admirable."

"It does? It could easily be seen as motivated by self-interest."

"How so?"

"I am interested in the advancement of medical science for self-serving ends. Everyone else and their suffering—pardon me, but you will—can be damned to hell, for all I care."

Lisa was adamant in his defense. So much so it brought color to his lean cheeks.

"If that were the case then all a gentleman of your means need do is wait for medicine to advance, without you lifting a finger to help. After all, you are fortunate to be able to deal with your affliction in a most civilized manner and make yourself as comfortable as possible. You need not involve yourself personally in the medical field, and most particularly not in the running of a charitable fund that seeks to relieve the sick poor of their burden of illness, free of charge. Besides," she rattled on, warming further to her topic, and because his gaze remained fixed on her eyes, "a gentleman such as yourself need not show an interest in the sick poor at all. There are any number of charitable trusts to which you could give of your time and attention, and your wealth, that have nothing to do with poor relief, or medicine. And yet, here you are, a trustee of the Fournier Foundation. And so I do not believe you wish to consign anyone to hell, least of all the poor, sir."

"And I do not think you, Miss Crisp, have anything to concern yourself about your French language skills. With practice I could have you speaking like a native, so that not even my mother would guess you were from this side of the Channel, and not that."

"Oh? I don't? Could you? Is your mother French?" she asked in a rush, shy at his praise and because mention of his mother made their conversation that much more personal. And not least, because she had asked three successive questions. But she saw the absurd in her response and laughed behind her hand, confessing, "You may find me a poor pupil, sir, because I would prefer to listen to you."

"But ... Surely the poor pupil is the one who does not listen at all...?"

When he continued to frown in thought, she blushed and said in a small voice before looking down at her hands, "Very true. I meant something else entirely..."

There followed such a long silence between them that she forced her gaze up to his face, and saw that he was looking at her intently, and she knew he understood the real meaning behind her confession. He smiled thinly, and something sparked in his dark eyes.

"Perhaps we should start an admiration society for French speakers —for two?"

She returned his smile, and said cheekily, "I will join. On condition you do all the talking."

He laughed and instantly put a fist to his mouth to stop himself.

"Will you tell me how you became interested in the Fournier

Foundation?" she asked quietly, gaze following his hand up to his mouth and noticing for the first time that he had removed his gloves. His fingers were long and tapered, the nails manicured, and he wore a heavy gold signet ring on his pinky, which was set with a carnelian intaglio engraved with a coat of arms.

"At the risk of boring you—"

"I beg your pardon, but you cannot bore me," she interrupted without realizing it, attention still focused on his signet ring and the significance of that coat of arms. And when he moved his hand and let his arm lie across the length of the back of the sofa towards her, she rallied, saying seriously, which was at odds with the light in her eyes, "As we are now members of this newly-formed French speaking society, and I have joined on condition and expectation that you do all the talking, I must listen to whatever you say. So you see, I won't be bored. Besides," she continued, knowing she was prattling but unable to stop herself because he was looking at her in an odd sort of way that made her happy and nervous at one and the same time, "you have such a lovely voice, you could talk on any subject and I would listen, and in whatever language you cared to address me in. Though I am sure that is nothing new to you, to be complimented. And although I have only heard you speak in English and French, I am confident you must speak other tongues, too. You are too well spoken to have limited yourself to two. At Blacklands I also learned to read, write, and speak in Dante's language. But since coming to live with the Warners I have had even less practice speaking that language than I have French. But you—I could listen to you speak in French all day…"

Again the silence stretched, but this time she could not bring herself to look up to see his reaction, such was her embarrassment at allowing herself to blather. Yet it was easy to blather in French, to him. She doubted she would have been quite so effusive or as candid in English. She kept her gaze to the embroidered front of his linen waist-coat, with its sprays of lily of the valley and matching covered buttons, and waited for him to speak. After all, she had given him permission to talk without needing any contribution from her.

He took her up on her offer.

"I do not recall a time when I was not interested in medical science," he reflected. "Perhaps, initially, my interest was piqued because of my affliction, and being constantly surrounded by physicians, almost from birth. The closet off my bedchamber was a veritable pharmacopeia. I had a resident physician until my teens, and I have never gone anywhere or done anything without my shadows. I have three. The one that belongs to me, and the two belonging to the lads, a far more convivial name for the minders who follow me every-where. And just like my shadow, I have learned to accept them as a matter of course. Their presence gives me a certain peculiarity amongst Society. Such a self-absorbed existence is as liberating as it is limiting.

"I am fortunate enough to have the means to be indulgent. Others —most others—will never have such freedom. But how the poor, debilitated by the falling sickness, and who must carry its stigma for life, are able to function in our society with any sense of dignity, I cannot imagine... But the foundation's *raison d'être* is to fund the advancement of medical science. It is a charitable trust for physicians, apothecaries, surgeons, and researchers, and their apprentices. I believe —the trustees believe—that the advancement of knowledge in the medical sciences is the only way forward to alleviating suffering, not only for the poor, but all mankind.

"But I fully appreciate my duties as a trustee are but a thimbleful's worth of effort when compared to those who dedicate their lives to treating the sick, and who spend their days toiling in the most barbaric of conditions, elbow-deep in human remains, all to improve our understanding. Nor can my efforts measure up against the comfort and reassurance you provide those wretches who visit the dispensary seeking relief, if not a cure, for their ills. One smile and a kind word must surely alleviate their pain, if only for that brief moment in time. And for many, that is more than enough to sustain them, to know they are thought of, and their ills believed, even if they are so self-absorbed, as indeed I was as a child, to take your smile and your kind word as a grand presumption."

"Sir, you are too kind—"

"I am never *too kind*, Miss Crisp. Nor should you be self-effacing. I give credit where it is due—well, I am much better at doing so nowa-days... Now that I am no longer a petulant boy, spoiled beyond permission."

"Petulant? Never! Spoiled? Yes," she agreed, head cocked and smiling into his eyes. "I can well believe that even as a boy you had a distinct advantage over your fellows, which meant not only did your parents and your siblings spoil you, I am very sure all those with whom you came in contact were only too willing to jump to do your bidding. Why, I would wager even your physician, your nurses, and your shadows were compliant to your boyish demands."

Henri-Antoine pulled a face, but he was not annoyed, despite the complaint in his tone. "Distinct advantage? Boyish demands? Dear me, Miss Crisp, whatever can you mean?"

"Oh, pray, sir! Surely you are funning with me. I have told you so already."

"I have not the slightest notion to what you are inferring," he said with a shrug, features schooled in what he hoped was an expression of neutrality. "And this despite being the proud owner of three full-length looking glasses, and five or more dressing mirrors." When Lisa giggled behind her hand, he added softly, leaning into her, "I demand that you give me a clearer explanation of your meaning."

His tone was playful but there was an intensity in his gaze that made her suddenly wary, and she shivered, swallowed and looked away.

"Please—please do not make me," she replied and in English.

That broke the spell.

He realized at once that their verbal sparring had gone too far for her; that she was, after all, quite young and innocent for all her worldly façade and maturity in dealing with the dispensary patients, and with him while in the throes of a seizure. For the second time in as many weeks he had lost his footing and overstepped the mark, which was unforgiveable; she with the power to unsettle him. He remembered that they were alone, and he a guest in her guardian's house. Had she been a young unmarried female of his own class, she would never have been left alone with him under any circumstances, and rightly so.

He sat back and let his arm drop to his knee, and remembered the package. But it did not seem appropriate to give it to her at that moment because she might misconstrue his intent. Thus he went to great pains to make conversation which he hoped would put her at her ease so she would be comfortable with him again. Following her lead, he reverted to English.

"My grandfather, my mother's father, was a physician, and a Parisian. Perhaps that is where I inherited my interest in medical science... It must be in the blood?" he mused, gaze on the diamond-studded top of his walking stick. "My grandfather the Chevalier was a gifted healer, and much to the horror of his noble parents he chose to study medicine, and not the law. Worse. Once he had graduated, he did not go into private practice to treat those of his own class, but used his healing gifts to help the poorest of the poor wretches in the hospital known as *La Salpêtrière*, where females of lowest repute, the insane, and those suffering from the falling sickness are incarcerated. Which is not surprising, given epileptics are thought by many to be one step away from madness—"

"That is unsupported prejudice. Dr. Warner will tell you so."

"Then he is one of our more enlightened medical men."

"He is, sir. But forgive me. I interrupted you telling me about your grandfather…"

"I will not tire you with the particulars of his medical career, as much as I know *you* would be fascinated by such detail. My grandfather came to the attention of the French Court, and was appointed personal physician to Philippe the Second, Duc d'Orléans, *le Régent* of France during Louis the Fifteenth's minority. My great-grandparents lived long enough to see that day, but thankfully not long enough to witness their son's downfall, and so they died happy… Again, let me skip forward to an incident… A lady at court, a German princess married to a French noble, went into early labor. My grandfather attended on her but alas the infant, a boy, died. That death ruined my grandfather's career. He was forced to leave France. He retired to the Italian states where he continued to practice medicine and to raise my mother on his own until his death at fifty-nine. My mother believes—thinking back on her childhood and on particular episodes where her father would shut himself away—that he was hiding his affliction—"

Lisa drew in a small breath and her blue eyes widened. "Your grandfather also suffered with the falling sickness?"

"That is my mother's postulation. Coincidentally, I bear one of his names… My parents could not have foreseen at my birth that I, too, would be a sufferer…" Henri-Antoine was pensive, then said with a note of wonder, taking his gaze from his walking stick to meet Lisa's, "I have not spoken about my grandfather in many years—with anyone… Nor have I behaved as a gentleman ought when I took my leave of you," he continued smoothly, seeing she was again comfortable in his company. "I ask that you accept this small token as my apology for my uncustomary discourtesy, and as a thank you for coming to my assistance at Lord Westby's townhouse."

He took the package from the low table and placed it between them on the sofa cushion.

"For-for *me?*"

"For you."

Lisa frowned at the package tied up with black ribbon.

"Please keep your frown for after you have opened it, if it is not to your liking."

Lisa's frown disappeared and she smiled into his eyes. "I am very sure I will like it because it is from you. May I unwrap it?"

Henri-Antoine waved a languid hand and sighed, though he was secretly pleased with her undisguised delight, and uncharacteristically apprehensive as to her reaction to his gift.

"Please do. It cannot unwrap itself."

"Very well then," she said, giving the bow a tug. "But I must warn you I am unused to receiving gifts—"

"It is a mere token."

"—of *any* kind. So I may shed a tear or two."

"Thank you for the warning. I will ready my handkerchief."

Lisa chuckled then gave her full attention to the package as the ribbon unraveled and the cloth fell open to reveal a rectangular wooden box. But it was so far from the ordinary as to be extraordinary. So much so that Lisa froze, speechless.

ELEVEN

When Lisa did not move or say a word, Henri-Antoine leaned forward, frowning.

"It is not to your taste, Miss Crisp...?"

Lisa shook her head and swallowed. She had never before seen such a beautiful object, and this one a writing box. This was her presumption given the diagonal cut to the lid and the drop handles at either end, though she had yet to be told or instructed on its function. She had seen a few finely-crafted boxes while at Blacklands, and envied those girls who were fortunate enough to own them. Her writing box had been made for her by one of the school's carpenters in payment for giving his son lessons in reading and writing. She still used it. A simple wooden box constructed from off-cuts, the writing slope covered with a piece of repurposed leather, and the hinges of a nondescript metal. She had been grateful to the carpenter for making it, for she would not have had the coin to purchase one herself.

But this writing box on her cousin's sofa... It was a thing of beauty. As beautiful an object as it was functional. A work of art, carefully crafted to be seen as well as used. It belonged in a great lady's boudoir, and to be taken by her when she went traveling in her splendid carriage-and-four, perhaps with a liveried footman employed for the precise purpose of carrying and caring for such a treasure.

Such was Lisa's reverence that she hesitantly and then gently caressed the lid, fingertips trailing over the gleaming red richness of the rosewood and the border of mother-of-pearl inlay, the fretting expertly cut and polished to represent foliage. The front face was similarly inlaid and here also was a polished brass lock. She wondered as to the where-abouts of the key because she itched to open it to see if it was as magnificent on the inside.

As if sensing Henri-Antoine held the key, she looked up through a mist of tears. He did indeed have it, but he put it aside to dig in a frock coat pocket for his handkerchief. This he held out to her.

"Th-Thank y-you," she muttered, swallowing hard. She patted her eyes and cheeks dry. "I-I am sorry. It-it is *very* beautiful, and cost you dearly, so I am a little overcome by it, and you, for gifting it to me. I never expected payment of any kind for assisting you in your distress—"

"And I would not insult you with payment, Miss Crisp. As to the cost, that is of little consequence to a man of my vulgar wealth. And this writing box was not the most expensive on offer, but it was the most tasteful. I hope you will pardon the presumption, I thought it perfect for you. But that is the least of my concerns. What does concern me is the rehabilitation of my reputation, which is beyond price," he drawled in a most superior manner. "Thus I must insist you accept this token so that I may feel better about myself."

His facial tick gave him away, and Lisa smiled and shook her head, not at all fooled by his haughtiness. She realized he was doing his best to make her feel at ease.

"Very well, sir. I should not like to be the cause of any further unease on your part. So I will accept your gift—pardon me, *your token* —with gratitude. Though I am mystified as to how you knew I am a keen letter writer. Or perhaps while you were investigating Dr. Warner's Dispensary for the foundation you discovered I am an amanuensis for the poor?"

"An amanuensis for the poor…? Indeed! You never cease to surprise me, Miss Crisp. No. I did not know. And why do the poor require your services as a scribe?"

She told him, and she wasn't sure what surprised him more: That she provided such a service, or that while most of the persons who came through the dispensary doors could read, they could not write. He was such a willing ear, that she then went on to tell him about sitting in her corner with her writing box, and the poor lining up to take advantage of her services in dictating to her letters they could not write themselves.

"So you see, this beautiful writing box will be put to good use, and be cared for very well indeed," she told him happily, allowing her fingertips to again caress the box, as if needing the tangible to make certain it was there, and hers.

He could see his gift had made her very happy, and that filled him with a sense of contentment, the unwanted apprehension he had been experiencing wondering if the box would please her vanishing as his gaze followed her fingers across the polished rosewood and mother-of-pearl inlay.

"It was your fingers," he confessed softly. "The ink stains—The ink stains to your fingers told me about your letter writing—No! You must not hide them away," he said more harshly than he intended when she snatched her hand away and made fists in her lap. "You should never be ashamed of the tell-tale signs caused by honest work. They are a badge of honor, are they not? And now that you have told me about your services as an amanuensis for the poor, I am more than ever delighted with myself at the appropriateness of my gift—pardon me, *my token*."

"*Delighted with myself?*" she repeated with a gasp, and then giggled at the absurdity of his pronouncement. She asked sweetly, "How is it, sir, that you know just what to say to put me at my ease?"

Henri-Antoine shrugged, as if he had no idea. But his attempt at nonchalance failed because he could not stop himself from smiling at her undisguised happiness.

"Ah. This is when I *should* tell you I've spent years cultivating social insouciance. But I know that would not impress you—"

"You are right. It does not."

"—so I must confess I do not have an answer where you are concerned."

"You do not?"

Lisa pouted, unable to hide her disappointment, and again Henri-Antoine found himself grinning. Only this time he forgot to mentally castigate himself for his lax behavior, asking her in a light tone,

"Would you like me to show you the mechanics of your writing box, or do you wish to discover for yourself what—"

"Oh yes! Yes! Please show me—*everything*," she interrupted excitedly.

She hopped off the sofa, slipped off her mules so she could better sit on her haunches, and careful not to crush the skirts of her gown she sat on the carpet in front of him. Before he had time to even put aside his walking stick, she was settled, back straight, hands in her lap, with chin up and eyes bright awaiting his instruction.

He held out the key. "Would you do the honors?"

Lisa nodded, and was up on her knees to turn the small but surprisingly heavy brass key in the lock. And as he folded back the lid until it lay flat on its polished brass hinges, she leaned ever forward, mouth at half-cock in amazement that what was revealed inside the writing box was even more luxurious than its outer casing. With the two halves now lying flat, the slope to the writing surface was evident. This was covered in a bright red leather bordered by a tooled frame stamped in gold. Here was the place to lay each sheet of paper and write in comfort, the red leather surface set within a framework of ebony facings inlaid with mother-of-pearl filigree work. At one end was a long segmented storage compartment, one for quills, another for nibs and associated paraphernalia, and at either end a place for an inkwell. And there were two, of cut glass with silver stoppers.

Henri-Antoine removed one from its place to show Lisa how the mechanism worked in the silver lid to stop the ink from leaking, and how to unscrew it. He then gave it to her to try, which she did without any difficulty. But when he put out his hand to take the inkwell to put it back she hesitated, and looked up at him wonderingly. Her voice was barely above a whisper.

"You've had the lids engraved with my initials."

"Yes. Did you have someone else in mind…?"

She shook her head, too overcome to say more, and pushed the little bottle back into his hand.

Next he tugged gently on a small red leather tab in the center top edge of the writing surface and the entire half of the box lifted like a second lid to reveal a compartment underneath.

"A place to store your paper," he told her. "But wait! Let me astound you further—"

"Can you? I am more than a little tongue-tied as it is."

"I can tell…" he quipped.

He put this lid back into position and pulled on a second tab at the end in front of the quill compartment and inkwells, and lifted back the writing surface as he had done before. This half also revealed a compartment. And he beckoned Lisa closer and to pay attention to what he was doing. He ran his fingers along the rosewood panel below the compartment, and just as Lisa blinked, the panel came away in Henri-Antoine's fingers. Lisa took a breath, surprised, and if it were possible, her eyes grew rounder when he removed the panel entirely and showed her the brass spring latch that held this panel in place. When pressure was applied to a particular spot, the catch released and the panel came away freely. She was about to ask why, when, having removed the panel, all was revealed.

"Three secret drawers with bone handle pulls, neatly concealed behind the wood panel. Tiny, but large enough to hold little notes, or keepsakes. And only you know they are there—"

"And you," she said, smiling up at him. She reached in and slid open one of the drawers, and then tried the next, and finally she slid open the third. "Oh," she said, peering into each drawer with a feigned sigh of disappointment. "I thought... I thought perhaps you might have left me a note—"

"A note? Did you? Is this writing box not enough—Oh! Ah! I see," he muttered, realizing too late when she clapped a hand to her mouth to hide her smile that she was teasing him. He made a quick recover, however, saying on a drawl, his tone at odds with the mirth in his dark eyes, "If I'd not had those silver lids engraved, you ungrateful wretch, I'd think about returning this—"

"Oh no you don't!" she said fiercely, hands splayed covetously across the leather writing surface. But then she had a sudden thought and sat back on her haunches with her chin up, to say loftily, "By all means, sir. Take it. Though I warn you that in doing so you will lose any advantage you had, and you will no longer feel better about your-self. And—*and*," she stressed when he went to speak, continuing when he pressed his lips together, though it was obvious he was trying to suppress a grin, "I can draw but one conclusion from such petty retribution. That despite assurances to the contrary, you are as petulant and as indulged as you ever were as a boy. I am certain that is not how you wish to present yourself to me, is it?"

He shook his head obediently. Then in an about-face he nodded, which had her gasping and again sitting up, balancing on her knees, feigning affront. But her display fell flat when she became unbalanced and fell forward, only for him to catch her by the upper arms. And once he had her he did not instantly let her go, though he kept her at arm's length. He stared into her flushed face, all humor extinguished.

"It is only fair I warn you, Miss Crisp," he said quietly. "Petulance and acting the pampered brat remain two of my better qualities."

She held his gaze. "I do not believe you."

He let her go and sat back, eyes anywhere but on her. She stayed silent and still, the feeling of his fingers about her arms lingering longer than was pleasant. And then she rallied, suddenly aware of the passage of time. They had been in the drawing room alone together for so long she was certain the trustees had had enough time to not only have a comprehensive tour of the dispensary, but must have ascended to inspect the anatomy theater and the preparation rooms. And he, whoever he was, because he had yet to confide in her his name, and she had never asked, was surely conspicuous by his absence.

The writing box was still open and pulled apart, and when she went to put it back together, he came to life and offered to help. His manner and tone gave nothing away of his thoughts. She asked to be shown how to work the spring-loaded catch so she would be able to remove the panel that concealed the secret drawers by herself. He obliged and had her practice several times until she was proficient. This interval gave them both the time and opportunity to return to the easy manner they found they enjoyed in each other's company. So much so that, when the door to the drawing room opened quietly to admit a trustee, Henri-Antoine and Lisa were so absorbed in the writing box and each other that they were oblivious to all else.

Lisa was up on her knees, head over the box, practicing one last time to release the hidden spring-loaded catch, while Henri-Antoine was so close he could count every dark lash framing her blue eyes. And while he was acutely aware of her he was very sure she remained oblivious to him. Her concentration was on being able to use the catch to reveal the hidden drawers, and then be able to successfully replace the panel. He quickly returned his thoughts to the task at hand and soon they had their heads together peering into the writing box's every nook and cranny, while he found himself giving her an account of his visit to Toulmin and Gale on New Bond Street, and how he had returned later that same night to retrieve the box once the silver lids of the inkwells had been engraved, the proprietor only too willing to keep his premises open well into the small hours to make certain the writing box was prepared to his client's satisfaction.

It was no surprise then that when the couple were addressed, they both jumped and turned as one to the doorway.

"APOLOGIES FOR THE INTERRUPTION, BUT WE'RE WANTED upstairs," Jack said chattily to Henri-Antoine.

He had waited until his best friend had finished recounting his visit to Toulmin and Gale, which also gave him the leisure to observe the girl kneeling on the carpet at Henri-Antoine's feet. He would not have recognized her from their brief meeting in the passageway at Westby's townhouse. He had been too distracted by Henri-Antoine's diminished health to notice much about her, except that she was young and pretty and far too self-possessed for a girl dealing with such a situation. Such self-possession reminded him of his Aunt Deb, and he never thought he would ever know another woman quite like the Duchess of Roxton.

In the light of day, with her cheeks delicately tinged with color, and her eyes bright, dressed in a simple floral cotton gown that was molded to her long slim arms and trim figure, this girl was even prettier than he had first thought. And then she smiled at him in recognition, and her lovely smile lit up her features. He mentally corrected himself: She wasn't pretty, she was beautiful, as beautiful and as sunny as a spring day.

"Hello," she said, scrambling to her feet, allowing Henri-Antoine to help her up. She brushed down the skirts of her gown, looked about for her mules, slipped them on her stockinged feet and came across the room to drop a simple curtsy in greeting. "Today is full of surprises. Are you a trustee, too?"

Jack made her a bow, and could not help smiling. "I am. I'm only sorry that under the terms of our visit I cannot properly introduce myself, Miss—Miss—?"

"Miss Crisp. No matter. Your friend Harry hasn't introduced himself either—"

"What the devil—!" Henri-Antoine exploded, unable to contain his incredulity. He was utterly flummoxed. Jack's idiotic grin did not help his mood. He strode over to join them, and ignoring Jack, demanded of Lisa, "For how long have you known—"

"—your name? Since my visit to Lord Westby's residence. Jack—" She looked at Jack. "That is your name, is it not, sir?" When he nodded, she continued. "Jack called you Harry that night, and so I presumed that to be your name."

For reasons he could not quite fathom he was not pleased to hear his name and Jack's tripping off her tongue with such familiarity. It was one thing to be at his ease with her when they were private—though thinking about this he was made uncomfortable by his social lapse—and he was annoyed with Jack for the interruption, and with her for compromising his judgment. And so he tried to restore order—the way his life ought to be conducted—and failed miserably.

"That is not my name," he enunciated coldly. "That is what *he* calls me. And Jack is not *his* name. That is what *I* call him. So remove your self-satisfied smile and no, you may not address us on such familiar terms—"

"Now hold on, Harry," Jack said, rushing to the girl's defense. "Jack is what everyone calls me. And I'm not the only one who calls you Harry. Most of the family does, except your mother, and—"

"Keep out of this!" Henri-Antoine snapped, not taking his gaze from Lisa.

Jack threw up his hands and took two steps back. But he needn't have bothered to come to Lisa's defense because she was not upset in the least. In fact, if he had felt himself an intruder upon entering the room, he most certainly knew he was one watching these two verbally spar. But while she was enjoying every minute, Henri-Antoine was becoming increasingly uncomfortable as those seconds ticked by. If someone had recounted this scene to him, he would not have believed it possible, not of Henri-Antoine, whom he had always assumed he knew better than anyone—apparently not.

"You're irritated because you wanted to tell me your name yourself, and now you cannot," Lisa replied to Henri-Antoine. "Though why you wish to keep your name a secret... And you cannot use the Fournier Foundation rules as an excuse. This is your second visit. And I was good enough to tell you my name on your first visit—"

"But not your age. You still haven't told me your age. Nor do I see that there is anything in that to make you smile," he grumbled. "I am being perfectly serious."

Lisa took a step closer so Jack would not overhear her. "Yes, I see that you are. And employing two of your *better qualities* to try and make me do your bidding will not work. I will not be coerced by such underhanded means."

Despite his best intentions to remain grave he was quickly realizing he could not conjure any defense against her.

"You, Miss Crisp, are a shameless baggage," he drawled softly, looking down into her upturned smiling face. "Nor can you coerce *me*, with your sweetness and light. I have been burned once too often, and I am immune to such feminine wiles."

Lisa blinked at him. "I am not entirely certain I understand your meaning, sir."

He believed her. And he was very likely to be burned by her if he remained in the orbit of her flame for much longer. He so wanted to take her in his arms and kiss her... That thought snapped him out of his reverie. And although he came to a sense of his surroundings and occasion, he was left feeling slightly inebriated. He wondered if he were experiencing the onset of an impending seizure, he was so whey-brained and disorientated. But this sensation was different from anything he had ever felt before, and that disturbed him most of all. So much so that he turned away and went over to the window, needing space and time to help him determine if he needed to excuse himself and send for the lads.

The drawing room door opened then to admit Minette Warner, and with her was Michel Gallet. She was fluttering her fan and saying something over her shoulder in response to the major domo. But when she turned into the room and was confronted with her cousin and two gentlemen, her smile fell away. Her face flooded with color and her mouth set in a prim line. She looked Lisa over, shot a glance at Jack, then one at Henri-Antoine, then fixed on the sofa and a pretty, filigree-worked wooden box sitting on a cloth and a length of black ribbon.

"How surprising to find you entertaining our guests in my absence, Lisa," Minette Warner said with a tight smile. "You may return to your room, where you were told to remain, and finish packing for your journey. And do make certain you remove that gown. You do not want it ruined before you have even arrived at your destination. The cotton is fragile, thin at best, given it has been worn many times before by Henriette. You could very well have put holes in the fabric already."

Lisa bobbed a curtsy, embarrassed to be caught out by her cousin, though she had done nothing wrong, and mortified to have the secondhand nature of her gown discussed openly, and before a gentleman who was always dressed with all the sartorial elegance of one attending a ball. Still, anything she said would sound petty, and it was her cousin's home and she a member of her household through the Warners' good graces. So she remained silent and went to collect her writing box off the sofa.

"Leave it. I'm certain it can't be yours—"

"Forgive the interruption, Madam," Henri-Antoine said with icy politeness. He wasn't sure what made his blood boil more: The condescending tone in which this woman spoke to a girl who lived under her roof, who was clearly not a servant, or watching the light go out of Lisa's eyes as she was being lectured to. "The writing box does indeed belong to Miss Crisp. No doubt she will put it to good use in her duties as amanuensis—"

Minette Warner was so surprised she forgot her manners and scoffed, "I hardly think writing letters for the poor requires such an expensive and ornamented writing equipage. And I am certain you will excuse me when I point out that, as Lisa is not of age, it is not her place to accept gifts from persons unknown to her guardian."

Henri-Antoine bowed his head with extreme politeness and smiled thinly. Jack did not like that smile at all, and he waited for his best friend to go in for the attack. And if he didn't he was certainly willing to do so to put this creature in her place.

"I agree—" Henri-Antoine began, and was rudely cut off.

"There, Lisa. Now run along."

"I agree that you cannot have thought through your response," Henri-Antoine stated, completing his sentence. "Nor do I excuse you for pointing out the obvious, or for making the inference there was anything improper in the gift-giving." And while Minette Warner was opening and closing her mouth to try and find the words to reply to such a set-down, he turned to Lisa and said smoothly, "And when you have put away your writing box, Miss Crisp, return here to join us in the dining room. The trustees may have questions regarding your duties in the dispensary."

Lisa stopped in front of him, the writing box hastily wrapped up and clutched to her chest.

"I am already in more strife than I can easily explain away in coming here to the drawing room," she whispered.

"The same strife you would've been in had you come out to my carriage when I called upon you that first time?"

Lisa nodded. "And you will only compound that by having me attend a dinner party to which I am not invited."

"I am invoking my right of request as a trustee. And if the good doctor and his dragon lady wife want the foundation to fund his enterprise, then they will not object to your presence at dinner."

Lisa stood her ground.

"Sir, this is one battle from which I ask you to retreat. Do not make me attend. There will be—consequences... And tomorrow I embark on my journey, which at least will give my cousin the time to forgive, if not forget, my infraction."

Henri-Antoine looked into her eyes. She did not blink or look away. "If that is your wish."

"It is."

"Very well. Then I will forgo your company... Are you away long?"

"A fortnight."

"Will it be a pleasant fortnight?"

Lisa's smile returned. "It will. I'm attending a friend's wedding."

"How coincidental. So am I." He jerked his head in Jack's direction. "He's getting leg-shackled."

Lisa turned to look at Jack, and then she looked back at Henri-Antoine with wide eyes and lips slightly parted, as if she'd had a sudden thought that was too good to be true. Henri-Antoine's facial tick surfaced watching her. They looked at each other and Lisa knew then that he, too, was having the same thought. Voicing it was unnecessary. The smile in their eyes was enough to communicate such an outlandish thought: Wouldn't it be the most wonderful coincidence imaginable if they happened to be attending the same wedding!

Little could they have known then that their wish was about to be fulfilled, bringing with it its own joys and tribulations that neither could have anticipated, but which would ultimately change their lives forever.

TWELVE

It was still dark when Lisa and Becky were woken to ready themselves to be taken to the Bell Savage Inn at Ludgate Hill, where they would board the Southampton stagecoach for the journey into Hampshire. A hackney was waiting them in the street, and their luggage was already secured. So they quickly splashed cold water on their faces, tidied their hair and dressed. Capes, bonnets, and gloves on, they went downstairs and scrambled up into the hackney, only to find themselves joined by Dr. Warner, who was waiting for them, and who gave the order to the *jarvie* to be off.

"I—we—Mrs. Warner and I—could not in good conscience allow you to go off on your own," he confessed. "Our minds will be much easier if I see with my own eyes that you are put on the coach, secure an inside seat as was paid for, and that you have everything you need for a pleasant journey."

"Thank you, sir. That is very kind," Lisa replied, stifling a yawn into her gloved fist. She forced herself to be more awake than she was. "I must confess to being apprehensive about the journey, but more so about finding our way at the inn. So your thoughtfulness is appreciated. When we are settled on the coach, I am certain we will be less anxious and be able to enjoy the scenery once the sun is up. Will the Bell Savage be busy at this hour?"

"Busy? Upon my word, it will be, very much so," the physician replied gravely, warming to his topic. "The night coaches will be drawing up in the yard at this hour, while the day coaches and their fresh horses are setting off in all directions. The inn itself is a sizeable establishment which advertises forty guest rooms and over a hundred horses in its stables. Not only are there coaches coming and going, but wagons loaded with all manner of merchandise for the counties, piled so high they require teams of eight horses to pull them along. And those with more money than sense hire their own private vehicles to take them where they please..."

Lisa wondered how the physician could be so wide-awake, for surely he'd had very little sleep after a full afternoon and dinner with the trustees of the Fournier Foundation. And she knew he always spent a few hours in the evening writing up his notes or designing some new experiment or other in the garret laboratory. But here he was at three in the morning as if it were the middle of the day, and as always with her, garrulous. She did her best to concentrate on what he was telling her.

"And if all that isn't enough to dazzle the eyes and ears of even the most jaded traveler," he said, still on the topic of the Bell Savage Inn. "There are the stable hands shouting to one another across the yard as they spring into action when a coach arrives, and those employed at the inn who come and go with baggage and refreshment for the travelers and the coachmen. And there are the team of boys, who for a tip, dash about directing persons to their correct vehicles, assist with carrying portmanteaux if you let them, and who will try and sell you an orange for the journey at an extortionate price. When the sellers of oranges and apples, hot pies, and bread are hawking their produce out on the street at half the rate!" He was pensive. "It is such an exceedingly busy and noisy place it is not surprising accidents often occur... Many years ago, before I married the second Mrs. Warner and moved to Gerrard Street, I had a practice at Ludgate Hill... I received the corpse of a boy from the Bell Savage, still warm. He'd been pinned between a heavily-laden wagon leaving the yard and the wall, and was crushed in the archway... Lower torso flattened, both legs broken, feet severed by the wheels... Died almost instantly. Thank God. They said he was ten years old, small for his age, but it was my opinion he could not have been more than six years old. Perfect skull with excellent teeth, and with the secondary set yet to erupt and still in his jaw. Young William's skull still assists me in my lessons..."

"Was the visit from the trustees and the dinner a success, sir?" Lisa asked, hoping to change the topic from talk of corpses and perfect skulls. For while she was used to such conversation with her breakfast, Becky was not. The girl's eyes were round with horror, and if she had been drowsy with sleep when they set off in the hackney, she certainly was not now. "Do you think they were suitably impressed...?"

"Visit? Dinner? Trustees? Aye!" Dr. Warner replied, suitably diverted. "I had a most productive discussion with my colleagues, Drs. Willan and Blizard. I could see they were more than a little envious of the facilities I offer my anatomy students. Which bodes well for their report. And Dr. Bailey is a most distinguished physician, with the manners of a gentleman. I had heard it so, but to be in the presence of the man himself proved the rumor. And no wonder! He was once the personal physician to none other an exalted personage than the fifth Duke of Roxton, a most formidable old aristocrat—"

"—husband of the Duchess of Roxton, to whom Aunt de Crespigny was lady-in-waiting?"

"The very same. You can imagine how well received this news was by Mrs. Warner. It was most gratifying for us both to have such a gentleman to dine at our table, and one familiar with His Grace's family. Naturally he was circumspect about his years with the Duke and could not be drawn on the subject—indeed he was most diffident —despite Mrs. Warner's best efforts to have him recount one or two small anecdotes."

"I am sure Cousin Minette did her best, sir," Lisa said with as much seriousness as she could put into her tone, all to stop herself rolling her eyes imagining her cousin's efforts at the dining table to entice Dr. Bailey to talk about his years as the physician of a duke, and not just any duke, but the one duke her cousin's mother had served. And no doubt Cousin Minette had found the appropriate moment to tell him and the other trustees all about her own connection to that ducal house. That would not have endeared her to anyone.

Dr. Warner sat forward with a smile. "And I must share with you something about that estimable young gentleman with the profile of a Roman Caesar who took it upon himself to speak with you in the drawing room, that I am sure will impress you as it did me."

"Yes, sir?" Lisa asked, again doing her best to appear grave. Only this time it was because she felt her face warm at the mention of he who had still to tell her his name, though she knew Jack called him Harry. She did not suppose Dr. Warner had discovered his name... "What did you learn?"

"Only that he has met *Dottore* Lazzaro Spallanzani himself!"

Lisa was deflated, and puzzled.

"*Dottore*—Spallan—Spallan*zani*...?"

"The very man! Imagine!"

"I wish I could, sir. You will have to tell me more about him."

"Spallanzani is a most brilliant teacher and one of the greatest minds of our time. His theory of the spontaneous generation of microbes is most illuminating. But his greatest works are in the areas of fertilization and the processes of human digestion. He was made a Fellow of our Royal Society for his contributions to science."

"And a most worthy honor it would seem from his scientific labors," Lisa offered, not being able to contribute any scientific knowledge to the discussion. A glance at Becky, who had a look of disgust at the words *human digestion*, and she was forced to stifle a smile. "And one of the trustees had the honor of meeting him, you say?"

"Not one trustee but two. While on the Grand Tour, both young gentlemen took it upon themselves to visit the good *dottore*. Although it was the gentleman with the visage of a Roman coin who was the catalyst for the visit. He has a keen interest in the scientific and the medical."

"Which is perhaps why he is a trustee of the Fournier Foundation...?"

"Indeed! Yes! No doubt," the physician replied buoyantly, only to become suddenly grave. He sat forward and asked conspiratorially, "He did not, by any chance, tell you his name...?" When Lisa shook her head, he added with a nod, "I did not think so... But Mrs. Warner did wonder, and wished me to ask you... She noticed he wore a ring—"

"—set with a carnelian stone engraved with a coat of arms."

"The very one! Mrs. Warner recognized the coat of arms immediately as belonging to the Hesham family, of which the Duke of Roxton is its head. She said she would know it anywhere, for she had seen it painted on the side of the Duchess of Roxton's carriage when she visited her mother upon occasion—"

"He is a member of the Duke of Roxton's family!?" Lisa blurted out before she could stop herself.

"That is the most likely explanation for him wearing such a ring. Who else but a family member would dare to do so otherwise? And if that is so, it would explain his connection to Dr. Bailey, and be a reason why he is a trustee—Ah! Here we are! Now, before you step outside, you must take this," he said and handed her a package that Lisa had not noticed but which had been beside him on the seat. "Your new writing box—"

"My new writing box?" Lisa interrupted, mind still reeling with the knowledge about the owner of the carnelian-set gold ring, and wondering at the precise nature of his relationship to the Hesham family. "Pardon, sir, but Mrs. Warner said I had to leave it behind at Gerrard Street, it being too valuable—"

"She did. But I have countered her decision, for it was the wrong one. You must and will have your gift. It is a most beautiful writing aid, and this journey is the perfect opportunity for you to use it, too. I took the liberty of stocking it with a few sheets of paper, and your quills, and filled the inkwells—Ah! What is this! Dear me! Dear me! There is nothing to upset you, dearest girl," he said with a nervous laugh when Lisa threw her arms about his neck and hugged him, muffling her thanks into the upturned collar of his coat. He patted her shoulder, sat back, and put the writing box wrapped in a cloth bag into her gloved hands, adding with a smile, "No tears, Lisa. You are to enjoy your time with your school friend. Do you hear me?" When she sniffed and nodded he smiled and flicked her flushed cheek, then dug in a pocket of his coat. He next pressed into her hand a small velvet pouch. "You may have need of this for the journey. Use it wisely. Now quickly put it away, in a pocket under your petticoats if you have one on—"

"Sir, there is too much in here," Lisa said in a small voice, feeling the weight of the bag. When he waved his gloved hand, she quickly dug in under her cape for the slit in her petticoats that let her find the pocket tied about her waist. She put the pouch away and withdrew her hand to grip the writing box, and said with a watery smile, "Thank you, sir. You are too kind, and too generous."

Dr. Warner leaned in to whisper near her ear. "There are some fifteen shillings and a few pence. Tip the driver and the guard the going rate, a little more if they do you a kindness. Procure refreshment for you and Becky—"

"But, sir, Cook gave us apples and oranges, and we have bread, almond biscuits, and orange cake. Becky has it in her satchel. We won't need—"

"If you do not have need of it now, you may have need of it later…"

Lisa blinked at him. There were tears in her eyes. "It is too much, sir."

He smiled and surprised her. "It is not nearly enough for all the hours you've spent in my dispensary aiding and comforting patients. Do not ever think I have been unaware of your efforts. In the dispensary and," he added with a chuckle, as the door to the hackney was wrenched open, "at breakfast when I am at my most loquacious! Now, let me see you both to the Southampton coach."

The yard of the Bell Savage was every bit as noisy and as busy as the physician had described. The noise more thunderous and jarring, the movement of animals, people, and vehicles more hectic and frenetic, if that were possible. They had been set down in the middle of the inn's yard. Both girls immediately looked up at the tallness of the buildings with two floors of open galleries running along both sides. People were coming and going along their length, and guests were hanging over the balustrades watching the activity below, all under the honeyed glow of a hundred tapers.

Such was their preoccupation that they would have been lost had not Dr. Warner taken Lisa by the arm, and she in turn hooked her arm through Becky's. They then moved snake-like through the hustle and bustle of passengers and servants seemingly going in all directions, following four young boys carrying Lisa's and Becky's trunks between them, and making a path as they went, shouting at the top of their lungs to *Make way! Make way!*

Soon they were standing before a large coach with its roof strapped with luggage, and the outside passengers crowded about eager to climb aboard. The horses were being attended to, the coachman's box still without its driver, so there was still time for the two girls to be settled. Inside the coach were already seated three individuals, a husband and wife, and between them a young boy, not much older than poor Young William when he had lost his life and his skull became a teaching aid for Dr. Warner.

The physician was talking to the head porter and that gentleman was listening with all the gravity of one being addressed by a duke. He glanced over at Lisa and Becky standing to one side of the physician, nodded, and then Lisa saw Dr. Warner press something into the palm of the man's hand—no doubt a coin for his cooperation—and him nod and smile and doff his hat in understanding. Then Lisa and Becky's trunks were put aboard, but not up on the roof with the rest of the luggage, but inside the carriage under the seat where Lisa and Becky were to sit. With their luggage carefully stowed and the seat back in place, Lisa and Becky were invited to board. It would not be long before the coachman was up on his box, and with the outside passengers seated, their journey would begin.

Becky scrambled up inside, Lisa turning to give Dr. Warner another hug of thanks.

"I'll write, so that you know we arrived safely."

"Do that, my dear. If you have the time. But do not waste it in writing to us. Enjoy every minute of your stay. It could be the one and only time you have the opportunity to mix in such exalted circles, and to visit such a wondrous place as Treat, if Mrs. de Crespigny's descriptions are to the life. Remember everything you see and do. Write that down. Share it with us when you return. Mrs. Warner can hardly wait to hear all about it."

Lisa smiled and nodded, swiftly kissed his cheek and with a quick look over her shoulder, she climbed up into the coach. The door was shut on her back before she was seated, she setting the writing box in its cloth bag on the seat beside her between her and Becky. There were to be no other inside passengers, and so they had the luxury of space, for which Lisa knew she had the good doctor to thank. She nodded to the couple and their son, and they nodded back, but were so dour-faced, and she too tired and overwhelmed to engage in conversation that she remained mute. Instead, she concentrated on what was happening outside, both she and Becky giving a jump of fright when the passengers began to climb up on the roof, and the carriage to rock to and fro with the movement. The couple across from them smiled knowingly but said nothing, as if it were not new to them.

Lisa looked for Dr. Warner, but he was lost to the jostling crowd of passengers, those eager to board, and those having been set down to be on their way. No doubt the physician was wanting to return home as soon as possible, to his breakfast, his newspapers, and his day in the dispensary, and perhaps before his wife knew his whereabouts. Lisa was sure he had come to see her off with Cousin Minette none the wiser. And for that Lisa would ever be grateful. She wondered when he would be notified if his application for funding had been approved or rejected. And that made her think about her handsome gentleman with the profile of a Roman Ceasar and his connection to the Hesham family. It did not surprise her to think he was member of a ducal house. He had the bearing, the manners, and the arrogant self-assurance—and from his clothing and accoutrements, the wealth, too—of a duke. But the Duke of Roxton was the premier duke in the kingdom. He did not just have wealth and power, he was the epitome of both. And that deepened the mystery of her gentleman's connection to such an illustrious nobleman. But most of all she wondered if she would ever see him again. As if wanting tangible proof that he would seek her out, she put her hand to the writing box, and that provided her with some comfort that she had not seen the last of him.

But uppermost in her mind as the final preparations were being made on horses, carriage, and coachman, was that she was on her way to be reunited with Teddy. That still seemed a dream, despite now sitting inside a coach about to depart the Bell Savage. That thought made her smile and she snuggled into her corner of the interior, still aware of the racket and activity outside in the busy yard, but it slowly fading into a homogeneous drone. The thumps above her head had ceased, so the outside passengers were also ready to be off. Then finally there was movement of the coach as the horses set to, and the vehicle lurched forward, the driver maneuvering the horses behind a line of carriages all waiting to move off under the archway. They would then go their separate ways out into the environs of Ludgate Hill, then further into the streets of a city that never slept, the Southampton stagecoach heading southwest into a countryside that was new to both girls, and eagerly anticipated.

Finally, Lisa and Becky were on their way.

When Lisa woke, the coach had left the city behind. She had no idea as to how long she had slept, though she had a vague awareness of the carriage coming to a standstill upon several occasions, of thumps above her head, and of people scrambling down and then up again. But she had been too tired and drowsy with sleep to fully wake. Becky was still asleep in her corner, but the couple across from them were wide-awake, the boy leaning against his mother, who had her arm around him, with his eyes closed.

Lisa was still tired, but awake enough to take a peek out the window at the morning sky, which was streaked with clouds. Yet it was a lovely sunny day, with no hint of rain. This boded well for travel along dry roads, and for the passengers holding on above her head atop the roof, who would continue to have dry clothes, rain not adding to their woes of traveling in the open air.

The fresh green of summer was everywhere to be seen along the roadside, in the hedgerows, the open spaces of rolling hills, and in the forests farther afield. Surprisingly to Lisa, the road was not deserted of people. But there was every reason for it not to be, as the coach was trundling along the London to Portsmouth road, one of the busiest thoroughfares in the kingdom, and it would remain on this road until Guildford, and a change of horses. That town was still hours away yet. Most of the travelers they passed were on foot and headed towards the city. Possibly they had walked all night. A few men on horseback passed by. And then the coach moved around to overtake an open wagon being pulled slowly by eight horses, and which was full of carousing men.

"Sailors headed for their ships," the woman stated, answering Lisa's thoughtful frown when she sat back. "It will take a good three days before they see the harbor, and when they join their ships, they'll be at sea for months."

"Thank you. I see then why they are enjoying their time while on land…"

There was a long silence, but Lisa sensed the woman was still staring at her, as if trying to get her measure. She knew this was so when the woman asked, "If you don't mind me making conversation, are you and your friend traveling all the way to Southampton?"

"No. We alight at Alston."

"Alston? Now there's a pretty village in a pretty part of Hampshire. Isn't that so, husband," she added in a loud voice, with little regard for her son or Becky, who were still asleep. If the husband had been dozing, he wasn't now. "Alston—it's a pretty village."

"Aye. Very pretty. The church with its set of bells is particularly worth a visit. And the town is not too distant from Treat, the Duke of Roxton's seat. I think *Paterson's* gives the exact mileage."

"Such a grand establishment as His Grace lives in must be in every guide book in the country," the wife opined. "Now, had it been built in King Harry's time, he'd have found an excuse to confiscate it for himself, make no mistake. He'd not have liked to be outshone by one of his nobles. Possibly would've locked up the Duke for treason."

"But not this present duke, wife. His Grace is a God-fearing family man, just like His Majesty. And he's humble into the bargain, and has upon occasion stopped in at the Crown to take a pint. Is that not so, wife? King Harry would've had him for a friend, I'll wager."

"I don't disagree with you, husband. But King Harry would have been jealous to think the Duke had a grander house than he ever did. And he would've been envious that His Grace has sired eight children, and six of those healthy sons, too. Imagine!" said the wife, warming to her topic. "Though he cannot match His Majesty's fifteen children. So our present king has nothing to be jealous of there. My grandmother was the proprietress of The Crown in Alston, after my grandfather passed on," she confided in Lisa. "And then we took it on for a time, did we not, husband? And that is why he can say the Duke is a humble, God-fearing man for a noble, because he was the one who poured him that pint. Did you not, husband?" And then she said to Lisa with a superior smile, "Which is why we know so much about His Grace and about Alston, you see. Such a pretty town…"

"Here, wife. I've marked it in *Paterson's*. Let me read it to you," the husband said, having dug in a pocket of his coat and pulled out *Paterson's British Itinerary*. He leafed through the pages. "Treat is listed between the noble estates of Traine and Trebursey. And it's shown on the map, too." He then removed a folded piece of paper tucked in to hold a place at this particular page, and looked to his wife, and then said to Lisa, "But *Paterson's* don't give a good description of these fine noble establishments. Just where they are located. But this does, and so I kept it, thinking I'd like to take a tour of the grounds one day. For although we lived but a few miles from the estate, we never did make a

visit. Did we, wife? We thought there'd be plenty of time for that...
But then we had the boy, and he's not always at his best—"

"Sea air. That's what the doctor said he needed," interjected the
wife. "One day he'll be as right as rain."

"—so we moved to Southampton," the husband said, finishing his
sentence. "We own a boarding establishment on Canute Road—"

"—which is in the fashionable part of town. It's always booked out
for weeks ahead. A proper respectable establishment it is. With breakfast and dinner served every day, and a special dinner on Sundays."

"We make a stop in Winchester on our way to and from
Southampton to visit our daughter Sally, who's married to a curate.
Our other daughter, Molly, she's our eldest, she and her husband Fred
are in charge of our boarding establishment while we take the boy up
to London to see what his physicians can do for him—"

"But there's no change in him. Which is a good sign. So says the
physicians. He's no worse and no better."

"When it's warm enough, I take him in to the sea baths," said the
husband. "I don't care too much for the salt water, but he loves it—"

"—and the smell of the salt. He'd leave the window open all night,
even on a cold winter's day, if he had his way..."

Lisa regarded the boy with a soft smile. He looked to be asleep,
which didn't surprise her, given their early start, but she wondered if he
might be awake and listening, but preferred to stay snuggled up to his
mother, who was warm and comforting, particularly when he was
feeling poorly. The jolting of the carriage would not make him feel any
better. The parents mistook her frown for one of concern for herself
and were quick to reassure her.

"The physician says you can't catch what he's got."

"Now, Mother. That ain't strictly true. One of his doctors says you
can catch it, and another says you can't because it's all in his head. Not
that he imagines what he's got, but that it's his brain that's to blame. To
tell you a truth, I don't think they know theirselves why he gets such
headaches. But he does. And what I can tell you is that we've never
caught it off him, nor has Sally and Molly or their families. And none
of our guests have ever complained of fainting spells and the like. Not
that he's much around the guests..."

"If you don't mind me asking, does your son suffer with childhood
megrims or are his symptoms more akin to those who are afflicted with
the falling sickness...?"

Mother and father looked at one another and then at Lisa. Their
startled and wary looks begged the question as to how she, who was
not much more than a girl, knew about such things.

Lisa then felt compelled to tell them a little about Warner's Dispensary, and about Dr. Warner, adding with a reassuring smile, "So you see, I am not at all concerned for my health, or my companion's, either. And I would like very much to hear what that piece of paper has to say about the Duke of Roxton's estate…"

"Yes! Yes! The paper," said the husband, taking his gaze from Lisa, whom he thought an extraordinarily confident young woman, and that it was a crying shame that such beauty was wasted tending to the sick poor. Still, if he'd been ill, he could think of nothing nicer than having this ministering angel tending to his woes. On that thought, he quickly cleared his throat and read aloud the description of the ancestral home of the dukes of Roxton:

"Treat. Seat of the dukes of Roxton. Five miles southwest of the village of Alston in the county of Hampshire. A substantial mansion fashioned in the Palladian style by architect William Kent. Said to be the largest privately-owned home in England. Originally an Elizabethan manor house. Much altered by Henry, fourth Duke of Roxton, the 'architect duke', at the turn of the century, and completed in all its glory by Renard, fifth Duke of Roxton. The Grand Gallery has an excellent selection of paintings by well-known artists from Holbein to Kneller, and grand portraits of the family abound. Of particular note is the full-length portrait of the fifth duchess by the French artist Jean-Honore Fragonard. The library is on two levels and said to have no equal in the kingdom. A grand ballroom with three chandeliers, a gilded music room, and several state reception rooms are open to the public on particular days.

"The grounds are much altered since Queen Anne's time. Gardens, lake, and immediate surrounding parkland are the work of Capability Brown. Many follies in various fanciful architectural styles can be found throughout the extensive grounds, and those not locked up may be viewed by the public. There is an artificial lake of considerable magnitude that can be crossed at various sites by one of three stone bridges. Small islands abound, with the largest, Swan Island, once home to a hermit and said to be haunted by his ghost. Worthy of note is the magnificent family mausoleum, final resting place of the dukes of Roxton and various Hesham family relatives. It has a grand domed roof set with a glass oculus, and is built on the highest point on the estate. A good vantage point for taking in the surrounding countryside, the mausoleum is a beacon to travelers, for it can be seen from many miles hence. The interior is dominated by a lifelike statue of the fifth duke. Not open to the public, except on foundation day. A small remuneration to the housekeeper for a tour of the public rooms within the house is expected. The grounds may be accessed when the family is not in residence by calling at the Gatehouse Lodge at the northern entrance. Crecy Hall, a restored Elizabethan manor, and its parkland, abuts the eastern shore of the lake, and was once part of the Roxton estate. It is presently the English residence of the Scots duke of Kinross, and is strictly off-limits all year round. No exceptions."

"Oh look!" exclaimed the wife before Lisa had time to thank or comment to the husband for reading out a most illuminating description of her destination. The wife then pointed to the window. Her husband and Lisa followed her extended finger. "There! There, between the trees. Do you see it?"

And they did see it. A grand building with an equally grand portico held up by four fat columns. It stood proudly atop a hill of rolling lawn, much higher than the surrounding trees, so that it was easily visible from the road, and no doubt for miles around. The husband and wife enlightened Lisa about the mansion and its history as she kept her gaze out the window.

"That's Claremont—"

"—built by a rich nabob. What was his name...?"

"Clive. Lord Clive of India."

"Ah! That's right! Made his riches out on the subcontinent and brought it back here and built that house."

"It's said that from the top floor you can see as far back to London as St. Paul's—"

"All the way to St. Paul's?"

"All the way to St. Paul's, wife. And you don't have to take my word for it. Molly's Fred's uncle said it. You ask Fred when we return home if it isn't so. But for all that, I don't believe Clive's mansion can be matched against that belonging to His Grace of Roxton."

Lisa turned away from the window with a smile, the house now disappearing from view behind a clump of forest as the stagecoach rounded a bend.

"From the description you read me, I do not doubt you, sir. The Duke of Roxton's seat is beyond anything I can imagine."

"If you have the time and opportunity, and the coin to pay the housekeeper, I am certain it would surely be well worth the journey. You wouldn't regret it."

"Oh, I believe you, sir. And I will, and have no regrets."

THE JOURNEY BETWEEN CLAREMONT, WHICH WAS ON THE outskirts of Esher, and the town of Guildford, the next scheduled stop, gave the stagecoach's occupants plenty of hours to become better acquainted. Lisa and Becky shared their fruit, slices of orange cake and almond biscuits with the husband and wife, who formally introduced themselves as Mr. and Mrs. Fuller, and their son Master Samuel. To this feast the Fullers added bread, cheese, chutney, and some fruit, too. And then Samuel and Becky played several hands of snap with playing cards the boy had purchased in London with his pocket money, while the couple dozed and Lisa admired the view, before she, too, fell asleep with the rocking of the carriage.

When she woke, the stagecoach had pulled in at the White Hart Inn at Guildford, to change horses and to drop off and take up passengers traveling further south. All passengers alighted, to use the facilities, to sit down to a meal, and to take a stroll along the High Street to stretch their legs, before once again clambering aboard to take a seat on the roof, or for the Fullers and Lisa and Becky, to resume their seats in the relative comfort inside the coach.

Yet, the companionable company the girls and the Fuller family had formed after many hours of travel together in such a confined space was disrupted when, upon climbing back inside the coach they found it occupied by a gentleman seated in a corner, the collar of his coat pulled up around his ears, and a felt hat pulled down over his eyes. His chin was on his chest and he looked to be asleep.

The girls and the Fullers all looked at one another, Mrs. Fuller muttering what the others were thinking.

"Oh dear. This is most unfortunate."

The Fullers all returned to their seats, and Lisa gave Becky the window, while she took the middle seat next to the sleeping gentleman. Not even the thumping above their heads, as the outside passengers scrambled up to find a space on the roof, disturbed the stranger in his corner. And then Lisa had a sudden thought, one that made her sick to the stomach and her heartbeat quicken.

"My writing box! Becky! I left it on the seat. It's—it's not here!"

"It must be, Miss," Becky said. "No one would dare touch it."

Everyone except the stranger shifted about in search of the object in question. Though it was unlikely that anyone had sat on something that was clearly large enough to be avoided. And just as Lisa was feeling bereft and wondering how she would ever explain such a loss to the gift giver, the stranger sat up and produced from under his arm the cloth bag that had within it Lisa's rosewood writing box.

"Oh, thank you!" Lisa exclaimed, smiling at the gentleman and hugging the box to her bodice.

He tugged at the front of his hat, and without a word went back to sleep. Yet this would have been impossible, for no sooner had he dropped his chin than there was a crescendo of noise outside in the yard that could not be ignored. Stable hands ran every which way, shouting out commands, many of the passengers on the roof of the coach moved about to get a better view, unsettling the delicate balance of the entire group, while the coachman needed all his strength and skill to keep a firm grip on the reins of his six horses, who were unsettled by the unexpectedness of the new arrival.

A sleek, high-set carriage, pulled by four thoroughbreds and accompanied by six outriders in livery, entered the yard with the speed and arrogance of their arrival taking precedence over everyone and everything else. That the carriage swept up beside a stagecoach that was about to depart barely registered with the driver, the outriders, and the occupants of this conveyance. Everything about this latest arrival at the White Hart Inn proclaimed a master with wealth and social position, from the latest in carriage construction, with its light body set on springs to make for a more comfortable ride, the black-lacquered and gold-painted panels and embellishments, to the horses, which were magnificent matching grays in their brightly-polished brass tack, and the outriders resplendent in black and silver livery. Which was why the passengers of the stagecoach leaned forward to take a better look at the carriage, the horses, and most of all to discover who it was that traveled about the countryside in such state.

The passengers on the roof of the stagecoach had a better view than those inside, for although the carriage was driven up between the coach and the inn, it came to a halt a little further along, leaving the Fuller family, Lisa and Becky, and the stranger who had sat up, to watch the outriders dismount outside their window and then stride off, and this while the stagecoach was slowly pulling away from the inn to the road leading south towards Winchester. There was no opportunity to see these new arrivals for they exited on the far side. Yet their shouts of laughter, as they stepped down onto solid ground, were heard across the yard but soon lost in the accompanying noise of the moving stagecoach.

Everyone within the coach sat back, dissatisfied. But Lisa did not need to see these new arrivals to have a good idea who owned the carriage. She recognized the livery, and two of the outriders. They were the same two bear-like footmen who had accompanied the gentleman who had gifted her the magnificent writing box when he had visited Gerrard Street. She was not mistaken, and she began to wonder if indeed her wish would be fulfilled and they were indeed attending the same wedding. For why else would he and his servants be traveling this same road towards Alston? And had not Mrs. Warner recognized the coat of arms of his carnelian intaglio as that belonging to the Duke of Roxton? And so if he was a family member, it stood to reason he was indeed attending the wedding of her best friend Teddy. And as it was his friend who was getting "leg shackled", then this friend had to be none other than Sir John Cavendish, Teddy's intended. He said his name was Jack... She had met Teddy's future husband. Lisa's eyes opened wide with amazement and shock at this unlikely coincidence. She turned to stare out the opposite window, lest the Fullers think her staring at them.

And just as she thought she could not be any more surprised, with the stagecoach now free of the inn and trundling along the road, the stranger removed his hat and tousled his hair so that it no longer remained plastered to his scalp. Lisa's gaze shifted from the view to the stranger's thick head of hair. It was a vibrant copper red, the same color as Teddy's. She must have stared at him hard, for he turned and looked straight at her, and she felt another shock. His hair was not only the same color as Teddy's but he had the same straight small nose, which was too feminine for a man as far as she was concerned, though it suited Teddy very well. Nevertheless her best friend shared her hair and nose with this gentleman, who looked to be in his mid to late thirties, if her reckoning was correct. He had to be in some way related to Teddy. She was so sure of this, and so astounded by it, that she just came out and asked him.

"Excuse my forwardness, sir, but I must ask you: Are you on your way to attend the wedding of Miss Cavendish to Sir John Cavendish?"

THIRTEEN

THE STRANGER GAVE A START TO BE DIRECTLY ADDRESSED. HE darted a glance at the other occupants of the carriage, and saw that the couple had sat forward at the girl's question.

Lisa waited for his response. When he shrugged and pulled a face she realized he was about to deny all knowledge of the wedding and Miss Cavendish, even though she had seen his startled reaction to her question. He did this by pretending he did not understand a word of what she had said.

"*Excusez-moi, mademoiselle. Je ne comprends pas l'anglais.*"

Lisa was more than ever convinced he knew exactly what she had asked. Besides when she had exclaimed at having lost her writing box he had quickly found it next to him on the seat. And when she had thanked him, he had tugged at his hat in reply. So he understood enough English to understand her question. Perhaps he was being cautious because he did not wish his private business discussed among strangers. After all, he did not know her, and he certainly did not know the Fullers. She was certain that even if the Fullers knew some French, they would not be as conversant as she, so she persisted with the stranger, and spoke to him in his own language. Reasoning that if she was truthful and open with him, he might just be the same with her.

"Then I hope you won't mind if I persist, and ask you my question in your preferred language," she replied in French, and continued smoothly, as if she had not seen his surprise or that he was peering at her keenly. "The reason I asked if you are attending Miss Cavendish's wedding, is because I am. I beg your pardon. My name is Miss Crisp.

I was at school with Miss Cavendish—Teddy—and I have not seen her in two years. But I have a most excellent memory for names and faces. And I do recall Teddy telling me about an uncle who lived in France. She had never met him, but that her mother told her that this uncle—who is her mother's brother—has the same color hair as Teddy and her mother. She called the color 'Fitzstuart Fire'. She also told me that there is a family ring called the 'Fire and Ice', the fire represented by a ruby, and ice represented by a diamond. But please excuse me, I am rattling on at you. And if you are not Teddy's French uncle, then you must think me quite addle-brained, or at the very least a most forward female to speak to you so freely, and you may quite rightly snub me."

The stranger continued to peer at Lisa for several seconds, and then, after another glance about at the others, who were either dozing again or looking out at the view, replied in French, saying with the hint of a smile,

"You have a remarkable memory, Miss Crisp. As remarkable as your French language skills. It is gratifying to know Teddy attended a school that provided such excellent tuition in the language."

"It did. But that does not mean all the girls took advantage of what was on offer, or indeed had a natural aptitude for language. I do. I don't say this with arrogance, but as fact, M'sieur. But if you do indeed know anything of Teddy, you know her interests lie anywhere but in a classroom."

The stranger gave an involuntary bark of laughter. But he soon had his features under control, and all he would say was, "If you will excuse me, Miss Crisp, I shall keep my own counsel until Alston. I have had a long and arduous journey from Cheltenham, where I spent time visiting with my ailing mother, whom I have not seen in many years. But if you care to continue our conversation on the way to our destination, I will oblige you."

Lisa readily complied, and let the stranger sleep, and he did, in his corner, soundlessly, until they reached Alston, which was indeed a picturesque village as attested by the Fullers.

Lisa and Becky and their trunks, and the stranger with his satchel, were set down in front of the Swan Inn on the High Street. The girls said their farewells to the Fullers, and to Sam, who gave Becky an impromptu hug and made her promise to visit him in Southampton. The Fullers then gave Lisa their trade card, and Lisa thanked them, and Becky said she would write. Leave-taking was then conducted in a rush, which suited Lisa because she would not have known how to respond to the Fullers had they asked her why she had not made her destination known to them when they had spoken about the Duke of Roxton's estate.

For no sooner had Lisa and Becky taken their leave of the Fullers than they were approached by a gentleman in the somber attire of an upper servant, followed by two footmen in livery. The Fullers knew instantly to whom the livery belonged, and they stared at Lisa and Becky anew to see them greeted by servants of the Duke of Roxton. A carriage awaited the girls in the yard of the Swan Inn, ready to take them to Treat.

Lisa invited the stranger to join them, and he gladly accepted, though he did not offer her or the upper servant his name upon entering the carriage. And again he sat in his corner as the servant, who introduced himself as assistant to His Grace of Roxton's secretary without giving his name, spoke to Lisa at length about her stay on the estate, and the upcoming nuptials of Miss Cavendish to Sir John Cavendish. She must have glanced one too many times about the interior of the carriage, which was a compact vehicle but beautifully appointed throughout, with deep blue velvet cushions, satin buttons in the upholstery, and silk blinds with a delicate fringe, for the assistant secretary felt compelled to comment.

"This is Her Grace's estate carriage, used only to make short trips, to the village on fete days, special days at the local Alston school, of which Her Grace is patroness, and to visit such persons in the local environs as Her Grace deems worthy of her time."

"It is a beautifully appointed vehicle," Lisa replied with a smile, gloved hands in her lap. "And gives a most superior ride."

"This is a superior road," the stranger in the corner quipped, and in perfect English, without opening his eyes.

No one commented, though Lisa kept her smile from widening with difficulty. The assistant secretary then handed Lisa a sealed packet which he said she did not need to open now, but it would be beneficial for her to read the entire contents and familiarize herself with the protocol sheet and the two maps, as soon as practicable upon her arrival at the Gatehouse Lodge, where she would be residing for the duration of her stay.

Lisa stared at the fat packet and at the wax seal, and then across at the assistant.

"Protocol sheet? Maps?" she enquired, requiring more information to understand what he was talking about. "Excuse me. It has been a long day, and I am a little tired."

The assistant coughed into his gloved hand and explained.

"A protocol sheet is a most necessary and instructive instrument if one is unfamiliar with the—um—*intricacies* of the customs, and the order of precedence, and the minutiae of the daily interactions of persons of position of a large estate, particularly the estate of a duke whose mother is a double duchess, and whose step-father is also a duke in his own right. As I'm certain you, Miss Crisp, can appreciate, when the niece of a duke weds, the guest list is one long list of titled relatives and friends. All will be known to one another, and so it is helpful for those who have had little or no—*interaction*—with such exalted persons to know the difference say, when addressing an earl, and when addressing a viscount—"

"It would, but the examples you give are not good ones," stated the stranger, opening his eyes. "Both are addressed as 'my lord', whether they are the Earl of Big Breeches, or Viscount Hot Head. So how would she know? How would anyone unless they were related to the said Lord Big Breeches or Lord Hot Head?"

Lisa clapped a hand to her mouth to stop herself from laughing out loud. But she could not stop the twinkle in her eyes. The stranger, who was sitting across from her, smiled and winked before dropping his smile and saying to the affronted assistant secretary, "Please don't let me interfere in your instruction. Though I will add for Miss Crisp's benefit, so that she may feel more comfortable knowing that as this is a family wedding, and the Duke of Roxton is a family man first and a nobleman second, he will not be standing on ceremony with any of his guests, the Earl of Big Breeches and Viscount Hot Head not withstanding. If I know anything of the man, he values good manners and honesty above precedence and posturing."

"And you know His Grace well, do you, sir?" the assistant secretary asked stiffly, not expecting an answer.

"I should. I am his first cousin once removed."

The assistant secretary goggled at him, and then realizing his bad manners quickly looked away and down at his hands. There was a long silence, in which the stranger turned to stare out the window; then the assistant said diffidently to Lisa, "There is also a day-to-day itinerary included in the packet, with certain events organized in the lead-up to the wedding ceremony and wedding breakfast and the ball. Guests are not obliged to take part in any of these, but are most welcome to join in where that is possible, or just to be a spectator at such events as the gentleman's cricket match. You will find one or two events that have been marked to your particular attention, and these you are to attend, as a guest of the bride.

"Also included are two maps contained within the packet which I hope you will find most useful. One is of the estate's immediate landscape environs, with various landmarks, follies, and such of interest inked in, which you may visit if you have the time during your stay. The second is a map of the big house—that is what the house occupied by His Grace and his family is referred to by family, to distinguish it from—

"—the little house...?" suggested the stranger in a voice which told Lisa and the harassed assistant secretary he was being facetious.

"—Crecy Hall, the home of His Grace's mother, the Duchess of Kinross, and her husband, the Duke of Kinross," the assistant secretary continued as if the stranger had not spoken. "The map included shows the rooms in the big house which are open to guests, so that if you find yourself lost, or in difficulty navigating your way about, then the map will come in most useful."

"What?" asked the stranger. "What happened to the army of footmen, or has Roxton resorted to employing only mute fellows at such posts?"

"Not at all, sir. It was thought that perhaps some guests might feel less intimidated if they were to have a map to find their own way about, rather than ask one of the footmen, who is not to leave his post, to show them the way."

"Oh yes, having a map is an excellent notion. Thank you," Lisa said, feeling she should say something in defense of the hours that must have gone into preparing and drawing up such maps for each of the guests who were unfamiliar with the estate. "And you are quite right. Approaching a footman in all his finery would be an unsettling experience. And I dare say," she added with a cheeky smile and glance across at the stranger, "that if they were not regular guests of His Grace, then Lord Big Breeches and his friend Lord Hot Head would benefit from such a map, too."

The stranger gave a huff of laughter.

"They could then swan about the rooms as if they were indeed familiar with the place?!" He leaned in and confided to Lisa. "Thing is, even family members get lost in such a monstrous place from time to time, so there's no shame in you having your map front and center." He looked across at the assistant secretary. "Is there anything else you need to tell Miss Crisp?"

"No, sir. Everything else is detailed in the packet."

"Good. How's your French?"

"I beg your pardon, sir. My French?"

"Do you speak it?"

"A little."

"But not well?"

"Not well, sir."

"Then you must excuse Miss Crisp and me for the next little while," he said and turned and spoke to Lisa exclusively in French. "I beg your pardon for not being more forthcoming in the stagecoach. I do not know how much Teddy knows, or what she has told you about her French uncle, but perhaps you would be kind enough to tell me what you have been told, so that I do not repeat myself. And I would appreciate your candor, Miss Crisp."

"Very well, sir. Teddy and I had no secrets at school. She only knows what her mother chose to tell her about you. Hence, I knew about your similar coloring, and that you live in France." Lisa met his steady gaze. "One thing her mother was most adamant about was that you were not a-a—*traitor* to your conscience, whatever your-your —*treasonous* actions toward His Majesty during the war in the American Colonies. And that you were pardoned in your absence after the signing of the Treaty of Paris because, as Teddy put it, you are related to practically everyone who is in government."

"Thank you. The latter is not strictly true. I was pardoned for my actions in aiding the American cause, but I am related by blood to only half of those in government, and most of those I would not own to knowing."

Lisa frowned in thought.

"You need not answer this if you do not wish to, sir, but as you have been pardoned, why is it that you seem to be in hiding, or, at the very least, moving about the country by stealth?"

"How perceptive of you, Miss Crisp. Old habits. Though that is not strictly true. There are still those within government who wish me harm because, in their eyes, I will forever be a traitor for my support of the colonists. I will never alter the opinions of such men. But I do not seek to do so. In truth, when I departed England for France almost ten years ago, I had no wish or expectation of returning. I was persuaded to do so by my cousin and my father-in-law upon their recent visit to France."

"For Teddy's wedding?"

"Yes. It seemed the perfect opportunity to see family members before I take mine to live permanently in the new united states of America. To see my mother one last time; she is very poorly. To be reunited with my sister, to make peace with my brother—"

"—the revolutionary war hero?"

"Ah. So you *do* know my family's history! Yes. And to meet their families. I would tell you my name," he added on a note of apology, "but I fear that in the telling it would soon be communicated, not by you, but the mere mention will alert other ears within the confines of this space, and in turn alert M'sieur le Duc, my cousin, and I want to be the one to surprise them."

"And so you should, sir." Lisa smiled. "Teddy's wedding is certainly going to be a memorable occasion for everyone."

"Just so, Miss Crisp," said Teddy's uncle reverting to English, and then, after a quick look out of the window, surprised the occupants by knocking on the backboard above his head, signal for the driver to pull up the horses. He collected his satchel, set his hat firmly over his head of red hair, and said to Lisa, "Up ahead the carriage will leave the avenue of trees and turn left to take you to the Gatehouse Lodge. If you look out the right window you will have an uninterrupted view across the lake to the big house. It is a breathtaking sight, and it never grows old. I envy you your first view of Treat. No matter what you have read, or been told, nothing can quite prepare you for the sheer scale of the place. It is simply beyond belief, and this from a man who has spent the last nine years living on the doorstep of the Chateau of Versailles. Ah, if Louis could but see how the Duke of Roxton lives!" He tugged the front of his hat. "We shall meet again very soon, Miss Crisp."

With that, Teddy's uncle exited the carriage and disappeared through the line of trees on the other side of the road. The assistant secretary knocked again for the driver to continue. Lisa did not wish to miss her first view of the big house, but her gaze was still out the left window, and she voiced her thought aloud, not expecting an answer,

"I wonder where he is headed…"

"There is a right of way just beyond those trees along the top of the ha-ha that runs all the way to the adjoining estate of Crecy Hall," the assistant secretary informed her. "Home of the Duke and Duchess of Kinross—"

"Oh! Oh! Miss! Miss! Look! *Look*," Becky burst out and gasped, sliding along the seat and then crossing to sit opposite Lisa so she too had an excellent view out the windows to the right.

The two girls pressed their noses to the glass, mesmerized. It was just as Teddy's uncle had said, and yet what he had said seemed inadequate to the sight presented them. As the carriage veered left, leaving the avenue of trees which continued on towards the lake, they trundled along a graveled drive which gave a clear view across rolling acres of lawn down to the wide blue waters. On the other side of the lake, the rolling lawns continued sloping upwards to a hill, where sat perched a palace. For that was what it was. A grand central Palladian building, with enormous fat columns rising up three floors from a grand staircase, that was almost the width of the building, and to support an impressive pediment carved with statues, sat proudly front and center of this colossal collection of buildings that extended left and right from this imposing central structure. Also three stories high, there were rows and rows of windows that seemed to go on forever before turning a corner and continuing on, for how far, Lisa could not see. Her line of sight was broken by a second avenue of trees, now with only glimpses of the palace atop its hill seen between the green foliage. And then the carriage crossed a stone bridge and turned in through a set of gates and on up a circular drive that was lined with standards of white roses. It came to a stop in front of a quaint—everything else after glimpsing the palace of Treat could not be called anything else—Elizabethan two-storey cottage with turned chimney pots and gargoyles atop the fanciful battlements.

Their carriage was not the only one pulled up outside the entrance to the Gatehouse Lodge. Another vehicle, an open buggy pulled by two horses, with a driver up front and two footmen in livery up back, was patiently awaiting its occupants.

Lisa and Becky were set down with their trunks behind this vehicle, and there they waited, watching their carriage depart, and it was almost at the entrance gates before there was any movement from within the manor. And then a great deal happened very quickly, leaving Lisa and Becky tired and mute but fascinated spectators to a family leave-taking.

A boy with a mop of red curls dashed out of the house into the sunshine, and climbed up into the waiting buggy and slid along the seat to the end. A second, younger boy, with a head of black curls, was not half-a-dozen steps behind and scrambled to climb aboard. When he had difficulty in doing so, the older boy quickly slid back down the seat and stuck out his hand and hauled the younger boy up beside him. He made exaggerated groaning noises, to impress his brother. Both boys did not sit, but stood waiting, looking back to the house with eyes wide with excitement, as if their party was not complete for what was to be a grand adventure.

A servant appeared next with two small leather satchels which he put up behind the seat at the feet of the liveried footmen; another followed with a larger satchel, and this, too, went in with the others. Next out of the house strode a tall, well-built gentleman of middling years, dressed in a plain linen frock coat and top boots. He put up a hand to the two boys who jumped up and down with excitement and called out for Papa to hurry! Hur-*ry*! But their papa did not immediately go to them. He turned to the house and waited to be joined by a small woman with an abundance of bright copper hair, and who had an infant to her hip. He kissed the baby's rosy cheek and then one chubby hand that was held out to him, before gently kissing the woman's forehead and then stooping to kiss her mouth. It was a lingering kiss and it brought color into Lisa's cheeks. She dared not look at Becky, and she could not look away from a couple that were clearly very much in love.

"Two nights sleeping in tents in the woods," the gentleman stated with a smile and a shake of his head. "I can't believe I allowed Roxton and Strathsay to persuade me. I don't know who is more excited, they or our combined seven rascals. You know where I'd rather be."

"I do. But that's not to say you won't enjoy every minute of it, just as much as Roxton and my brother," the woman threw at him with a laugh and touched his cheek. "And you couldn't disappoint your sons. They've been talking of little else for days. But do be careful. And if there is even the hint of rain, come back. I couldn't bear it if any of you caught a cold right before Teddy's big day. Now, give your daughter another kiss and off you go before David and Luke jump themselves right out of that carriage."

The gentleman held the infant up in his outstretched arms, which made the baby gasp and then giggle, before he brought her down to kiss her chubby cheek then hand her back to her mother. He ignored the shouts from his sons, to say to his wife,

"Do you know this will be the first time we've slept apart since—

"—we were married. Yes, I do know that," she answered gently and went on tiptoe to kiss his cheek. "I shall be bereft."

She then brushed past him and went over to the carriage to see her sons settled, the infant in her arms squealing with delight when her brothers pulled faces to make her giggle.

The sudden noise of a window being flung open with force had everyone looking to the house and up to the first floor. Hanging half out of an open window, her long red hair falling in tangled waves either side of her face, and her arms waving back and forth to get the attention of those below, was a young woman with bright eyes and an even brighter smile.

"Papa! David! Luke!" she shouted, and then shouted their names again so they all looked her way. "Have a wonderful, wonderful time! Don't sleep a wink! I love you! I'll miss you all!"

The two boys waved and shouted back. The gentleman blew her a kiss. Her baby sister giggled—she was still watching her brothers making faces, and the little lady holding the baby took a deep breath and smiled but said nothing.

The buggy was gone off down the gravel drive and peace had descended once more on the Gatehouse Lodge, and the girl with the long red hair remained in the window, arms folded on the ledge, chin on her fist, gaze on the middle distance.

Lisa and Becky had gone unnoticed throughout the entire family farewell, standing mute with their backs up against the wall, trunks at their feet. But they were not invisible for long. For no sooner had David and Luke's mama turned to re-enter the house with her infant daughter than she noticed the two travel-weary girls. Lisa was staring up at the girl in the window. Becky was staring at the beautiful little lady in her floral-painted petticoats with the happy baby in her arms.

And then the girl in the window went to pull down the sash and happened to look below, and directly into the upturned smiling face of her best friend from Blacklands, and who was waving up at her. She couldn't believe her eyes. She pushed the sash back up and leaned out.

"Lisa! Lisa! Lisa! You're here at last! Mama! Mama! It's Lisa Crisp! It's Lisa! Wait! I'll be right there."

PART II

THE COUNTRY

FOURTEEN

TREAT, ANCESTRAL HOME OF THE DUKES OF ROXTON

"Oh dear. Have you been standing there awhile?" Lady Mary apologized, going forward to greet Lisa. She smiled. "So you are Lisa Crisp. Here at last. Did you have a pleasant journey?"

Lisa dropped a respectful curtsy, quick to realize when Teddy had shouted from the window that this fascinating little lady was her mother and, she remembered, the daughter of an earl; Becky followed her lead.

"Not long, my lady," Lisa replied. "And, yes, we had a very pleasant journey. Thank you."

"Leave your trunks and your bag with your maid—she'll be taken care of by the housekeeper—and come inside."

"I beg your pardon, my lady," Lisa said politely but firmly, remaining beside Becky when the Lady Mary went to turn away. "Becky is not my maid in the strict sense of the term. She is a seamstress who agreed to accompany me for my stay, and to-to—be of assistance to me."

"Oh? I see," replied Lady Mary, a glance at Becky. "Then we had best find a girl who can help Becky give you that assistance. Perhaps Becky can still remain with the trunks until the housekeeper comes, who will show her where everything is so she is comfortable and so she can be a help to you during your stay."

"I don't mind bein' Miss Crisp's maid for the duration," Becky stuck in, feeling she had to say something given Lisa had just made it plain she was not a servant, *in the strict sense of the term.* "It's all new to me and I'm just 'appy to be 'ere."

Lady Mary blinked, unaccustomed to being addressed by a servant whom she had not addressed first, but then smiled thinly and said evenly, "Yes, I see that you are…" Then said to Lisa as she shifted the baby in her arms, "I've heard a great deal about you, Miss Crisp."

"Have you, my lady?" Lisa replied politely, giving the cloth bag containing her writing box into Becky's safe keeping, and quickly falling into step beside the Lady Mary, who had turned to go inside.

"All of it from Teddy, of course, and all most complimentary. My daughter says she would not have survived her time at Blacklands without your friendship. So for that alone, I am eternally grateful. She has always referred to you as her Blacklands sister…"

"And now she does indeed have a sister."

"Yes! A surprise to us all, but quite the most wonderful surprise. This is Sophie-Kate, and she is five months old today."

"She is a beautiful baby, my lady."

"Yes… Yes, she is," Lady Mary said on a sigh of happiness and turned to the housekeeper who had come out under the portico, a male servant behind her. "Mrs. Rogers, here is Miss Crisp finally come at last. Her friend Becky is with her to act as her maid. If you would take Becky in hand and find one of the upstairs maids to chaperone her—perhaps Meg would do—so she knows what is to be done, and where everything is to be found, that would be a great help to us all."

Mrs. Rogers shot a glance at Lisa which swept over her from half-boots to small peaked bonnet, and then out across to Becky obediently standing by two trunks that had seen better days, and while she nodded to her mistress without a change in her expression, Lisa saw the disapproval in her gaze.

Her throat constricted to be summed up and then dismissed so summarily. But the uncomfortable feeling vanished the moment she entered the small vestibule behind the Lady Mary and to the sight of Teddy rushing down the winding staircase, so happy to see her that it brought tears to her eyes.

Teddy scooped Lisa up into her embrace and both girls hugged and cried and hugged some more to be reunited after a separation of two years. There was not a dry eye in the vestibule, the Lady Mary smiling through her tears to see her daughter so happy as she handed her baby daughter to her nurse, who also had a tear in her eye.

"May I take Lisa up to my room before supper, Mama?" Teddy asked, holding Lisa's hand. "We have so much to talk about, and I need to tell—"

"Perhaps allow Miss Crisp—"

"Lisa. Mama, you must call her Lisa, after all she is my Blacklands sister. Aren't you, Lisa?"

"Very well. Lisa has come a very long way in one day," Lady Mary replied patiently. "So you should do her the courtesy of allowing her to freshen up and perhaps take a dish of tea—"

"We can do all those things in my room—"

"As I was about to suggest, but—"

Teddy kissed her mother's cheek. "You are the most wonderful mama in all the world!"

"Thank you, my darling. But do not tire Lisa out on her first day. There will be plenty of time for the two of you to become reacquainted. And don't be late down for supper. You know how Granny Kate is one for punctuality, and how keen she is to meet your friend from your school days."

"Promise!" Teddy announced. She smiled at Lisa. "Come on, Blacklands sister! I have so much to tell you! But first," she added after she had led Lisa up the narrow winding staircase to the landing, and opened the immediate door to the right, which was her apartment, "I want to hear everything about what you've been doing since I last saw you. And I do mean *everything*."

LISA MANAGED TO WASH HER FACE AND HANDS AND TIDY HER hair, and enjoy a cup of tea and a slice of seedy cake, while giving Teddy an account of her last two years living with the Warners in Gerrard Street. Teddy curled up on the window seat and listened attentively, and whatever her private thoughts about her best friend assisting in a dispensary for the sick poor, she showed most aversion for life in a great city, unable to fathom how anyone could live in a place where there were few open green spaces, where there were so many people that one could simply not escape the hordes, and where there were more buildings than trees. She had found Chelsea too overrun with people, and could not wait to return to the peace and tranquility and pace of the Cotswolds.

It was Granny Kate—formidable mama of Teddy's step-papa— who showed a keen interest in Lisa's duties within a medical dispensary, asking her all sorts of questions at supper, most impressed that she acted as an amanuensis for the poor. And Lisa could understand why, given Granny Kate was blind, and thus having someone to read out her letters and to write them was very important to her. She told Lisa that she dictated all her letters to her companion, who also read the replies to her, Teddy often taking on this task whenever she was asked to do so.

"But I am only given letters to read out that Mama, Papa, and Fran —that's Granny Kate's companion—will allow me," Teddy revealed. "Which are all very interesting, but not as interesting as those from Granny's particular correspondents, who commit to paper an exchange of scandalous anecdotes from their youth, and are thus unfit for the eyes of a young lady; so Mama tells me."

"Your mama is quite correct, Teddy," Granny Kate replied primly. "But I think you'll find that the stick in this mud is not so much your mama but your step-papa. He has given me fair warning that those correspondents, and such anecdotes, are for my ears only, and most definitely not for your eyes."

"But as they are anecdotes from your youth, Granny, then you must have been a young lady at the time you behaved in such a scandalous manner."

Granny Kate chuckled and had no answer for this. Neither did Lady Mary.

"Teddy, it is time to steer the conversation in a different direction," her mother advised gently, putting down her silver knife and fork and pushing her plate forward. She nodded to the butler, the signal it was time to remove the dishes and bring the coffee pot.

"I don't know what surprises you more, Teddy," Granny Kate said with a laugh, ignoring her daughter-in-law's directive. "That I was once young, or that I could ever be involved in scandalous behavior."

Teddy squeezed the old lady's fingers, kissed her cheek, and whispered near her ear, "I believe both." She sat back and put aside her napkin. "And one day, after I am married, I won't take no for an answer and you will tell me *all* about it. May we be excused, Mama? Lisa has had such a day and is worn thin, and we still have much to talk about... I hope you don't mind sharing my bed," she asked Lisa when they were back upstairs in her bedchamber ready for bed.

A maid had warmed the bed sheets with the copper warming pan, a fire crackled in the grate despite it being the first month of summer, and a tray holding two mugs of hot milk had been placed on the window seat. Both girls were in their nightgowns and banyans, and Teddy stood before her dressing table, brushing her hair free of tangles.

"Why would I mind?" Lisa responded with a smile, sitting on the edge of the mattress of the four-poster bed watching Teddy brush and then braid her hair. "It will be like old times. Although this bed is far larger than the cots we slept in at school. But I am only sorry to put you to so much bother."

"It's no bother. It's just that this is such a small house—"

"Is it?"

"It's a gatekeeper's lodge. The entire structure would be swallowed up in one wing of Papa's house at home, and Abbeywood must be three times this size. But it's not the size that matters. It's that we can all stay here as a family, and I wanted you here with us. Which is why we are all sharing. The rest of the extended family and guests are over at the big house." Teddy gave a snort of laughter. "Big house! What a gigantic understatement! You must have thought so too when you first saw it. I am very sure if I were to ascend in one of Signore Lunardi's balloons and look down upon the earth, Treat would be the most enormous structure to be seen for miles and miles! And I cannot wait for you to see inside Uncle Roxton's palace! You'll simply be dazzled blind by the twinkling lights from chandeliers in the ballroom alone."

"I am already dazzled and I have only seen the palace from across the lake. No doubt the ballroom will leave me speechless."

"Oh, it will. But you're not to feel too overwhelmed because I expect you to stand up and dance with every gentleman who asks you."

"That is very kind of you to think I will be asked. But I am so out of practice—"

"Then we must make certain you are practiced by the time of the ball. I will not have you sitting in a corner, Lisa Crisp! Not when you are the cleverest and prettiest girl in the room. Your turn," she announced, tossing the hairbrush on the dressing table and pulling out the dressing stool for Lisa to sit upon. She patted the padded cushion. "Come along or our milk will grow cold. Oh! I have a better idea!" She brought the tray over to the dressing table. "We shall have it while I brush your hair." When Lisa obediently sat before the looking glass, she removed her friend's little lace cap, and then began taking out the multitude of pins that held up the coils of Lisa's waist-length hair. She suddenly paused and looked at Lisa's reflection. Her friend's lips trembled of their own accord, and she had lowered her gaze, so that her dark lashes covered her eyes. "Do you not want me to brush your hair?" Teddy asked curiously.

Lisa shook her head, and then she could no longer hold back the pent-up emotion of this longed-for reunion. She put her face in her hands and cried. It was such a simple gesture—Teddy offering to brush her hair—and so evocative of their schoolgirl friendship that it meant the world to her. She sniffed and sat up and looked at Teddy through the looking glass and did her best to smile.

"I do," she said with a watery smile. "I do *very much*... It's only... No one has... No one since-since school, since *you*, and—forgive me," she apologized, dropping her gaze. "I'm being foolish... I must be tired..."

Teddy put the hairbrush aside, dropped to her knees by the stool, and gathered Lisa into her arms and held her tightly. She kissed her and sat back and smiled.

"Never foolish, dearest Lisa. I remember you telling me once how you never did get hugs and kisses when you were a child."

"Not until I met you, and not since, my darling Teddy."

They stayed that way for a few moments longer, and after Lisa had dried her face with one of Teddy's handkerchiefs and they had both taken a few sips of hot milk, Teddy set to brushing Lisa's hair. And while her bristle brush went down the length of Lisa's chestnut hair repeatedly in long even strokes, Teddy told Lisa what she had been doing with her time since she had left Blacklands some eighteen months ago. Adding with a sigh, "My life is not half as exciting or as interesting as assisting a physician in his dispensary is it? And I thought I would marry Jack as soon I left school. I could see no reason for waiting. For what? Jack had returned from his years abroad, and was ready to settle—"

"—after all those years pondering paintings...?" Lisa asked airily with a cheeky knowing smile.

Teddy blinked and stopped mid-stroke on a gasp. And then she burst out laughing.

"Oh good grief! How like you to remember me telling you what mama had told me! Were we such naïve little beings as to think the reason boys were eager to run off abroad was so they could stand before a bunch of musty old paintings?" She gave a snort of incredulity and resumed brushing. "If Jack Cavendish did any pondering it wasn't in an art gallery. Particularly not when this pondering was done in Harry's company. I'd wager Harry has tossed more coin into bordellos in France and Italy, and every country in between, than any other young man his age."

It was Lisa's turn to gasp.

"Teddy! How can you say—"

"Because I know Jack, and I know Harry. There is good reason Harry has earned the nickname 'satyr's son'. It's not only because he has a great look of his late father. His salacious conduct with actresses and other men's mistresses, and his behavior while he was abroad, suggests he has every intention of emulating the legendary scandalous habits of M'sieur le Duc before he married Cousin Duchess."

"How-how can you know this?"

Teddy held Lisa's thoughtful frown in the looking glass reflection, and then she shrugged and said, "You think as a bride I should be ignorant of the habits of young virile men? That just because I live in the wilds of the Cotswolds where there are few people I would have little idea of how boys behave when they finally become young men?"

"I do not dispute that we know something of young men and their habits. And I am not blind. I do see the poor girls who walk the streets hawking their favors. And I have read reports in the newssheets about titled men and their mistresses. But I confess to being thoroughly ignorant of the-the—*process*…" She looked at Teddy under her lashes and added, ears burning, "You once told me that growing up on a farm you've always known about how life—*begins*. So, no, I do not think you are ignorant. Though I suspect as a young lady you are supposed to avert your eyes to such *processes*…"

"As a young lady, yes. But what a poor farmer would I be were I to do so? A farmer needs to understand the breeding behavior of his animals—his prize bulls, rams, and stallions—just as he—or in my case *she*—needs to know when to plant the fields, and with what crops."

"You've always been so practical, Teddy."

"And you, Lisa Crisp, have always been such a romantic."

Both girls smiled and then giggled, and with Lisa's hair now plaited and tied off with a ribbon, they climbed into the big four-poster bed and snuggled in under the covers, a single silver chamberstick on the bedside table and the fire providing the only light in the otherwise still, warm room. They were happy to lie there facing each other, reveling in their reunion and this renewal of a friendship that stretched back to when they were twelve years old.

"So you are not at all worried about the bridal night?" Lisa asked in the silence.

"Not worried. Nervous. I can't imagine being utterly ignorant. That would make the prospect of that first night unbearable. And I would be very worried had Jack not spent his time *pondering* on the Continent. Mama says it is important for husbands to know what they are about when making love—"

"You spoke about making love—with your *mother*?" Lisa was astonished. She could not imagine the self-possessed Lady Mary discussing anything so intimate as lovemaking, and with her daughter.

Teddy was unperturbed. "Who else would I ask? Mama says I can ask her anything, and so I do."

"Oh, I think your mama is the most marvelous person, Teddy. You are very fortunate."

Teddy grinned. "I am. I could not want for a more wonderful

mama." And then she became serious again, and said levelly, "Mama says it is important for husbands to know how to please, and be pleased by their wives. She says I am not to worry if on the first night everything does not go to plan, but that if Jack and I are honest and gentle with each other it will all come together eventually. She says lovemaking that first time is like the first time you bake a cake."

"Bake a-a *cake*?"

"Yes. That even though you might have all the right ingredients and you follow the recipe for the most wondrous cake imaginable, it doesn't necessarily mean the cake will turn out precisely as you expect. And to not be disappointed with the result. It is still a cake. And that to make a wondrous cake sometimes takes practice and then once you perfect the ingredients and the recipe, it will be a wondrous cake every time. She said the most important thing to remember is to enjoy the making of the cake together."

Lisa thought about this for a moment, frowning, and then confessed, "I have no idea how to make a cake, or about lovemaking for that matter, but I am confident your mother's advice is very wise. And from the little I saw of her with your step-papa when he and your brothers were off on their expedition in the woods, they love each other very much."

"Very much. And they have got their cake recipe just right, haven't they, because I now have two little brothers and a baby sister."

The girls giggled, plumped their down-filled pillows and settled in again. There was a long silence, and then Teddy whispered,

"Are you still awake?"

"Yes."

"I'm not keeping you from sleeping, am I? I know you've had a very long day—"

"I want to stay awake for as long as I can so we have as much time together as possible. Two weeks will go by too quickly otherwise."

"Do not worry about that for now," Teddy assured her. "I have something to tell you, but I need to talk it over with Jack first. And now Mama has met you she thinks it could work—"

"Plan? Work? About *me*?"

"Yes. I'm certain Jack will agree. He is so kind, and loving, and such a gentle soul."

"Are you not amazed that everything you told me when we were at school has turned out the way you said it would? You said you would marry Jack, and here you are about to marry him! I am so happy for you, Teddy. You know that, don't you?"

"Yes. You more than anyone else know how much I wanted this to all come true." Teddy chuckled into her pillow. "It's as well I like the way he kisses, too, or I may not have been as happy."

Lisa sat up on an elbow. "Kisses? You've kissed Jack? When? Oh! Don't answer that! Forgive me. I should not have asked—"

"Of course we have kissed, silly. But you may be shocked when I tell you when we kissed the first time—I didn't tell you at school because I knew you would think me shameless."

"Oh? Why would I think you shameless?" Lisa asked in a small voice, lying back down on the pillow.

"Because you, my dearest Blacklands sister, were always one for doing what was right. You follow rules, and you never do anything to upset anyone."

"You mean I was quite the most uninteresting girl in the class."

"But the cleverest, and the most beautiful of all of us."

"Teddy, that is the second time tonight you have said so, and I do love you for saying it, and you told me that at school, too. But you are my best friend, and best friends think of each other as beautiful, as I do of you. But no one else has ever said that of me, ever."

"Mama said it. Tonight, in fact. I heard her describing you to Granny Kate. She used the word beautiful and said you had a face that was uncommon. The sort of face that reminded her of a painting she had once seen up at the big house, in the Gallery. A face worth painting."

"How lovely of her! I think I shall ask your mama to adopt me. But please, we were not talking of me, but of the first time you kissed Jack."

"I was fourteen—"

"*Fourteen.*"

"I knew it! You *are* shocked."

"I am not—Oh! Very well. I am. Only because I thought the first boy you ever kissed was Jamie Banks behind the Chelsea Bun House."

It was Teddy's turn to sit up on an elbow. She was surprised and mystified. "Jamie? Jamie Banks? Why would you think I had kissed Jamie? You liked Jamie."

"We liked to discuss science together, and his wish to study medicine at university. And we talked about his apprenticeship at the Physic Garden. Topics which would have bored you silly, Teddy."

"He liked you very much, Lisa."

"I liked him. I foolishly kissed his cheek…"

"Violet told me."

"She did?

"But whoever said I kissed Jamie behind the Chelsea Bun House is a liar. I could no more kiss Jamie in the same way as I kiss Jack, as I could my own brother were he the same age. It would be positively vile. I like Jamie. But he is my cousin—"

"I know. He is your uncle Dair's natural son. I remember you telling me all about him before you introduced me to him that day when we were at the bun house and he was with his school friends. But Teddy, Jack is your cousin, and you are about to marry him."

"But it's different with Jack. I've loved Jack since I was ten—if any ten-year-old can know they are in love. But I did know it by the time I was fourteen. But Jamie is like a brother. And why would I kiss Jamie when I was in love with Jack? Did you think I could do that to Jack?"

"No. I could not imagine it... But I remember how upset you were when he told you his plans to go off wandering abroad, and how he would be away for years and years. And Jamie is handsome—"

"He is. Very. But I still have no wish to kiss him *in that way*."

Lisa put out her hand to Teddy and they interlocked fingers. "I would never have thought it possible had I not been told by someone I believed. But thinking back on that episode, which I have done too often that surely it is not healthy, I now think it was told to me to make me feel as if my kiss was worth less. Does that make sense?"

"It does. Girls can be the most horrid creatures imaginable when they are jealous. To think some spiteful cat told the headmistress about your kiss... I was beyond grief-stricken when you were made to leave Blacklands. You do know I tried to find you after your departure?"

"I have all your letters now, and read them many times. Thank you for persisting. Thank you for finding me."

"I did not find you. Cousin Duchess—my mother's cousin—she found you for me. She is the most kind-hearted, loving fairy godmother in all the world, and when you meet her you will agree. She cannot wait to meet you."

"I cannot wait to thank her for finding me because I am very sure if it had not been through her efforts we may never have had this reunion. And I would not now be here with you, and about to see you finally marry your Jack."

"How could I marry Jack without you here by my side, dearest Lisa? You are my closest friend, and you cared for me at school, and I would never have passed one exam if not for your tutoring. If girls were permitted to use their brains in the same way boys are, then you could have achieved anything equal to what Jamie is doing. He is about to head off to university to start his study to be a physician, and I wish you could have gone and studied with him."

"I am very happy for him. And thank you for thinking me clever.

But after assisting in the dispensary I do not think I could be a physician. A willing sympathetic ear to the problems of others, yes, but I do not possess the fortitude for anatomizing..."

"Jamie's here for the wedding. He is one of Jack's attendants. I know he is keen to see you again."

"Is he?" Lisa replied calmly. When Teddy lifted her brows and smiled, she did not return the smile but said seriously, "I want to see him, too. But please, Teddy, you must promise not to try and match me with your cousin. He was only ever a friend, and that is all he will ever be. And I am certain he feels the same way."

"As you wish. But I do so want you to fall in love and marry, Lisa Crisp. For you to be as happy as me."

"I want that too. But I fear it is more wishful thinking than a likely outcome."

"Why do you say so? When you do fall in love and marry, we can confide in each other as we did at school, but as married women, about our husbands, about our babies, and—"

"I can wish about marrying one day, and that may come true. But I'm afraid I must leave the babies to you, dearest..."

There was a silence between them again, and then Teddy said in a small voice, "Has there been no change in you since school?"

"No change."

Another silence, and then Teddy sighed and pressed Lisa's fingers and said with a buoyancy she did not in the least feel, "In one way that makes you even more special. Monthly courses are beastly, and I do not understand why human females must endure such a ghastly business, when female animals do not. But I will endure them because I do want babies—"

"And I want you to have babies because then I will be an aunt—of sorts."

"Oh yes! And a godparent. I will have you for my baby's godmother."

"That would be lovely, and an honor. Thank you."

"So what vile toad of a girl told you I kissed Jamie?" Teddy asked, thinking it best not to belabor the point about babies, knowing Lisa was not likely to ever have a baby of her own, though Teddy was not without hope that her friend might just still do so, after she had found a gentleman to marry her.

Lisa rolled over onto her back and stared up at the pleated canopy. She hesitated to answer because the truth would expose the carry-tale as a liar. And that liar was one of Teddy's friends, Violet Knatchbull. She and Margaret Medway had been the bane of Lisa's life at school, all because they did not think her worthy of their friendship, and most definitely not worthy of being the friend of Theodora Cavendish, the niece of a duke. And with Teddy's denial at kissing Jamie, Lisa was very sure Violet had fabricated that kiss in the hopes it would put a rent in Lisa and Teddy's friendship.

Almost from her first day at Blacklands, Violet had made it her mission to prize Teddy and Lisa apart. Something she did not succeed in doing until their final year, when she witnessed Lisa kiss Jamie Banks' cheek and told the headmistress. How did she know this? Because Violet had gloated about being the one who'd had Lisa expelled.

Lisa was sure Violet and Margaret would be at the wedding, if they were not already here to share in the fortnight of celebrations, so it would serve no purpose to expose Violet as the liar, and she did not want to cast a shadow over Teddy's celebrations. So she stifled a yawn and closed her eyes and snuggled in, hoping Teddy would take it as a sign she was too tired to share any more confidences that night.

She would focus on tomorrow and the start of her magical two weeks in this magical place, and soon she drifted off to sleep, dreaming not of palaces and ballrooms, but of a rosewood writing box, and the handsome gentleman with a pair of fine dark eyes who had given it to her. When he gazed upon her in a particular way, he made her happier than she ever thought possible. She hoped the Jack and Harry she had met at Lord Westby's townhouse and who had visited Gerrard Street were the very same Jack and Harry Teddy spoke of, and who would be here at Treat; Jack, the man Teddy was to marry, and Harry, his best friend, with his velvety voice and visage of a Roman coin, whom Lisa dreamed of kissing, and with whom she was very sure she was falling in love.

If only dreams could come true…

FIFTEEN

LISA WOKE LATE. SHE HAD NEVER SLEPT SO SOUNDLY, NOR
woken with the sun so high in the sky. She had a recollection of Teddy
rising, and of water being splashed about, and women talking in
hushed tones. And then, far off, doors were opened and closed, and
there was movement outside on the gravel drive. A carriage arrived,
and then it left. But that seemed to have happened hours ago.

When she padded through to the small dressing room, she found
her clothes set out on the chaise: One of the floral gowns expertly
altered by Becky, stays, petticoats, matching mittens, and her half-
boots, which had been polished and set ready with a pair of fresh
stockings. Also laid out were items new to her: A flimsy white apron of
finest linen, a wide-brimmed straw hat, and a folding fan. She had
never owned a fan before, though she had been instructed on how to
use this most essential of feminine accoutrements while at school.
Other girls had reveled in practicing how to flutter a fan like a lady.
Lisa had thought it a great waste of her time. Now she was glad she
had at least paid attention.

"You're up, Miss!" Becky announced, coming through via the
servant door carrying a brass can of hot water. She stepped aside to
allow a girl in a mob cap, about the same age, and who carried a
similar brass can, to come in after her. "This is Meg, and she's ever so
'elpful. There's a tub behind that screen at your back, Miss, and once
we 'ave you bathed and dressed, I'll fetch your breakfast, which you're
to 'ave in your room, on account of the late 'our. Miss Cavendish said
you're not to worry 'bout sleepin' late. She wanted you to. She's gone

across to the big 'ouse with her mama and granny to welcome some new arrivals. Now, let's get you ready. You've a big day ahead o'you."

"ARE YOU CERTAIN LADY MARY SAID THE PAVILION?" LISA ASKED Becky, as they strolled up a leafy laneway that connected the Gatehouse Lodge with the Kinross estate of Crecy Hall.

"I am, Miss," Becky stated without hesitation. "All I was told was to follow this path to its termination and we'd know the way from there. Ain't this the prettiest walk?" she added with a sigh, looking up and about at the tall avenue of beech trees. "I've never seen anythin' like it. Then again, I've never seen anythin' like anythin' 'ere before, anywhere."

"It is very pretty, and quite magical," Lisa agreed with a smile, ignoring her nervousness at her first public engagement to enjoy the moment. For it was a perfect summer's day, with a powder-blue sky where drifted wisps of white cloud. And a slight breeze off the lake stirred the bright green leaves on slender black branches of the beech that provided a dappled shade from the hot sun.

She supposed she would not have been so nervous had she not discovered from Becky that when she and Meg had set to unpacking her trunk late the night before, the Lady Mary's personal maid had interrupted them, going through the entire contents before marching off to inform her mistress of items found to be wanting. Hence the straw hat, which was now tied over Lisa's freshly-washed and braided hair, the flimsy apron covering the front of her floral gown, and the fan that dangled from its cord about her wrist. There were other items to come, and, according to Becky, the Lady Mary's personal maid was most critical of the gown Lisa had hoped to wear to the wedding and the ball. It would never do, and something would have to be done.

Lisa just hoped that she, unlike her wardrobe, did not prove a sad disappointment to Teddy's relatives and friends. But Becky's infectious wonderment soon had her putting these misgivings to the back of her mind, as they came to the end of the avenue and stepped into a wide open space and the wondrous sight of an Elizabethan manor house, its banks of mullioned windows sparkling in the sun. The manor with its turned chimney pots and fanciful gargoyles at each corner was a much larger version of the Gatehouse Lodge, or more correctly, the lodge was a tinier version of this substantial mansion. Set atop a terraced fragrant garden that overlooked the lake, the approach from the tree-lined avenue from where Lisa and Becky emerged provided a view of endless green lawn rolling down to the water's edge, where rowing boats bobbed at a jetty.

Lisa and Becky stared at one another, as if needing confirmation from each other they were indeed seeing the same idyllic scene. And as they walked out from under the dappled shade and into the sunshine, their wonder increased as a pretty pavilion came into view. Set atop a small hill, and overlooking the lake, it had a high domed roof supported by marble columns, and a set of wide steps open to the elements which gave access to its large interior.

"Don't be nervous, Miss," Becky said encouragingly when Lisa paused in the middle of the lawn, drew in a breath and squared her shoulders. "You look a picture. No one could say otherwise."

"Thank you, Becky. If we can get through this first day of introductions, I am sure we shall enjoy ourselves all the better. Let's see who awaits us..."

But when they arrived at the pavilion, they found it devoid of guests and family members, and with only servants going about the business of decorating fat columns with ribbons, and setting chairs and tables in place. Lisa and Becky took the opportunity to admire the pretty pavilion from its set of steps, looking up at the painted ceiling, and out across the marble flooring to the costly fabric-covered chaise longue and chairs, and to one side the scatter of large cushions arranged about a long low table of polished mahogany. They were left wondering at the whereabouts of the guests invited to nuncheon, and if they had arrived much too early for the event.

Before Lisa could ask the question, Becky reiterated, "'er ladyship did say the pavilion. Per'aps everyone is still inside the 'ouse?"

"Perhaps that's so. You stay here in the shade, while I take a walk across to the terrace. I may find some of the guests wandering about. If people begin to arrive here, come find me. Otherwise, I shall return shortly."

Becky did not feel comfortable sitting on any of the furniture, it was all too grand, and what if a guest arrived and found her there? So she waited until Lisa was off across the lawn and sat on the top step, back up against a fat column, ignored the cluster of servants going about their duties, and admired the view. She was intent on committing it all to memory so she could tell her Aunt Humphreys upon her return to the city.

And while Becky watched swans gliding past and ducks swimming in and around the jetty and the bobbing row boats, Lisa crossed to the terrace where she found winding stone steps leading up through the gardens to the house. But something made her turn away from the steps and walk further along the edge of the gardens until she came to a large oak tree halfway between the gardens and the lake. It was a majestic tree and very old, and there, supported in its lower heavy branches, was a tree house fashioned to resemble the quarter deck of a sailing ship. She was so fascinated by this that she walked up under the oak's branches to take a better look, and finding her straw hat partially obstructed her view, she removed it, and let it dangle by its ribands at her side. She had walked halfway round the tree with her chin pointed in the air before she became aware she was not alone.

A little girl was watching her. She was standing by a swing, holding on to one of two ropes affixed to either side of a damask-covered seat, the ropes rising high up into the branches of the oak, where they were affixed. She did not move or acknowledge Lisa in any way. In fact, her brow had furrowed, and her gaze was solemn. She was a beautiful child with large brown eyes that were slightly oblique, like a cat's, and a rosebud mouth in a heart-shaped face framed by dark honey ringlets threaded with fat silk ribbons. But for all her beauty, it was at her clothing Lisa stared at most. The girl was dressed in a round gown of finest cotton, painted in vivid colorful detail with cherry blossoms and little song birds. Underneath the gown were bright white cotton petti-coats edged in delicate lace, and on her feet she wore matching slippers in the same cloth as the gown, tied off with silk bows that matched her pink hair ribbons. She looked to be dressed for a grand occasion, but Lisa suspected that such exquisite clothing was everyday wear for the children who lived in such a magical place.

Lisa came over to her.

"Hello. My name is Lisa."

"Hello."

"What's your name?"

"Don't you know who I am?"

"No. But I should, shouldn't I."

"Everyone knows who I am."

"Do they? Everyone but me, it seems."

The little girl looked Lisa over. "Are you a lady's maid?"

"No. I'm a guest staying at the Gatehouse. I arrived yesterday for Miss Cavendish's wedding."

"I've never met anyone who doesn't know who I am."

"How fortunate for me to be the first stranger you have encoun-tered," Lisa replied with a smile, doing her best to remain unnerved by the child's solemn questioning air.

But she had dealt with worse in the dispensary when children, ill or injured, wanted nothing to do with anyone who might make them feel worse than they already were. She wondered why the girl was alone, for surely a child possessed of such noble self-assurance and dressed in the expensive attire of the privileged few would be surrounded by a veritable army of nurses and maids.

"Do you wish to be here by yourself, or do you have friends coming to join you at the swing?" she asked.

The girl surprised her by choosing to answer her in French, and it made Lisa wonder if when she was petulant the girl spoke in the language that was second nature to her.

"I wanted to be alone because I am never alone. And so I ran away."

Lisa was unperturbed by the girl's assertion she had run away. In this idyll there did not seem to be anywhere to run off to where she would not be easily found. Unless she were to swim across to the island out in the middle of the lake, or take up oars and row herself away.

"Then I will leave you to be alone," Lisa replied evenly in French, and turned towards the pavilion.

"*Attendez! Ne partez pas!*"

Lisa turned at the girl's order for her to stop and wait, and waited.

"I would like you to stay—please." She regarded Lisa curiously and asked again, "Do you *honestly* not know who I am?"

"Honestly." Lisa smiled. "Unless of course you are a fairy princess who lives here under this oak. And as I have never been formally introduced to a fairy princess, I do not know if it is polite to curtsy, or should I kiss your hand, too?"

Something in what Lisa said made the girl giggle. She shook her head and then with her chin tilted up and a superior smile full of secrets said, "I don't live under a-a *tree*. I live over there in that house."

"Of course you do. It is a very fine house. A fairy princess could live in such a house."

"But I am not a fairy princess. I'm a *marchioness*, and one day I will be a duchess."

Lisa hoped she did not appear as startled as she felt to discover a girl, who looked to be no more than seven or eight years old, to not only be ennobled, but who was also acutely aware of her status. Yet, there was nothing conceited in her declaration. It was said as a matter of fact. Just like her presumption that everyone should know who she was.

"How splendid," Lisa replied with a smile, masking her astonishment. She made a fuss of putting aside the wide-brimmed straw hat and fan, lifted her petticoats to her ankles so she could sink onto the grass, and then looked up at the girl. "Would you like to sit with me?

Here, sit on my gown, so that your pretty petticoats are not ruined."
Adding when the girl eagerly took her up on her offer, "I should think
that as a marchioness who will one day be a duchess, you still must
have a Christian name, yes? Perhaps you might like to share this with
me, now we are no longer strangers to one another...?"

The girl considered this for a long moment, and such was the
solemnity in her expression that Lisa was quick to stifle a smile, lest the
child think her insincere or laughing at her. She could see the girl was
weighing up whether she should trust this stranger with information
that everyone else in her world knew as a matter of course. But once
her mind was made up to put her trust in Lisa, there was no holding
back her confidences. It was as if she needed to verbalize the explanation to make sense of it to herself. Lisa was certain the girl had never
had to think deeply about her family connections before; those
connections, like the existence of the sun and the moon, were just
there, and everybody in her world knew it to be so. But now, thinking
about them and trying to explain them to another, she realized her
family ties were possibly beyond the comprehension of a stranger. So
she gave it her best effort, and Lisa patiently listened, giving the convo-
luted explanation the gravity it was due. Surprisingly, in the end it all
made perfect sense to them both.

"I have three Christian names," the girl stated. "Elspeth. Henrietta.
Jane. Maman and Papa call me Elsie. And so do my big brothers. I
have two. Roxton is much older than me. He's a duke. Henri-Antoine
is my younger brother but he's also a lot older. And I have a big sister,
too, and her name is Sarah-Jane. But she is not Roxton and Henri-
Antoine's sister. She is Papa's daughter, not Maman's. She lives in
France and has four children, three girls and a boy. Her husband,
Cousin Charles, is here for Teddy's wedding. But Sarah-Jane could not
come because she is still nursing her baby. His name is Benjamin
Franklin Fitzstuart and Papa says Baby Benjamin was named after a
very important man called Benjamin Franklin. Papa says he is more
important than him, even though my Papa is a duke, too. And
everyone knows that after the king and his ministers, dukes are the
most important men in the country."

She leaned in to Lisa and said confidentially, "Maman told me that
she corresponds with Benjamin Franklin—not the baby, the old man.
And that whatever Benjamin Franklin's greatness in the world, Papa
will always be the most important man in the whole world to us."

"That is as it should be," Lisa replied earnestly, and said no more
because she could see the girl had more to say.

"When we were in France in the spring, Maman and Papa and I

lived in a house near Sarah-Jane and Charles, and every day we walked up the avenue to call on them. The houses there have blue shutters on the windows and high archways so the coach can pull right up at the door, which is not at the front of the house but at the side in the courtyard. The house was near the palace where the French King lives, and where Cousin Charles does important work for his new country. Maman once lived at the palace, but that was very long ago when another king ruled France.

"We went to France so Papa could meet his grandchildren, and I could meet my sister. Papa cried when he saw Sarah-Jane, and that made me cry, too. But Papa says his tears were happy tears so I was not to be sad. He told me he had not seen Sarah-Jane since before I was born. It is strange that I have a Papa who is a *grand*papa when he does not look like a grandpapa. He has no gray hairs at all, even though Maman has many. But hers are silver. And she has been a grandmamma since Freddie was born, and he is twice my age.

"Sarah-Jane and Charles call me Elsie. Roxton's children do too. They live over in the big house. Maman says as most of my big brother's children were born many years before me, it is polite for me to let them call me Elsie and not Aunt Elsie. Maman lived in the big house when my brothers were little like me, and she was the Duchess of Roxton. But now she is the Duchess of Kinross and so we live here, and sometimes we live in London, and then there are times when we go to a big house with turrets that is on a lake called a loch very faraway in a country called Scotland. But it is still not as big as the big house that Roxton lives in. I like it here at this house the best, even though there are much better places to hide over in the big house. Henri-Antoine knows all the best hiding places, and so does Jack. You can call me Elsie, too, because we are no longer strangers. And because I would like you to be my friend… If you would like to be my friend…?"

"Thank you. I would like to be your friend very much, Elsie. And because we are friends you may call me Lisa. And thank you for telling me all about your family, which I found most interesting because I do not have a family of my own—"

"No family?" Elsie's eyes widened. She was intrigued. "None at all?"

"No brothers or sisters, and no mother or father. My parents died when I was about your age—"

"I'm eight years and six months old."

"Then yes, about your age."

"And cousins. Do you have any cousins?"

"I have three female cousins. Two are married, and the youngest is twelve—"

"Julie is twelve, and she wants to be a duchess one day like me. Which is why she is sometimes not nice to me. Maman says that's because I will be a duchess regardless of who I marry, but Julie must find a duke to marry her. I think she will find a duke, because Julie is very pretty and she has a great look of my Maman; everyone says so."

"Then I am sure a duke will want to marry her."

"Are you sad not to have any brothers and sisters and parents?"

"I was sad when I was your age. But I am not now because I keep myself occupied helping other people, and I have friends, and my best friend in the whole world is Miss Theodora Cavendish. I am sure you know her."

Elsie smiled and nodded. "Teddy? I do! I like Teddy very much. She makes me laugh."

"Me too. She is always happy. So you see I am blessed to have such a good friend, and you are blessed to have a Maman and Papa, and two brothers, and a sister, and many cousins. All of whom must love you very much. I cannot wait to meet them all."

And there was one member of Elsie's family in particular she was looking forward to meeting again, and who she was more than ever convinced had deliberately kept his nobility from her, and for reasons she could only speculate. Perhaps, like Elsie, he assumed she would know who he was without the need to inform her? Perhaps he did not feel the need to make himself known to one who was a social inferior. Perhaps he had just been amusing himself with her... But her intuition told her that these excuses did not ring true, that he did like her, and as much as she liked him, and so there had to be another reason he had made such an effort to remain anonymous. Whatever his reasoning, she would not speculate further and wait for him to tell her himself... She glanced at the swing.

"Now that we are friends, would you like me to push you on your swing?"

"I am not to swing by myself. Two of my maids and a footman must be here with me."

Lisa screwed up her mouth in response to such prescriptive coddling before she realized what she was doing. Elsie saw this and giggled.

"Henri-Antoine does that, too. So does Papa. But they do not let Maman see them do it because they do not wish to upset her. When they are with her they do as they are told—"

"—and when they are not, sometimes they are naughty?"

Elsie put a finger to her lips and said in a loud whisper, "I am not to tell…" She grinned and nodded. "Very naughty."

"I do not know how much time is left to us before we are discovered… But perhaps we could be a little bit naughty, too?" Lisa asked airily, a pointed sidelong glance at the swing.

Elsie was up off Lisa's petticoats, but instead of turning to the swing she rushed over to the base of the oak and scooped up two dolls which Lisa had failed to notice were propped against the trunk. Both were outfitted in court gowns of silk and embroidered with spangles that would have been the envy of any grown woman. One doll had black hair and was dressed in plum brocade, the other was blonde and wore a gown of ivory silk, and both were much loved.

"This is Mademoiselle Yvette," Elsie said, holding up the doll with the blonde hair. "And this," she said, holding up the doll with the black hair, "is Signorina Simonetta."

Lisa curtsied. "It is a pleasure to meet both your friends. Shall we sit them just over there in front of the swing so they can watch you, or shall they take turns with you?"

"They will take turns. Mademoiselle Yvette will be first, because she is my newest doll and Simonetta has had many swings."

"That is fair."

Elsie placed Signorina Simonetta sitting up a few paces from the front of the swing, arranging her dress to cover her stockinged legs, and placing the doll's hands in her lap. She then returned to Lisa, who was holding Mademoiselle Yvette. And when Lisa was sure Elsie was sitting securely on the swing's padded damask seat, and her hands were tight about the ribbon-covered rope, she put the doll beside Elsie, tucking it in securely with a quantity of the girl's cotton petticoats.

They had enough time for Signorina Simonetta and Mademoiselle Yvette to take turns on the swing with Elsie, and then on the third turn, both dolls watched on while Elsie went higher than she had ever been swung before. She was so excited that she was like any other child who enjoyed the wind in her hair and the thrill of going up in the air so that the toes of her slippers tipped the blue of the sky, heart racing and breath held, knowing that in the blink of an eye the swing would fall back again, and she would feel the drop in the pit of her stomach, and gasp every time.

Lisa came around to the front of the swing, letting it slow of its own accord, and sat cross-legged in the grass, with both dolls in her lap, watching Elsie enjoying her freedom. And because she was facing the swing, she was oblivious to the activity behind her. If Elsie saw the small battalion of women headed her way, she chose to ignore them, intent on remaining on the swing for as long as possible, and doing her best with the movement of her stockinged legs to propel the ride herself to make it last as long as possible, now she was no longer being pushed.

Lisa was so engrossed in watching Elsie enjoying herself without a care in the world that she only became aware that they were no longer alone when a cloud moved in front of the sun at her back, or so it seemed, leaving her in shadow. In truth someone had come to stand directly behind her, blocking the sunlight. And then before she could turn to see who had cast her in shadow, a wave of women surged forward, either side of her, in a flap and rustle of petticoats and concerned chatter, all of it in French.

She scrambled to her feet, assisted by a firm hand about her upper arm. When she was let go she brushed down her petticoats, before turning about and looking up and straight into the face of the gentleman who consumed her dreams and who was never far from her thoughts.

"Hello," he said in that deep purr peculiar to him, and in something of the same cheeky manner in which she had greeted him in Gerrard Street that day he had visited as a trustee of the Fournier Foundation. If he was surprised to see her here at his family home, he had made a herculean effort not to show it.

"Hello," she echoed, also remaining calm and in control, mostly because she was not surprised at all to see him. Yet, being in his presence and in such close proximity she was unable to say anything further, and so allowed her gaze to flicker over him from linen stock to top boots.

She had admired his sartorial splendor of richly-embroidered frock coats and waistcoats in his urban setting, but out here in the country amongst the leafy greenery and fresh air, he looked relaxed and his lean face had a healthy glow. He was very much in his element, and although dressed for comfort in tight buff breeches and a pale lemon-yellow linen waistcoat over a white shirt and plain stock, he was no less splendid. But it was his free-flowing dark hair which brought a warmth to her throat. Without pomade and ribbons, it fell loosely across his brow and down to his shoulders. On any other man such lack of restraint would have bordered on the effete, on him it made his masculinity crackle.

"Is this a fortuitous contrivance, Miss Crisp?" he drawled. "Or a spectacular coincidence? Are you a guest of the Cavendish wedding?"

"I am," she replied steadily, aware of his tease, hands behind her back, with chin up and smiling into his dark eyes. If they had not been surrounded by others, she would have kissed him there and then. "And fate cannot be contrived, can it?"

He took a step closer. "Fate? I am inclined to think you are a practitioner of the dark arts, and are a witch."

"A witch? But you are the one who inhabits a magical world conjured by sorcery. Are you not then a sorcerer?"

"Touché. Tell me again: How old did you say you were…?"

Her smiled widened. "And by what name did you say I should address you—my lord?"

He did not flinch. "If you know that," he murmured, "then you know the rest, *witch*."

Lisa suppressed a grin, lifting her brow in puzzlement, but there was no hiding the light of triumph in her blue eyes. "But it would be prudent to have the information that has been imparted to me confirmed. Though I am very sure my source is impeccable."

His tone lost its playfulness. "I would have told you—eventually."

She continued to tease him. "Here? Or elsewhere? And when?"

"You're the witch, you tell me."

"Ah, but as a sorcerer you should have the answers."

His top lip twitched and her gaze dropped from his dark eyes to his mouth. That mouth she so wanted to kiss. She would. She must. It was not a desire, it was a need. Her eyes lifted again to his and she drew in a breath. The look in his dark eyes was no less hungry. He was thinking the same wicked thoughts. Instead of being shocked, she was elated.

"I did not know you would be here," he confessed. "But I dared to put my hope in wishful thinking."

"That is fate."

They took a step closer and were within a hand span of one another, acutely aware of each other yet mindful they were in a public space. Their private reverie was intruded upon and they were dropped back into the here and now when Elsie broke from being fussed over by her nurses and maids. She pressed her dolls on a maid and rushed over to the couple and tucked her hand into her brother's fingers.

Touch made him look away from Lisa and down at his sister.

"Henri-Antoine, this is my new friend Lisa. I want her to be invited to Maman's picnic in the pavilion."

"As a guest, she already is, *mon petite chou*," he replied gently.

"Are you staying for the picnic?" she asked hopefully.

When the clutch of women took a step toward their charge, Henri-Antoine stopped them with a dark look, and they quickly retreated to the oak to await His Lordship's pleasure, and where two of his ever-present shadows lingered at a respectful distance. He went down on his haunches before his sister, not at all concerned Lisa was present and would hear every word of their discourse. He spoke to Elsie in French, their preferred language.

"Maman's picnic is a female-only affair for all of Teddy's friends and relatives, and of course that means you, too."

"But Maman would let you stay if you asked her. Papa is at home."

"So he is. But your papa will do as he is told and remain well away from the pavilion for the duration of the picnic. And I too must respect Maman's wishes. Remember what was threatened at breakfast?"

Elsie giggled

"Maman would never banish Papa to sleep in his dressing room, silly. There's no bed for him in there."

"I think it was an idle threat, too." He kissed the back of her hand. "I understand your wish to be alone better than any other, *mon petite chou*. But when you run off without telling anyone, and your ladies they cannot find you, Maman becomes frantic. I know the last thing you wish to do is upset her."

"I do not want Maman to be upset, and I do try to do as you say and ignore them all," she said, a glance over her shoulder at the half-dozen women obediently waiting by the tree trunk. "But they fuss too much. I tell them not to, but they do not listen. So I run away to breathe. You must make Maman understand."

"She is trying her best to let you breathe, *ma chérie*. You are the most precious thing in the world to her and to your papa. She has no other daughter but you, and you are your papa's only heir. Which is why your women they are protective to the point of suffocation. But I will talk to Maman again, and to your papa, and perhaps we can contrive to make your breathing easier, *hein*? All Maman asks is that you tell her, or someone—anyone—when you wish to run away."

"But how is that running away if I tell someone? Did you tell Maman when you ran away and hid in the big house?"

Henri-Antoine could not help smiling. He shook his head.

"I did not. But I always had Jack with me, and so Maman she was not so worried. If anything were to happen to me, Jack could raise the alarm. If you go off by yourself, who is there to do that for you?"

"But you were a very ill little boy, Henri-Antoine. That is what Maman told me. So she had cause to worry. I am not ill. Papa says I am a better swimmer than Sarah-Jane ever was. He says I have the heart of a tiger! But you do not even row on the lake without your bears at your back—"

"Bears?" He flicked her flushed cheek. "Is that what the lads look like to you?"

Elsie nodded and smiled. "But they do not dance like the bears I saw in Paris."

He winked. "They would if I told them to."

Elsie giggled, but then shook her head. "You would not make them. Maman says your lads help *her* to breathe."

"So they do. Which is one good reason I have them as my shadow."

"And if you were ever to fall ill again, yes?"

"Yes. If I were to fall ill again."

"I have never seen you without them except at table when they wait outside the door. I want you to have them because they look out for you, but do you not sometimes wish you could breathe without them?"

Henri-Antoine rose up to his full height on a sigh, gaze still on his sister.

"I wished for that every day when I was your age, *mon petite chou*. But I am old enough to be wise to the truth: I cannot breathe without them, and neither can our Maman. So I accept them, and do my best to ignore that they are there. But your life will be very different to mine. On my honor. One day you will be old enough to do as you please, and no one will be able to stop you from walking out from under the shadows of your women. For the present—for Maman and your Papa—you must strive to do your best to ignore your shadows, without being cruel or unkind in doing so, because they only have your best interests at heart, and do what they are told to do. If you accept this is the way life must be until you are older, then they will be gone, just like that," he said with a snap of his fingers. "As if by magic, you will no longer see them, even though they are still there. Can you understand that?"

Elsie cocked her head and squinted in thought. "You mean in the same way as the footmen who open all the doors, and the maids who clean out the grates before first light, and the laundresses who wash our clothes, whom I do not see at all but who are there every day, and who Maman says are most necessary to our comfort, and deserving of our gratitude."

Henri-Antoine lightly touched the tip of Elsie's little nose and wiggled it gently. "I see that you do understand."

Elsie smiled and grabbed her brother's hand and pressed it to her cheek. "I wish you were staying for the picnic."

Henri-Antoine glanced at Lisa but said to his sister, "I wish that too. But Jack and Freddie and the twins are waiting for me at the big house. We are having our own—er—picnic in the billiards room." He looked across at Elsie's maids and nodded, signal for them to approach. "But I shall see you in a day or two—I am sorry, *ma petite*, but Miss Crisp must remain here," he added when Elsie took hold of Lisa's hand, her ladies ready to return her to her mother. "I shall not keep her long. And then she will join you at the pavilion."

"Promise."

"Promise."

He watched Elsie take back her dolls from one of her maids, and go off across the lawn with her female entourage following close behind. He then signaled to the lads, who were still kicking their heels by the oak, to move on, which they did, to the stand of willows by the water's edge. They had come by skiff across to Crecy Hall the day before, and would return to the big house the same way. His valet Kyte and his overnight bag had already done so via horseback. He knew not only Jack and his three nephews would be waiting him, but also Seb and Bully, but he had some unfinished business with Miss Crisp first, and they could wait; this could not.

"Come with me," he ordered, taking hold of her hand and striding off towards the oak.

"You do realize, my lord, that when Elsie lets it be known I am here, and that you are here, and that we are alone, questions will be asked. I could find myself in the awkward position of having to account for myself."

Undaunted, he walked on and around to the far side of the enormous tree, glancing about him, as if he had lost something, and still holding her hand.

"Getting yourself into an awkward situation did not seem to bother you when you took it upon yourself to enter Westby's house, did it?"

Lisa gaped at his back. Her mouth worked for several seconds and then she blurted out in a guilty rush, "I beg your pardon, my lord, but—"

"My lord? No, no, no, Miss Crisp. It will not do. I much preferred it when you called me sir—"

"—that was an entirely different circumstance—Oh? You do?"

"I do. But I would also prefer you not to call me sir, either. And you are right. Entering Westby's house was an entirely different circumstance. Your friend stole something of mine—"

"Stole? She did no such thing! In your distraction, you dropped the catalog into her basket. She was none the wiser and I offered to help her return it before she was wrongly accused of stealing—" Lisa blinked. "If I am not to call you my lord or sir, then how am I to address you?"

He let go of her hand, confident that they could not be seen, from the house, or by anyone approaching from the direction of the pavilion. He took a step toward her, and she backed away and came hard up against the tree trunk. He smiled to himself. He had her right where he wanted her.

"In my distraction?" he asked with a frown of incomprehension. "Whatever can you mean, Miss Crisp?"

Lisa decided now was not the time for dissimulation. She met his gaze openly.

"It is hardly surprising you dropped the catalog into Becky's basket when your mistress was standing before you naked but for a pair of stockings held up by pink garters—"

"Pink garters? Were they?"

He took a step closer.

"Yes! They were pink, and your mistress stole them from Becky—"

"She is not my mistress."

"I beg your pardon. That is true. She is Lord Westby's mistress, and your lover."

"And I must beg your pardon. She is no longer my lover."

"Oh? I see."

"I don't think that you do."

"I may be ignorant of many things, but I do understand that gentlemen—noblemen—have mistresses and take lovers, and it is none of my business, my lor—sir—"

"Henri-Antoine. That is my name. And that is what I wish you to call me."

"I cannot call you by your Christian name!"

"Why? If when we are private I call you Lisa, then surely you can call me Henri-Antoine?"

Lisa unconsciously shook her head but then closed her eyes on a sigh for the briefest of moments hearing him say her name. She wished he would say it again so she knew it was real, that he had indeed said it and it wasn't because she was suddenly heady due to his closeness. He had his hand to the trunk, gaze fixed on her, and hair falling into his eyes. She was sure her heart was beating faster; that her blood was pumping too hard and drumming in her ears. Becky would say she was feverish. What had Becky called him—"bewitchin' 'andsome"? He was that, and much more. And if she didn't move away from his orbit that instant she was very sure she would do something she would later regret, but which at that very moment she wasn't thinking about the future, or regrets, or consequences. She wasn't thinking logically at all. All she knew was that if she didn't act upon her impulses and satisfy a need, she might just go mad. In one last ditch effort to bring herself back from the brink of social ruin, she swallowed hard and asked curiously,

"What do you mean *I don't think that you do?*"

"I currently do not have a mistress, nor have I had a lover since that night you and your friend the haberdashery assistant returned the catalog she did not steal—"

"Becky did not steal—Oh! You said that." She blinked up at him and resisted the urge to gently brush the hair out of his eyes. "Why—why are you telling me this?"

He moved closer. "Because it is all your fault, Lisa Crisp."

"My fault?" She was nonplussed.

He nodded slowly, gaze fixed on hers. His upper lip twitched and his mouth parted slightly as he tried to suppress a grin at her complete lack of awareness as to his meaning. He tried to sound disconsolate, and gave a practiced sigh for good measure.

"Whatever am I to do with you?"

"Do? Do with me?"

She knew what she wanted to do with him, and that was kiss that perfect mouth, and the consequences could go hang. No wonder his mistress—who was no longer his mistress—had dropped her clothes there and then for him. To her astonishment she had the urge to do just that, here and now. But she would settle for a kiss. One kiss would be worth the consequences, whatever they might be—she would find that out soon enough—if only to stop this all-consuming desire that threatened to overwhelm her body and soul.

And then it happened. Thought succumbed to need, as if by magic —she a witch and he a sorcerer in this magical place. In one fluid movement her arms slipped up about his neck and she leaned into him. On tiptoe, with her body pressed against his, as if needing anchorage, she tilted her chin, closed her eyes, and let her mouth find his.

Surrender.

SIXTEEN

HE WAS RARELY IF EVER SURPRISED, BUT HE WAS BY HER. AND HE had been since their first meeting at Gerrard Street. Now this. She had kissed him first!

He'd had every intention of kissing her. Reason he had brought her around to the far side of the oak, out of the potential prying gaze of guests and servants at the pavilion picnic. But intention had almost crippled him. He wanted their first kiss and everything about the moment to be perfect. It was to be a memory for them to cherish. And then she had stolen his initiative and kissed him.

Startled, he was slow to respond, not only because her kiss was unexpected, and thus the moment he had planned was lost, but because he had never been kissed first before, and never on the mouth. And never in such a spontaneous, rather awkward manner which he supposed sweethearts who had never kissed before would share a first kiss. It was a barely there, tentative touch of her lips to his, and it made him wonder if she had ever been kissed before, and presumed not. Just as he presumed her to be innocent of the carnal delights of the bedchamber. Which was why he had hesitated, and why he had planned the execution of this, their first kiss.

And then he surprised himself. For while he believed himself to be an attentive and experienced lover, he knew he was prescriptive in certain particulars, which was the reason for his hesitation. He had never been needful of indulging in the extravagance of kissing on the mouth. It was too deeply personal. And intense emotion had played no part in satisfying his carnal appetite, until now. Which was why this moment with Miss Lisa Crisp held such significance for him. He not only wanted to kiss her, he needed to kiss her, and in the sort of reverential way that she would not only derive just as much pleasure from the act, but gain some understanding of the depth of his feelings.

He surprised himself further by realizing he was being utterly selfish in wishing she had not taken the initiative from him. It required great courage for her to be the one to kiss him first, to lay her feelings bare in that way. In doing so she gave him the choice to accept or reject her, and without consequence to himself, because she was not of his world. In his world, a girl did not find herself alone with a man, and she never permitted him to kiss her unless they were engaged, or, as in Jack and Teddy's case, the promise of an engagement between cousins had been on the horizon for years, and welcomed by both families, so there really was no going back from that.

But not for him. He was a free agent. He could kiss who he liked, and damn the consequences, particularly for a girl like Lisa, with no family, no pedigree, and nothing to offer him. She could not expect anything from him in return, certainly not marriage. His honor did not oblige him to offer her his name. Had she been of his world, there wasn't a girl who wouldn't want to marry the son of a duke, and not just any duke, and he not just any son. His brother was a duke, his nephew would be a duke, his stepfather was a duke, and his half sister would be a duchess in her own right one day, and there was his maman who was a double duchess. He was as steeped in aristocratic privilege as was possible, and he could, quite rightly, have any female he wanted, to bed, if she were a member of that fraternity of high class whores who catered to men of his ilk, or to wed, if she were the daughter of the nobility with a pedigree that matched his own. But he didn't want to bed a whore, and he did not want to wed a nobleman's daughter. He had made up his mind. No one would do for him but Miss Lisa Crisp of Gerrard Street, Soho...

All this had raced through his mind as she let her arms fall away from his neck to take a step back only to find she had nowhere to go, with the oak behind her and him standing so close. He glimpsed the confusion and hurt in her blue eyes as she lowered her lashes and her chin, to say in a small voice, as her throat and cheeks stained with an embarrassing blush,

"The-the picnic... They must be wondering where I—"

"Lisa, your—"

"There is no need for you to-to say anything. I was the one who presumed—"

"—your kiss was perfectly lovely."

Her gaze flashed up to find him smiling down at her. It was a gentle smile which softened his whole face and made her heart give the oddest leap. Her brow cleared, and so did the hurt. She smiled hesitantly. "Oh? It-it was?"

He nodded. "I'm the clumsy clod; I hesitated."

"Why?"

He huffed and grinned and then shook his head.

Her smile faded. "Should I not have asked? Is it impolite to do so? Forgive me for not knowing the rules, or how precisely I should act, because I only arrived yesterday, and still have much to learn about—"

"Never second guess yourself. Like your kiss, you are perfectly lovely. I do not want you to be anything but yourself." He caressed her cheek with the back of his fingers. "Miss Crisp, presently of Gerrard Street, previously of the Blacklands School for young ladies, where I presume you became friends with Teddy…?"

When she gave a start and stated the obvious, he grinned.

"Yes. We are best friends."

"Naturally."

"But how did you—"

"—know? It did not take a mind the size of the moon to put the pieces together once you told me you went to a boarding school for young ladies in Chelsea. Only one boarding school—Blacklands—is appropriate. And only one girl who went to Blacklands who is about your age—which I have now calculated to be eighteen or nineteen—is marrying in the country this week—Theodora Cavendish, the irrepressible Teddy."

"I am so relieved you know all about Blacklands, and my friendship with Teddy, because although my mind is not even the size of a-a balloon, least of all the moon, I did wonder if the Jack Teddy was marrying was the same Jack who is your best friend. You see, I do believe in fate, even if you think me a-a witch."

"You've bewitched me!"

"Have I?"

Again he laughed, this time at the wonderment in her voice. He chucked her under the chin. "How could you think otherwise? Perhaps now you will tell me your age?"

She wrinkled her little nose. "Surely I do not need to, because as a sorcerer with a mind not quite the size of the moon, you already possess that information."

He inclined his head at her reasoning. "Very well then. Indulge my curiosity and set my mind at rest that you are nineteen, or closer to that age than you are eighteen."

"I do look younger than my years—

"What?!" He gave a theatrical start, hand to his chest, and pretended to be stricken. "Don't tell me! You're five and thirty!?"

Lisa gave an unladylike chortle and hung her head.

"This is not a laughing matter, Miss Crisp! You are a witch and have put me under your spell if you are in truth a middle-aged woman—"

"—with warty hands and a warty nose!" She became serious. "Teddy is nineteen and Jack must be your age—"

"I am eight-and-thirty. I just look younger than my years, too."

"Don't be ridiculous. If you were a sorcerer and you'd told me you were a hundred and thirty-eight, I would've believed you. Eight-and-thirty? I'm not convinced. Jack is five-and-twenty, so you must be too."

"Would it have bothered you had I been eight-and-thirty?" he asked with a frown, and then he shook his head and put up his hand. "You do not have to answer. I *am* being ridiculous."

"Because that was the age your father was when he fell in love and married your mother?"

He did not ask how she knew this, presuming Teddy had told her, but he did nod, and for some reason even this simple acknowledgment made his throat constrict with emotion. "He—he died too early, and she—she was too young..."

She saw him hard swallow, and sensed speaking about his parents, his father in particular, was not easy for him.

"What does age—what does any impediment—matter, when two people fall in love? All that matters is that they are together."

He stared at her hard and she was taken aback by the fierceness in his expression.

"A selfish expectation without thought to the consequences."

"They could not have predicted the future when they fell in love. All they had was the expectation—selfish or otherwise, though I do not think it selfish to surrender to fate—that their future happiness was dependent on each other."

He lost his harshness and pinched her chin. "There is that word again," he said with a sigh. "Fate." He peered at her. "So you are nineteen?"

When she rolled her eyes at his persistence he laughed out loud. She gave a practiced sigh of her own.

"If it will stop you pressing me further on the matter, then I will tell you I am indeed nineteen, but I am older than my years. Dr. Warner says I am an old head on young shoulders."

"Dear me," he drawled, taking a step back and allowing his gaze to sweep over her from boots to coiled braids. "If that is what an old head looks like, I am giddy with anticipation as to what awaits me below your lovely shoulders—*Mon Dieu*. I said that out loud," he muttered in French, when she clapped a hand to her mouth in astonishment to hear him vocalize his yearning. He bit his lip as his face fired red. For the first time in his life he felt as gauche as a drunken sailor. "Forgive me—I should not have—"

"—said the truth?"

"—been an uncouth fiend."

"Is it uncouth to express your desire for me, to me? For surely I may also do so, to you?" She smiled, adding shyly, "I think you are perfectly lovely—in every way."

"You do have an old head on those shoulders," he quipped, appeased that he had not shocked her. "I've never been called lovely before, and I accept your compliment because it is said with sincerity and without artifice."

"You did tell me to be myself," she teased. "So you will have to accept my compliments, too." She tilted her head and asked thoughtfully, "You will be yourself with me—always—won't you?"

He met her gaze openly. He knew her qualifier referred to his bouts of falling sickness. He also knew that as soon as he had taken her by the hand and led her behind the oak there was no going back, so he did not hesitate in his reply.

"I will do my best. It will take time, for I am by nature aloof. And I do my utmost to keep my seizures from my family, and have done so for years. To not do so—with you, will require *adjustment*. Curiously, I find I have no desire to hide anything from you."

She took a step closer again, and rested her palms lightly to the front of his linen waistcoat. She was certain there were tears behind her eyes.

"Thank you. Thank you for your honesty, and for trusting me. That makes me very happy..."

He lifted her chin with the crook of one finger and stared into her blue eyes rimmed with tears. "You, Lisa Crisp, make me happy. Are those happy tears...?"

She nodded and smiled tremulously. "So why—why did you hesitate to kiss me?"

He leaned in and his breath tingled on her lips as he murmured, "Because I wanted my kiss to be perfect."

"Perfect?" she echoed softly. "With such a kissable mouth, how could it not be?"

"Kissable? Is it?" he muttered, taking her face gently between his hands and lowering his mouth to hers. "Then let us see if I can live up to your expectation…"

If they were aware, it was not of time or place, but only of each other. They remained sheltered and unseen by the ancient oak's wide trunk, bodies pressed together, Lisa gathered up in Henri-Antoine's embrace, she with her arms once more about his neck. And having enjoyed their first tentative kiss, tenderness and hesitancy gave way to satisfying desire. The couple yielded to a fervent longing that had simmered since his first visit to Gerrard Street, and nothing and no one was going to stop them savoring the moment. And when he gently opened his mouth on hers and she followed his lead, an unfamiliar spike of pleasure shot through to her core that was so strong she could only equate it with pain. She had never experienced anything like it, and thought she might faint.

He felt her shudder against him and had she not still been in the moment, and enjoying this wonderfully exploratory kiss as much as he, he would have broken off at once, thinking he may have taken this their first kiss one step too far. Or perhaps she had become aware that they were now not alone, that his fine fellow let him know that while he understood there would be no relief for him here, under this oak, he still lived, proud and strong, and this despite a woeful performance at Burke's, where he had failed to show the slightest interest in the exotic beauties offered him. And Henri-Antoine had seriously questioned if there were something wrong with him.

It was no one's fault but his own. Sheer obstinacy had made him go to Burke's after the unscheduled visit to purchase the rosewood writing box. How he thought he could indulge in satisfying his carnal appetite when his thoughts had been conquered by a girl in a plain linen gown with ink-stained fingers, he put down to intransigent pride. He made it through the door of the bath house, was offered the pick of the evening's beauties and was halfway through undressing when his thoughts wandered to the engraving of her initials to the silver stoppers of the inkwells; he couldn't wait to give her his gift, hoping she would be delighted with it. That was that. He lost interest in Burke's, in satisfying or being satisfied by a bevy of beautiful whores, however skilled. He threw on his clothes and strode out of the establishment, startling his shadows, who were settling in for what they thought was a long night, and scrambling after him as he walked off down the street to clear his head. To add insult to injured pride, he woke the very next morning, having had his dreams invaded by Miss Lisa Crisp, with his fine fellow in all his sizeable glory letting him know the problem did not lie with him.

Kissing this most delectable creature in his arms was the first step of many until she was his, body and soul. He had never met anyone like her, and was certain he never would again. For in the space of a few weeks she had managed to annoy, madden, bother, delight, charm, fascinate, and finally invade his every waking thought. It was time for him to wrest control, or he would go mad, and he had the perfect solution, one that would suit them both.

"IF IT WERE MY CHOICE, I WOULD STAY WITH YOU UNDER THIS oak until the stars appeared," he told her, leaning his forehead against hers and smiling into her eyes. "But for a little while longer, until Jack and Teddy are wed, we must bow to the dictates of others. After that, our time will be our own."

"Will it?" she asked sluggishly, forcing herself out of the daze of the most wonderful feeling she had ever experienced. She was sure her lips were swollen. They certainly tingled. All of her tingled.

"It will," he assured her. "I've given your situation—"

"Situation?"

"—living in that house with those people, a great deal of thought. You won't mind giving that up will you?"

"Giving it up? What?" she asked, finally fully coming out of a delicious haze. She leaned against the tree, hands in the middle of her back and took a deep breath. She mentally shook her brain to try and make sense of what he was telling her. "I—I don't understand."

"Helping in the dispensary. Being an amanuensis for the poor. You won't mind not doing that anymore."

"Why would I give it up? Yes, I would mind."

"I see…"

"I don't think you do. Helping in the dispensary gives me purpose. Without it I have none. My education at Blacklands, if I am honest, was excellent for a girl who hoped to become the wife and helpmate of a merchant, or a banker, or a-a diplomat. Or if my cousins had permitted me to do so, take up a post as governess. But fluency in the French and Italian languages is good for nothing when I am nothing—"

"Never say that," he cut in coldly. "If you want to continue on with such projects then I will arrange it, but you will have to do so in a supervisory capacity, not in the day-to-day activities of a dispensary."

"Oh? Could I do that?"

"Certainly. Dispensaries with patients who need the services of a scribe are yet to be identified. After my—our visit to Warner's Dispensary, the benefits of the sick poor having access to an amanuensis became evident. Warner sets great store on the power of the mind to aid in patient recovery. If the ill feel better within themselves, they are more likely to respond to treatment and heal that much the quicker."

"I agree. The sick poor can barely afford to eat, and they certainly can't pay for medical care, so how can they engage a scribe? But a letter home to a loved one, to family, and in their own words, does make them feel better. I have seen it time and again. It is a small service, but it means so much to them."

"Warner would not have thought it possible, or made his observations about the benefits of the power of the mind to help in the healing process, if not for you. And he readily admitted it at dinner."

"He did?"

"He did. How could he not? He is dedicated to his vocation, and an excellent observationist."

"You give the sick poor a good deal of your thought, too."

"That surprises you. Because I am a nobleman?"

"I am not prejudiced. A selfish disregard for others is not the preserve of your class," she said with a cheeky smile, which cleared his brow in an instant. "My cousins are entirely self-absorbed. Minette married Dr. Warner, who has dedicated his life to the sick poor and their diseases, in spite of his chosen profession. He is wealthy and much respected, and she wanted a comfortable life."

"I do not condemn her for that. But I do for her spiteful behavior towards you."

"She is the nicer of my two cousins. She does try to temper her jealous spite. Henriette does not." She shook her thoughts free of her cousins, not wanting them to spoil her time in this magical place, and so said, "You can arrange for these scribes to be paid—"

"Through my—through the Fournier Foundation."

"And I could assist you—the foundation—with this endeavor?"

"Yes. There is much to be done and a great number of projects I— the trustees have under consideration which they wish to fund. I thought you might like to become involved...?"

"And if I am to no longer assist in Dr. Warner's Dispensary, how and where would I become involved in your—in the foundation's charitable works?"

"From Bath."

Lisa stood tall, stunned. "*Bath*? Why Bath?"

"I have a small estate on the outskirts of the town. A quaint Queen

Anne house set in parkland. There is a stream at the bottom of the garden, and it is surrounded by woodland, and has several hectares of farming land attached to it, which is tenanted."

"It sounds delightful, but why would I need to go to Bath?"

He met her gaze openly and said flatly, "You could not remain in London. I won't have you subjected to gossip. That's not how I want you to live—"

"—to live?"

"—as my mistress."

And there it was, out in the open between them. Honesty showed her a future. What else had she expected from him? Marriage? Perhaps, for a fleeting second, she had hoped he might ask her to marry him. But she was level-headed enough to know that outcome was impossible. Still, to hear him say it. To have him ask her to be his wife would have proven the depth of his feelings for her. Then again, in good conscience, she would have had to refuse him, and that would not have come easy, for her or for him.

She was thrilled and disappointed in the same breath, but ultimately she was happy, because his offer was as close to a declaration of love and commitment as an orphaned, penniless nobody of no family could ever expect from a wealthy eligible bachelor who was the second son of a duke from one of England's ancient families.

Paramount, she wanted to be with him, and if that meant being his mistress and living in a quaint Queen Anne House on the outskirts of Bath, then so be it. Her only worry was how to break the news to Teddy, and if, after Teddy was given this news, would she speak to her ever again? She did not doubt that Jack and Henri-Antoine would remain best friends, but could Lady Cavendish, niece of a duke, be friends with the mistress of her husband's best friend? The thought of losing Teddy when she had just found her again brought the tears back to her eyes. She quickly sniffed them away and tried to smile. This was not the time to think of Teddy, that dilemma could wait for another day, possibly after Teddy had married. She would not spoil the wedding celebrations or Teddy and Jack's big day with news of her imminent fall from grace. No doubt Henri-Antoine was expecting an answer to his offer, so she put a halt to her ruminations and looked up at him, and was startled.

The blood had gone from his face. He was chalk white. She wondered if he was experiencing the onset of a convulsion. But he seemed to be in control, too in control. His jaw was clamped shut and his dark eyes regarded her with an unblinking stare. It was as if he was forcing himself to remain calm when he was anything but. In fact, he looked terrified. A flash of insight provided her with the answer. He was petrified of what her answer would be, that she might refuse his offer... He did genuinely care for her, and deeply. It was writ large in his features. She impetuously kissed his cheek.

"And you will visit me in this quaint house on the edge of town," she said buoyantly.

He heaved a sigh of relief and briefly closed his eyes, wiping a hand down his handsome face. He nodded.

"I hope you will visit often," she said in the silence, because he was still too affected to speak.

He put his hands to her waist and drew her to him, the color returning to his face. He kissed her forehead.

"So often it will be as if we are not living apart, but in the house together. I plan to stay for weeks at a time—"

"When you are not needed here, with your family, or required in London?"

He nodded. "We will be a couple in every sense."

"In every sense...?" she asked curiously.

"In every sense that matters."

"Oh! Yes, I see..."

He started to make plans for their future, saying aloud, "You will need pin money."

"Will I?"

"Yes. You must have an allowance, so you have money of your own."

"And you mean to give me this allowance—this pin money?"

"I do."

She would save as much of that as she could for the day when he no longer came. For a gentleman with a pedigree must marry, and marry well, and he would want a family of his own one day...

"And a dress allowance," he stated. "For as many dresses as you desire. I would like to see you in satin and silks."

"That would be lovely."

Good. She would save most of that money too. How many dresses would she need out in the country? Perhaps if she saved enough she could travel on the Continent? She'd always wanted to visit Constantinople, a wondrous city on the edge of the civilized world, and a place full of medical marvels and learning, according to Dr. Warner.

"And you must have a personal maid."

"I've never had a personal maid. Perhaps a female companion, too? For when you are not with me..."

"A companion. A personal maid. An upstairs maid. A butler. A housekeeper. A cook, and a footman. It will give me great pleasure to spend my wealth on you."

"You overwhelm me with your generosity…" She looked at him keenly. "But you do mean it—about assisting you with the work of the Fournier Foundation—because I cannot be idle in Bath, and I do have many ideas I wish to share with you, and with the Foundation, on how best to provide for the dispensaries and the physicians—"

"After receiving my offer, *every* girl I know would be calculating how best to spend my largesse on themselves, but not Miss Crisp," he interrupted, smiling at her note of hesitancy and look of uncertainty. He gently touched his nose to hers. "She wonders how best she can serve my foundation, and help me go about distributing my wealth amongst the sick poor."

"Is that so wrong?" she asked, the note of hesitancy still in her voice because he was looking down at her in a way she could not accurately interpret.

He shook his head. "No. Everything is right about it—Everything is right about you…"

She smiled and kissed him on the mouth, and he folded her into his embrace, and they shared a long lingering kiss, to seal their bargain. He then let her go, and she took a few steps away from the oak, brushing down her flimsy apron and her petticoats and fussing with her hair. It was as if these mundane actions would calm her, for she had just made the most momentous decision of her young life. Perhaps in this magical place she was a witch and he a sorcerer, for she could never have imagined while in London agreeing to such a scandalous proposal to become a nobleman's mistress.

But there was no thought of reneging. Not even when they parted, and Henri-Antoine headed off to the jetty, and she took the long way round to the pavilion via the terraced gardens. Every step closer to the pavilion and the sounds of female chatter was a step away from him, and she wished with all her heart she was still in his arms and they had remained under the oak until the stars appeared.

SEVENTEEN

THE PRETTY PAVILION BY THE LAKE WAS FESTOONED IN A RIOT OF silk ribbons in pastel shades of pinks, yellows, and blues. The fat marble columns were wrapped in sashes tied off in large bows, chairs were similarly adorned, and so too the large tubs bursting with color and the heavy scent of summer flowers. Ladies in flowing gowns of painted cotton with layers of diaphanous petticoats and tiers of delicate lace cascading from elbow to wrists, had draped themselves on chairs, or on tapestry ottomans, and languidly fluttered fans to push the cool air coming off the lake across their white *décolletages*, while engaging their nearest neighbor in conversation. The low mahogany table was lost under the weight of baskets of seasonal fruits, pretty little cakes, macarons, and pastry delicacies contrived by the hand of a master pastry chef. And all served on plates of porcelain rimmed in gold and emblazoned with the ducal coat of arms of the dukes of Kinross.

A blanket spread on the lawn and scattered with cushions was in the shade at the base of the steps, occupied by Elsie and three little girls about the same age. They had with them their dolls, and child and doll were both dressed in their summer finery, their gowns and abundance of shiny hair a miniature mirror image of the clothes and coiffures of their mothers, aunts, and cousins up in the pavilion. They were enjoying a feast of their own on small plates and cups that matched the Kinross porcelain dinner service, watched over by nurses, maids, and governesses who hovered at a discreet distance—not too close to their charges, but close enough to be called if needed.

And snaking in and around these pampered and privileged females,

in the pavilion and on the lawn, were a small battalion of liveried footmen, in their distinctive peacock-green wool frock coats with silver
braiding and buttons, offering trays of delicacies, tumblers of fruit
punch, and flavored ices. They came and went with food and drink
from the main house at the top of the terrace in a steady stream, much
like ants coming and going from the nest.

Lisa encountered them as she came along the path of the second
tier of the terrace between the hedgerows and tended garden beds, and
she held back while several footmen rushed up the stone steps in
pursuit of more ice from the ice house. With the path clear, she took
the stone steps down to the lawn, and there found several more
footmen waiting for her to pass, carrying empty trays.

She kept her head down, thankful she was wearing the wide-
brimmed straw hat. It covered her mussed hair, and shaded her face
from the sun and the cursory sly glances of footmen and upper maids.
She wondered if her lips were swollen and bruised, for that is how they
felt. They still tingled from his kisses. She pressed her lips together,
hoping to somehow hide her mouth and the telltale signs of her
shameless behavior, which was a thoroughly idiotic notion and one
that caused her to blush at her own naïveté. What was a passionate kiss
behind a tree when she had agreed to an immoral relationship with
Lord Henri-Antoine Hesham?

She was suddenly thirsty and hoped one of the army of footmen
would offer her a tumbler of cool lemon water. She would then
find somewhere to sit at the far end of the pavilion, where no one
would notice her, and no one would engage her in conversation.
And there in her corner she would silently observe the dazzling
spectacle of fresh porcelain-skinned beauties in their sumptuous
fabrics of incalculable cost. Their braided hair threaded with silks
and pearls. And as if they were a commonplace thing, there were
strings of pearls about their wrists and about their throats, and
stitched into their silk bodices, and onto their silk slippers. And
with their fluttering fans of ivory and pearl and tortoiseshell, there
was an elegance and ease of movement in their wrists and to their
swanlike necks that to Lisa it was as if she were witness to a carefully choreographed piece of theater, representing aristocratic privilege and plenty.

What she could not have foreseen was that the little girl whom she
had befriended at the swing was waiting and watching for her arrival.
The ramifications of being the new best friend of the most important
little girl at the party, as well as the best friend of the bride to be, were
soon apparent when she found herself the unwanted center of atten-

tion, and every conversation paused, and every pair of eyes looked her way.

As soon as Elsie saw Lisa coming down the terrace steps, she put her dolls aside and jumped to her feet. She rushed across the lawn, brushing down her crumpled petticoats as she went and almost toppling face first into the grass, such was her excitement. Her three young relatives looked about to see what was the matter, and her chief lady-in-waiting sent two of her maids scurrying after her. Her absconding was not immediately apparent in the pavilion, but then one of the three little girls jumped up, too, not to follow in Elsie's footsteps but to go up into the pavilion seeking her mother, Deborah, Duchess of Roxton, with the news of the latest arrival before anyone else could make the announcement.

"I've waited a very long time for you to come," Elsie stated, standing before Lisa, with a concerned frown. "Were you lost?"

"Yes. A little," Lisa fibbed, and hoped her smile at least appeared genuine. "I'm sorry you had to wait. I must have turned right instead of left in the gardens. I never was very good with my compass points."

Elsie accepted this explanation and taking hold of Lisa's hand walked with her across the lawn.

"We've had pistachio ices, and there's lots of cake. Julie ate two helpings of vanilla. Tina likes the lemon tarts best. She's eight. Harriet is six. She spilled strawberry punch on her gown and cried, because it is her very best gown. Would you like a slice of chocolate cake, or do you like vanilla, like Julie?"

"Perhaps after I have something to drink. All that walking about the gardens in the sun has made me parched." She looked down at Elsie and said conspiratorially, with a quick hunch of her shoulders, "I may have a slice of each."

This made Elsie smile, and she led Lisa across to the edge of the blanket and introduced her to Lady Christina Fitzstuart, whom everyone calls Tina, and Lady Harriet Hesham, whom everyone calls Harriet. She could not say where Lady Juliana had run off to. Tina knew. She announced Julie was in the pavilion, adding by way of explanation to Lisa, who had such a lovely face she was sure there would be no harm in confiding in her that, "Julie doesn't like sitting with us. She says playing with dolls is for babies, and that now that she's turned twelve, she's an adult. But her mama has her sit here because she isn't an adult yet—"

"Mama says she must keep an eye on me because I'm her little sister," Harriet added, squinting up at Lisa.

"And she plays with our dolls," Elsie said in support of Tina and Harriet. "You can sit with us and have your punch, even though you're an adult, can't you, Lisa? Teddy does."

Lisa was startled by two footmen who suddenly materialized at her elbow. One held a tray of tumblers and a pitcher of fruit punch, and the other was there to pour out and hand her the tumbler. She was so thirsty she took a sip of fruit punch without really tasting it, and partially numbed her tongue and her lips, before looking into the tumbler and discovering shaved ice floating in her drink. She had never had ice served in a drink before. In fact, she had never had a flavored ice or ice cream. Her Cousin Minette had received a most exotic porcelain ice pail for storing ice cream as a wedding gift, and informed Lisa that ice creams, flavored ices, and crushed ice added to drinks in the summer months were all the rage amongst the nobility, who built icehouses on their estates to store ice. Lisa was certain then that this estate must have an icehouse, and no doubt the big house across the lake had one, too. She made certain to savor this new experience, drinking the rest of her fruit punch slowly, for it was delightfully refreshing, and just what she needed after the walk through the terraced gardens, and helped to settle her after her encounter with Henri-Antoine.

And because the wide brim of her straw hat shielded her face, she kept her chin lowered in the hopes of not catching the eye of those up in the pavilion, hoping she might be able to spend a little time with Elsie and her young relatives, to make up for her tardiness. But she was not given the opportunity to take up Elsie's offer of sharing cake on her blanket because Teddy pounced on her. She had rushed down the steps and put her arms about her.

"Here you are! We all thought you'd been lost and were about to send out a search party." She untied the ribbons holding on Lisa's straw hat and removed it, and quickly tidied Lisa's hair by repinning a few strands come loose from their pins. "We must have you looking your best to meet Cousin Duchess and Aunt Deb and Aunt Rory. And then I have another surprise for you." She turned and bobbed down and hugged Elsie to her and said kindly, "Thank you for letting me borrow your new friend for a little while. I want her to meet your mama. And perhaps when all the introductions are over with you can come up into the pavilion and sit with us while we have our coffee? Julie is there already." And before Elsie had time to nod in agreement, Teddy kissed her swiftly on the cheek, and swept Lisa away, up the steps and into the pavilion to meet her female relatives.

All this was accomplished within minutes, without giving Lisa time to think too deeply or prepare herself for meeting the one person who had made such a difference to her life. Not only had the Duchess of Kinross sponsored her enrollment at Blacklands, she had then gone to the effort of discovering her whereabouts, and ordered Lisa's aunt to give assurances of her attendance at Teddy's wedding. What did one say to such a wonderful woman? A simple thank-you seemed wholly inadequate. And if all this weren't enough to make Lisa anxious, there were the years of listening to her Aunt de Crespigny's stories about the fairy tale world she had inhabited as lady-in-waiting to this most beautiful, kind, and loving noblewoman, which had elevated Mme la Duchesse to mythical status within the de Crespigny household. And here was Lisa, who never expected she would know what such a mythical creature looked like, least of all be in her presence, was about to be introduced to her.

"Here she is, Cousin Duchess!" Teddy announced brightly, bringing Lisa to stand before four women and a young girl, all sitting close together on an arrangement of comfortable chairs and a chaise longue.

Lisa managed to curtsy without faltering but did not know at which noblewoman she should direct her gaze. Her cousins' warning reverberated in her ears, and it effectively made her mute: *If you dare say or do anything that might interfere or diminish the special bond between Mama and Her Grace, we will hate you for the rest of your days.*

The only woman Lisa recognized was Teddy's mother. The Lady Mary was seated at one end of a silk upholstered chaise, a cushion supporting her arm in which she held her baby daughter to her breast. Lisa stared and then quickly looked down to the baby basket beside the Lady's Mary's silk slippers. Not because she had never seen a baby suckling before—often women came into the dispensary with a child clutching at their skirts and a baby at their breast—but because she never expected to see a noblewoman in layers of costly silk, with her bodice unhooked, feeding her infant, and at a social gathering.

Teddy gave Lisa's hand a reassuring squeeze, which brought her gaze up from Lady Mary's silk slippers, and made the necessary introductions.

"This is my fairy Godmother, Mme la Duchesse d'Kinross. She is the kindest, most loving godmother a girl could ever wish for, and I will never be able to thank her enough for all she has done for me, but most particularly for finding you, dearest Lisa."

When Antonia Kinross blew her a kiss, she grinned and blew one back, and Lisa's gaze swept over the Duchess, who reclined on cushions at the far end of the chaise in a cloud of cotton petticoats, a low-cut cotton caraco jacket buttoned across her ample breasts. Her mass of honey-blonde hair was generously streaked with silver, most notably at the temples, and she had a pair of fine green eyes that were reminiscent of Elsie's in shape if not in color. But it was to her mouth—at the cupid's bow—that Lisa was most drawn. Here was the feminine form of Henri-Antoine's very kissable mouth.

"And the most wonderful mama to me you've already met, oh! and Sophie-Kate, of course," Teddy continued, which caused Lisa to quickly look away from the Duchess to be introduced to a second duchess. "And this is my Aunt Deb, the Duchess of Roxton, who is also Jack's aunt, too. Which makes her extra special. She and Uncle Roxton have eight children. Imagine! *Eight*. Almost a cricket team—"

"Not quite, Teddy dear," Deb Roxton said with a light laugh.

"And I am the Lady Juliana Antonia, the eldest girl," volunteered a very beautiful young girl leaning against the Duchess of Roxton's chair. She had honey hair and green eyes just like her grandmother, and wore a round gown of pale pink silk. She had her mother's nose, but in every other respect she was a miniature version of Antonia Kinross. "Everyone calls me Julie. You can too."

Lisa bobbed a curtsy and managed to say evenly, "Thank you, Julie."

Lisa glanced at Julie's mother and thought this Duchess had the prettiest dark red hair and kind eyes that were slightly familiar, and then she recalled Teddy had mentioned her Aunt Deb was also Jack's aunt (though she looked too young for that) and realized Jack had those same eyes. She found it difficult to believe such a fresh-faced majestic woman was the mother of eight children.

"What you should have said, *ma belle-fille chérie*, is not quite a cricket team—yet," Antonia Kinross quipped, green-eyes alight with mischief. "I am very sure my son Julian he has ideas of increasing that number to a cricket team, and there is little you can do about that, my dearest Deborah. What will be will be."

This had the other noblewomen chuckling behind their fans and Deb Roxton opening her mouth to comment but thinking better of it and pressing her lips together, a heightened blush to her cheeks.

"And this pretty fairy is my Aunt Rory," Teddy said, turning to a noblewoman with white blonde hair, fine features, and welcoming blue eyes, and who was dressed in lemon-yellow silks. She fluttered a fan that Lisa was very sure, if she had the leisure to inspect it more closely, was painted all over with the fruit of the pineapple plant. "Aunt Rory is the Lady Strathsay and married to my Uncle Dair. We think Uncle Dair must have plucked her out of his garden, because she is quite the loveliest flower I have ever seen."

"And you are my favorite niece in the whole world, Teddy dear," the Countess of Strathsay replied with a smile, and because she was sitting closest to Teddy, reached out and grabbed her hand and squeezed her fingers. "I—we—are all so happy for you that Mme la Duchesse was able to find your friend, and in time for your wedding."

These noblewomen—including the Lady Mary, who had looked up from feeding her infant who had fallen asleep at her breast—all directed their gaze at Lisa and smiled benignly and fell silent, no doubt in expectation of Lisa offering a suitable reply. But Lisa remained mute, despite replying to the Lady Juliana. This was not only because she was nervous at being presented to two duchesses, a countess, the daughter of a duchess, and the daughter of an earl—more nobility seated before her than she ever would have expected to encounter in her entire lifetime, least of all in one sitting—but also because these women looked to be sweet, kind, and unassuming. No doubt their preeminent position at the apex of society gave them the confidence to be themselves and to presume they would be treated with the respect and deference their positions demanded. But for Lisa, it was their genuineness, not their status, that most affected her. She had few females in her life who were unpretentious, and even fewer who had shown her genuine warmth and kindness, Teddy being one of them, and the other being Becky, and that thought brought bittersweet tears of happiness.

Being part of such a world was beyond Lisa's reckoning. Being on its fringe and looking in was delightful enough, and she was grateful for this glimpse, however brief. It would provide her with a lifetime of memories and, being ever practical, a grounding in his family, should Henri-Antoine wish to talk to her of his relatives when he came to visit her in his Queen Anne house on the outskirts of Bath.

She now knew what Henri-Antoine meant when he'd commented that he came from a family of exceptional beauty. And no wonder he was affronted when she had giggled, thinking his response absurd. But his assertion was not unreasonable. He had not been exaggerating about his female family members. Still, she did not think him a thorn. It made her eager to meet the husbands, fathers, brothers, and male cousins of these women, to see if they were masculine equivalents worthy of inhabiting this fairy tale.

Lisa's preoccupation lasted only a matter of seconds in the lingering silence and Teddy was about to speak on behalf of her tongue-tied friend, when Antonia addressed Lisa in English with her decidedly French enunciation, "Was your journey a pleasant one, *chère petite?*"

This brought Lisa's eyes up to the Duchess's face and they widened momentarily in surprise at the directness in Antonia's gaze. The gentleness in the Duchess's tone and the kindness in her smile were genuine, but they also masked an intent, for Lisa was certain she was being acutely scrutinized by Henri-Antoine's mother. She wondered if there were more to it than just discovering precisely what sort of girl her goddaughter Teddy had befriended at Blacklands, and what, if anything, her Aunt de Crespigny had said about her that could be confirmed or discarded. More worryingly, she wondered if the Duchess had some knowledge of her son's interest in her, and would not have been surprised to learn that Elsie had told her mother she had left her brother in conversation with her newest friend. This increased Lisa's nervousness tenfold.

"Thank—Thank you, Mme la Duchesse, I had—I had a-a most pleasant journey," Lisa replied haltingly though she did her best to suppress her unease, swallowing hard to clear her throat which made her voice more breathless than intended. She dropped another curtsy, gaze again flickering up to those steady green eyes, before politely lowering her lashes, the heat in her face having nothing to do with the warm summer weather.

"Teddy tells us you traveled down by the common stage, Miss Crisp," the Duchess of Roxton said in her straightforward but pleasant manner.

"*Comment? Ce n'est pas possible!*" Antonia demanded, reverting to her native tongue. "How is it you were put on the common stage when I specifically instructed Gabrielle—your aunt—to have a diligence hired to convey you here."

"I assure you, Mme la Duchesse, it was no inconvenience to take the stagecoach," Lisa replied diplomatically in French.

"But wasn't it crowded with all manner of travelers?" asked the Duchess of Roxton with concern. "The stagecoaches I have seen on the London road are so overbooked that persons are sitting on the roof, which cannot be safe."

"Pardon, Your Grace, but those passengers who sit on the roof do so either because that is the only ticket they can afford, or it is by choice, because it is twice the fare to take a seat inside the carriage."

"Good grief. I had no idea," the Duchess of Roxton replied, genuinely startled.

"Gabrielle she should not have put you on a common coach, and there is no excuse for it," Antonia grumbled. "It is a wonder she did not have you sitting on the roof!"

Lisa suppressed a smile. "To be fair to my aunt, I do not think she had any part in my travel plans, Mme la Duchesse."

"That I believe, *ma petite!*" Antonia retorted. "No doubt it was her daughters she entrusted with your voyage."

"Yes, Mme la Duchesse," Lisa replied, her nervousness evaporating at the Duchess's outrage on her behalf. "As thrilling as an outside seat atop the carriage would have been, for all of five minutes, the other thirteen hours would've been terrifying. So I am grateful to Dr. Warner for securing us inside seats."

Antonia leaned forward, hands in the lap of the many layers of cotton petticoats, her green eyes wide with horror. "*Thirteen* hours? *Mon Dieu!* But that is diabolical!"

Teddy giggled at Antonia's look of disgust. "Mayhap to you, Cousin Duchess, because you have the most luxurious carriage in the kingdom." She confided to Lisa, "Mme la Duchesse's carriage has seats that can be turned into not one, but two beds!" before announcing, "I'd love to travel on the roof of a coach, at least once. How thrilling to think that at any moment, and on any bend, the entire coach might overturn and we'd all end up in the shrubbery!"

"With broken bones, or a cracked skull, or no skull at all," Lady Mary stated with a shudder. She appealed to Lisa. "Is that not so, Miss Cr—Lisa?"

"It is, my lady," Lisa agreed. She grabbed Teddy's hand and turned her to face her. "Promise me, and your mama, your godmother, and your aunts, that you will never travel on a common stage, and *never* on the roof."

Teddy rolled her eyes and looked mulish, but then she smiled and kissed Lisa's cheek before turning to her most senior female relatives. She bobbed a curtsy. "I promise and double promise!"

As everyone was breathing a sigh of relief, Teddy said to Lisa, "Cousin Duchess may never have traveled on the roof of a coach, but she has done something far more thrilling—She was held up and shot by highwaymen! Isn't that so, Mme la Duchesse?"

"It is. But it was a very long time ago."

"She was just *seven*teen—

"Almost eighteen," Antonia gently interrupted.

"*Almost* eighteen," Teddy corrected, barely pausing for breath. "Highwaymen held up M'sieur le Duc's carriage on the Versailles road. And they shot her, here." She placed her palm against her collarbone. "And M'sieur le Duc he had to staunch the bleeding and get Cousin

Duchess to Paris as fast as he could so a physician could remove the bullet."

"That must have been terrifying for you, Mme la Duchesse," Lisa said breathlessly, eyes wide. She could hardly believe it possible.

"It was," Antonia admitted, and then surprised Lisa by smiling and giving a shrug. "But only after the bullet it struck me. Before that, when we were held up by highwaymen, I thought the entire episode the most exciting thing that had ever happened to me! And of course I was not at all worried because I was with Monseigneur—"

"—who shot those brutes dead!" Teddy said with relish. "And deservedly so."

"How bloodthirsty you are, Teddy," Antonia complained without heat, and quickly put up her fan to hide a spreading smile. But nothing could hide the twinkle in her eyes.

"I now know where she gets her sense of adventure," the Lady Mary commented as fact. "I hope you do not mind that I told Teddy all about your misadventure, Cousin Duchess."

"Not at all, Mary." Antonia's green eyes sparkled and she revealed her smile. "I imagine that M'sieur le Duc he told you this story when you were a girl, and that you were just as fascinated by it as Teddy. Though perhaps your first thought was not one of wishing you had been held up by highwaymen."

"That is so, Cousin Duchess. But I am very sure it was Teddy's first thought."

"Mama! How can you say so," Teddy complained with a pout, and then she laughed behind her hand and confessed, "That was my *second* thought. My first was wishing I had been kidnapped from the Versailles palace by M'sieur le Duc d'Roxton!"

Antonia rolled her eyes and sighed. "How many times has this story been told and how many times me I must correct it. I was—"

"—*not kidnapped by Monseigneur. I arranged for Monseigneur to kidnap me*," Deb Roxton, Lady Mary, and Lady Strathsay all repeated independently but in unison. They gave a start, gasped in surprise at their unified response, and then burst into giggles.

Antonia smiled with satisfaction to hear her own words repeated back to her, color in her porcelain cheeks. But there was nothing conceited in her manner.

"*Bon*. That is the truth of it."

The merriment amongst these doyennes of society paused conversations taking place in the pavilion amongst the coterie of female guests, and they strained to hear what was being said around the Duchess of Kinross's chaise longue. Their interest had already been

piqued by the arrival of Theodora Cavendish's friend from her school-
days, a girl whose face and name could not be placed, and thus her
family connections were unknown to them. This circumstance was not
only unheard of, but mystifying. But two amongst their number, who
were also Teddy's school friends, could put a name to the stranger. And
while Lisa was being introduced to Teddy's female relatives, they took
it upon themselves to tell all they knew about Miss Lisa Crisp to
anyone who was listening, and that was everyone seated around them.

Thus by the time the Duchess of Kinross was enquiring of Lisa
about her journey to Treat, every ear in the pavilion was tuned to, and
every eye judging, the newcomer, from her plain half-boots to her
faded floral petticoats, the astonishing sight of ink stains on the fingers
of her right hand, to her unadorned hair. And with the newly-imparted
knowledge that Miss Lisa Crisp was an orphan of no particular family,
and if the two school friends were to be believed, had left Blacklands
under a cloud. The only explanation as to why Miss Cavendish had
befriended such a girl had to be out of a sense of charity, and that was
to be commended. Still, having this Lisa Crisp come amongst them
was unsettling. It was as well she had a healthy, scrubbed, and clear
complexion, and was above average in looks. That helped to settle their
unease, though Teddy's two school friends were left irritated by this
begrudging assessment, for despite being pleased with themselves at
having spread gossip about Lisa Crisp, they disliked hearing her
described as *surprisingly pretty and pleasingly robust for a poor girl*, when
the cost of their hair adornments alone could've provided Lisa Crisp
with food and shelter for a year.

ANTONIA DIRECTED HER GAZE BACK TO LISA AND ASKED, STILL
concerned about her journey, "Please to assure me, *ma petite*, that your
many hours in the common coach were uneventful, yes?"

"They were, Mme la Duchesse," Lisa replied, more at ease since
these illustrious ladies had fallen into a fit of laughter repeating the
Duchess of Kinross's assertion about her kidnapping on the Versailles
road. "I have never been further from London than Chelsea, so everything along the way captured my interest."

"I hope you and your companion were not too inconvenienced
with having to share your carriage with others?"

"Not at all. There were only the one couple and their young son
inside the carriage with us, Mme la Duchesse. They were returning to
Southampton from London, where they had taken their son to visit
with his physicians."

"That is quite a journey to undertake to seek out a physician."

"It is, Mme la Duchesse. But in my limited experience, devoted parents will do whatever it takes in the hopes a physician can offer them a cure for their child's affliction or, at the very least, provide some relief with medicinals—"

"Affliction?"

"The little boy suffers with the megrim," Lisa explained. "His physicians are not certain, but they theorize his headaches may be another manifestation of the falling sickness."

Antonia sat up, fingers tight about the sticks of her fan.

"If it is the falling sickness, then me I pity them, because there is no cure," she stated bluntly. "One can go all the way to Constantinople, and the physicians there they have no clearer idea than they do here how to treat such a despicable illness."

Lisa met her gaze openly, alerted to the possibility that the Duchess, who had stated there was no cure, was well aware her son still suffered seizures. And this despite the precautions he had taken to conceal them from his family, particularly his mother. And thinking on it, why, as a loving mother, would she not know? The aristocracy lived with an army of servants catering to their every need and whim. It only required one servant to break the confidence of his master for his mother to remain informed. And if the Duchess did not allow her little daughter to breathe—as Elsie explained her mother's overprotective coddling—she certainly would be just as worried and protective of a son who suffered a life-long illness, albeit from a distance, now he was an adult.

Lisa decided to test her assumptions, adding quietly, holding Antonia's gaze,

"I imagine it is heart-wrenching as a parent to watch your child suffer such seizures, and to remain a silent witness when that child chooses to suffer alone must be unbearably difficult…"

Antonia's fan paused mid-flutter, green eyes fixed on Lisa. If she was taken aback by this indirect reference to Henri-Antoine's illness, she was even more surprised to discover Lisa had intimate knowledge of it. And yet, she forced herself to remain impassive. So when she spoke there was no change in the timbre of her voice, and she quickly and deftly took the conversation in another direction.

"That is very true. Your French tongue, it is very good. I had supposed Blacklands, it being a French boarding school, you would have excellent teachers in the language."

"We did, Mme la Duchesse," Lisa replied. "And may I say again how grateful I am to you for-for sponsoring me and-and—" She shuddered in a great breath and dashed tears away, "—for-for finding me…"

Antonia leaned forward with a smile. "I hope those are tears of happiness, *ma petite*. And now you must stop thanking me and enjoy your time here—Teddy, *ma chérie*," she said to Teddy, who was now holding her baby sister against her shoulder, "your school friends they must be eager to be reunited with Mlle Crisp, yes?"

"Oh, yes! Come, Lisa. I have a surprise for you!" Teddy replied, returning Sophie-Kate to their mother.

She blew a kiss to her female relatives and turned away, taking Lisa by the hand. She led her through the crowd, weaving her way around ottomans and chairs and small clusters of guests, young and old, who were enjoying the plates of little cakes, sweetmeats, and ice-filled drinks, and who were seated further back in the pavilion, where it was cooler, and the breeze off the lake found its way between the fat columns. She finally came to a halt before a matron in an overlarge frilly cap, seated with two young women Teddy and Lisa's age.

Lisa knew these two: The Honorable Violet Knatchbull, and the Honorable Margaret Medway. Known as *The Honorables* at school, and privately by Lisa as *The Horribles*. She was not surprised they were guests at Teddy's wedding, though a small part of her hoped they would be unable to attend so as not to spoil her visit. She did her best to hide her disappointment, for if there were two girls at Blacklands who had caused her the most distress, it was Vi and Meg. Both were daughters of career diplomats on postings abroad and had been placed at Blacklands because no other seminary for young ladies would have them. They were troublemakers and distant cousins, and did their utmost to hide their sour dispositions, and their dislike of Lisa, from Teddy. And because Teddy did not have a wicked bone in her body, she failed to see the true nature of *The Horribles*. And Lisa would be the last person to tell Teddy that Violet and Meg were the carry-tales who had informed the headmistress Lisa was seen kissing an apothecary's apprentice behind the Chelsea Bun House.

She supposed it was too much to ask that in the two and a half years since she had left Blacklands, *The Horribles* may have changed for the better. Within a few minutes' conversation, Lisa knew this for wishful thinking. She did her best to ignore their snide remarks. She was not about to let them ruin her stay.

"What a surprise to see you again, Lisa. Teddy told us you'd been found," Violet Knatchbull said with a brittle smile. "Meg and I could hardly believe the news when Teddy wrote and told us! London is such a vast place, that you could have been living down any back alley, doing who knows what, never to be seen again. But here you are!"

"Not a back alley. A dispensary for the sick poor."

"Good—grief!?" Violet gave a start, a hand to her bosom in shock. "You've not got a contagion, have you?"

"What? Lisa ill?" Teddy scoffed. "She's never been ill, ever. No, silly. Lisa was assisting the physician at the dispensary."

Violet and Meg stared at Teddy, speechless, and then at Lisa, Violet finding her voice to say silkily,

"Working with the poor hasn't done you any harm. You haven't changed at all, not even your clothes. I'm sure that gown was your Sunday best dress when we were at school, wasn't it?"

"You haven't changed either, Violet," Lisa commented with a straight face and a quick smile. "That gown is very pretty, and the perfect shade of green. Green always did suit you."

Meg stifled a laugh behind her hand at this backhanded compliment and nudged Violet before saying to her aunt, who was looking Lisa up and down through her quizzing glass,

"This is the poor girl I was telling you about, Aunt. She was at Blacklands with Vi and me, and Teddy. Miss Crisp was reportedly the cleverest girl in the school, which I suppose, when you think about it, being poor and with nothing better to do with her time than fill her head with the nonsense we were taught, she ought to have been—"

"Clever never got a girl anywhere worth getting," the matron announced stridently. She peered at Lisa with one magnified eye. "The wonder of it is—how do the poor enter such an esteemed institution?"

"The same way as everyone else," Lisa replied cheerfully. "Through the front gates."

The matron gave a start and drew in a breath and Violet and Meg held their breath too, hoping to see Miss Lisa Crisp get her comeuppance for her impertinent reply from such a stickler for form as the Dowager Marchioness of Fittleworth. But then her ladyship burst out laughing. It was such a genuine laugh full of good humor that Lisa decided the aunt, unlike her nieces, was genuine, too, and she liked her all the more for it.

"Hahahaha! Through the front gates! Hahahaha! I do approve of a gal with a sense of humor!"

Lisa smiled and dropped a curtsy to her ladyship, and having found the perfect excuse to quit the company of the matron's sour-faced nieces, said to Teddy, "Please excuse me, dearest. I spy Becky, and I must make certain she is being looked after..."

And off she went, back straight and hands clasped under her small breasts, and made her way through the crowd across the pavilion to where the maids, nurses, and footmen were congregated, waiting to serve and be of service. And when she put up her hand to Becky and Becky waved back, Violet and Meg could hardly believe their eyes that Lisa Crisp had quit their presence in preference for the company of servants. They both hoped the Dowager Marchioness was also making note of this social solecism, but to their frustration, their aunt had dropped her quizzing glass back on its riband and was talking to Teddy.

"I was hoping your grandmother would be here, Teddy. I did not see her up at the big house. Then again, the place is so vast one could go a week without seeing another guest! Or is she arriving in the next day or two?"

"Granny won't be coming to the wedding, my lady," Teddy explained flatly.

Lady Fittleworth sat up. "What? The Dowager Countess of Strathsay *not* attend her granddaughter's wedding? This is the event of the season! Is she unwell?"

"No. Oh, I should correct myself. Not so unwell she was unable to make the effort to attend."

"What does your mama say to it?" Lady Fittleworth demanded stridently. "More to the point, what does His Grace of Roxton say? What does *his* mother say? What possible excuse could Charlotte Strathsay have for *not* being here?"

"Granny insists I be given away at the church altar by Uncle Dair, because as Earl of Strathsay, he is head of my family. And if not Uncle Dair, then Uncle Roxton, because he is the head of all our families. Granny said any man less than an earl or a duke giving me away would be treating our union and our guests with less than the respect due our lineage and the lineage of our guests. At least that is what I *think* she said in her letter of complaint to Mama, which she also sent to Uncle Roxton and to Uncle Dair."

"And what was their reply to such a severe letter of complaint?" Lady Fittleworth gave an irreverent snort and answered her own question. "I can guess what your Uncle Dair told her. As a former military commander he would've been blunt to the point of rudeness. And your Uncle Roxton, while being more diplomatic, would've put Charlotte in her place."

Teddy smiled. "They did. Particularly because Granny blames Mama for my choice, when the choice was mine to make. After all, I'm the one being married!"

"Of course you are, child. So who is walking you down the aisle and giving you away at the altar?"

"My step-papa of course. Uncle Dair and Uncle Roxton agree he should have that honor. Of course Mama and Jack think so too. So that's all that matters."

"It is all that matters," Lady Fittleworth agreed with a smile, and made a show of looking about her as if she had lost something or someone. "I do not see your Granny Kate—"

"Oh! That reminds me, my lady," Teddy interrupted. "Granny Kate is here, but not here at this picnic because she finds crowds are not to her liking these days. But she does very much wish you to visit her. So I am to invite you to dinner tomorrow evening at the Gatehouse Lodge. Silvia is making her special dishes, and Granny Kate told me how much you enjoy all things Italian, most particularly the food, and how you once lived in Leghorn—"

"The best years of my life!" Lady Fittleworth exclaimed on a sigh, and clasped her hands together. "Thank you, child. I accept the invitation with great pleasure. I remember your Granny Kate as a gracious hostess. And when Fittleworth was consul in Florence, we often had her to stay with us, too." She grabbed Teddy's hand, pulled her closer and said confidentially, "You must not misconstrue me, my dear, for I do enjoy the occasional all-female gathering, but the decided lack of male company here today makes for a dull affair, particularly for my nieces. They need any and every opportunity put at their disposal to meet and make a favorable impression on a suitable suitor. They are pretty enough, but possess waspish tongues, and to their great misfortune do not possess a defining feature—such as your glorious red locks, or Miss Crisp's beauty. Your friend might be poor but she has a face any painter would wish to immortalize with his brush. And I like her direct approach; men, no doubt, do too."

"Aunt! How unkind you are," Meg Medway whined, blushing. "Unlike Miss Crisp, who I am very sure has never had an offer made to her, despite her-her *beauty*—for how can the poor be made offers when they have nothing to offer—I was made an offer just last week—"

"Which you should have accepted," Lady Fittleworth stated bluntly. "Knatchbull isn't the brightest candle in the sconce—after all he did offer for *you*—but he does have an income of a thousand a year and every expectation of inheriting his father's pile, even if it is badly in need of repair; the winds in Wales are brutal on man, beasts, and buildings!"

Meg pulled a face of disgust. "Marry Vi's brother? I can do better than Bully Knatchbull."

Violet glared at her friend. "You didn't tell me Bully had made you an offer. I'm glad you didn't take it. Bully can do better. Much better."

"Enough, wasps!" Lady Fittleworth demanded, lightly rapping each girl on the back of the hand with the closed sticks of her fan. She turned to Teddy with a roll of her eyes.

"How you tolerated these two at school, I shall never know! But do pity me because I have been instructed to have them married off before their parents return from abroad in the new year. So I hope Roxton and the other fathers and their cubs are now returned from their expedition into the woods, so that all the gentlemen may join the ladies for the rest of the week's activities before the wedding ceremony and the ball...?"

Teddy smiled at Violet and Meg who lost their disgruntled demeanors at the prospect of male company at future social gatherings, and reassured them and their aunt.

"This is the only all-female gathering, I assure you both. From tomorrow, all the men and boys will join us for the organized events, and as you are staying at the big house, you may even see them at the breakfast table, and most assuredly at all the dinners."

"I heard mention of a cricket match...?" Violet asked hopefully.

"Between the Duke's eleven and the guests' eleven," Teddy told them.

"Vi is hoping Lord Henri-Antoine will play."

"He does. With Jack, on the Duke's eleven," Teddy told Meg.

"Did you hear, Vi?" Meg taunted her with a snigger. "Lord Henri-Antoine will be playing at cricket. Perhaps he'll ask you to marry him after the match?"

Violet blushed, but embarrassment did not stop her retorting, "Perhaps he will! I have more chance of him making *me* an offer than him offering for *you*!"

"Westby said if Lord Henri-Antoine offers you anything not to take it because it will end with your ruin," Meg retorted. "And that it most assuredly won't end with him giving you his name—"

"Dear me, girls! Enough," Lady Fittleworth demanded. "Whatever Lord Henri-Antoine's unsavory proclivities, this is not the time nor the place to air them! You forget we are within earshot of his dear mama and his aunts, and Teddy is his cousin."

"Thank you for your consideration, my lady. But what Meg says is true," Teddy stated bluntly but without rancor. "Henri-Antoine isn't the marrying sort, and if he does eventually settle, it won't be until he is middle-aged, like his papa before him."

"I tried to warn you," Meg taunted Violet. "Roxton's brother offering for you is as likely as—oh! As likely as Lord Henri-Antoine offering marriage to any other female in England—Why, even poor Lisa Crisp has as much chance as you—"

"*Lisa Crisp as much chance as I?*" Violet was affronted and scoffed. "Sometimes, Meg, you make the most outrageous statements. Your brain is the size of a-a *peppercorn*. At least Lord Henri-Antoine is aware of who I am. Whereas he wouldn't know Lisa Crisp from a-a *hedgehog*! He certainly has no idea she exists."

Violet Knatchbull's emotive assertion was put to the test the very next evening when Henri-Antoine, Jack, and Lady Fittleworth were guests to dinner at the Gatehouse Lodge. Yet no one who enjoyed Silvia's excellent Italian dishes could've foreseen that events of that evening would result in a confrontation at the cricket match the following day that would have far-reaching consequences, for Lisa, for Henri-Antoine, for Teddy, for Jack, and for the couple's impending nuptials.

EIGHTEEN

With the return of Mr. Bryce and his young sons from two days and nights spent out in the woods, the Gatehouse Lodge was no longer quiet and still. Servants, male and female, ran up and down stairs filling hip baths with soapy water. Nurses scrubbed clean the tired and aching bodies of their young charges, while their father found a few moments' respite soaking in a tub in his dressing room. In the kitchen, Silvia and her assistants were preparing an Italian feast, while footmen under direction of the butler were trying their best to arrange the required number of chairs, and settings of china, silver, and glasses, around a dining room table that usually seated half that number. This problem was eased somewhat when Granny Kate's companion Fran retired early, and Lady Mary decided her sons had had enough excitement in two days to last them the rest of the year. The boys would have their meals in their room and be put straight to bed. A warm bath and hot food would see them asleep well before the guests arrived.

"May I also be excused, my lady?" Christopher teased his wife, when she told him their sons were now in bed, having eaten a huge helping of Silvia's pasta. "I should like you to tuck me up in bed, too."

Lady Mary kissed him and smiled. She had come to his dressing room to see if he had fallen asleep in his bath, to find him in his shirt-sleeves, tousle of damp auburn curls falling about his shoulders, the hair riband between his fingers. She took the riband and tied back his curls.

"You look tired. But no, you cannot be excused. We have guests to dinner."

"Are you surprised I'm tired after two sleepless nights with a pack of brats who never slept! Roxton and your brother fared much better than I—"

"They are younger than you—"

"Thank you for the reminder, darling. But I will have you know I outlasted both of them on the second night, and was the one to keep the fire alight."

"Of course you did." Lady Mary kissed him again when he drew her into his arms. "And no doubt they are both asleep in their tubs—"

"Dair, mayhap, but not Roxton," Christopher said with a huff of laughter. "The poor fellow returned home to a storm. His eldest three had a night of it with Jack and Harry and their friends, and outdid themselves by drinking and smoking until they were sick."

"As only a sixteen-year-old and his two fourteen-year-old brothers can! But I'm surprised at Frederick. He's always been the level-headed eldest son."

"He possibly still is. But even Roxton was young once! Frederick has lost the use of his voice from smoking too many cheroots, and the twins—well one drank enough to pass out on a back stair and couldn't be found for several hours; the other cast up his accounts all over his father's billiards table."

"Oh dear. Poor Roxton. Poor Deb…"

Christopher grabbed the brown linen frock coat from the chair where his valet had placed it.

"And from what Deborah told us of the number of bottles of wine and fine brandy consumed, I'm very sure Jack, Harry, and their friends are all nursing sore heads today."

"Serve them to right, but they had best not be poor company this evening. Teddy is so looking forward to seeing Jack, and she and her school friend have been occupied all afternoon with what gowns to wear."

"That's a turnaround for Teddy, which must give you some pleasure, for she rarely has time for such feminine fripperies when at home."

Mary took the frock coat from Christopher and helped him shrug into it.

"I wish I could say I had something to do with it, but it is all Lisa's influence. Teddy is determined to see her dressed as befits her beauty. The poor child brought gowns with her that no self-respecting maid would wear. I am certain they are third-hand at best.

Though she seems to be grateful to have them, which makes me wonder what pretty gowns, if any, she had at her disposal in London."

Christopher turned to his wife.

"Did I hear Teddy say the girl was assisting in some capacity in a physician's consulting rooms?"

"A dispensary for the sick poor. I suppose it is no small wonder then that she has no gowns worth wearing."

"Then you must approve of Teddy's plan for her friend's future?"

Lady Mary was surprised. "Oh? How do you know? Teddy only told me of it last night, and you've been away in the woods." When Christopher smiled down at her and then lightly kissed her forehead, she gave a little sigh. "Of course. She would have discussed it with you before anyone else, before me, or Jack. It's all right. I'm all right. I'm glad she confides in you. And no doubt she was concerned about what I would think, so told you first."

"Yes. And you'd just had Sophie-Kate... But she was most concerned about what Jack would think."

"Was she? Jack has only ever wanted what makes Teddy happy. She is very fortunate in that regard."

"In every regard. Jack will be a devoted husband, an excellent son-in-law, and in due course, a wonderful father. We could not ask for a better mate for our daughter."

Lady Mary nodded and mechanically set to straightening the bow in her husband's stock, mind preoccupied.

"I do know that. I just hope... As a newly married couple... This idea of Teddy's for Miss Crisp is the right one at this time..."

"I have yet to meet this beauty in rags, but I'll certainly let Teddy know if I have any reservations in that regard. Jack must come first in all things, and their marriage is what is most important. Though," he added, snatching up his wife's fingers and pressing his lips to the back of her hand, "There is something far more important on my mind this very minute—"

"As much as I would dearly love to tumble into bed with you, Mr. Bryce, we have a dinner party to—"

Christopher affected an expression of smug satisfaction. "My dear Lady Mary, I am heartened by your ardor, but for once I was thinking with another organ entirely. I'm famished."

Lady Mary rolled her eyes and gave him a playful shove. "Men! If it's not one organ, it's the other!" She bustled to the door, turned and said, "Did I mention as well as your future son-in-law and Harry coming to dinner, your mother has invited Lady Fittleworth?"

Christopher's brow furrowed. "Fittleworth? Where have I heard that name before?"

"Her husband was consul in Florence... They visited with your mother when you lived in Leghorn..."

Lady Mary suppressed a grin at Christopher's lack of recall, color in her cheeks. She had heard all about the Fittleworths from Kate, and in particular Fanny Fittleworth's infatuation for a much younger Christopher, which his mother found hilarious in the extreme. Mary predicted her husband's reaction would be the polar opposite, and had the satisfaction of seeing the blood drain from his face when he finally made the connection. She quickly closed the door on his expletive-loaded response.

Lisa and Teddy had spent the afternoon in Teddy's bedchamber having Lisa pinned in and out of a selection of gowns that to Lisa seemed to have been conjured up as if by fairy dust, but which had in truth come from the wardrobes of the Duchess of Roxton, the Countess of Strathsay, and Teddy's own clothes press, all three being of an approximate height to Lisa. The gowns were made from the sheerest cottons and the lightest silks in the most radiant array of colors she had ever seen, with delicate embroidery in spangles and metallic thread to sleeves, bodice, and hems. And there was such yardage in each gown that Lisa was certain three gowns could be cut from one in any other household. Accompanying these gowns were an assortment of matching under-petticoats, delicate white lace *engageantes*, stomachers covered in silk *eschelles*, as well as several chemises with lace edging worn to be seen at the low cut *décolletage*.

Teddy was insistent Lisa choose three gowns, all to be altered to fit her slim frame. The most ornate, with spangles, would be reserved for the wedding and the ball following the wedding breakfast, the second and most immediate gown to be worn that very evening to dinner, a third of summery cotton would be perfect for the cricket match tomorrow. And once the gowns had been selected by Teddy and Lisa, Lady Mary and her personal maid were called to give their final approval. And then Becky was set to work with her pins, her needle and thread, and her expertise.

By the time Becky had finished altering and sewing the first gown, it was time to pin Lisa into it. Just as Becky had done with the cast-off gowns the cousins had given Lisa to use, this robe à l'anglaise of chocolate-brown silk fitted Lisa's lithe frame perfectly, the elbow-length sleeves molded to her long slim arms, and the bodice hugged her narrow back and small breasts, the little white lace edge of the chemise just visible along the neckline against her white skin. With the addition of tiered lace and blue silk bows at her elbows and a stomacher covered in matching bows, Lisa looked the part of best friend to the niece of a duke.

She was nervous to be joining the family for an Italian feast. It would be her first formal dinner, and not eaten alone in the back parlor of Gerrard Street, since her days of communal dining at school. And it would be the first time gentlemen and guests would be present. She was particularly anxious at meeting Teddy's step-father, having heard all about the dour Squire Bryce who had dared to reach up from his world to marry the daughter of an earl, much to the disapproval of Teddy's Granny Strathsay, and because Teddy loved him as if he were indeed her true father. But what made her even more nervous was discovering that Jack and Henri-Antoine were coming to dinner. She wondered at the reception she would receive from the former, and how she was to conduct herself with the latter, and what he might think of her dressed in silks.

Sensing her nervousness, Teddy put her arm through Lisa's, and they came downstairs and walked into the drawing room arm in arm. Lisa could not remember ever hearing the sound of adult laughter or such incessant chatter in a drawing room. Everyone was taking drinks before dinner and not speaking in English or French, but in the Italian language.

"Don't concern yourself, I can't speak the language as well as I ought, though I am much better at understanding what is being said," Teddy confessed near Lisa's ear. "As I recall, you used to practice your Italian language skills with the drawing master. Oh! And here's Jack. He'll speak in English with you. His Italian is inferior to mine, and having been on the Grand Tour, he has no excuse." Her smile died seeing the tiredness in her betrothed's eyes, and she said with a frown, stepping up to him, "You look green, Sir John."

He made her a bow then kissed her hand. "I am, Theodora, but I do not deserve any sympathy. Last night Harry, Seb, Bully, and the rest of the fellows succeeded in getting me as drunk as a sailor."

Teddy swiftly kissed his cheek. "Then you most certainly will not have any sympathy from me, or from Miss Crisp. And here she is." Teddy turned to Lisa, still holding Jack's hand. "You needn't worry that because we are formal you must be formal, also. It's just that everyone calls us Jack and Teddy, so we thought we'd call each other Sir John and Theodora. And as I won't allow anyone else to call me by that vile name, Jack saying it makes it very special. But as you are my best friend, and I am certain he will agree, you must call him Jack. And you," she added, turning back to Jack who was looking at Lisa with a smile, "my dear Sir John, will call her Lisa when you know each other better."

"Miss Crisp! How utterly delightful to see you here!" Jack announced with a bow. "When Harry told me that the Miss Crisp of Gerrard Street in Soho was the very same Lisa Crisp who is my Theodora's best friend, well, I thought he was the drunk one! I can't tell you how happy I am for you both. And for you to be part of our wedding celebration."

"Likewise, Sir John," Lisa replied with a smile and bobbed a curtsy. "To be here with Teddy... To see her married to you... To share in your happiness... It is a dream come true for—"

"—all of us!" Teddy announced. "I hope you brought your viola with you?" she asked Jack. "We are to have dancing after dinner, and I do so want Lisa to hear you play. He is a splendid musician," she said to Lisa. "And has composed something just for me which I am not permitted to hear until our wedding day."

"How can it be a wedding gift if you hear it before the wedding?" Jack said with a grin. "And when don't I have my viola?" He looked at Lisa, a glance at Teddy, and spoke his thoughts aloud. "I hope you won't mind me saying this, Miss Crisp, but that shade of brown sets off your hair most becomingly. And the blue silk ribbons are a perfect match for your eyes."

Lisa thanked him for the compliment, brimming with happiness. It had been another wonderful day, just like the day before. Spending it with Teddy, being part of her family, seeing her and Jack so happy together, and now this gathering for dinner. She wasn't sure if it was the warm reception she had received, and the fact that Teddy was so loving and generous, or that it was this gown and the feel of the silk between her fingers, but suddenly she felt special, almost beautiful, and Jack's compliment made her heart swell. All that remained to make it perfect was to find herself seated next to Henri-Antoine during dinner.

"You see, Lisa!" Teddy exclaimed triumphantly. "I told you the brown and blue work well together on you. She does look divine in chocolate silk, does she not, Sir John."

"Divine," Jack agreed, then leaned in to Teddy's ear and said in a whisper, "Though, for me, nothing will ever surpass your ruby tresses and those freckles on your nose."

Teddy turned her head and looked up into his eyes. "Five more sleeps. Are you counting too?"

He nodded, and they would have kissed but for Lisa's uninten-
tional interruption, which saw them move apart when she bobbed
another curtsy and said merrily,

"Thank you, Sir John—"

"Jack. You must call me Jack," he interrupted, standing tall. He
glanced around the room, looking for Henri-Antoine, then said to Lisa
with a smile, "I insist. You are practically a member of the family, is she
not, Theodora?"

"She is, but you must hush now on that score, or you will spoil the
surprise," Teddy told him stridently, a finger to her lips and a significant glance at Lisa. But she need not have worried her best friend had
overheard her caution, because her mother had approached with her
stepfather and was introducing them.

Jack again looked about to see where Henri-Antoine had got to,
because he had been at his side when the two girls had swept through
the door, and then vanished. He had so wanted to see his reaction to
Miss Crisp in her silk gown. She had been quite pretty in her floral
petticoats when he had visited Gerrard Street as part of the Fournier
Foundation, but this gown showed off her lovely form, and that she
was not pretty at all, but breathtakingly lovely.

It was only when everyone had moved through to the dining hall
and were being seated that Henri-Antoine reappeared, one of his lads
following up behind, carrying a large parcel that looked to be the shape
of a framed canvas, wrapped in cloth. This was leaned up against a wall
by the sideboard, out of harm's way, and with no further comment,
and Henri-Antoine was directed to sit on Lisa's right hand, while Lady
Fittleworth was placed on her left. Teddy and Jack with Granny Kate
sat opposite, with a chair left vacant on Lady Mary's right. Lisa was
given no time to glance Henri-Antoine's way, for while everyone had
taken their seats Jack remained standing and was waiting for conversations to cease. When he had their attention, he looked down the
length of the table at Christopher Bryce, and receiving a nod from
him, he addressed the gathering.

"I know we're all eager to taste Silvia's delectable dishes, so I will be
brief," he said looking about the table. "Though I cannot be held
accountable for the aftermath of this speech, and so I have apologized
in advance to Silvia should we need a few moments to compose
ourselves and regain our appetites. And I will also apologize on behalf
of myself, Uncle Bryce, and Harry, because we know what you, my
dear Aunt Mary, and you, dearest Theodora, and you Granny Kate, do
not, and have kept from you for three nights. But I am assured that
none of that will matter once the surprise is revealed."

"Surprise?" Teddy interrupted, eyes wide. "Oh, I do love surprises. Is it animal or vegetable? Do we all get to guess?"

"No guessing required, Teddy," her step-papa said quietly. "Though perhaps, Jack, you may care to ask her ladyship one simple question…?"

"Yes, sir." Jack turned to Lady Mary. "Aunt Mary, what have you been saying for months is the one thing missing that, if it could be obtained, would make our wedding celebration perfect in every way?"

Lady Mary looked down the length of the table at her husband, then across at her daughter, before looking up at Jack. She did not hesitate in her response.

"To have my brother—Teddy's Uncle Charles—here with us."

A hush came over the room. No one moved or spoke. Everyone, except the Lady Mary, was looking across her shoulder to the door behind her. At mention of her brother's name, a footman opened this door and into the room stepped a man of middling height, with a head of flaming hair that was a beacon to his familial connections. And with the same nose as his elder sister, there was no mistaking his kinship. Here was the stranger who had shared the coach, but not his name, with Lisa from Alston to Treat, and who had disembarked before the black-and-gold iron gates to wander off in direction of Crecy Hall.

"Mary?"

The Lady Mary's name was uttered just as Teddy jumped to her feet. But she did not go forward. This reunion was first and foremost between a brother and his sister, and no one wanted to spoil that moment.

Wide-eyed and shaking, the Lady Mary swiveled about on her chair at her name said by a beloved voice she never thought to hear again. She saw the gentleman standing just inside the door and froze. She was disbelieving. But when he smiled and took a step forward, she scrambled up so fast her chair fell back and hit the floor. She rushed up to him, threw herself into his arms, and was gathered up in her brother's loving embrace.

She sobbed and he submitted to her outpouring of joy and relief and disbelief, overcome by this reception, which was much more emotive than his reunion with his elder brother, the Earl of Strathsay, his cousin the Duke of Roxton, and meeting for the first time his brother-in-law Mr. Christopher Bryce. All three men were jubilant. It was the first time brother and cousin had seen Charles in almost a decade, and Christopher welcomed finally meeting his brother-in-law. But as is the way with men, they tempered their finer feelings amongst themselves and in front of others, in particular because of the presence of their young sons who were all huddled about the campfire in the woods, a wide-eyed audience of seven little boys.

Christopher Bryce went forward and shook Charles's hand and offered his wife his handkerchief. The Lady Mary was still so overcome to see her youngest brother that she was only too happy to be comforted by her husband, as Teddy rushed forward to be introduced to the uncle she had heard so much about and had never met. And within a short interval of Charles Fitzstuart's surprise arrival at the Gatehouse Lodge, he was seated at his sister's left hand, dinner was upon the table, and everyone was enjoying Silvia's delectable dishes.

And while brother and sister became reacquainted, and exchanged news that may have not made it into their correspondence over the years, or had yet to be written, they held hands. Lady Mary occasionally touched Charles's cheek, he squeezed her fingers or kissed the back of her hand, as if touch was needed as assurance that this was not a dream, that indeed they were both in the same room together. And both could not stop smiling.

They were left alone, everyone else getting on with eating, drinking, and chatting amongst themselves. It was under the cover of this general chatter, with Lady Fittleworth recalling a particular anecdote from a wedding she and Granny Kate had attended at the consulate in Florence, and with footmen coming and going with covered dishes and topping up wine glasses, that Henri-Antoine finally turned to Lisa and engaged her in conversation, silver knife and fork placed on his plate and pushed aside.

Lisa had been just as caught up in the reunion between the siblings as the rest of the dinner guests, but with food and conversation came a return of her acute awareness that on her right sat Henri-Antoine. She pretended an interest in the food, but one sidelong glance at him and she lost her appetite for the mushroom-stuffed pasta. If the upturned cuffs of his lavender silk frock coat were any indication, then he was dressed resplendently. The silk was smothered in an intricate embroidery of honeysuckle, vine leaves, and tiny bees, and the white lace ruffle that covered his wrists was delicately paper-thin. So when she turned at her name, her lashes remained lowered, and she noted that the front panels and the buttons of his frock coat were similarly embroidered, the lace stock under his square chin matching the lace at his wrists. And how could she not fix on his mouth after he briefly touched a linen napkin to his lips.

"You are staring at me without blinking, Miss Crisp," he observed as he put aside the napkin. "Which makes me wonder—Do I have spinach caught between my teeth?"

Lisa's gaze flew up to his, startled, and then she clapped a hand to her mouth to stifle a giggle.

He smiled and winked. "That's better. I like it when you look me in the eye. It allows me to admire your fine eyes. And now I see that they do indeed match the blue of the silk bows to your gown. Which, by the way, is very pretty."

"Teddy and her mother have been most generous."

"And with the expertise of their seamstress, too. I'd no idea the small of your back was so narrow—"

"My lord! You can't say—"

"I just have. Now don't jump. Give me your hand."

He let his slide under the table and she followed his lead. And when they found each other's fingers and fumbled, then held on, neither could stifle a smile. And while he was searching out her hand, he made certain to look the other way, holding his glass for a footman to refill. He rested their entwined fingers on the skirts of his frock coat which covered his silken thigh, set the glass down after taking a sip, and turned to her with an expression that suggested they were the merest of acquaintances.

Before he could say a word she quipped, "That was expertly done. So expert in fact I suspect you've done this sort of thing before. Possibly not with a maiden, but with a mistress, or perhaps another man's wife…?"

Taken aback, he almost spat his wine across the table, only managing to swallow it down hard at the last moment, then cough into his fist before taking a deep breath. He followed this up with another sip from his glass to calm himself. He squeezed her fingers, and when he could speak said curtly,

"Don't be absurd! I've never—"

"Good. That is gratifying." She frowned and squeezed his fingers in return and regarded him with such a serious expression that he wondered what was the matter. "Now that I have kissed you, the thought of you holding hands with another makes me sad."

"Does it?" he drawled, schooling his features to remain neutral, though he could not stop the sudden onset of lightheadedness at her admission.

He wondered if he was still feeling the effects of the previous night, for though he had tempered his drinking and smoking to ensure his health remained robust, he had not fallen into bed until almost dawn, and then slept most of the day away. But then he realized this feeling had nothing to do with smoke-filled rooms and late nights and everything to do with Miss Lisa Crisp. When she continued to regard him with a frown, he said gently,

"I never want you to be sad. You do know that don't you?"

She nodded and her frown lifted. She took a swift glance about the table, saw that everyone was otherwise occupied, and said cheerfully, "Perhaps it is the wine making me sad, or happy, or both. I may have drunk a little too much, too quickly. It isn't the same as drinking tea or coffee or fruit punch, is it?"

"Were you not permitted wine in Gerrard Street?"

"There was no cause for me to drink it. I've never dined in the dining room. And I suppose the Warners did not want me drinking wine on my own."

"You ate dinner alone?"

When she nodded it was his turn to frown, but like her, he did not let it linger. He was enjoying holding her hand too much to let his anger with the Warners and her life with them ruin their evening. He leaned sideways as he picked up his glass, hoping this action would mask his intent of confiding in her, and said while looking out across the table, and not at her,

"I missed your company today."

Her fingers shifted in his, which made him look at her. She smiled and confessed,

"And I missed you... I had hoped you would be at Crecy for nuncheon."

"That had been my intention. But my days are not my own while there are guests for the wedding. Elsie's disappointment at my absence was tempered by your presence. She likes you."

"I like her. And she loves you very much. You are a devoted brother."

"She is my sister. How could I not love her?"

Lisa looked down the table to where the Lady Mary and Charles Fitzstuart were deep in conversation, heads together and peering at a miniature portrait in a gold frame. Three similar portraits were on the table before them. Lisa supposed these were of his children back in France with their mother. She turned to Henri-Antoine with a smile.

"I have yet to meet your elder brother, but I suspect you and he are also close."

"In sentiment, if not in age. He is fifteen years my senior, and I am fifteen years older than Elsie. In many ways we grew up as you did."

"As I did?"

"As an only child."

"The gap in your ages allowed your mother to devote herself singularly to your infancies. But whatever the differences in years, you will always have each other."

"I visited Elsie before I came here tonight, to apologize for not being at nuncheon, and she could not wait to share with me your good deed."

"My good deed?"

"As scribe for Simone, her night nurse."

"That was to be a secret between Simone, Elsie, and myself."

"My sister keeps no secrets from her parents, or her brothers."

Lisa inclined her head at this. "I did not expect she would, though I had hoped she might for Simone's sake. The poor girl is frightened out of her wits at losing her position within your mother's household and being sent back to France—"

"Why? All because she cannot form her letters? My mother would never be so callous for that reason alone. Simone should know this, as should all the servants in my mother's household."

"But Simone knows the importance your mother—and Elsie's papa —place on education, particularly the education of their daughter who is to be a duchess one day. She also knows Elsie is surrounded by persons who can benefit her upbringing. As someone who can read but not write, she feels inadequate."

"My mother and Kinross place great importance on education, that is true, but just as important to them is truthfulness, loyalty, and- and feelings. What is the worth of an education to a person if that person is a liar, a cheat, and has a heart of stone? But do not look so worried. Simone will be taught to form her letters, my mother will see to it, and then she will be able to write to her family, and she will feel more at ease." He sipped at his wine and then added, unable to hide his smile, "Elsie was particularly taken with your pretty writing box. Thank you for showing it to her. She now wants one of her own, and it must be as pretty and have as many secret drawers as the one owned by her friend Lisa."

"Perhaps she will receive one for her ninth birthday…? And why would she not want one of her own. It is the most beautiful writing box in all of England, and I shall cherish it always, and because it was a gift—"

"A mere token."

"—from you," she concluded and gave his fingers a harder squeeze than he anticipated, which made him flinch in surprise. She giggled. "Forgive me, but it is a gift, not a *mere* anything!"

"My dear Miss Crisp, you may have just damaged my fingers and tomorrow I am required to bowl at the cricket match—"

"You bowl with your left hand? Teddy is left-handed too."

"I see that is of more interest to you what hand is dominant than if you have bruised my fingers."

"Rot!" she retorted and pouted. "You have lovely hands, but your fingers are still much stronger than mine, so—"

"Lovely hands? As lovely as my kissable mouth…?"

Lisa felt her face grow hot under his steady gaze. So she showed him her profile, chin level with the table. "I will not feed your vanity, be you thorn or no!"

Far from taking offence, he laughed out loud before he could stop himself, and hissed in her ear, "Witch! The sooner I can get you to Bath the better!"

She turned her head at that and found him so close that their noses almost touched. They stared at one another, breath held, and she said in a whisper something that left him nonplussed and wondering.

"That may not be soon enough for—"

"Harry? Harry!"

It was Jack, and he wasn't the only one looking across the table at Henri-Antoine and Lisa Crisp in expectation of having their attention. Pudding had come and gone, and the table cleared of all but the coffee pot and cups and saucers. Hearing his name, the couple sprang apart, their entwined fingers pulling free, both keeping their hands under the table, as if by showing them there would be tell-tale signs of their illicit hand-holding.

"Uncle Bryce says you have an announcement to make," Jack said with a sheepish grin at the couple. "And now is as good a time as any to make it, because after coffee we'll all be moving back into the drawing room. Apparently there will be dancing, and I am required to practice the minuet—"

"—for the ball," Teddy interrupted. "Granny Kate and Papa have volunteered to be our orchestra. Although, I think—and Mama agrees —it would be an excellent notion if Papa and I were to dance the minuet first, so Jack can see how it is properly done."

"Indeed?! Am I such a bad dancer?" Jack asked indignant.

Henri-Antoine pushed back his chair and stood. "You are, Jack. You have two left feet. Mr. Bryce could offer you some pointers."

"Thank you! Thank you *very* much!" Jack said without heat, but his facial expression was one of such affront that it had everyone laughing at his expense.

"What have you there, Harry?" Teddy asked, intrigued, when Henri-Antoine picked up the large parcel wrapped in cloth one of his lads had earlier brought into the room; he propped it on a chair facing the table. "Is this another surprise?"

"Yes. Another surprise." Jack's two left feet were instantly forgotten. "But a rather small surprise. Nothing can compete with the appearance of Cousin Charles."

"That is very true," Teddy agreed, and she leaned over and gave her uncle a swift kiss on the cheek. "Nothing will ever quite surprise us again, Uncle Charles. Will it, Mama?"

Lady Mary smiled and shook her head. "No. Nothing, my darling... But I feel for poor Harry—"

"Oh, don't you worry about *poor* Harry!" Jack scoffed. "Apparently *I'm* the one who cannot dance!"

There was general laughter which considerably lightened the mood, and all attention focused again on the wrapped parcel. Henri-Antoine looked to Teddy.

"This is for you both, but most particularly for you, Teddy. So I am confident Jack will allow you the honor of unwrapping it."

Teddy and Jack looked at one another and then at Henri-Antoine. It was Teddy who voiced what Jack was thinking too.

"But you have been generous to a fault, Harry. So much so that Jack and I can never ever thank you enough for what you have done for us, that this gift is surely too much."

"This is but a token—"

"His lordship only deals in tokens, not gifts," Lisa quipped.

Only after she had spoken and there was a heavy silence, all eyes shifting to look at her in surprise, did Lisa realize she had voiced her playful taunt out loud. So much for not drawing attention to herself and staying in the background as her cousins had instructed. What would Henri-Antoine think of her forwardness? What would Teddy's family think? She dared not look his way. Her face felt hot; mortified, she lowered her lashes and looked at her hands in her lap.

"That is very true, Miss Crisp," Jack agreed buoyantly, breaking the silence. And in an effort to make her feel comfortable again, and to relegate her outburst to the commonplace, he added with a grin, looking at his best friend, "Tokens or gifts, call them what you will, you have always been the most loyal and generous of men, Harry. And I raise my coffee cup to you."

Henri-Antoine gave a short bow. "Perhaps you should reserve judgment until you see what is under the cloth. Though, before you unwrap it, I have one stipulation: This is to hang in your Mount Street townhouse." He looked at Teddy, who had come to stand beside him. "Not to make you homesick, Teddy, but to make you more at home."

Everyone leaned forward in their chairs as Teddy, with Henri-Antoine's help, carefully removed the cord, and then peeled away the felt wrapping. What was revealed was a painting in a heavy gilt frame. It was a landscape, a morning scene, with a spectacular use of contrast between light and dark to capture the radiance of the dawn. Light filtered through trees and across the undulating hills of a Cotswold countryside in early spring, and drew the eye across the canvas to an Elizabethan manor house built from indigenous yellow stone that seemed to glow.

Granny Kate asked what those few at the table did not recognize, grumbling,

"Will someone enlighten this blind old lady what we are all looking at!"

Christopher quickly apologized to her, and in an under voice described the painting, while Teddy, after the initial shock of gazing at the most wonderful work of art she had ever seen, threw her arms around Henri-Antoine. Jack was out of his chair, and did likewise. Both had so many questions, as did the others around the table that Henri-Antoine was urged to tell them everything he knew about the painting. But then Teddy looked to her stepfather and then at her mother, and finally at Henri-Antoine, and said with a knowing laugh,

"Ha! That gentleman you told me was a surveyor come to check the boundaries and do work for you at Brycecombe Hall, he wasn't a surveyor at all, was he?"

Christopher smiled, a glance at Lady Mary. "He was not. I did wonder when you might enquire why a surveyor in a flamboyant black felt hat and carrying about a sketch pad did not have his waywiser with him. And as I recall, you were rather rude to him when he set up his easel and paints."

"He wouldn't show me what he was about," Teddy countered with a pout. She looked to Henri-Antoine. "And it was you who sent this chap in the black hat to paint Abbeywood?"

"I commissioned Joseph Wright, yes," Henri-Antoine told her.

"Good—Lord! Wright of Derby was down at Abbeywood?" Jack exclaimed. "This is too much. Too, too much, Harry," he muttered, shaking his head as he continued to stare at the painting.

"It's done now. And turned out rather nicely," Henri-Antoine replied, points of color in his cheeks the only sign of his embarrassment at such an effusive response to his gift. "And Jack has the perfect place to hang it, Teddy. In the morning room, so you will see it at breakfast. The color palette is perfectly complemented by the curtains and wallpaper Jack chose."

"I do? It does? I chose?" And when his family laughed, well aware it was Harry and not Jack who would've had the greatest hand in decorating the Mount Street townhouse, he blustered, "Yes! Yes! Perfect spot! Perfect spot for this marvelous creation." He leaned in to his best friend and said under his breath, "Now I know why you made me keep the space above the sideboard clear…"

Teddy did not hear this aside because she had gone over to Lisa, pulled her out of her chair, and brought her to stand with her before the painting, a hand about her waist and holding her close.

Everyone followed her lead, and now the entire family, except for Lady Fittlewood who chose to remain beside Granny Kate and drink tea and give her a running observation, now stood in a semi-circle admiring the painting.

"What do you think of our painting, Lisa?" Teddy asked.

Lisa gazed at the landscape in oils.

"It is wonderful, Teddy, and Mr. Wright is a gifted painter. I see in this painting why you love Abbeywood so much. It is just as magical a place as Treat, but in a different way—in an untamed way, as God intended."

"Well said, Miss Crisp," Christopher Bryce agreed. "That is very true."

Teddy put up her brows, and smiled at Lisa, a smile she knew well from their school days that indicated she was about to say or do something outrageous. It put Lisa on the alert, and she felt her smile widening in anticipation.

"Is this Wright of Derby a painter of significance?" Teddy asked with feigned wonder. "I can *see* that he is a superb craftsman, but I love Abbeywood, so anything to do with Abbeywood is wonderful to me, and I am the first to admit I know nothing of paintings, so I am not the best judge, am I?"

"Significant painter?" Jack repeated, almost shrilly. "Theodora! The man has exhibited at the Royal Academy. He painted *The Orrery* and *An Experiment on a Bird in the Air Pump* and—

Teddy shuddered. "Sounds frightful."

"—in my opinion," Jack added, warming to his topic, "is the greatest living exponent of *chiaroscuro* there is! Isn't that so, Harry."

"It is, Jack."

"Chiar—*oscuro*, Jack?" Teddy enquired, another mischievous sidelong glance at Lisa. "Whatever is *chiaroscuro*?"

"It's a painting term for a technique on how an artist uses light and dark to highlight the subject matter of his work," Jack explained seriously, seemingly the only one who was unaware that Teddy was teasing him. Even Granny Kate heard the inflection in her voice, alerting her to Teddy's playfulness. "If you look here, at the way he has managed to capture the contrast between the light and the shadow on the stonework—"

"Dear me, Sir John Cavendish," Teddy interrupted. "I am staggeringly impressed. All those years wandering about abroad were good for something after all. You actually did ponder in front of paintings, when all the time I thought—"

"Teddy!" her mother cut in stridently.

"What? What did you think?" Jack demanded, face aglow at Teddy's spreading smile. He said to Henri-Antoine, "What did you write in your letters home?"

"My dear fellow," Henri-Antoine drawled, affronted, though his top lip twitched. "I have no idea what you or Teddy are talking about."

Teddy and Lisa burst into a fit of the giggles at Jack's red-faced embarrassment, and hugged each other. They could not help themselves. But no one minded. In fact everyone was all smiles to see these two friends so happy, and soon the girls had calmed, and were dabbing dry their eyes.

Christopher Bryce suggested they all remove to the drawing room, where the furniture had now been pushed to the walls and the carpet taken up in readiness for dancing.

Teddy grabbed Jack's hand.

"Let's tell her and everyone now, before the dancing."

Jack nodded and smiled. "If that is your wish."

"Jack and I have one last surprise for you," Teddy declared.

She waited for her family to fall silent and look her way, then grabbed Lisa's hand and drew her back to her side. She put her arm through Jack's, and after looking up at him with a smile, announced, sandwiched between her husband-to-be and her best friend,

"Jack and I have made this decision together, and it is one we want you all to embrace. We hope it won't come as a surprise to any of you, and we sincerely hope that after giving our decision due consideration, you will see that it is the best outcome for all of us." She smiled at Lisa and then again addressed her family. "Jack and I have decided to begin our married life by sharing it with another, one who is like a sister to me in all but blood. Lisa is to come live with us, and be part of our life, and share in everything we do. Not as a companion, or a servant, or a dependant, but as one of us." She looked at Jack and then impulsively kissed his cheek. "Of all the wedding presents Jack could possibly give me, this is the most wanted. We hope you will think so too."

NINETEEN

IT WAS A GLORIOUSLY SUNNY DAY WITHOUT A CLOUD IN THE SKY. The air was crisp. A light breeze rustled the tops of the trees. Swans glided along the surface of the lake. Children ran about playing and laughing on the gentle slope of the lawn, watched over by nurses and attendants, while their parents sat under marquees in the shade. Servants who had not drawn the short straw to be in attendance on their masters were at their leisure to enjoy a picnic lunch under their own marquee. Everyone was focused on the cricket match in progress on the south lawn. The Duke's Eleven, captained by his son and heir, and comprising family members and household servants, were out in the field, while the Gentleman's Eleven, captained by Lord Strathsay, and made up of a team of noble guests, had won the toss and elected to bat.

Lunch was called, just as the best batsmen for the Gentleman's Eleven, Jamie Fitzstuart-Banks and Bully Knatchbull reached a fifty-run partnership. Both teams came off the field to great applause and joined the spectators for a well-earned feast and a welcome respite in the shade.

Lisa and Teddy, who were under the marquee closest to the field, were soon joined by members of the Gentleman's Eleven—Lord Westby, Bully Knatchbull, Jamie Fitzstuart-Banks, and several of their teammates, Teddy's two school friends, Vi and Meg, sweeping up to do their best to monopolize the time of those gentlemen they considered worthy of their attention. Notably absent from this group were Jack and Henri-Antoine, for although they were part of the Duke's Eleven,

Teddy had expected her betrothed to seek her out, and Lisa had hoped Henri-Antoine would do likewise, as she had not had a chance to speak with him since Teddy's shock announcement to her family the night before.

Lisa's astonishment had been profound. She had no words, for Teddy and Jack's generosity, for their family's ready acceptance of her to be part of their lives, but most of all she had no idea what to say to Henri-Antoine. But before she could even turn to look his way, everyone swarmed forward to welcome her into the family and he had disappeared out into the night.

She could not remember dancing with Mr. Bryce or Jack, but she had. And she had danced with Teddy's Uncle Charles, too. There was lots of laughter, and music, and everyone was so happy.

Later that night, when she and Teddy were drifting off to sleep, tucked up in Teddy's bed, her friend had been so full of excitement for a future which now included her in all her plans, that Lisa did not have the heart to deflate her enthusiasm. She was in such a state of emotional turmoil she hardly knew what her future would hold.

Her predicament left her at a loss to know what to do or say, for anything she said or did would surely be misconstrued.

She had hoped to clear her thoughts with a good night's sleep, which would allow her to be rational and formulate a plan. But the morning did not provide her with clarity or relief, and she was soon swept along in the wake of Teddy's happiness. What could she say or do but join her and hope that an answer would present itself after the wedding ceremony, for she would not—for anything in the world—ruin Teddy and Jack's big day. Resolved, she did her best to be involved, and to remind herself just where she was and whom she was with. The day was cloudless, the aspect of the monolithic Palladian house as backdrop to this summer idyll magical, and, all things considered, she had never felt prettier in her new floral gown, or happier, in the company of people who cared for her.

She had just handed off her plate to a footman and accepted a tumbler of iced punch when she was mentally shaken from her musings by a tall young man with a broad chest and a head of coal-black curls that fell about his handsome angular face. He looked familiar... She gave a start. She knew who it was, but although he had been pointed out to her while he was out in the middle of the field batting, only now, with him standing before her, did she finally recognize the friend from her school days in Chelsea. She was so happy to see him.

"Mr. Banks! I hardly recognized you. How quickly boys grow into men."

Jamie Fitzstuart-Banks smiled and flushed. He made her a short bow.

"The pleasure is mine, Miss Crisp. You have not changed at all."

Lisa laughed. "Oh dear! Should I be worried?" she teased.

"I always thought you the prettiest girl to ever step outside the gates of Blacklands," he stated. "Most importantly for me, you were the cleverest."

As ever with him, he was frank, with no hint of flirtation in his words or manner. He treated her as he found her, and he had never defined her by her sex. She was someone he could talk to about his interests, which was possibly why she had always been comfortable in his company.

"Would you care to take a walk, Miss Crisp?"

She could see no harm in taking a stroll with him, now nuncheon was over, and Teddy was deep in conversation with *The Horribles* and a couple of other guests with whom she was not yet acquainted. Besides, she wanted to hear all his news, and they could not talk freely while Vi and Meg had an ear to their conversation.

"I would like that very much. Let me fetch my hat."

They exited the marquee without another word or look at the other young people congregated in the shade, Lisa with her wide-brimmed straw hat secured by a silk ribbon tied in a bow about her coil of braids at her nape. She held her tumbler of punch at her bodice, and Jamie walked beside her with his hands clasped behind his back, shirtsleeves rolled to the elbow, and waistcoat unbuttoned and hanging loose because he was still feeling the effects of the summer's day after his stint at the crease.

Soon they were so deep in conversation while strolling the perimeter of the cricket field, recalling their school days and visits to the Chelsea Bun House, that neither noticed how far they had strayed from the marquee, or that it was almost time for the game to resume and Jamie to return to the field with Bully Knatchbull to continue batting. Nor were they aware of the attention they had attracted, not only from the marquee where their mutual friends were gossiping amongst themselves, but also from senior members of the Roxton family. And one member in particular, whose brooding silence was nothing new to his family, but whose preoccupation with Miss Lisa Crisp was being keenly monitored, not only by his brother and his mother, but by his best friend.

. . .

"I MUST CONFESS," JAMIE SAID WITH A DIFFIDENT SMILE, "THAT when Teddy wrote and told me your whereabouts had been discovered, I was overjoyed, for you both, but also for myself. You did not take your leave of me. In fact, you disappeared from Blacklands so thoroughly it was as if you had not been there at all."

Lisa was contrite. "I am sorry I was unable to say my farewells. I was not permitted to leave you a letter. I did think of writing to you at Banks House. I knew your family would pass on a letter from me but... I thought it best for you that I cut all ties."

He stopped in the shadows of a stand of shade trees and looked down at her. But as he could not see her face he bent his knees to peer under the brim of her hat.

"But—Miss Crisp—"

"Lisa. And I have called you Jamie since our school days. That should not change, surely, now we are older?"

"Yes, of course. Lisa. Why would cutting ties be best for me? We were good friends. No! We were the best of friends. I've never known a friend quite like you. Apart from my mother, who listens as only a mother can, you were the only other person who encouraged my wish to become a physician. Did you think your expulsion from Blacklands would change our friendship?"

She shook her head and tilted her chin up so he could stand straight and still see her face.

"No. But I knew that if you discovered why I had been expelled you would do something chivalrous, and that would be foolish. I could not allow you to jeopardize your schooling. You are by far the cleverest boy—excuse me—*young man*—I know. And you must fulfill your wish to be a physician. Tell me: You have now graduated from your Physic Garden apprenticeship, have you not?"

He smiled. "I have. And I know this will mean something to you —" His smile widened into a grin. "I was awarded the Hans Sloane medal for my efforts."

"Oh, Jamie! That is wonderful news! Such wonderful news." She set the tumbler at her feet and clapped her hands, and impulsively gave his arm a squeeze. "I am so proud of you!"

He grabbed her hand and held it for a moment.

"I knew you would be pleased for me. Thank you."

"Your parents must be so proud, too."

"They are. I do believe I am the first person in my mother's family to gain a qualification. As for Papa... His Lordship laughed out loud. Not in a derogatory way, because he has always been supportive of my scientific endeavors, but because, as he said, if he had managed to sit still in a schoolroom for more than five minutes, his tutors would've given him a medal."

"And your stepfather, the botanist. He must be pleased to have another scientist in the family."

"He is. And two of my brothers have followed in my footsteps and are now apprenticed at the Physic Garden. But the person who showed the most enthusiasm, just like you, is my step-mama—"

"Lady Strathsay?"

Jamie nodded. "Do you remember me telling you about Her Ladyship's cultivation of the pineapple? I think she secretly hoped I would further my studies in botany and perhaps take on the curation of her pinery."

"If only so you could be nearer to your father, and to be better known to your half-brothers and sister perhaps?"

Jamie's brow cleared. "I'd not thought of that... There may be some truth in it..."

"And now you have completed your apprenticeship, I hear you are still keen to pursue your medical studies?"

"My determination has not changed. And I am happy to report that I have been accepted to Glasgow University's medical school, and will depart for the north in the autumn."

"I am so happy for you. I know how much you wanted this. I trust your family are reconciled to your choice of vocation and are supportive?"

"They are. And although Papa was a military hero, he has no wish for any of his sons to go into the army. But I am not convinced he sees medicine as the ideal vocation for the son of a nobleman, regardless of my irregular birth. Law or the Church, or even the Foreign Office would be his preference. And he no doubt could've got me in the door with one word. But he is not against my choice, and has agreed to fund my studies."

"I am glad for you he has," Lisa assured him. "There is so much work to be done in every facet of medicine, that your scientific mind cannot be lost to any other sphere of knowledge," she added seriously, warming to her topic. "And I hope that with his son studying medicine, Lord Strathsay—and indeed your Roxton relatives—will take a greater interest in medical science. Much could be achieved if only those in positions of power and influence, and who have the means, chose to become patrons of such worthwhile medical endeavors."

"Well said, Miss—Lisa! You always were passionate about helping those less fortunate than ourselves."

"Oh, do forgive me if I am lecturing," Lisa apologized with a light laugh. "I suppose it is because I know from experience what it is to go without. And I have heard firsthand about the pitiable funding meted out to medical research from Dr. Warner's breakfast lectures."

"When Teddy confided you'd been helping in Warner's Dispensary for the sick poor, I admit I was not surprised. Your concern for the plight of the poor combined with your interest in my chosen vocation, I often wished if any one person could attend medical school with me, it was you."

"You will make a far better physician than I ever could. As I said to Teddy, I have no stomach for anatomizing, whereas, if I remember correctly, you took great delight in telling me how you investigated the internal organs of a cow your grandfather had just slaughtered—"

"A sheep. Ha! Yes! Your face went green, though you did make an effort to remain interested. I must have been a dead bore at times."

"Never a bore. Though I could have had less description on how you pulled out its entrails while they were still warm and moving to investigate the contents of its stomach."

They laughed, and in his joy at their renewed easy-going camaraderie, which he had missed since their school days, and because he had always considered her like a sister, he confided, "You may decry the lack of patronage for medical science by our social superiors, but it should please you to know that there are those amongst my esteemed noble relatives who already do take a concerted interest in its advancement. I've been sworn to secrecy, but I will break my confidence for you because I know how much it will mean to you. I've been offered a position upon enrolment in my medical studies as a trustee of the Fournier Foundation, a foundation that—"

"—provides funds to physicians who tend to the sick poor, and to anatomical schools. Yes, I am intimate with the foundation's work. Dr. Warner has applied for such funding, and I had the opportunity to meet a number of the trustees."

"Then you are aware the foundation is wholly financed by the Duke of Roxton's brother—"

"—Lord Henri-Antoine?" Lisa interrupted, and hoped in her surprise her voice remained steady. "I had a suspicion… Though I was unaware it was his wealth alone that provided the means for the foundation to function."

"His Lordship was willed an enormous inheritance by his father, it is said because he knew his son would never be able to pursue the usual careers open to second sons due to his affliction. You are aware—"

"Yes."

"Good. I assumed, as Teddy's friend, you would. It's the family's open secret. Everyone knows about it but no one ever mentions it. I remember as a boy asking why His Lordship is followed everywhere he goes by Goliath-like brutes, and why no one else noticed them lurking about in the shadows. I guess I thought I had conjured them up! Papa set me straight."

"And His Lordship has taken you into his confidence about the Fournier Foundation...?"

"He did. Only recently. Once he learned I was off to Glasgow. I suppose he wanted to be certain I was serious about pursuing a career in the medical profession."

"I'm so glad he did. Having a student physician on the board is an excellent idea. For how else can the trustees know the plight of medical students if not from a student himself?"

"Do you know, that's what he—what Lord Henri-Antoine said! He has this idea of offering scholarships to students identified as outstanding candidates to study as physicians but who are struggling to pay their way. And once they finish their studies, they would be bonded to a dispensary or a hospital for a number of years, as a way of repaying the foundation for its financial assistance. I already know a couple of fellows who could greatly benefit from such a scheme."

Lisa smiled and nodded, and was suddenly inexplicably touched to learn Henri-Antoine was intent on implementing such a scheme.

"That is—that is such a worthwhile use of the foundation's funds... I am—I am so glad to hear it. I hope—I hope he is able to find the funds to implement such scholarships—"

"Oh, don't you worry about that!" Jamie said with a grin. "The interest alone from the capital he invested provides over two thousand pounds annually for the foundation's work. And that's without touching the interest from the principal he himself can draw on to live. So I should think Lord Henri-Antoine will be able to do whatever he wants without any hardship whatsoever, don't you?"

Lisa's eyes widened. She could barely comprehend such a staggering sum in interest, so she found herself incapable of calculating the principal, or even wanting to. She had surmised that Henri-Antoine was wealthy, but not to what extent. Somehow it seemed impolite and too personal to dwell on such particulars. But she did wonder how Jamie had come by such figures, and he told her without her even having to ask.

"My goodness!" she muttered. "I had no idea..."

"Not many do. He didn't tell me. Why would he? I overheard my father and His Grace discussing the foundation, and of course my ears pricked up. But I know you would never break a confidence—"

"Never…" She looked up at him. "I think it for the best if you not mention to anyone that we discussed the foundation, or that you know anything about Lord Henri-Antoine's personal finances. For his sake, as much as your own…"

He made her a small bow. "You have my word."

She nodded and smiled. "Perhaps we should head back…? Won't you be called soon to resume playing?"

"Yes! Yes! We must! I'd forgotten all about the match."

He picked up her empty tumbler, and kept hold of it so she would not have to carry it, and they turned and started back the way they had come, Jamie walking on Lisa's right to shield her from the sun.

"I cannot tell you how many times I went to the bun house in the hopes of seeing you there," he confessed. "I wished by some miracle of circumstance you might appear. I bought countless buns in the hopes you would…"

"There were many times when I too wished to visit the Chelsea Bun House, just to see if you, too, were there. But you must believe me that it was for the best that I stayed away."

They walked on in companionable silence and when they were just a few feet from the shade of the marquee, Jamie turned to Lisa, back to the huddle of persons who were watching them intently.

"I wonder if you would do me the honor of allowing me to write to you from Glasgow?"

"I would like that very much."

"But you aren't going to tell me what happened that forced you to leave Blacklands, are you?"

Lisa untied the ribbons of her straw hat and removed it, saying with a smile up at him and a shake of her head, "It is unimportant. What is, is that we have found one another again, and we can continue our friendship."

"Oi! Banks!"

It was Bully Knatchbull, and he had stepped out of the shade of the marquee with a cricket bat under each arm. He made Lisa a quick bow of acknowledgment and then thrust one of the bats at Jamie.

"Come on! The game awaits, and our captain wants a word…"

SEVERAL OF THE FEMALE GUESTS, VIOLET KNATCHBULL AND MEG Medway amongst them, followed the players to the edge of the playing field where preparations were taking place in readiness to resume the match, directly in front of the marquee where sat the most senior members of the Roxton family. And as they fluttered their fans in the summer sunshine, chatting amongst themselves and pretending a disinterest in the game, their admiring sidelong glances from under their straw hats were directed at both teams, who were in close proximity. The plethora of manly physiques were shown to advantage in knitted breeches and shirt fronts without cravats, and sleeves rolled to the elbow allowed for plenty of bare skin, increasing the tempo of fan-fluttering.

Bully Knatchbull and Jamie Fitzstuart-Banks were in conversation with Lord Strathsay, while Jack, who had the ball, was talking with his captain, Freddy, Lord Alston. This left Lord Westby and Henri-Antoine, who were preparing on the fringe of the group, to be pounced on by Vi and Meg. They were encouraged to come closer by Lord Westby, not because he was interested in flirting with either of them, but because he sought to use them to gain his revenge on Lord Henri-Antoine. He had waited this opportunity for a very long time, and he was certain he now had the means by which to cause his friend the kind of angst he had experienced when Henri-Antoine's brazen affair with Peggy Markham had turned him into a cuckold.

He had noticed Lisa from almost the moment she had appeared at the cricket match, and made enquiries about the fetching little beauty. But it was what Vi and Meg confided about the girl to anyone who would listen, coupled with Henri-Antoine's interest—all through nuncheon he had sat in brooding silence watching Jamie Fitzstuart-Banks and Miss Crisp stroll the lawn's perimeter—that set him on his present course of action. He glanced at Henri-Antoine now, and sure enough, his gaze was fixed on the girl—if that wasn't infatuation, he didn't know what was! Knowing Vi and Meg were within earshot, he asked in a loud, but noncommittal tone,

"Jack! I say! Who's the pretty wisp of a thing talking to your bride?"

Jack looked up from inspecting the cricket ball, handed it to Freddy and came over to join Henri-Antoine and Seb Westby. He followed Westby's gaze across to Teddy and Lisa, but before he could ask him to repeat his question, Violet Knatchbull answered.

"I told you, Westby. She's the poor girl who was at Blacklands with us—"

"—and got herself expelled," stuck in Meg Medway with a snigger.

"However did she manage to do that?" Westby asked with feigned surprise, a glance at Henri-Antoine. "She don't look the type to get herself into trouble... And being a pauper, she couldn't afford to, could she? Whereas you, my dear Vi," he drawled and winked at Bully

Knatchbull's sister, "are all sorts of trouble, you and Meg both. And no doubt cost your papas a pretty penny to get you out of trouble, too."

Both girls giggled and appeared bashful behind their fluttering fans.

"She's not worth your effort, Westby," Henri-Antoine stated flatly, tearing his gaze from Lisa and pretending an interest in adjusting the diamond-encrusted shirt buckle keeping his shirt front closed.

Westby put up his brows. "Is she not, Harry? And you would know this—*how?*"

"Jamie Fitzstuart-Banks certainly thinks she is," stuck in Meg with a smug smile, and yet when Henri-Antoine glared at her, dropped her smile and her gaze.

"Why would Banks think—" Westby began and was cut off.

"You're becoming a bore, Westby," Henri-Antoine enunciated coldly.

Jack looked from Henri-Antoine to Seb and back again, and hissed at his best friend's ear, "What's going on? What pauper? Who was expelled from what?"

"It doesn't matter," Henri-Antoine said through his teeth. "Drop it."

"I caught her kissing Jamie Banks behind the Chelsea Bun House!" Violet burst out in a much louder voice than she intended, and gave an involuntary nervous laugh.

"Did you indeed, Vi?" Westby purred, and with a lift of his brows encouraged her to continue.

"I was never more shocked, and neither was the headmistress. And did the proud little pauper deny it? Not her! She confessed to it. Bold as you please. And then refused to give *him* up to save herself. She'd have remained at Blacklands if only she'd named him. More fool she!"

"Dear me, Vi," Westby drawled with a heavy sigh of false sincerity. "More fool she, indeed."

"I don't know whom you're telling tales about, but I don't like it one bit," Jack grumbled.

"And what's worse," Vi added in a breathless whisper, ignoring Jack's censure now that she had several pairs of male eyes fixed on her, including the unwavering gaze of Lord Henri-Antoine. "It happened more than once. We saw them behind the shop too many times to count. Isn't that the truth, Meg?!"

Meg looked about at the silent faces, and then at her friend who was glaring at her in a way that told her to agree or face the consequences of her displeasure later. "Yes! Yes! It's all true. Every word." She nodded, then nodded again, adding with a contemptuous sniff, "And they weren't sharing a bun back behind the shop, if you get my meaning."

"Well!" Westby said with exaggerated emphasis, adding with tongue firmly planted in his cheek, and another sidelong glance at Henri-Antoine. "It looks as if our hero of the hour not only knows how to handle his bat, but his tongue—"

"Shut up, Westby!" Henri-Antoine snapped, his gaze on Vi and Meg. "As for you two…"

Vi and Meg smiled saucily, huddling together and bobbing curtsies. Emboldened by Lord Westby's misplaced encouragement they were thrilled when England's wealthiest bachelor and the brother of the Duke of Roxton had finally turned his singular attention their way. They had misjudged his mood entirely, which made his blunt denunciation all the more devastating.

He stared at Meg. "You're a bitch. And you," he said with undisguised disgust, gaze transferring to Vi, "you're worse. You're a bitch and a snitch. A pox on you both."

"Egad, Harry, that was uncalled for, surely?" Westby complained with a sad shake of his head as Meg Medway and Violet Knatchbull burst into tears and fled, howling, up the slope of the lawn towards the marquees. Privately, he was enjoying every moment of his friend's discomfort. "Unless," he goaded, "you, like our hero Banks, has some —um—prior *experience* of Miss Crisp and her oral talents that you'd care to share—"

"That's it, Westby—" Henri-Antoine growled, taking a step toward Westby with fists clenched.

But at the mention of Lisa by name, Jack came to life, shouldered past Henri-Antoine and stood over Lord Westby.

"No one has anything to share about Miss Crisp," he seethed, glaring at Westby. He took a menacing sweep about him. "No one. Not now. Not ever. Or you'll answer to me. Got it?"

There was a deathly silence amongst the group, in marked contrast to the noise and activity surrounding them. And then, just as Teddy and Lisa announced their arrival with flushed cheeks and smiles, Henri-Antoine turned on Jack with a sneer, hands still clenched into fists.

"Got it? Oh yes, you've given us all a mind's eye full of just what you've got yourself, Jack Cavendish."

Jack blinked. He flushed scarlet at the inference. And when Henri-Antoine went to turn away, he grabbed his arm and pulled him back around.

"I don't like your tone!"

"I don't bloody well care!"

"Take back what you said! Take it back!"

Henri-Antoine pulled his arm free. "Go to hell!"

He stormed off. Jack would have followed, but Teddy caught at his arm and held on. It was Lisa who went after Henri-Antoine. She picked up her petticoats, and rushed across the lawn as he strode out towards the cricket pitch. She only managed to catch him up when he suddenly stopped, looked to the sky, closed his eyes, and took a deep breath. He stood there like that, as a statue, with his face warming in the sun, for several seconds before sensing someone was behind him. He dropped his chin and let out a breath.

"Go away! Damn you! Leave me in peace!"

TWENTY

"I will. If that's what you want. But first we need to talk."

Henri-Antoine swiveled about to face Lisa. But if he was surprised she was the one who had followed him he did not show it. In fact, he stared at her, dark eyes expressionless, as if she were a stranger, and kept his lips pressed together. He wasn't going to be the one to start a conversation, not with her.

She swallowed down her nervousness and refused to cower. It was time to be brave. So she came closer, removed her fingers from her petticoats, straightened her spine, and held her hands close against her bodice. She hoped that by effecting a pretense of restraint she could remain in control and not allow her feelings to bubble up and overwhelm her. In a small way his aloofness helped; living with her cousins' intransigence meant she was resilient to offence and not easily overwhelmed.

"You left the dinner early. I hope it was not on my account, or because you were unwell."

He stared at her for so long she thought he was not about to reply. And when he did, his response sent her spirits plummeting, yet she would not let him see how much he upset her.

"I left because there was nothing to keep me there."

"Oh? The prospect of watching Jack dance with his two left feet, or standing up with me, was not inducement enough?"

"No."

"I wish you had stayed."

Again he said nothing, and again she waited. They stood a few feet apart, both with so much to say, and yet said nothing. That they were now the actors in a deeply personal performance being played out in an open-air theater to a rapt audience did not occur to them. Everyone from the cricket players on the edge of the field, to the family and guests under the marquees on the hill, the handful of upper servants at the windows and those under their own marquee, to the gardeners resting in the shade, and the local tenant farmers and their families who had walked across to join in the day at the Duke's invitation, all eyes were on the Duke of Roxton's enigmatic brother and the poor girl from Soho.

It was Lisa who broke the silence.

"You're angry with me. I do not know why that is when I—"

"Spare me your indignation, Miss Crisp. I neither have the inclination or patience for your garbled excuses."

"My-my *garbled*—excuses? I have not the slightest notion what excuses, garbled or otherwise, you think I possess."

"Let's end this here and now. Put in simple terms: You accepted a better offer."

"Accepted a better—*offer?*"

He rolled his eyes and clenched his jaw. "Are you intent on repeating everything I say?"

"I find that I must because I have no idea what you are talking about."

"So you have just said, Miss Crisp—"

"Am I no longer Lisa to you?"

His voice was cold. "You are no longer anything to me, Miss Crisp."

It was her turn to press her lips together, and to stifle a sob. She tried to hide that his words sliced deep, but she could not conceal the desolation in her eyes, which instantly filled with tears. She tried to blink them dry, and took a breath, but she could not stop them rolling down her cheeks. She kept her gaze on his chest and the small diamond-encrusted heart-shaped shirt buckle.

"His lordship is-is—retracting his-his offer of a house in the country, pin money, and a companion?" she asked in what she hoped was a light tone, and with a watery sniff. "Does His Lordship forget he made such an offer and that I accepted it in-in good faith?"

He took a step closer. "Retracting? *Good faith?* You dare to imagine you are the injured party? Say it like it is. You received and accepted a better offer."

"No. I-I will not. You cannot make me say what it is not—what is not true."

He threw up a hand in frustration. He was suddenly dry in the mouth, and the sun beating down on him was making his eyes ache and his temple throb. What was worse, she was crying, and he hated himself for making her miserable. But the way he was feeling physically, and the unalterable fact she'd been taken from him, made him say harshly, "For God's sake! Are you pretending you didn't know? That you had no hint of what was to come last night. That the announcement was to you as a bolt of lightning that appears as if from nowhere? You cannot think me that buffle-headed!"

"It *was* as you say—a bolt of lightning, and it-it—*hit* me, as it must have you, suddenly and without warning. It was a-a shock. And it was *not* an offer. How can it be an offer when I was not given a choice?"

He grunted his disbelief.

"You made no protest to the contrary."

Her gaze flew up to his and she blinked away her tears. Her voice was clear and strong and full of indignation.

"And how does His Lordship propose I was to do that? I was in shock. Nor was it the time or place to say anything to the contrary. Teddy and Jack were so happy, and so were their family. You must see that, surely?"

He did see it, and she made perfect sense, but he did not want to see it, and nothing made sense to him anymore. He was in shock himself. Teddy's announcement had hit him as if he had been struck by lightning. One minute he saw a future, sharing his country manor house with Lisa, and the next, that future and she were taken from him, he left with nothing. He felt swindled, and the demon on his shoulder wanted him to believe that she could not be entirely blameless, that she must have known something of what Teddy proposed—after all they were best friends. And so he let the demon persuade him that she had led him on; she was just like the rest of the females from the lower orders who threw themselves at him. They wanted what they could get out of him. They did not want him for himself, and they certainly would not want him if they knew he was cursed with the falling sickness. And if he'd not had position and wealth, what was he, and how wanted would he be? But he was pragmatic. He'd wanted what they could give him, too, and that had suited his carnal appetites just fine at the time.

But Lisa… He had thought her different in every way…

Intuition. Common sense. His finer feelings. All warned him the demon was wrong. But after the salacious gossip he had just been fed about Lisa and Jamie Banks—which he would have considered baseless had he not spent a brooding half hour watching them take a stroll together—he was inclined to think there was a grain of truth in it. They had walked close together and there were several times when she had touched his arm, and he hers, and they had talked and talked and not stopped for breath. Jamie had carried her tumbler for her, and he was a strapping young man just like his father, and just as handsome, and knowing their backgrounds, he was certain they shared a mutual interest in the medical sciences.

The deterioration in his health, Teddy's shock announcement at dinner, and the mental image of Lisa in comfortable conversation with the physically robust Jamie Fitzstuart-Banks, set him on the path to self-destruction. He let the demon have its way.

"Bravo, Miss Crisp. I am almost convinced by your performance. As convinced as I was at the oak tree, when you led me to believe you had never kissed another. But there, too, I allowed myself to be taken in."

Lisa blinked at him, mortified.

"You think—You think I have-I have kiss-*kissed* another the way I kissed you?"

"Have you?"

"Need you ask me that?"

He put up his chin. "Need you hesitate? You either have or you have not."

She swallowed, sadness making her shoulders droop, and let the tears course down her cheeks. Her voice was barely above a whisper.

"I have not, sir."

He put up his brows, surprised.

"Indeed. Perhaps not behind an oak tree, but behind the Chelsea Bun House…?"

"Behind the—" Her gaze flew up to his again and her throat was instantly dry. "You hold against me one kiss between a girl and a boy who look upon each other as brother and sister?"

"Brother? And-and *sister*? I watched you taking a stroll with our batting hero—as did everyone else here today. I doubt anyone thought 'there goes a brother with his sister'—"

"I don't care what anyone else thinks—I care only what *you* think."

He scoffed. But far from her words appeasing his jealousy, which subconsciously he knew was ridiculous in the extreme, he was left even more wretched by his own outlandish assertions against her. *What was wrong with him? Why was he being such a facile reptile?* Being aware of his appalling behavior towards her did nothing to stop it continuing.

"Perhaps you should have thought about *me* before you went for a stroll with *him*."

"I was unaware I needed your permission to-to—do—Oh! To do anything at all! But I am glad this is now out in the open between us, because I intend to continue my association with Jamie—and yes, I do call him Jamie and he calls me Lisa—because he is a dear friend—"

"Who you kissed behind the Chelsea Bun House. Some friendship."

"I was seventeen, and he the same age, and I kissed his cheek. He was—he still is—just a boy."

"If you are so determined I should know about the *friendship* between the two of you, tell me why you refused to give his name up to your headmistress at Blacklands."

Lisa sniffed and dug in her petticoats to pull the handkerchief from the pocket tied around her waist under her skirts. She dabbed at her eyes and patted her cheeks dry before continuing.

"You seem to infer I have something to be ashamed of. I do not. If I had given his name up, Jamie would most certainly have lost his apothecary's apprenticeship. Physic Garden apprentices and Blacklands girls were forbidden to socialize on any level. Which is why when we met on a Sunday at the Chelsea Bun House, we would take our bun to the lane at the back of the shop and there sit and share our bun and talk, oh! about all manner of topics, but mainly science."

Henri-Antoine frowned at her, incredulous.

"You willingly gave up your schooling—let yourself be expelled— all to save Jamie from expulsion?"

She flushed scarlet, not only at his disbelief, but because by his tone she sensed he thought her action, far from being noble, was foolhardy.

"I did. It was the right thing to do, and I stand by my decision. Jamie will one day be a brilliant physician. I have always thought so."

"I agree. He is also an exceedingly handsome young man."

Lisa resisted the urge to roll her eyes at his masculine persistence at stressing Jamie's physicality, and presumed this to be all part of his male reasoning as to why she would choose to be friends with Jamie. She thought about pointing out that when she had first met Jamie five years ago, he was thin-shouldered and spotty-faced. Instead, she did her best to cajole him out of his sullen moodiness, hoping that with playful teasing he would calm himself enough to finally see reason. For only with a cool head could they discuss what was to be done about

the predicament in which they now found themselves, since Teddy's
announcement of the night before.

"I do not disagree with you. But—" She regarded him with a tilt of
her chin and a tremulous smile, "—he does not possess a kissable
mouth. I have no desire for him to kiss me in the way you kissed me…
I wonder… As you now know who I have kissed, perhaps you would
care to share with me the names of the females you have kissed over
the years?"

He stared at her, outraged, as if she possessed two heads.

"Don't be absurd!"

"Because you cannot tell me or will not?"

"I will not."

"But you do remember their names…?"

"I have never considered the act of kissing a commonplace thing.
So of course I remember."

"I should imagine then that making love is even less commonplace,
or I had hoped to find that out—with you. Though you have had
many lovers, have you not?"

"If you expect me to name my lovers, you are to be vastly disappointed!"

"Oh? Because there are too few, or too many?"

When his jaw swung open, and he stared at her with outraged
amazement that she could dare make such a suggestion, she felt the
laughter bubble up in her throat, and she quickly put up a hand to
smother her giggles.

Her laughter was infectious and he found himself smiling. She had
such a lovely laugh. And a lovely smile. And such beautiful eyes. She
was clever and noble and all that was good with the world. He wanted
to scoop her up and feel her in his arms and smother her with kisses.
And she had this gift, this way of taking his anger and his frustration
and by turning it inside out, he saw how petulant and petty and thoroughly unreasonable he was being. All he wanted to do was laugh
along with her.

But he needed to do something to alter this situation they were
now in, convinced she was better off without him, and that Teddy's
offer was the right one for her. Because despite his shock and anger,
hurt and bitterness, at losing her, he had spent the previous night
struggling to find a single reason why she should not live with Teddy
and Jack. And because he had decided that this was the way her life
should be, not the way he wanted it to be, he needed to do that something here and now, so she would walk away from him, knowing she
had made the right decision. He could then stop feeling wretched,

about himself, but most importantly so he could stop feeling anything at all for her.

"It would seem that having a vast experience of women does not make a man immune to the wiles of a predatory female, particularly one who is pretty and lacking in experience," he drawled, and avoided looking at her. "Therein, no doubt, lay my downfall. I strayed from my usual preference, lost my head, and made an offer I would not have, had I been thinking with my brain."

Lisa's smile faded.

"I'm not entirely sure what you are talking about, but I sense you think I somehow tricked you into offering me a house in the country where I would live as your mistress?"

Her blunt summation made him sound absurd, and it was absurd, but he gave himself permission to allow bitterness to feed his demon. He inclined his head in agreement and then added to the absurdity by saying with a sniff of disdain,

"No doubt to someone like you my title, my pedigree, and my wealth were like shiny objects dangled before a cat: Irresistible, and for the capturing."

"Someone like me...? Oh! You mean as an orphaned pauper living on the charity of her relations. As for irresistible and for the capturing..." She blushed scarlet, incensed by his outrageous assertion. "I do not know what saddens me more: That you think me so shallow of character that I agreed to be your mistress because I am dazzled by your wealth and privilege, or that you are so shallow of character that you must needs bolster your conceit by trumpeting your pedigree as son of a duke. As for your wealth—It is, quite frankly, unfathomable to me. I have all of fifteen shillings to my name, and that was given to me, most generously, by Dr. Warner. So in truth I do not have even one penny that is mine."

He contradicted himself by saying coldly, "When we first met I did not fling, or as you put it *trumpet*, my name or my consequence. In fact, you were clueless as to my identity."

"When we first met," she reminded him gently, "you were in no position to fling anything at me."

It was his turn to blush scarlet. She was right. Their first encounter had not been at Warner's Dispensary when she had refused to go out to his carriage, it was at Westby's townhouse when he was in the throes of a full-blown seizure. She deserved his thanks and his gratitude for taking care of him, but in his present destructive state of mind, and with the sun blazing in his eyes and his throat becoming drier by the minute, he allowed himself to hurtle back to a time before his father's death, when he was a sullen, petulant boy, full of resentment and self-consequence, who privately, desperately, wanted to be like every other boy, but most of all like his best friend Jack, and knew with bitter certainty he never would be.

"Ah! Here it is! Voiced at last! I wondered when Miss Crisp, the dispensary assistant who has never been ill a day in her life, would find the moment to remind His Lordship that though he is a duke's son and wealthy beyond her comprehension, he is less than whole, and he certainly is not *wholesome*. He has frequent moments of monstrosity and madness which he cannot control, and never will be able to control, and he will spend the rest of his days a slave to his affliction. And were it not for his illustrious relations, he would have been committed and now be chained up with the lunatics in Bedlam, and there left to rot, an exhibit for curious paying visitors. Thank you, Miss Crisp. Thank you so much for your timely reminder. It can serve as your exit clause. You can sigh with relief knowing you have accepted the better offer. Your life with Teddy and Jack will be vastly different to the one I would have subjected you to, and you may live it without—"

"You are being self-pitying for its own sake, and I won't let you degrade yourself or me with such nonsense!"

Her sagacity made him want to laugh at his own irrationality, and her tears made him wretched. He wanted to fall to his knees and weep at her feet and beg forgiveness for such a ludicrous display of infantile behavior. He had no idea what had come over him to allow himself to display such raw emotion. His conduct was not only childish and disgraceful, it was unforgiveable. And here she was, behaving as she always did, with the utmost decorum and majesty. Perhaps he did belong in Bedlam. At the very least, locked away from good society, and most of all, far, far away from her. He didn't deserve her, and she certainly deserved better than him. And with his head pounding and his eyes hurting, and welling with panic at that feeling that at any moment he was about to spiral out of control, he convinced himself he had lost her forever, and set about satisfying his self-destruction.

"You should be flattered to have received two offers in two days. I have never offered any female what I offered you, and Teddy most certainly would never offer any female but you with what she and Jack are willing to provide."

"You cannot compare the two."

His gaze swept over her and fixed on the little lace edge of her chemise just peeking above the top of her low-cut bodice, inviting the eye to caress her small perfect breasts. He sneered and looked up into her eyes with undisguised lust.

"You're right. You wouldn't have to work on your back for Teddy."

His vulgar inference fell flat. "Work on my-my—*back*…?"

Oh God. How had he descended into such crudity, and with her? He would never have been that coarse with a whore. He was a monster. He certainly was no gentleman. He felt ill and pitiful and utterly helpless. He sensed the latter feeling had less to do with her and everything to do with his physical deterioration. And with this awareness he did what his father had always told him to do when in the public gaze: Remain calm. Signal for help the way he had been shown. Breathe. Soon he would be in a safe place, out from under prying eyes, and out of harm's way.

From the corner of an eye he saw they had company, and his first thought was that it was the lads come to take him away. But he had yet to signal them. And then his confrontation with Lisa was brought to an abrupt halt. Suddenly, and without warning, Jack marched up to them. He grabbed Henri-Antoine by the collar and shoved him backwards, taking him as far from Lisa as he could manage without them both tripping and falling to the ground. She followed them, and tried to offer an explanation, but Jack was in no mood to listen, even to her.

"That was a piece of filth I never thought I'd hear from the mouth of a gentleman," Jack snarled in Henri-Antoine's ear. "Lord! You've outdone yourself this time, Harry! You've descended into the cesspit!"

THE DUKE'S ELEVEN HAD TAKEN TO THE FIELD. THE BATSMEN for the Gentleman's Eleven, Bully and Jamie, were at the crease swinging their bats, ready to play. Mr. Frew, officiating umpire, was at the bowler's end, behind the wicket. Marc Gallet had the ball, ready to bowl. It only remained to have Lord Henri-Antoine and Miss Crisp removed from a position where they could be hit with the ball, so play could commence. Jack elected to break up their heated argument. He had gone on ahead of the rest of the players to alert them that they were not only providing fodder for the gossips and causing the family concern, but there was a cricket match to get underway.

He walked up to the couple in time to hear the end of Henri-Antoine's heated diatribe, followed by Miss Crisp's measured reply. He had then stepped forward to make his presence known when he heard something out of his best friend's mouth he never thought he would ever hear a gentleman say to any female, least of all to Teddy's best friend. Lisa Crisp might not have been born of noble parents, she may not have been a gentleman's daughter or even the daughter of a squire for that matter, but as far as he was concerned she conducted herself in every way as if she were in truth a lady, and better than some females who had been born to the title.

That the couple was in the midst of what was clearly a lover's tiff, opened wide his eyes, and he was prepared to give them some latitude, and thus had waited a few moments until there was a break in their exchange. But Henri-Antoine's tasteless insinuation prompted him into action, and if he wasn't already angry enough to think Miss Crisp had been subjected to baseless gossip by an argument conducted in full public view, her tear-stained face and evident distress had his blood at boiling.

So what had been a heated argument between a couple in the middle of a field, had now inflated into an enraged altercation between two best friends, with Miss Crisp helplessly watching on, mortified to be the subject of their furious disagreement. And it happened there, on the field, amidst the cricket game, with family and friends, servants and tenants, leaving the comfort and shade of their marquees to swarm as one along the edge of the field toward Jack and Henri-Antoine and Lisa Crisp, to have a better view and hopefully hear what all the fuss was about. The only ones to miss out on this impromptu diversion were the children, the Duchess of Roxton having the presence of mind to order their nurses and maids to round up any little person twelve years and younger and herd them indoors for ice cream and cake.

HENRI-ANTOINE TWISTED OUT OF JACK'S HOLD AND PUSHED him off.

"If you hadn't stuck your nose in where it's not wanted you'd have been spared my cesspit tongue! Go away, Jack," Henri-Antoine complained. "I don't want you here. This is—was—between Miss Crisp and me, and none of your concern, so off you trot—"

"Be *damned* it's none of my concern!" Jack huffed. He went right up to Henri-Antoine and said in a low voice in the hopes Lisa would not overhear him, "You'd best tell me your intentions toward Miss Crisp."

"Intentions?" Henri-Antoine shrugged. "I have none."

"Good. Then stay away from her."

In an about-face, Henri-Antoine stared at Jack with astonishment.

"*You* are telling *me* to stay away from *her*?"

"You're damned right I am!"

Henri-Antoine glanced at Lisa, who stood some feet away, hugging her lithe frame in distress, and in a blinding moment of clarity, he saw in Jack the means to bring about the annihilation of his good character so all ties would be severed with Miss Lisa Crisp. He goaded Jack in an undervoice dripping with arrogance, "It's a bit late in the day to be chivalrous where she's concerned. She's agreed to become my mistress. I'm to set her up in my house in Bath. Interesting times, ahead, eh, Jack."

"Be damned you will!"

Henri-Antoine pulled a face and drawled, "Yes, I probably will be. But until then, I'll have a nice girl to come home to when I'm in the country."

"I won't let you do it!"

"What? Why? Wake up, Jack! She's a penniless orphan whose family were in service to mine. It's more than most servants can expect out of life. Don't worry. I'll look after her. Clothes. Fripperies. The occasional trip to town." He smirked. "As long as she does as she's told and continues to please me—"

"You're a self-centered muckworm. You know that?"

"Yes. I am. And you've always known it. So?"

"She's Teddy's best friend, for God's sake!"

"You are marrying Teddy. I am making Teddy's best friend my mistress. They are mutually exclusive propositions. If Teddy wants to write to her, I'll not object."

"I will!"

"And Teddy will do as you say? Good luck with that!"

When Henri-Antoine turned his back and waved a hand, as if in dismissal, Jack took two strides, grabbed onto his shirt and spun him about. And before Henri-Antoine could pull out of his grasp, he snatched up a handful of his shirt front and jerked him up against his chest. The two men were nose-to-nose and eye-to-eye.

Jack's voice was low and menacing and flat. "If you think for one moment I will allow that girl into your bed all to satisfy your selfish carnal wants, you do have ballocks for brains."

"It's not your decision, is it?"

"This isn't the Middle Ages. Just because she's poor and has no family, and her antecedents were vassals of the Dukes of Roxton, you look upon her as fit only to serve as your concubine? Shame on you! Shame. On. You."

"Have you done with the morality tale?" Henri-Antoine drawled, and for good measure rolled his eyes and sighed. He pretended an interest in his attire, and whined, "You've ruined the fibres of this shirt, and perhaps crushed the shirt buckle, which was a gift from the management of Burke's in appreciation of my *assiduous* patronage."

Jack's lip curled with repugnance. "You think it something to boast about, being the saytr's son?! Well I'm done with you. And I don't know why we're arguing. The decision's been made. She's coming to live with Teddy and me. And there isn't a damn thing you can do about it. And unless you treat her with respect, and accept that she is part of *my* family, you won't be welcome at Abbeywood. Ever."

And when Jack let him go with a contemptuous shove and opened wide his hand as if he no longer wanted the touch of him, Henri-Antoine smiled to himself and delivered the final verbal sword thrust to his own demise.

"Well. Well. Jack Cavendish. You cunning fox! I doff my hat and bow most humbly to your libidinous dexterity. Not one, but *two* virgins to warm you up at night. Who's the satyr—"

Jack planted his fist into his best friend's face.

TWENTY-ONE

With the best friends throwing punches and grappling with one another, the cricket match was abandoned. Players rushed over to watch the spectacle. They were soon joined by guests and family who swarmed across the field. And while some of the ladies fell back so they would not have to witness the bestial behavior of two young men having a set-to, the gentlemen and boys flocked to join the cricket players who had formed a tight circle around the fight, shouting encouragement with every swing, thwack, and thump.

Forgotten on the sidelines was a horrified Lisa, who quickly averted her gaze the instant Jack landed the first sickening blow and blood began pouring from Henri-Antoine's nose.

The fight was finally broken up by Lord Strathsay, the Duke of Roxton, and Christopher Bryce. Jack and Henri-Antoine were pulled off one another and held back on opposite sides of the circle, heaving in great breaths, Jack still combative, Henri-Antoine with head down and bleeding into the grass. The Duke instructed the disappointed cricketers, spectators, and relieved family members, to return to the marquees where afternoon tea was to be served before changing for dinner and an evening of music. And with the aid of his army of servants dispersing the crowd, as well as providing a barrier between onlookers and boxers, soon the guests and cricketers and family members drifted back across the field, chatter all about the astonishing events leading up to and including the set-to between the groom and his best man. Everyone wondered what this would mean for the upcoming wedding.

When Teddy arrived, she took one look at Jack's bloodied shirt front and the split to his lip, and satisfied he was not seriously hurt, turned away in disgust to gather a distraught Lisa to her. From the comfort of Teddy's embrace, Lisa dared to glance over at Henri-Antoine. His shirt front was also spattered with blood, and blood glistened about his nostrils and mouth, which was strangely blue, and there was a gash to his top lip that looked to be swelling before her eyes.

Not one to faint at the sight of blood or injury or disease, and thought good in a crisis at Warner's Dispensary, an overwrought Lisa was oddly sensitive to seeing Henri-Antoine's blood spilt. She took one look at his busted lip and fainted, slipping through Teddy's arms to collapse in the grass.

Lord Strathsay, who was helping the Duke keep Henri-Antoine propped up, immediately crossed to assist Teddy with Lisa. Gathering the girl into his arms, and with his niece at his side, he strode off to the marquees, seeking shade and refreshment, and where he hoped to find his Countess, who was also known to be good in a crisis.

And while Lisa's faint caused the family alarm, it was a needed diversion for those guests still milling about because they turned their backs on Henri-Antoine to watch the girl be taken away by the Earl, and thus were unaware of His Lordship's collapse. Henri-Antoine had turned to his distressed mother, to assure her there was nothing to worry about, he was not greatly hurt. But the Duchess did not believe him. She had arrived in a flurry of silken petticoats and greatly agitated, which meant she was talking in a rush of French no one but her sons could possibly understand. She demanded both boys be taken up to the big house immediately to be examined by Roxton's personal physician. Henri-Antoine was protesting this was unnecessary when his body stiffened, he blacked out, and fell forward.

The Duke caught him before he fell flat on his face, and laid him in the grass at their mother's feet, who knelt beside him, a cool hand to his brow. But while the Duke was able to stop his brother's fall, there was nothing he could do but watch on helplessly as Henri-Antoine's entire body convulsed and writhed before them. And when Antonia briefly looked up at her eldest son, her tears of anguish brought tears to his own eyes.

It was the first bout of falling sickness mother and son had witnessed in over a decade. And Antonia thought herself prepared for such an eventuality. After all, she was aware that her younger son still suffered from infrequent bouts of his illness, though she allowed him the dignity of pretending ignorance. Discreet enquiries and regular secret reports from loyal servants kept her informed. What mother would not keep a close eye on all her children, but most particularly on a son whom she had nursed from birth until his thirteenth year through so many attacks that if he went a week without one, they began entertaining fanciful notions he was cured. But he wasn't cured, and he never would be. And watching him as a twenty-five-year-old man surrender to such an uncontrollable illness, she realized she had forgotten just how frightening and horrid such an all-consuming attack was on the body and mind of the sufferer, and what a torment it was for his loved ones who could do nothing but be mere spectators to his suffering and indignity.

And while the Duke of Roxton conferred with the Gallet brothers on what was to be done, not only with his brother but with his nephew, the Duke of Kinross finally found his wife. Pushing through the small group of dedicated servants he joined her on the grass, and took her in his arms, providing her with some comfort while they kept vigil over her tormented son.

Matters progressed swiftly when four of the eight lads employed to shadow their master arrived to look after him. Henri-Antoine's valet Kyte and his major domo Michel Gallet took matters in hand, and everyone from the Duke of Roxton to the Duke and Duchess of Kinross, to the footmen currently shielding His Lordship from prying eyes, were required to bow to their expertise and their master's wishes. So the family, however reluctantly, soon found themselves following the guests to return to the marquees, leaving Henri-Antoine to the care of his minders.

When Jack tried to go to Henri-Antoine, Kyte and Michel Gallet warned him off, and it was only after Christopher Bryce took him in hand, that he finally complied. And when he tried to offer his apologies to his Uncle Roxton and to Cousin Duchess, they were in an unforgiving mood. The Duke told him to go clean himself up; he was a disgrace; there would be plenty of time for him to explain himself later that evening in the quiet of the Duke's library.

For the Lady Mary and Christopher Bryce and their family, the day ended there. Everyone thought it for the best if the girls were taken home to have an early night. And while the Duke and Duchess of Roxton had obligations to their guests, the Duke and Duchess of Kinross with their daughter decided to return to Crecy Hall. And so three carriages crossed over the main stone bridge across the lake for the short journey along the tree-lined avenue, the adult occupants subdued and still stunned by what they had just witnessed between two young men who had been best friends and as close as brothers could ever be for sixteen years, and hardly a cross word exchanged between them.

Teddy and Lisa remained mute on the journey to the lodge, and later when they went up to Teddy's room. Neither wanted supper. And so after their baths, they were put to bed, each with a mug of hot milk. And while Christopher tucked in his sons, the Lady Mary sat with the girls for a while. She brought Sophie-Kate with her, which offered Teddy some comfort because she loved to have cuddles with her baby sister. But despite the color returning to her face, and the bath helping to soothe her, Lisa was still so much affected by events that she fell asleep exhausted without saying her prayers or her good-nights.

Her appetite had not returned the next morning when she went down to breakfast, the last of the family to do so, and where she found Teddy, who insisted she have a slice of toast and a cup of tea. She learned that Mr. Bryce had already left for the day with his eldest son David, to go hawking with the other gentlemen and boys old enough to ride unassisted. Uncle Roxton and Aunt Deb decided that the men would spend the day as far away from the big house as possible, while the ladies and girls would remain indoors occupying their time in more leisurely pursuits: Embroidering, dabbling in water colors, walking the Long Gallery, enjoying a musical recital, and watching the children rehearse their dance steps and musical pieces to be performed at the wedding breakfast. Of course there was little the ducal couple could do to stop the gossiping about the previous day's extraordinary turn of events, but while Deborah presided over the teapot, she kept a keen ear out for any disparaging or inflammatory remarks, helped in this endeavor by the Countess of Strathsay.

"And we are to spend our day here, doing whatever we please," Teddy said buoyantly. "Which will make for a nice change."

"You wish you were out hawking too, don't you?" Lisa said with a smile, nibbling on her toast.

Teddy grinned. "I do. But I also wish to spend the day with you, and Jack."

"Jack? He did not go hawking?"

"No. That pleasure was denied him. He must apologize to you for—"

"Oh, Teddy, no. Please," Lisa said with a self-conscious frown. "I could not bear it. It is I who should be apologizing to him—"

"Nonsense! Besides, he wrote me the most wonderful apology letter." With a smug smile, Teddy held up a folded sheet of paper, its red seal broken. "It was delivered at first light, so he must have spent *all night* composing it. And this was after his scolding from Uncle

Roxton, who summoned him to his library, which apparently is the worse summons to receive. It strikes dread into the hearts of those who must walk the length of the library with hundreds and hundreds of books peering down from a great height as if they are persons in a courtroom, and with the judge—that's the Duke—seated behind his big desk, sour-faced and waiting to berate you for your infraction. So Jack says. And he has only ever had that happen to him once before, but he says the experience stays with you so you hope it never happens again!"

Lisa blinked. "But His Grace seems the most amiable of men, and Her Grace, too, is quite lovely. One does not have to be in their company long to see that they love each other very much, and adore all their children equally."

Teddy's eyes shone.

"There's lots of cake-making going on in that family that's certain!"

Lisa gasped, clapped a hand to her mouth and then could not help herself and giggled. When she found her breath, she said with a smile, "You are the wickedest girl I know! But also the most loving. Thank you for making me laugh."

Teddy poured them out a second cup of tea.

"You're very welcome. I do like to see you smile, Lisa. And you are not to concern yourself. None of what happened yesterday was your fault. Jack didn't tell me what Harry said to you to make him furious, but if you need to confide—"

"Thank you. I don't—I don't want to speak about—about that yet," Lisa confessed, losing her smile and putting her hand out across the table. When Teddy took hold of her fingers and smiled in understanding, she smiled back. "Let's have our tea first..."

She was relieved not to be made to speak openly about Henri-Antoine, because she was sure if she did she would barely be able to speak at all, or become a blubbering mess. And although she was desperate to know that he was not greatly harmed, and was safe, and how Jack had fared, she did not ask, again because it was still too raw. So instead she asked,

"I hope His Grace wasn't too harsh on Jack?"

"Jack accepted the rebuke, and once he had explained matters to Uncle Roxton they both agreed that while Jack should have shown more restraint and not hit Harry, he was provoked. And this," Teddy announced, holding aloft the letter again and then kissing it before putting it away in a pocket, "is quite the most romantic letter Jack has ever written to me. So I shall keep it always. And he explained everything, and I forgive him. In fact, I love him even more, if that is possible, for being so chivalrous."

"He did? He was? You do? He explained it all in that letter?"

"No, silly. His letter was about us. He gave me his explanation in person, as was proper. He's here. We had breakfast together before Papa set out with David for the big house. He's outdoors with Luke, who was most upset at being too little to go hawking with his big brother. So Jack and Luke are out playing in the wagon, Jack running it up the hill and then he and Luke getting in it and coming down at a speed, which I am very sure is sending Mama's lovely hair gray, however much she smiles and tries to appear as if she hasn't a care in the world."

"Do you know, Teddy, that as well as being very pretty, your mama is the most composed person I have ever met. I do not think anything or anyone ever ruffles her feathers."

Teddy stood and pushed in her chair. Lisa did likewise.

"She is. And it doesn't. Oh, except for Granny Strathsay. But she ruffles all our feathers. Mama and her brothers had the most appalling upbringing, so she said she would never allow her children to be treated that way." Teddy's eyes widened. "Imagine if you can, sitting for hours with a book on top of your head, all to keep your back straight, and being beaten if you let it slip off. No wonder my uncle Dair climbed out the schoolroom window!"

"You would've too, given half the chance!"

"Yes, and climbed onto the tree next to the ledge, too." Her smile became superior. "I'm still the best tree climber in the family. Come. We need some fresh air, and Jack wishes to see you…"

They linked arms and then Teddy led Lisa to the back of the house, through the kitchen, where she gave Silvia a kiss, and then through the kitchen garden, where she waved to Carlo who was in conversation with the gardener supervising one of the kitchen hands collecting vegetables, and then on out the back gate, to the other side of the stone wall to an expanse of lawn at the base of a small hill, which provided a natural privacy barrier. From atop the rise, there was a good view into the walled gardens of the Gatehouse Lodge, and in one direction was picturesque Crecy Hall, and in the other, the big house dominating the landscape in which it sat.

Teddy and Lisa joined the Lady Mary, who had a hand up to the peak of her straw bonnet to further shade her eyes from the sun, and was standing by a haycock with two of the outdoor servants. Their attention was focused on Jack and four-year-old Luke who were seated in a wooden wagon that had large wheels at the rear and smaller wheels up front, all with a number of spokes missing. And by the messy state of the haycock, this wasn't their first or third run down the slope, and if they kept at it there was every chance of the wagon falling apart altogether.

Jack had his long booted legs stuck outside either side of the wagon, and Luke was cross-legged, back snug up against his cousin, and with both hands holding firm to the wooden frame. Jack had control of the pull bar with one hand, and his other arm was around Luke. With Luke nodding he was ready, Jack dug his boot heels into the grass and gave an almighty push so that the wagon sped forward with the weight of his body. Down the hill it rattled, its occupants holding on tight, the wind in Luke's face forcing the black ringlets out of his eyes, and Jack steering as best he could at speed and with little control, and only his feet as brakes.

It was luck rather than steering that kept the wagon on course, and once again it came to a thumping stop into the partially-destroyed haycock. Both occupants were left covered in straw and laughing, Luke with excitement, and Jack with relief to have survived another run. He breathed an audible sigh when the Lady Mary confirmed that was indeed the final wagon ride for today, ignoring Luke's repeated pleas for just one more run down the hill. His mother was firm. Luke needed to be cleaned up. Did he forget he was accompanying his mama, Sophie-Kate, Granny Kate, and Fran across to the big house? Best of all he could go off and play with his cousins, most particularly the young twins, Will and Tony, who were the same age. And yes, Otto and David would not be there because they had gone hawking with their papas, so there was no chance of those two rascals spoiling the younger boys' fun.

"I wonder if we'll have twins…" Jack mused, watching Luke run off ahead of his mother through the gate.

"Twins? I hope not!" Teddy said with a snort of incredulousness.

"Why not? Uncle Roxton and Aunt Deb have two sets, and your Uncle Dair and Aunt Rory have a set, too."

Teddy carefully removed a hay stalk from Jack's hair, but then she gave him a playful shove.

"Just because I have two aunts who've had twins, doesn't mean I will, or even want to. If you want twins, Sir John, *you* birth them!"

"If it meant you need not be in any pain or discomfort, I would!" Jack stated fiercely and grabbed her to him. He kissed her forehead, and then her mouth, both with an unusual tentativeness because his bottom lip had a small split and was swollen and was thus tender to the touch. "Unfortunately men are relegated to playing a bit part in that drama, and that is as a quivering jelly."

Teddy smiled up into Jack's eyes, one of which was showing signs of bruising. "But my quivering jelly…"

Suddenly, they came to a sense of their surroundings and Jack let Teddy go. It was not only because Lisa was there, it was the fact the situation yesterday still needed resolution, and a great deal had been left unsaid. The moment Jack had taken Teddy into his arms, Lisa had turned away and wandered a little way off pretending an interest in the grass to give the couple some privacy. Now they came up to her, and sensing there was unease between them, Teddy said to Lisa,

"Don't be alarmed by the bruise or the cut to Sir John's lip. And on no account are you to offer him any sympathy. He brought it all on himself."

"Theodora is quite right," Jack replied good-naturedly. He bowed to Lisa with great courteousness. "But I do owe you an apology for my ungentlemanly conduct. The argument I had with Harry should never have come to blows, and never before an audience, and most definitely not before you, Miss Crisp. Can you forgive me?"

Lisa took the hand he held out to her, and looking down saw that his knuckles were grazed. She lightly covered his hand with hers and held it a little longer saying, after a hard swallow, and bravely meeting his troubled gaze, "You did what any man who professes to be a gentleman would do in coming to the aid of a female who is being verbally assaulted. As for the fight…" She let go of his hand and glanced at Teddy before saying with a sad smile, "How could you not have reacted in the way you did, when you were goaded to it?"

"Goaded to it?" Teddy repeated, puzzled, but was not given the chance to say more when Jack jumped in, eyes bright.

"That's what I said to Uncle Roxton! And I didn't say Harry provoked me all to shift blame. I said that thinking about the fight and what started it, I'm convinced Harry made me as mad as hell fire so that it was impossible for me *not* to hit him!"

"I have thought about it, too," Lisa mused. "Over and over. All of it. And your physical response to his words was precisely what he wished for—

"And I fell into his trap! More fool me!"

"Why would Harry *want* you to hit him?" Teddy asked, puzzled. "That's nonsense. I know he can be moody and exasperating, and there are times when I do not understand him at all, but he has never been so obnoxious that Sir John has ever wanted to hit him." She looked at Jack. "You said he made an ungentlemanly remark about Lisa, and that's what provoked you to strike out at him." She then looked at Lisa.

"And it did seem to us up on the hill that the two of you were having an argument…" She looked from Lisa to Jack and back again, and put a hand to Lisa's arm and asked in a low voice, "Did he—did he make an improper advance? You were both very friendly at dinner, and perhaps he received the wrong impression altogether. He is a flirt, and you are exceedingly pretty, and—" She looked to Jack. "He did, didn't he?!"

But Jack wasn't looking at Teddy. He exchanged a look with Lisa which let her know he was well aware Harry's mood had everything to do with her, but he was not about to betray her. Instead, he threw up a hand and effected exasperation.

"I don't know precisely what was said," he lied. "I just didn't like his tone and manner. He can be intolerable at times, and struts about as only the son of a duke can! Miss Crisp ain't used to such overblown hubris, nor should she have to tolerate it. And Harry has this habit of doing the contrary thing for the simple pleasure of watching you squirm. Which is well and good for persons who know him, like me! And I've always tried to keep in mind that his affliction does play its part in his—"

"Illness cannot be used as an excuse to be rude," Lisa interrupted. "And so I have said many times to the patients at the dispensary. If they wish treatment and any sympathy at all, then they need to be mindful."

"I do not doubt you keep Warner's patients in check, Miss Crisp," Jack said with a smile, which dropped into a frown when he added, "But I should never have hit Harry. Never. I fear it brought on one of his attacks and—

"I do not think it helped, but it certainly did not bring on the attack," Lisa countered. "It is my considered opinion—and I am no expert, I can only go on instinct and observation—an attack was imminent. It was only a matter of *when*, not *if*. So you should not feel any guilt it was you who brought it on. I believe he knew it was coming. Having you hit him no doubt brought the episode forward, but it would have happened anyway. That he provoked you to hit him was shameful. That he had you hit him knowing he was experiencing the onset of a convulsion was unconscionable, but—and you know him much better than I, and so can correct me—such behavior was most uncharacteristic."

Jack nodded, and could not help a spreading smile, though he gave a little jump when his lip suddenly stung as a reminder of his foolhardiness. He agreed with everything she said because he knew, as she did, what had motivated his best friend to act in such an irrational and self-destructive manner. Teddy still did not, though she sensed there was something neither Jack nor Lisa was telling her.

"How clever you are, Lisa," she said wonderingly. "When you make such observations, it disheartens me that females with intellect cannot pursue professional lives."

"Yes. For then I might have some hope of looking after myself, rather than needing to live off the charity of relatives who do not want me, and friends who do. Which brings me to your most generous and loving offer of having me live with you, and I am so pleased you are both here now for me to speak to you about—"

"We both arrived at the notion separately. Neither of us coerced the other. And we both want this outcome very much," Teddy assured her. "Is that not so, Sir John."

"It is."

Lisa nodded, but could not stop the tears welling up.

"I cannot tell you how much your offer means to me. When I was orphaned I became an unnecessary burden on my father's family. And there is some truth in that, isn't there? They did not know me, so why would they want me? So to have friends who want me to live with them, to be part of their family, means more than I can possibly tell you. But..." She went forward and took hold of Teddy's hands, and spoke to them both, "I hope you will understand that if I do accept your most wonderful offer, it is because I made the decision to do so, freely—"

"Of course! We never meant to compel you, Miss Crisp," Jack interrupted.

Lisa smiled. "I know you did not, Sir John. It was made with the best of intentions."

"Though perhaps we should have announced it more sensitively. Or not announced it at all, until we had spoken to you first...?" He glanced at Teddy, but said to Lisa, "I do believe Miss Crisp was not the only one who was startled by our announcement last night."

Lisa found herself blushing. "I see that you do understand."

Teddy looked from Lisa to Jack and back again. She was at a loss. "You do not want to be with us?"

"I do. It's that—"

"Miss Crisp must make that decision for herself," Jack explained and felt his face grow hot when he cautioned her. "Though I do hope... I trust that you will... That when you make your decision, you will not accept anything less than what you deserve, Miss Crisp."

Teddy presumed they were referring to Warner's Dispensary.

"Would you prefer to continue working with the poor to living with us?"

"I love you with all my heart, Teddy, and I have come to love your family, too. And you can be assured, both of you," she added, holding Jack's gaze, "that when I make my decision, it will be the right one for everyone." She smiled at Teddy. "But *my* future can wait until *your* future is well and truly secured by the wedding breakfast and ball. Of more immediate concern is putting matters to rights between you, Sir John, and His Lordship. And I believe I may be able to help. Though I will need you, Sir John, to take me to him."

"I wish I could, but I cannot. The only persons who know his whereabouts are his major domo, his valet, and the lads."

"Oh? He is not at the big house? I assumed he had an apartment..."

"He does. But he's not there. And even if he were, no one gets past Gallet, Kyte, and the lads until Harry gives the word. And I do mean *no* one," Jack apologized. "Not the Duke. Not his mother. And I never have in all the years I've known him. That lot are loyal to a fault and you can threaten all you want but they won't budge. Reminds me of the devotion of his father's servants. Given the choice, they'd rather crawl over hot coals than be disloyal to their master."

"I should still like to test the assertion. Will you take me to Mr. Gallet?"

"I can, but I'm afraid it won't do you any good. After one of his attacks it takes Harry a couple of days to come to his senses, and then we don't see him until—"

"A couple of days?" Teddy was aghast. "He doesn't—We don't—have a couple of days! The wedding is the day after tomorrow."

"Then we must see what we can do to ensure he makes the ceremony," Lisa stated.

When both Teddy and Lisa stared at Jack expectantly, he threw up his hands and acquiesced. "Very well! I will take you to Gallet. But do not tell me you were not warned of the outcome."

"Then you'd best prepare the hot coals," Teddy said stridently. She had no idea what it was Lisa thought she could do, or why she would want to go near a man who had subjected her to verbal abuse, but uppermost in her mind was her wedding. And if Lisa could get Harry to the church on time, then she was prepared for her best friend to do whatever it took to get him there alongside Jack. "One way or the other, Gallet will tell Lisa Harry's whereabouts, because I am getting married, with or without you, Sir John Cavendish!"

Jack didn't like to point out to his beloved she could not marry without him being present. Instead he did as he was told, and an hour later he and Lisa were in the marble vestibule of Lord Henri-Antoine's apartment in the north wing of the big house. Michel Gallet's stony face when a footman showed them into the drawing room told him he may just have to send for a bucket of hot coals.

TWENTY-TWO

It was the first time Lisa had been inside the Duke of Roxton's palace. So far all events had been held outside, or at Crecy Hall, and had matters not deteriorated at the cricket match, she would have had dinner in the state dining room. But her interest in the interior would have to wait. What she most wanted was to know Henri-Antoine's whereabouts, though she had an idea where he might be, but only his major domo could confirm it. Jack took her through a labyrinth of spacious marble corridors, up a wide curved staircase, and along a gallery with a parquetry floor and too many paintings to count up upon its walls. Her overall impression from this glimpse inside the big house was one of unparalleled opulence. The Palladian exterior was jaw-dropping, the interior almost beyond belief.

Lord Henri-Antoine's apartment was no different. And when a footman showed them into a drawing room furnished in crimson velvet and silk they were met by a man dressed in marked contrast to his surroundings, in a dark blue suit, and who, at Warner's Dispensary, had tried to cajole Lisa out into the street and into Lord Henri-Antoine's carriage. If he was surprised to see her, he did not show it. But she was surprised to see him and said in French before Jack had a chance to demand Harry's whereabouts,

"You have a twin at Crecy Hall, do you not?"

"I do, mademoiselle. My brother Marc he is major domo to M'sieur le Duke et Mme la Duchesse d'Kinross."

"And you hold a similar position with her son. That is convenient."

"How so?"

"I wondered whose eyes Mme la Duchesse uses to keep an eye on her son, and now I know. It is through your eyes, yes?"

"I cannot confirm or deny what mademoiselle says. What I can tell you is that as His Lordship's major domo, I work for him and no one else."

"Look here, Gallet," Jack stuck in, feeling he should contribute, "Miss Crisp needs a word with His Lordship. So if you'd be good enough to take her to him, we'll get out of your hair."

Michel Gallet bowed respectfully. "I regret to say, that is not possible, sir."

"You regret nothing. You just won't do it!"

"As you say, sir," Michel Gallet replied, and stood his ground.

Lisa dug in a pocket and pulled out the map of the estate she had been given on the carriage ride between Alston and Treat. This she showed to the major domo, who looked at it in some puzzlement, a glance at Jack, who was doing likewise.

"If you will indulge me for a moment, M'sieur Gallet. I made a study of this map, so that if I went for a walk, I might be able to do so without having to resort to it, though I kept it in my pocket should I need to refer to it. And do you know what surprised me most?"

The major domo shook his head. "No, mademoiselle. I do not."

"It was the number of follies and grottos within walking distance of the main house. Do you see how many there are? Perhaps there are more farther afield, but on this map alone there are eight. The one on Swan Island is not to be trespassed, but the others I presume are open to guests and visitors to the parkland alike?"

"I presume that to be the case, mademoiselle," agreed Michel Gallet.

"I was intrigued enough to enquire of the Lady Mary's brother, Mr. Fitzstuart, if he knew why there were so many, and he told me the ones within walking distance were all built by the fifth Duke. He remembered this particularly because he and his brother and sister spent their summers here, and these little outdoor buildings were constructed—"

"All great houses have follies and grottos. Some more than others," the major domo interrupted flatly. "I assure you, they are nothing to be surprised about."

"Aren't they?" Jack stuck in, suddenly on the alert because for the first time since entering the drawing room Michel Gallet appeared uncomfortable. He looked to Lisa. "Please continue, Miss Crisp. I'd like to hear what Cousin Charles had to say, because I spent my teens here, roaming the place with His Lordship, and there isn't a folly or grotto we haven't explored." He coughed into his fist. "Including Swan Island."

"That was my second thought while studying this map—that you, as His Lordship's best friend, would also know these follies and grottos well," Lisa said. "Mr. Fitzstuart told me construction on these particular follies—the ones closest the house—all began when the fifth Duke's second son was a small boy, and were all completed within a few years."

"Your second thought? Pray what was your first?" asked Jack.

Lisa answered with her gaze on the major domo. "That M'sieur le Duc d'Roxton was a nobleman of vision and compassion, and a most loving father...."

"He was, Miss Crisp. And you got this from looking at a map?" Jack asked with surprise.

"I did. For only a loving father who was thinking of his son's needs would have such little buildings placed within the landscape so that they were within easy reach. He had them situated so that his son could leave the safety of the house and explore farther afield knowing there was always somewhere for him to go where he could feel safe, and away from prying eyes. I do not doubt these places are interesting in themselves and are visited by family, guests, and visitors to the grounds. They are somewhere to sit and reflect on the landscape, to take a breath away from the sun and the heat, the rain and the wind. But their primary function was always to provide a safe haven for the Duke's second son. Is that not so, M'sieur Gallet?"

Jack stared at Lisa with something akin to stupefaction. "By Jove, Miss Crisp! You've opened my eyes. I never gave them much thought. They were just places Harry and I would explore. We even stayed overnight in a couple of them. Do I ever feel the ninny!"

Lisa smiled. "Oh, you need not feel the fool, Sir John. You said yourself, you have lived here most of your life, and thus you have never had to give any of this much thought. I, on the contrary, who have never been here, find everything fascinating, and it all requires a great deal of thought." She held up the map. "And you don't have one of these, do you?"

"I do not. Well?!" Jack said to the major domo. "How about it? Miss Crisp is right, isn't she? So which one of these follies is your master holed up in?"

Lisa indicated the Italian folly marked on the map. "I would hazard a guess it is this one, Sir John. The temple of Vejovis. Mr. Fitzstuart tells me Vejovis is the Roman God of healing. And this is the closest folly to where the cricket match was played." She glanced at the major domo, then back at the map. "And the cartographer was good enough to mark as being part of this temple, Neptune's Grotto, which Mr. Fitzstuart tells me is a plunge pool."

"It is," Jack confirmed with a nod. "It's fed by the lake. We never swam there. Harry hated the place because one of his early treatments was being dunked in the damn thing, as if being submerged in freezing water would cure him! He said he almost drowned. Frightful business."

"Will you take me there?" Lisa asked.

"You think he's there, even though I just said—"

"I do. Although he hated the plunge pool as a boy—and who can blame him—as an adult he would be aware that cold bathing is considered beneficial in the treatment of many ills."

"Now that I come to think on it, he recently had a folly with plunge bath built in the gardens of his house in Bath. With a cascading waterfall and water pumped from the river. I thought it one of his extravagant affectations."

"Like his walking stick with its diamond-encrusted top...? Unnecessary but adding to his consequence? But have you thought that perhaps the walking stick is just as necessary as the plunge pool?" She glanced at the major domo and saw that she had all his attention.

"His walking stick?" Jack frowned. "And how is that, Miss Crisp?"

"As well as an aid to keeping him upright should he suddenly be overcome by symptoms of his affliction, he uses it to signal without needing to say one word, to his minders—his lads as he calls them—and to you, M'sieur Gallet, should he need immediate assistance. Is that not so?"

"Egad! You do know him!" Jack announced with admiration. He addressed the major domo. "So, Gallet. If you don't take Miss Crisp to His Lordship, I will."

"I must point out that there is no guarantee His Lordship will see Miss Crisp. Or that the lads will admit her."

"Let's worry about that when we get there, shall we?"

Michel Gallet stood there as a statue, and Lisa held her breath hoping upon hope that her intuition had not failed her. But what she could not know was that the major domo was of the opinion that if there was one person whom his master would see, it was this girl standing before him. The first time he had visited Warner's Dispensary with his master, he had wondered what maggot had got into His Lordship's brain to want to visit such a health hell hole, and then there she was, sitting in her corner with her writing box, surrounded by the unwashed, ragged, and diseased poor, the sunshine in an otherwise bleak existence. And it wasn't that she was arrestingly pretty, because she was, but he'd seen some rare beauties hanging off his master's arm, here in England and on the Continent. It was that Miss Crisp's beauty radiated from within, and that was the rarest form of beauty of all, as far as he was concerned. And so what seemed like minutes was only a matter of seconds before Lisa was able to breathe again when the major domo nodded his agreement.

"But I take only Miss Crisp, Sir John."

Jack walked a few paces away from the major domo, signaling for Lisa to follow. And when she was standing before him, he said in a low voice, "If you go to the folly without my protection, and it is discovered that you went there alone, I cannot shield you from gossip—or from Harry. I say that with the deepest respect for you, and him."

"I know you do. And I am deeply touched by your concern for my welfare, but you must know—you of all people, as Henri-Antoine's best friend—you must know our feelings for each other."

"I do now," he said with a huff of laughter, color in his cheeks, gingerly touching the cut to his lip. "What I do not know is what the future holds for either of you. What I wish for may not be what eventuates, because Harry—"

"—is the Duke of Roxton's brother, and the son of a duke." Lisa smiled. "Do not concern yourself, Sir John. I may be young, and while I am not hard-hearted I am hard-headed. I know that to follow my heart, there will be consequences, and I accept that."

"All the same, Teddy and I would never abandon you. Remember that."

Lisa impulsively kissed his cheek. "Thank you. You are the kindest of men and I see why Teddy loves you. Now you must return to her, but please say nothing of this, yet. If I am to lose her good opinion, then let it be after you are married."

"Very well," Jack agreed, adding cryptically under his breath, "It's not a cliff, but an Italian folly will do just as nicely."

"I TOLD YOU. TOMORROW! GO AWAY!"

It was the sudden brightness in an otherwise darkened room that had him awake. In his half awake, half asleep state he was vaguely aware of the comings and goings on the floor below, and it gave him an odd sense of comfort. The lads brought food and clean drinking water, firewood to stoke the furnace, cleaned the place up, and emptied what needed to be emptied. And when they weren't moving about, Kyte came and went, taking away his clothing and replacing it with a clean set, which was just as well because he'd been left with only the shirt on his back. But as he was curled up in bed, he didn't need anything else...

But for all the comings and goings below him, no one trespassed into this room he used as a bedchamber. The folly was a rotunda on two levels, and there were windows all the way around, with a set of double doors that led out onto a narrow balcony. There were views into the forest from some windows and others gave a view out across the manicured gardens. His big four-poster bed was positioned in the center under the domed roof. All the windows had the curtains drawn to darken the room, but someone had uncovered one window and also pulled up the sash to let in fresh air.

Unless there had been a death in the family, he could think of no other reason for his servants' disobedience in bothering him. And it was this alarming thought that prompted him to roll onto his back. But he did not turn his head on the pillow to the undraped window, the light was too intense, but blinked up at the domed ceiling with its painting of a night sky full of twinkling stars. He lifted a hand mere inches off the coverlet, as signal the intruder had his permission to speak.

When the silence stretched, Henri-Antoine reluctantly squinted into the light, which made him wince, because of the bruising around his left eye. He was sure he must be running a fever. There in silhouette was a woman. He blinked. Surely he was hallucinating, but perhaps the apparition would at least be reasonable.

"The light hurts... Pull the curtain... Better. Now go."

He dragged the bedsheet up over his head, turned his back, and closed his eyes.

Lisa came over to the bed.

"I will wait downstairs. But I am not going away."

There was a flurry of activity under the bedsheet and then a hand was thrust out.

"No! Don't!"

"Don't wait downstairs, or don't go away?"

"Don't—don't go away..." The hand patted the coverlet. "Stay."

She sat on the edge of the mattress and took hold of his hand. She was surprised at how cold he was to the touch. Then again, there was no fireplace, and with the sun shut out, there was nothing to warm the room. It was a gloriously sunny day outside, almost too hot, but this folly was back in amongst the shrubbery, on the edge of a coppice, and so received little direct sun.

She looked about for another coverlet, but could not see one by the bed. So she went to get up to search, but his fingers tightened about hers.

"Stay."

"I intend to. But you're cold and you need more covering. There might be something downstairs—"

"No," came the muffled response. He slowly lowered the bed sheet to his chin and squinted across at her. "I don't need... I just need... I just need—you, and to sleep."

She pressed her lips together, overcome by his admission, and nodded, giving his hand a squeeze before letting it go. It disappeared under the sheet and he turned on his side and resettled. Without another thought, she got up onto the bed and lay down on top of the coverlet beside him. She shifted sideways until she was pressed up against his back, plumped the pillow and lay back down again. And with a hand to his shoulder, her face at his neck, and her body curled around his, which was wrapped head to toe in the bedsheet, she closed her eyes. She lay there for a long while, content and happy, before drifting off into a deep sleep.

When she woke it was several hours later. If he had moved at all, he had not disturbed her. As she had hardly slept the night before, she was not surprised she'd had no difficulty falling asleep beside him. He was still wrapped in the bedsheet, but it was no longer up around his head. He had an arm out, on top of the coverlet, and his shoulder length black hair fell across his pillow in messy disarray. She rose up on an elbow to take a peek to see if he was still sleeping and was surprised, not by the dark stubble to his chin and jaw line, but the bruising to his eye, and the cut to his lip, which was not as swollen as she expected.

She lay back down and shivered, realizing she was now cold, and that it was her fault for leaving the window ajar. She went to get up to close it, when her movement woke him.

"Get under the covers," he said drowsily. "Keep us both warm." When she hesitated that little bit too long, he woke enough to turn his head and say, "I am in no fit state to seduce you. I am weak... and... when we do make love, I want—I want to be at my best—for you... I should warn you... I'm only wearing a shirt... And you'll find this out soon enough: I have bony knees and hard, hairy legs."

Lisa smiled and blushed, but before removing her half boots she quickly went over and closed the window. In her stockings she rearranged the bed linen, so she could freely slip under the bed sheet and coverlet. And with his body no longer trapped by the bedsheet, she was acutely aware of the shape of him. She gingerly pressed herself along his curved length and snuggled in, and soon their legs were comfortably entangled.

He seemed to have drifted off to sleep again, for he was quiet a very long time, and then he said, "I must rest, or the headache lingers."

"Then rest."

"You won't go away…?"

"I won't."

"It's not—It's not Jack's big day, is it?"

"No. The wedding is the day after tomorrow."

"I thought…" He sighed. "Good. I don't want to miss it."

"He does not want you to miss it either."

"He forgives me?"

"He does."

"He is a dear man."

"He is. As are you."

"I am not," Henri-Antoine grumbled. He pulled her arm further across his body, to bring her closer, and to find anchorage. "I am a scoundrel and an arrogant wantwit… I'm still furious with you."

Lisa stifled a smile into his back, fearing she might giggle. But she could not hide the laughter in her voice.

"Yes, I saw how furious you were with me when you goaded Jack into striking you."

"You don't care, do you?"

"That you provoked Jack to hit you and then you hit him back? I most certainly do!"

"Not that, *witch*. You don't care I'm furious with you."

"Not a drop."

"I tried to warn you."

Lisa set her cheek between his shoulder blades.

"You did. Thank you."

There was a protracted silence before he said, "I'm sorry—sorry for everything… For what I said… I didn't mean any of it. It was despicable… I'm despicable… Staying with me will be your ruin."

"I am already ruined, my lord."

At that pronouncement, he unsettled them both by rolling over to face her and demanded she explain herself. Her response was to smile across at him and wonder how it was possible that even when he was unshaven and disheveled, with one black eye and a thunderous frown, he was still the most handsome man she knew. He might be overbearing, arrogant, uncompromising, and oft times inscrutable, but as she had discovered he was generous, compassionate, loyal, and loving, and all in all, the most complex person she had ever met, and she loved him. She was very sure she had fallen in love with him almost from their first meeting. She believed in fate, and had told him so. She also believed in being truthful, so she came right out and said it, and why not? She was here with him. She had agreed to be his mistress, and she could not wait for them to share a house, and a bed.

"Because I love you, Henri-Antoine."

He closed his eyes and turned his head on the pillow to stare unseeing at the stars sprinkling the ceiling, enjoying the few precious seconds to bathe in her declaration. And he found he was suddenly heady, as he had been when he had kissed her under the oak tree. He was so overcome with happiness, he grinned. But his grin made her frown and sit up on an elbow to stare down at him.

"I do beg your pardon if I have said something that makes you grin like a wantwit," she retaliated with a pout, feigning offence. "If this is how His Lordship responds to a declaration of love, then perhaps Jack did not hit you hard enough to knock the sense into you, as I had hoped!"

He chuckled, and reverted to his first language and said in French, "But *you* are the wantwit—*my* beautiful wantwit. You confess to loving a man who contrives to have his best friend hit him—to prove to you he is the last man with whom you should spend your life. You do this when he is as weak as a puppy and as woolly-headed as a lamb, thus he cannot respond as you deserve... His greatest wish is to show you he desires you, body and soul... And you wonder why I am smiling like a court fool?"

"If you expect me to feel sorry for your predicament—"

"Oh no! I feel sorry for yours!"

She gasped, and then laughed with him. And when she smiled down into his eyes he gently took her face between his long fingers, to draw her closer, and kissed her tenderly.

"You have made me very happy, Miss Lisa Crisp."

"And that makes me happy."

They snuggled in again, this time with his arm around her and her head on his chest, content to remain still and silent, and for long enough that they drifted off into a state between sleeping and waking. When he spoke, Lisa wondered if they had been asleep at all.

"I want to stay here, with you, forever."

"We would then become an entry in one of those guide books about grand estates—"

"Guide books? About grand estates? Are there such things?"

"How else are ordinary persons to know about how their betters live?"

"I had no idea."

"That's because you live inside one—"

"Inside a guide book?"

"Yes."

"Why would we feature in such a compelling read?"

"Because if we stayed here forever we would eventually die—"

"How morbid you are."

"You did say forever."

"I did."

"And so if we did stay here forever our skeletons would eventually be discovered, lying together as we are now. And such a discovery would be worthy of an entry in any guidebook. Possibly as a cautionary tale about lovers—or in our case, soon to be lovers—that it is never wise to remain in bed forever—"

"Not wise? Hang that! Who wants to be wise when I can be in bed with you?"

Lisa sighed and smiled and kissed his chest. She suddenly became pensive. Perhaps it was mention of death and dying. She wanted to know about his father. It was something he had said, and then done, when she had looked after him at Lord Westby's townhouse. It had remained unspoken between them but she wondered if now he might talk to her about it, and about his father, the illustrious fifth Duke.

"When you were ill as a child, was it your father who tended to you, because at Lord Westby's you—"

"Yes. I spent much of my boyhood recovering on a chaise longue in my father's libraries—"

"Libraries?"

"Here. London. Paris. Mostly here."

"And he would stroke your hair…"

"No matter what he was doing, he would leave it all to sit with me after one of my attacks… He'd recount stories of his youth… His voice soothed me… I still hear it in my head… He had this way of speaking —It was compelling. He was compelling. And his voice… Hard to describe, but if you'd heard it you'd never forget it…"

"Like your voice."

"Mine? Unforgettable?"

"No—"

"No? But you just said—"

"Your voice is-is—glorious."

He grinned. "Glorious?"

"You know it is! And I told you once before. Don't you remember? When you visited at Gerrard Street and gave me my most wondrous writing box. I said I could listen to you talk on and on in whatever language you chose." She smiled cheekily. "And Becky agrees with me. In fact she was the first to mention the hot chocolate—"

"Hot chocolate?"

"Your voice. That's what it sounds like. Your voice sounds like hot chocolate tastes: Smooth and delicious and-and just a tiny bit sinful."

"Hot chocolate? Sinful?"

He chuckled deep in his throat and then pulled the pillow over his face and held it there. Lisa wondered what was the matter until she felt his whole body shaking, and knew he was shaking with laughter. She pulled the pillow away and he blinked up at her and she glared down at him, blushing.

"I was not exaggerating," she said earnestly. "Or-or trying to-to flatter you."

"Heaven forbid!" He winced at the pain behind his eyes and pulled the pillow out of her fingers, but before putting it back behind his head said, "I was laughing with happiness, *witch*. You make me happy. Stop it!"

She smiled, and they both settled and were silent. He surprised her by confessing,

"When you stroked my hair at Westby's I thought... For one blinding moment I believed it was my father—"

"*Ne vous arrêtez pas, mon cher papa. Dites m'en plus.*"

"Is that what I said: 'Do not stop, dearest papa. Tell me more.'?"

"You did, and now I understand why."

"I-I blubbered like an infant!"

"Because you realized I was not him. Sentiment is nothing of which to be ashamed. You loved your father immeasurably. It is only natural you still mourn him... And you were young when he died, were you not?"

"He became ill just after my ninth birthday. I was twelve when he died. I thought—as a boy I thought—I thought I had infected him with my illness."

"Oh no! I hope your mother, your brother, his physicians, assured you that was not so."

"I told no one... But why not think it? Many physicians—who my parents consulted about my illness, my father's personal physician, in fact—all warned that the falling sickness is contagious—"

"Rot! If that were the case your whole family, and all your servants, would have caught it and suffer from it. And no one else in your family has it, do they?"

"No—"

"I rest my case! Oh, except your mother's father. But you did not catch it from him because he was dead well before you were born."

"Ah, but until it is disproved, there are physicians who will continue to believe we are infectious and demand our removal from society."

"And there are also physicians who think it is a manifestation of evil, a sign of madness. I know, because Dr. Warner told me in one of his morning lectures at the breakfast table. He is vehemently opposed to the postulation that the falling sickness is contagious or that it is a sign of evil—"

"Which is why I will fund his research, and his anatomy school."

"—but he does not discount the theory that when in the throes of a seizure, the sufferer is having a moment of madness."

"That could well be true. I do not know. I have no recollection." He turned his head on the pillow and met Lisa's gaze. "And because I do not know, who's to say that inside my head there isn't a monster—"

"I won't allow you to believe that!" Lisa said fiercely, and kissed him to stop his words. She smiled when he winced. "Forgive me. I forgot about your split lip. But as you brought that on yourself, I have little sympathy. But for the boy, yes, I feel for him, deeply. The death of a parent, particularly one so loved as your father was loved, is a most harrowing experience. Though my own father's passing was a blessing in disguise. It may have left me an orphan but I no longer had to put up with his drunkenness. I preferred the poorhouse to living with him."

"I always wondered," Henri-Antoine mused, only half in jest, "if being sent to a poorhouse was like me being sent to Eton…"

"A school for the sons of the nobility like a-a poorhouse?" Lisa was aghast. "If you think that, then you do live in a fairy tale! You have no idea what life is like in a poorhouse."

"No. I don't. But you, my sweet girl, have no idea about life at Eton. Brutal place. Full of bullies. Boys locked up together in such places are little monsters… For this boy who thought himself a monster, I was scared witless. Never mind I was shadowed by a physician; he was bullied too. If not for Jack, I'd not have survived. I lasted a few months, then my father rescued me. The experiment I could be like other boys my age was a miserable failure."

"I cannot imagine you were ever like other boys, and I am not referring to your illness. Just as you are not like other men, particularly not those your equal. What other nobleman thinks about poorhouses, and dispensaries for the poor, and how best to advance medical science, or wholly sponsors a foundation that supports this work, and offers scholarships to poor but brilliant students—"

"*The worth of a great inheritance is measured not by how it is kept, but in how it is spent.* Words of wisdom my father left me in a letter the day I came into my inheritance on my twenty-first birthday... I have a thudding headache. I must sleep now. While I do, reflect on whether you wish to spend your life with a man who will forever be debilitated. When I wake and you are gone, I will accept your decision. I won't seek out Jack and punch his nose. If you stay—there will be no turning back, for either of us."

TWENTY-THREE

When he came downstairs, it was late afternoon. He found the little table by one of the windows set for dinner. The French doors were wide. Just beyond the doors, where the path split left and right, the lads were seated on stools in the shade, playing at cards. He looked back at the table. It had two place settings. It gave him hope Lisa had decided to stay. But she was not at the folly, which had only this room and the one above, so nowhere for her to hide, if indeed she was being playful with him. There was only one other place she could be, and that the lads had positioned themselves at the fork in the path, to stop trespassers, gave him the answer.

He pulled the hair out of his eyes and went outside in his shirt and bare legs. The lads continued on with their card game as if he were not there. They were, after all, shadows, and he rarely needed to interact with them. Yet this time he came straight up to them, which had them instantly on their feet. But he gestured for them to sit and enquired, "You've kept the furnace stoked?"

"We have, my lord. Should've taken the chill off by now."

Henri-Antoine nodded and lingered. For the first time in his life he felt awkward and at a loss to know what to say to his lads, they who had been everywhere with him and so knew his habits intimately. None of that had bothered him in the past. It did now, because of Lisa. So it was a relief when one of them said levelly, "Mr. Gallet will be here with supper soon. But we were to tell Your Lordship that if we thought there was time, to send you to the grotto."

"And is there time?"

The lads looked at one another and then looked at Henri-Antoine and nodded. It was only when he went off down the path that wound its way through the coppice to Neptune's Grotto that they dared to grin at his back. They returned to their card game.

HE SAW HER DISCARDED CLOTHING BEFORE HE SAW HER. EACH garment was neatly folded and the pile placed at the base of the white marble statue of a sea nymph. It was one of Neptune's daughters, seated at the edge of the plunge pool with a jug pouring water forth from its spout and into the pool. Lisa was partially hidden from view by this statue, submerged up to her chin, one hand holding onto the stone ledge. He wasn't sure if modesty had sent her into hiding, or if she was playing hide-and-go-seek. Or indeed if she realized he had seen her. He suspected not. And if she had been any of the females he had bedded, he'd have stripped off and jumped right in, without a second thought.

He wondered how much, if any, male anatomy she had managed to glimpse while at Warner's Dispensary. He knew that in any given medical situation she would not have been prudish or squeamish. But that was with patients. And then he recalled that the lads said they were to send him to the grotto. So she was expecting him, and here she was in the pool naked. So there was only one course of action for him to take.

He stepped up onto the stone ledge where three steps descended into the water, wriggled his bare toes, and then pulled his white shirt up over his head, and dropped it beside her clothes. Naked, he mentally counted to five, so that should she blink in surprise she still could not help but see him in all his glory, even if now her eyes were shut tight on such a sight as her first full-frontal male nude. At least her response had not been to scream, laugh, or giggle. He hoped her eyes were wide open. That what she was doing was taking a good look at him from messy head of hair right down to his wriggling toes, and that she lingered on everything in between, most particularly on everything in between. He was arrogant enough to hope his was the first naked male body she had seen, and conceited enough to know he had an admirable physique. Previous lovers had fed his vanity, but as a member of Burke's he'd seen enough of his fellow members, in every sense of the word, to be comfortable in his own skin. Yet knowing Lisa was watching him, his past loves, Burke's, and his conceit became insignificant; she was all that mattered.

And just as he was about to step down into the water, she slowly waded out from behind the statue and came towards him. And when she was in front of him, she stood on the bottom step and rose up. The water lapped at her navel, and the long wet strands of her thigh-length hair floated around her and were plastered to her curvaceous loveliness like long tendrils of seaweed, providing the only tantalizing covering to her nakedness. She was the living personification of Botticelli's Venus, and her beauty left him speechless. And when she smiled shyly up at him and put out her hand in invitation, he did not hesitate to join her.

THE LADS REMAINED VIGILANT DURING THE REST OF THAT DAY and the next, while Lisa and Henri-Antoine divided their time between the folly and the pool, making certain the couple's time together remained uninterrupted by others. And there were others who tried to encroach. On several occasions guests from the big house, either on foot or on horseback, were drawn to this section of the grounds by the smoke from the furnace's chimney. It was as if the white gray plume rising up into the blue of the sky beckoned all comers, a signal of invitation, much like the warmth of a fireplace fire on a chilly night.

Those guests hoping to visit the Temple of Vejovis rotunda, to see the view from the first floor, or to watch for themselves how the furnace heated the water of the pool to bathing temperature, were adamant they had permission from the Duke himself to go wherever they pleased. And what pleased them was to see the inside of this particular folly, and to be permitted to visit Neptune's Grotto. One couple even pleaded it was a medical necessity that they take a dip in the pool's warmed waters. The lake water was too cold, despite it being a hot summer's day and the fact every man and his dog were taking a dip down by the boathouse. The couple would not take no for an answer. It was suggested most politely that they retire to the big house and find a bath for the purpose. They departed most reluctantly and with the threat that words would be said to His Grace.

And what about an urgent need to use the necessary house? There was a privy just beyond the folly, between it and the pool, secluded in the shrubbery. It was one of many little wooden necessary rooms placed throughout the estate for the convenience of guests and family alike. Again, the lads could not be persuaded, even going so far as to suggest any one of the thousands of trees on the estate as an excellent substitute for the privy, where the gentleman could find instant relief. But not here, not these trees, and not this privy.

The lads refused to be moved by any and all pleas, threats of prosecution, and even one threat of violence. Which was ludicrous, given their height and width, and the size of the muscles in their forearms and calves. All four looked to have the strength to lift a sedan chair with occupant, on their own, and without any effort whatsoever.

And then along came a party of young gentlemen and ladies on horseback who could not be persuaded to take their leave. They tethered their mounts, adamant they would see the folly, and they would take a look at Neptune's Grotto, even if only to dip a finger in its warm waters. And when they were politely but firmly warned off, they protested by strutting about in front of the lads evoking ancient ancestors, their lineage, and connections to every powerfully political personage in the kingdom. The lads said not a word, and remained unmoved.

And while the lads were being taunted, and thus distracted by this noble group, three of their number ducked around to the other side of the folly, through the shrubbery behind the privy. And by keeping low and moving by stealth, they progressed through the coppice, traversed a slope that took them below the level of the folly, to emerge unscathed and upright on a path that led straight to the entrance of the furnace, which was directly under the pool.

Here the three congratulated each other on their success at getting past Henri-Antoine's monoliths, and finding themselves exactly where they hoped to be.

"Hear that?!" Bully Knatchbull hissed. "I knew it! Someone is splashing about in that pool!"

There was indeed the sounds of water being splashed, and laughter, followed by female squeals, more laughter and more splashing.

"Not someone, Bully. Harry. It's Harry with someone," Seb Westby replied with a smug sneer. "Can't be anyone else. He doesn't go anywhere without those bears up behind him."

"Was the same when we were abroad," Bully confirmed. "But over there he said they were for our protection, from foreign types and the like. And come to think on it, they did have their uses. There were one or two times when they picked him up and carried him off home. Jack said Harry was drunk. That happened again in Rome... Not good with his liquor, is he—Harry, that is, not Jack. But here...Why does Harry need those bears at Treat? Not as if an Englishman is likely to attack him, is it?" He gave a snort. "Oh, except Jack! Hahaha—"

"Forget about his bloody bears, and concentrate on the matter in hand, Bully!"

"I don't see why he wouldn't want his Batoni Brotherhood to share in the fun of a splash in that pool. Seems only fair on a hot day."

"We told you why, Randal," his sister Violet answered, just as exasperated as Westby, and a roll of her eyes in his direction. "He's with a female. And after what we witnessed at the cricket match, we all know her name—"

"—and yours! He called you a bitch, Vi," Westby drawled with a raise of his eyebrows. "That's worse than had he called you a whore... He either detests you more than I thought, or his feelings for the pauper are stronger than I first supposed—"

"What you think ain't relevant, Seb! Harry can't go around calling m'sister that and get away with it. And neither can you—

"I didn't. He did."

"Which is why we're here, Randal," Violet explained. She pouted and batted doleful eyes at her brother, that had Westby rolling his at her performance, and said, "You want him to apologise for what he said to me, don't you? He should pay, shouldn't he? You can't let him get away with calling me such a horrid name."

"Of course he can't, Vi. But—Hang it! I don't like spying on a fellow when he's busy with a female. Poor form. I'd rather march straight up to him and strike him with my glove and demand satisfaction—"

"This is the 80s, Bully. Not the bloody 40s!" Westby argued. "Harry may look effete with his flowery clothes and his diamond-headed sticks and his bloody bears, but he'd kill you in a duel. Look at what he did to Jack's face with his fists! Now unless you want to put up your fists—"

"And ruin this fine nose?" Bully said with a snort. "Not on my life!" When his sister gasped at his cowardice he added darkly, "Still. He's got to pay for what he said."

"So we'll do this my way," Westby ordered. "We get eye-to-eye proof that the female he's with is the poor orphan, and then you leave the rest to me." He looked at Violet. "I promise you that by the end of the ball, you'll have your revenge, on him, and her, and so will I."

"You mean you'll have him apologize to Vi for what he said, don't you, Seb?" Bully asked, made nervous by the word *revenge*, which he did not like at all. "And I don't want any harm to come to that girl. She looks a nice sort, even if you say she-she is a-a whore."

"She is a whore, Randal."

"But you haven't proof, Vi," Bully argued.

"Your sister was at school with the orphan. The girl is poorer than dirt. If she had any brains, which we're told she does, then why wouldn't she make the most of this visit. It's her one and only chance to bag herself a fat-pursed lover."

"And they don't come much fatter than Harry's—"

"Eh? How do you know that, Vi?" Bully demanded, flushing. "Seb and I might know that because, well, we were on the Grand Tour with him, and fellows have to share all manner of lodgings and the like—"

"It was a figure of speech, you ninny!" Seb hissed. "And if we take a look—"

"Ah! Yes," Bully muttered, abashed.

"—over that wall," Seb continued, "I'll wager the pauper is discovering for herself the size of Harry's fortune."

"I want your word no harm will come to her," Bully demanded. "I won't go along with any of this, or look over that wall, if you intend to cause her a mischief—"

"She won't come to any more harm than she's already in. My word on it," assured Westby. "But Harry will get what's coming to him."

"Good. That's fair."

"Then it's settled. Can we get on with it before we're found out, or they're gone from here?" When Bully nodded, Seb turned to Violet. "You wanted to lead the way, so lead the way—"

"You're not looking over that wall!" Bully warned his sister.

"You are such a wet goose, Randal Knatchbull," Violet complained, and poked her tongue out at him. And with a hand to her straw hat, she ducked and went through the shrubbery, to climb the slope on the other side of the pool.

They emerged from the foliage directly behind a low privacy wall that screened bathers from the path used by servants bringing firewood to stoke the furnace. But as they were standing right up against the wall, it was an easy thing to peer over it and into the pool. All three looked at one another, listened for any sounds coming from the other side of the wall, agreed in low whispered conversation that they thought it odd that it had suddenly gone quiet and wondered if they should wait a bit longer until the bathers were otherwise occupied. To which Westby theorized with a lewd smirk that quite possibly they were.

That settled the matter. He and Bully immediately popped their heads up over the wall, and as they did not immediately pop them down again, Violet seized the opportunity to also take a peek. Her quick intake of breath, which sounded as if she were choking, went unheard and thus unheeded.

"My God—it's Pompeii all over again," Bully muttered under his breath.

"Lost your way?" drawled a voice at their backs.

Startled, all three spun about and found themselves being scrutinized by none other than their host, His Grace the most Noble Duke of Roxton.

THE DUKE WATCHED THE THREE TRESPASSERS GO ON UP THE path towards the folly, under escort of one of his brother's minders, an uneasy feeling in the pit of his stomach.

While all three had attempted to offer him muddled explanations for their trespass, there was nothing they could say in defence of their prurient curiosity in taking a peek over the wall into Neptune's Grotto, and they made no attempt to do so. And as the Duke did not mention it, it was as if it had never happened. He hoped his displeasure, and the fact Seb Westby's father had just arrived at the estate, would be enough to keep their mouths shut. The Duke of Oborne held the purse strings to his son's living and thus had great sway over him. One word from Roxton in Oborne's ear, and the threat of Seb Westby's debts not being paid might be enough to keep the young man's mouth shut.

But there was already too much wild speculation and innuendo being exchanged behind fluttering fans and over communal snuffboxes about what was behind the two incidents at the cricket match involving his brother. If any of it escaped the confines of the estate and found its way into the London scandal sheets, it would cause the sort of disgrace he abhorred. He'd spent the past sixteen years keeping his family's noble name above common gossip and out of the newssheets, and he wasn't about to let it be dragged down into the morass by a girl whose family was one generation removed from servitude.

Henri-Antoine fronting up to the chapel to stand beside Jack for the ceremony would do much to douse the flames that there was any discord between the two best friends. That they had come to blows could be dismissed as a piece of tomfoolery between two young men who had momentarily lost their heads and used their fists to settle an argument. At least no one knew for certain what had started the fight. But that incident did not greatly concern the Duke, because he knew Harry and Jack's friendship would endure beyond a few bruises.

But the other incident, the one involving the girl... The one where she and his brother had quarreled in full view of the world, and thus given every indication there was something between them, something unwelcome and unsavory—that incident greatly concerned him. What was he to do about it? What was he to do about her? And most importantly, what was he to do about his brother?

He knew Henri-Antoine to be no saint. There were plenty of

women of easy virtue who had come and gone in his life. He was known to frequent high class brothels, had indulged in all manner of vice while abroad, and was a member of Burke's, which appalled him. It was their father's murky past come back to haunt him as far as he was concerned. The fifth Duke's history had been so sordid it had stuck to him his entire life, no matter he was a devoted husband and father for his final thirty years. It was not the sort of reputation he wanted forever attached to his brother, nor associated with his family's name. He blamed himself for giving Henri-Antoine greater latitude to indulge himself, in every possible way, and all because of his illness. Had he been in full health, he would never have hesitated in demanding he curb his proclivities. But, in his brother's defence, he had kept his carnal habits buried so deep no one of his acquaintance, and most particularly not the newssheets, had ever had cause to call him to account for sullying his good name.

And now this! He would never have predicted his brother would lose his head over this girl, this Lisa Crisp of no family, no wealth, and no connections. He'd discovered that her wastrel father had drunk himself to death, that she had spent time in a poorhouse, and those relatives who owned to a connection were all in trade. If all this wasn't enough to cement her lowly background, of which there was little to be proud, there was the far more degrading connection—and the one that concerned him the most—that her aunt had been his mother's personal maid.

How could his brother have stooped to setting his carnal sights on a girl connected by blood to a personal maid employed by his own family? Henri-Antoine had crossed an unacceptable line, a line that was never to be crossed between master and servant. And from what he'd been told, his brother and this girl had gone far beyond mere flirtation. They were now shut away in his folly, showing a total disregard for him and his family, and their guests. And in so doing they were thumbing their nose at him—a preeminent peer of the realm, and head of the family—and his authority—here, where his word was law.

Something had to be done, and it had to be done at once

Precisely what he intended to do, he was not exactly certain. Buy her off and send her packing abroad came to mind, but that could wait until after the ball. Paramount was getting Jack and Teddy married with the least fuss, and no scandal. So the first order of business was having the girl returned to the Gatehouse Lodge this afternoon and under the pretext she had spent the past day and night at Treat. Already he had seeded the rumour she had taken ill and been isolated within the house for fear of spreading contagion, should it prove a fever. His physician and a servant were in on the ploy.

Once the girl was back at the lodge, his brother could do his duty by Jack as his best man. From what he'd been told by his brother's major domo, Henri-Antoine had made an excellent recovery from his seizure, and with only minor bruising and a cut to his lip from the fight, there was no excuse why he should not spend the evening with the younger gentlemen in preparation for the wedding tomorrow.

So with all this in mind, he turned to Michel Gallet, who had accompanied him to this secluded spot for the express purpose of keeping him informed of latest developments within the folly, and handed him a folded sheet of paper affixed with his ducal seal.

"Give this to him at once. And I don't care if you have to interrupt them. This must be done today. Best if she's removed under cover of darkness."

"If Your Grace insists."

"You foresee a problem? If so, I can send men to assist you."

"That won't be necessary, Your Grace. But…"

The Duke put up his brows and waited.

Michel Gallet met the Duke's unusual green eyes.

"She—Miss Crisp—she is not like all the others."

"She is not. The others knew their place. She does not because she has no place, and she certainly has no place being here. If there is nothing further—"

"There is, Your Grace." When the Duke said nothing but continued to stare at him, the major domo swallowed before speaking. "I have been in the employ of His Lordship for five years and thus I feel I have a measure of the man—"

"Gallet, Lord Henri-Antoine has been my brother for twenty-five years, not five. Whatever you feel you need to share with me, believe me, it is not needed or wanted. I appreciate your loyalty to him but—"

"Forgive the interruption, Your Grace, but my loyalty has and always has been to the family, your family, and thus to you both. And I would be doing you a disservice, as much as His Lordship, if I did not advise that to forcibly separate Miss Crisp from His Lordship will, in all probability, lead to an irreparable estrangement between you and His Lordship."

"Don't be absurd! Brothers don't fall out over a sly wench from the gutter!"

Michel Gallet straightened. "I beg your pardon, Your Grace, but I would advise you not to believe the common gossip being spread about Miss Crisp from malicious sources."

The Duke took a step toward the major domo, gloved hand clenched about his riding crop, and glowered down at him. "You—you *dare* to advise—*me* about-about this girl?"

"I do, Your Grace. Miss Crisp is poor, that is not in dispute. But she is, in my opinion, an estimable young woman—"

"Estimable? *Estimable?* Are you drunk or mad, Gallet? How can you defend her after what's—" The Duke thrust his crop in the direction of Neptune's Grotto. "—after what's been going on over there? Estimable young females do not behave the way she's behaving! Good God! Her behavior is-is—deplorable. The worst type of whore knows her place better than that trollop!"

"So it must seem to anyone who does not know Miss Crisp."

The Duke let his hand holding the crop fall back to his side. "And you know her, do you?"

"Better than those who seek to discredit her character—"

"Ye Gods! And you are of the opinion she has a character worth discrediting?" The Duke huffed his skepticism. His cheeks had gained color, finding this topic embarrassing in the extreme. "She should have thought about her character before she embarked on this quest to entrap my brother—"

"She did nothing of the sort!" Michel Gallet retorted, and immediately felt his face grow hot at his social lapse. "Pardon, Your Grace. But that is far from the case."

"Are you certain you haven't fallen victim to a beautiful face?"

"No, Your Grace," the major domo replied. "Miss Crisp is a beauty but she is also a beautiful person."

The Duke's reaction was to laugh but as the major domo appeared serious he resisted the urge. "Her actions would suggest otherwise."

"Her actions are those of a young woman in love. As such the consequences are irrelevant."

"What a romantic you are, Gallet!"

"I beg to differ, Your Grace," Michel Gallet replied and bowed respectfully. "My twin is the romantic. I merely offer you my observations as one who has come to know Miss Crisp, and who knows His Lordship intimately."

"Do you indeed, Gallet?"

"I do, Your Grace."

The Duke threw up a hand and capitulated. There was no harm in asking.

"What would you advise?"

The major domo did not hesitate in his response.

"That you allow me to handle this state of affairs. I will ensure Miss

Crisp is returned to the Gatehouse Lodge, and that His Lordship returns to his apartment, all in good time for the ceremony tomorrow."

"And if I do not let you handle it?"

"Then I am afraid, Your Grace, that there will follow an estrangement between you and His Lordship."

Michel Gallet held out the sealed note the Duke had given him for his master. Roxton looked at it but did not take it immediately. And when he finally did, and thrust it back in his pocket, the major domo dared to breathe a small sigh.

"So tell me, Gallet. Tell me the reason my brother and I would have a falling out over this girl from Soho."

Michel Gallet held the Duke's gaze and his voice was steady and clear.

"Because Lord Henri-Antoine is deeply in love with her."

TWENTY-FOUR

THEY LAY IN BED, BATHED IN CANDLELIGHT. STILL AND SILENT, and content to gaze at each other from opposite ends of the mattress. Lisa leaned against the headboard, hair tumbled about her bare shoulders, while Henri-Antoine was propped on an elbow by the bedpost. Between them was a jumble of bedlinen and pillows. He had hold of her bare foot and she was fiddling with a handful of her long hair, curling strands around her finger. Words were unnecessary. Everything that needed to be said or asked had been communicated in other, more vital ways. All doubt and hesitancy had evaporated, and so too had apprehension. They were completely at their ease and wildly happy, and that left them a little in awe of what had just occurred. Yet, he still felt the need to ask, given the occasion.

He gently pulled her toe. "Are you—happy?"

She nodded and beamed, adding for good measure, "Very."

And yet, while he was relieved and overjoyed by her response he was soon frowning and suddenly awkward. "I've never asked before... That was thoughtless and arrogant..."

"Oh? I imagine it was unnecessary for you to do so with your previous lovers. Was I supposed to tell you?"

"Tell me?" His top lip twitched. He kissed the bridge of her foot. "But you did, my darling, in the best way possible. And you have every time. It was just that this was—in the strictest sense of the phrase—our first time making love. And his first time with you..."

She regarded him curiously. "I hope he wasn't disappointed. You did make him wait."

He let go of her foot and sat up, and pulled the hair out of his eyes. "Disa—*disappointed?* How could you think that? He thinks you're the most marvelous, the most divine, creature he has ever had the privilege to pleasure. You've certainly ruined him—and me—for anyone else."

"Good!" She sat up off the headboard and crawled across the covers to his end of the bed to kiss him. Her blue eyes twinkled and she put her arms around his neck. "Because now that you have shown me all the delicious ingredients that go into making a most wondrous cake, I find that I enjoy baking with you very much. And I certainly do not want you—or him—making a cake with anyone else ever again!"

He tenderly brushed the hair out of her eyes. "Cake?"

She told him.

His laughter could be heard downstairs.

Michel Gallet didn't have the heart to interrupt, but he knew that he must.

THE SUN WAS NOT YET UP WHEN LISA ALIGHTED FROM THE Duchess of Roxton's carriage and was ushered into the Gatehouse Lodge by a bleary-eyed maid, who was resetting the fires. She tip-toed up the staircase and was on the landing when the Lady Mary appeared in her dressing gown, holding a taper. She took one sweeping look at Lisa and while her expression did not change Lisa became acutely aware that her attitude most certainly had. Gone was the warmth in her voice, and her manner was decidedly chilly.

"Is there to be a wedding today, Miss Crisp?"

Lisa bobbed a curtsy and kept her eyes lowered. "Yes, my lady."

"Then you had best get a few hours' rest. You have a big task ahead of you making certain my daughter has the happiest day of her life."

"Yes, my lady. My lady, I—"

"No. I do not want or care to know. Teddy's happiness is all that matters."

"Yes, my lady."

When Lisa finally slipped into bed beside Teddy, she lay there staring up at the canopy, not moving, hoping she had not woken her friend, and wondering what she knew and what to tell her. Michel Gallet had told her what to say, and she was mortified to think the Duke of Roxton had gone to the trouble of putting it about she had a fever and had been confined to the house until it passed. And so if he had done that, then he knew the rest. And if the Duke knew, then so did Henri-Antoine's mother... So much for staying in the background as her cousins had demanded of her. Still, she could not do anything to change their opinion of her now, nor did she want to if it meant never having spent time with Henri-Antoine at the folly. She had no regrets. What was required of her now was to get through the rest of her stay without causing a scandal, or doing anything that might interfere with Teddy's happiness.

"You've returned," a drowsy Teddy muttered, sliding across the bed to snuggle in beside Lisa. "Are you feeling better...?"

"Yes. Yes. Much better."

"I'm glad. Because I would have been very sad had you not been able to be with me on this of all days."

"I would not miss your wedding for anything, Teddy. You are going to be a most beautiful bride..."

"And Sir John a handsome groom."

"Yes! The handsomest! Now sleep."

Lisa turned her head on the pillow and tried to sleep.

TEDDY'S WEDDING DRESS WAS OF BLUE SILK, THE BODICE AND over-gown adorned with delicate white lace rushes, with *engageantes* at her elbows; the pearl choker about her throat had been presented to her at breakfast by her parents. Pearls strung on blue ribbons were threaded through the braids of her fiery hair, and diamond clasps and pearl-headed pins helped keep her coiffure in place. Lisa wore a similar gown in shell pink silk, the fabric without lace embellishment, except at the elbows, the bodice cut so low across her breasts that a sheer fichu was strategically criss-crossed over her *décolletage* and tied in a large bow in the small of her back. Matching pink ribbons adorned her hair, which was similarly styled to Teddy's, fat curls brought forward to cascade over one shoulder.

The girls and Christopher Bryce were the last to leave the Gatehouse Lodge for the Treat Family chapel. And by the time their carriage arrived at the big house, family and guests were seated and waiting, the groom and his four male attendants the most anxious of all, Jack pacing up and down before the congregation, clenching and unclenching his fingers. Henri-Antoine, far from offering soothing words of reassurance, teased his best friend mercilessly, and the two were soon bantering back and forth in their usual manner that had family and friends smiling and laughing along with them, none more pleased at this reconciliation than their immediate family.

And then there she was, Teddy as a beautiful bride escorted down the aisle on the arm of her proud step-papa. She could not stop smiling, and when Jack turned and saw her, he could not stop smiling either. And when she was brought to stand beside him before the Duke's chaplain, the couple gave a little joyous hunch of the shoulders, they were so happy. The bouquet was passed to Lisa to care for during the ceremony, once Christopher Bryce had done his part and gave Teddy's hand to Jack.

And while the service celebrated the coming together of two young people clearly in love, it was not lost on the congregation that this was a highly desirable dynastic union. It joined two branches of the same family, further strengthening the Roxton family tree. Theodora Charlotte Cavendish, as the new Lady Cavendish, walked down the aisle on the arm of her husband, Sir John George Cavendish, without the inconvenience of ever having to change her surname.

The newly-married couple left the chapel showered in white rose petals, handfuls thrown from baskets held by the young girls of the family dressed in their best silks. Lisa followed the couple and behind her were the groomsmen, the Duke and Duchess of Roxton, and the mother and step-papa of the bride, and finally the rest of the congregation spilled out into the expansive black-and-white marble paved courtyard. Bride and groom were surrounded by well wishers wanting to offer their congratulations, while the younger children were finally able to run about, watched over by their nurses and maids, the army of liveried footmen with trays of drinks doing their best to avoid these small personages dressed in outfits that replicated those worn by their parents.

Finding herself jostled to the outer rim of this circle of feathers and finery, Lisa retreated to stand by one of the enormous marble urns planted with topiary that were placed around the perimeter of this courtyard. Here she remained a spectator to the comings and goings of the liveried footmen; the little boys weaving in and out amongst the adults, chasing each other; the little girls in a cluster on the other side, twirling about so that their silk gowns lifted to show their white stockings, and throwing the remainder of the rose petals above their heads, so that the petals fell into their hair; and small groups of guests in non-stop conversation, laughing and chatting amongst themselves. And in the center of it all, a radiant Teddy and Jack, so happy to finally be able to begin their married life, and surrounded by their loving family and friends.

Lisa had never felt more alone in a crowd. London streets were friendlier than this. And while it was nonsense to think she was being deliberately forgotten, it was an easy thing for her to feel she was being shunned. And all the while she stood alone by the urn, in her peripheral vision she was acutely aware of Henri-Antoine, one of a group of young gentlemen in conversation by a set of open French doors. He was dressed in a pink ensemble, the matching frock coat and waistcoat smothered in gold thread and spangles; a pink ribbon tied back his hair, and he leaned lightly on his diamond-topped walking stick. It had not escaped her notice that Jack had chosen to wear a similar outfit in blue silk so that he matched Teddy's color choice, just as Henri-Antoine matched hers. It was fanciful for her to believe this was deliberate, but the romantic in her liked to think so, and it made her smile.

Yet she dare not look his way for fear she would be unable to hide her feelings, and with the growing suspicion that perhaps their time at the folly, as secluded as that spot was on the estate, had not been kept as private as she had hoped, the last thing she wanted was to draw attention to him or to her, or to them. This suspicion was realized, and a cold dread seized her when through the chatter and the laughter she heard her name mentioned on the other side of the urn, and by *The Horribles*. And while she could pretend to deafness and continue to smile and watch the activity in the courtyard, she could not help overhearing snippets, and she was certain said loud enough for her benefit: *Both naked*; *hedge whore*; *just another conquest*; *fortune hunting mopsqueezer*; *Chelsea Bun House all over again*; *athanasian wench*; *Roxton to have her gone by morning…*

"Miss Crisp, I thought you might care for a glass of wine? I do beg your pardon, did I startle you?"

Lisa mentally shook herself and looked about to find Jamie Fitzstuart-Banks at her elbow. He held two glasses of wine, and she readily accepted one and drank gratefully. Doing her best to ignore those on the other side of the urn, who were, no doubt, alert and listening that Jamie had sought her out, she turned her shoulder to them and smiled brightly.

"Thank you. Not at all. I was miles away. In London, in fact."

"Do you return to Gerrard Street soon?"

"Yes. Yes. I suspect in the next day or two. When a carriage can be arranged to take me to Alston for the stagecoach."

"I leave for Banks House in the morning. Perhaps you would care to journey up to London with me and my father's family?

"That is very kind in you. But I have my companion with me—"

"There are two carriages, and Papa and I always ride. So plenty of room for you and your companion."

"Thank you, but I would not wish to inconvenience Lord and Lady Strathsay and their children, or you."

"It is no trouble at all. In fact, it was Papa who suggested it, and my stepmama who agreed to it," Jamie admitted with a self-conscious smile and heightened color to his cheeks. "So you see," he said apologetically, "your travel is all arranged."

"I see that it is…" Lisa replied and made no further protest, though she felt color in her face, too, realizing her return to London must have been a topic of discussion within the family. Her departure arranged with the minimum of fuss or whiff of scandal attached to their good names, and that her separation from Henri-Antoine could not come soon enough for all concerned. "Please thank your parents. I will be sure to have our trunks packed tonight, if a servant could be sent to collect them and let us know the time for us to be ready in the morning, I would be most grateful."

Jamie bowed and soon excused himself, disappearing back into the crowd, his commission accomplished, and she finished off her wine and looked about for a footman to collect her empty glass. She revised her earlier estimation that she had never felt more alone in a crowd; this was the moment, knowing she was considered an embarrassment, and unwanted by these almost mythical beings in their fairy land; she almost wished the Duchess of Kinross had not made the effort to find her. But she quickly took back that sentiment because she loved Teddy and it was wonderful to see her married to "her Jack" at last. Nor did she regret her time with Henri-Antoine, or that she had given herself to him. She would cherish those few precious hours spent with him forever. And just as tears welled behind her eyes and she was castigating herself for her self-pity, small fingers slipped into her hand. She turned to find Elsie looking up at her with a frown.

"Are you sad, Lisa?" the little girl asked gravely.

Lisa went down on her haunches and kissed Elsie's cheek.

"Thank you for rescuing me. I was feeling a little bit lonely. But now you are here I am very much better." Lisa admired the girl's exquisitely-painted silk gown and the pearls threaded in her hair, and gently repinned a diamond pin that had come loose in her coiffure. "There. You won't lose that pretty pin. And you look beautiful in your gown, Elsie."

"You are too pretty to be sad, Lisa. I like your hair with ribbons in your braids. Henri-Antoine is wearing pink too. Did you see him? Would you like to sit at my table at the breakfast?"

"I would like that very much, but perhaps you have a special place at a special table?"

Elsie shook her head and then smiled and whispered in French behind her hand at Lisa's ear, "I do and your seat it is next to mine. Maman she promised me."

Lisa was genuinely surprised and delighted. "That makes me so happy. We shall have the most wondrous time together."

Elsie hunched her shoulders and held her hands close to her bodice, and she would have said more, except a hand placed lightly on her shoulder had her looking up and around. It was her older brother, and she said to him, "Julian, this is Lisa and she has a seat next to mine at the wedding breakfast. Maman promised."

"How delightful, *ma petite*. I wonder if you would allow Miss Crisp and me a few moments to talk?" the Duke of Roxton asked in French, and with a smile that softened his features making him appear almost approachable. It was clear he loved his little sister very much. "You will see her again as we are all going in to the State Dining Room very soon. She will find you there. You may wish to find Maman and tell her it is almost time. Would you do that for me, *ma soeur chérie?*" He waited until his little sister had skipped off into the crowd before turning to Lisa and saying conversationally, the warmth gone from his voice, "I am pleased you accepted the Strathsays' offer of a place in their carriage. Your return journey to London will be much more comfortable than the one coming here."

"Thank you for your consideration, Your Grace," Lisa replied levelly, hoping she sounded more confident than she felt. At least shaking knees did not make a noise. "And thank you for permitting me to attend Teddy's wedding. My stay here has provided me with a life-time of memories."

The Duke arched a brow at this, but as Lisa's gaze remained steady and there was nothing in her manner to imply she was being insincere, he made no comment, inclined his head and walked off, just as Teddy, with Jack in tow, pounced on her.

She hugged Lisa to her, kissed her cheek and grabbing her hand said, "Sir John and I won't allow you to hide behind the topiary! Come! We're going indoors for the breakfast, and you must sit with us—"

"I would love to, but I promised Elsie—"

"Oh? Then you must not disappoint her. But promise me you will sit with us when the pudding arrives. I'm certain Elsie will let you go then. Doesn't Sir John's eye look much better today?"

"Much better. And Teddy..."

Teddy looked around at Lisa from kissing her new husband's cheek and frowned when she saw she was making her curtsy. "Lisa? No! You do not curtsy to me—"

"But I must make my curtsy to Lady Cavendish. Is that not so, Sir John?"

"It is a lovely gesture, and you are Lady Cavendish now, my love."

"Walnut pickle to that!" Teddy pouted. "I won't have my best friend curtsy to me!"

"Walnut—*walnut pickle*?" Jack was surprised. He had never heard that expression before.

Lisa laughed and quickly put a hand to her mouth before saying, "Oh Teddy! I haven't heard you say that since Blacklands."

"I haven't heard you say it ever," Jack grumbled, feeling left out of the joke.

Teddy's eyes shone and she let Lisa explain. "Teddy used the expression at school to signal her displeasure. It always made me giggle, for it is quite harmless, and our teachers did not know what to make of it."

"Papa loathes walnut pickle," Teddy explained. "He knows. You say it to him and see if he doesn't laugh too."

"I will," Jack stated emphatically. "I'll mention it casually during the speeches." He grabbed Teddy's hand because everyone was making for the French doors, and said to Lisa, "You will join us for cake, won't you, Miss Crisp—"

"She most certainly will not!" Teddy said with a snort, and dragged Jack away before he knew what was happening.

Lisa watched the crowd part to allow the bridal couple to pass through the doors before them, her spirits very much lifted with this brief interlude; Teddy always had the power to make her feel better about anything and everything. And just as she decided it was time for her to join the throng, there was an almost imperceptible touch to the middle of her back. She did not need to turn around to know who it was.

"I wish we were seated together. No matter. Come the ball, my duties will be over. I'll find you."

Lisa's smile remained fixed nor did she react but she did take a small step so that his fingers were firm against her back. A slight tilt of her chin to her right shoulder, and she said, "I have the great honor of sitting with your sister."

"Excellent. Elsie will look after you. And Roxton is mistaken. The Strathsays will be leaving tomorrow without you."

"It's been arranged—"

"Over my dead carcass it has! You and I—*we*—have other plans. Give Elsie a kiss from me..."

. . .

TRUE TO HIS WORD, HENRI-ANTOINE FOUND LISA IN THE
ballroom not many minutes after the Duke's string ensemble had
struck up the music for the first dance of the evening, the minuet. The
bridal couple took to the dance floor, watched on by everyone. They
went through the intricate steps effortlessly, as a couple used to
commanding a public space all their lives, and not, as Lisa knew,
Teddy tucked away in the Cotswolds, a tomboy to the tips of her
fingers. But Lisa also knew that Teddy's step-papa was a most elegant
dancer, as he had proved at the Gatehouse Lodge and now, taking to
the ballroom floor with the Lady Mary, and it was he who had taught
Teddy to dance the minuet as fluidly and as elegantly as if she were
dancing upon a cloud.

Lisa however had never danced in public, only at school, so when
the couples took to the dance floor and Henri-Antoine came up to her
she had this terror he meant to have her dance with him. It must have
been writ large on her features because he smiled and winked and
leaned in to say at her ear, "The terrace is deserted."

"I thought you were about to ask me to dance," Lisa confessed with
a laugh of relief when they were outside.

She had her hands to the balustrade and was looking up into a late
afternoon sky. When he made no reply she turned to discover he had
stepped away from her. He bowed and held out his hand. She shook
her head.

"No. I cannot. I have not danced since school—"

"No excuse. We can hear the musicians well enough, and should
darkness descend, there is enough wax burning out here to illuminate
St. Paul's. Come. Take my hand."

"I do not doubt you dance beautifully, but I am gauche and—"

"You danced the other night with Cousin Charles and with Jack,
did you not?"

"I did. But—"

"If you managed to dance with Jack's two left feet, you can dance
with me."

"That was in the obscurity of a dining room. This—this is vastly
different."

"I did not bring you out here to save you from public embarrassment. I want you all to myself."

"That is what I want too."

When she placed her hand in his he dared to raise it to his lips.

"Then ignore the world on the other side of those windows. Listen
to the music and concentrate on me, as I will be on you."

She smiled tremulously. "I would like nothing better than to forget

the world, and I can do that when we are alone together, and because
—and because, aside from Teddy, whom I love as dearly as I would
love a sister, you are all that matters to me. But you—you have family
and obligation and duty, and the world watches and whispers and
waits. I do not want to be the cause of any-any—unpleasantness
between you and your brother, or be an embarrassment to your
family."

He came up to her, still holding her hand, and his concern made
his tone harsh. "Embarrassment? Was something said to you? Did
Roxton—"

"No. No. He was most correct. I do not doubt he knows about us,
but he refrained from being impolite. But there are others here who
also know—"

"Let them!" he retorted. "My business is none of their affair."

She touched his cheek briefly. "It is one thing for us to share a
house in Bath, away from the world, quite another for you to flaunt
your mistress under the noses of your peers at a ball. Not even the
Prince of Wales dare do that with Mrs. Fitzherbert, and it is rumored
he's married to her."

"The Prince is an infantile idiot," Henri-Antoine said. He glared at
her. "Is that how you think I see you? As a Mrs. Fitzherbert?"

"You? No. But I doubt even she has been called a-a *hedge whore*
and a-a *fortune hunting mopsqueezer*. I have no idea what to make of
an-an *athanasian wench*."

Henri-Antoine went very still. Lisa wondered if he had heard her,
such was the faraway look in his eye. And then he spoke, and his voice
was like ice. "Forgive me. You should never have been subjected to
such filth. I will deal with that presently. For now..." He mentally
shook himself free of his rage and smiled and bowed to her again. "The
music beckons. Come. Let us treat ourselves to an allemande..."

She smiled and curtsied and gave him her hand again. With the
formalities exchanged, he bowing to her, and she curtsying to him,
they joined hands and were soon dancing up and down the terrace. He
was exceptionally light on his feet and expert at guiding her through
the intricate steps, so that while their first run through was fraught
with missteps and mishandlings, at which they both smiled and
laughed as they fumbled on, their second dance was much more fluid,
Lisa gaining confidence with each turn and step. It was not long before
they were both smiling and concentrating less on their steps and on
each other as they took turns ducking under each other's raised arms,
and then dancing back-to-back, then face-to-face, and all the while
with their fingers entwined. It was as intimate as a couple could get

upon a dance floor without actually kissing. And they were so in harmony with each other and enjoying themselves that it was not long before the small number of persons watching them through the window had grown into a crowd.

It was only when they stopped to regain their breath, and Henri-Antoine went off to seek out a footman with a drinks tray, that the crowd at the windows reluctantly dispersed. Lisa retreated to the far end of the balustrade to await Henri-Antoine's return, her face flushed from dancing cooled by the breeze coming in off the lake, its surface shimmering in summer's dusky light. Dancing with Henri-Antoine had restored her confidence and her happiness, so that when she felt a tug on the bow at her back holding her fichu in place, she naturally assumed he had returned with glasses of refreshment, and was playfully alerting her to the fact.

When a second tug unraveled the bow, she turned around with a teasing scold, accusing him of undressing her, the fichu opening up from where it had been criss-crossed over her breasts, and now left hanging loose about her shoulders. But it was not Henri-Antoine. It was Lord Westby.

He was so close she could smell the spirits on his breath, and he came even closer. And when she tried to tug the fichu from his fingers he closed them into a fist and whipped the thin white strip of gauze from her shoulder, leaving her now heaving breasts exposed. She tried to quell a rising panic and kept her voice firm.

"My lord, I am cold. Please give me my fichu."

"Why? You don't need it. Everyone should see your bubbies. They're rather perfect." He lifted his gaze from her breasts to her eyes and smiled lewdly. "In fact, everyone should see all of you—I have. And I haven't been able to not see you since. You're such a responsive little thing. Lucky Harry, and now lucky me—"

"I should warn you, Lord Henri-Antoine will be here at any moment—"

"I'm waiting for him. It's time he returned the favor—"

"Favor?" she asked, with what she hoped was genuine curiosity, reasoning that if she could not threaten him she needed to keep him talking and Henri-Antoine would arrive before Lord Westby had a chance to act upon whatever demons were driving him. "What favor is that, my lord?"

"It's only fair he share you with me. I shared my mistress with him—"

"But I do not wish to be shared. Therein lies the difference."

"It's not up to you, is it?" he drawled with a smug smile, and set his hands on the balustrade either side of her hips, trapping her. He leaned in and attempted a kiss, but when she quickly turned her head, he settled for sniffing her neck and whispering near her ear, "If you act the whore, then you are a whore, and whores get what whores deserve."

Lisa grimaced and felt herself heave as his tongue tickled her ear. She tried to swat him away, and he grabbed her wrist and squeezed. Despite the pain and the fear of what he might do next, her voice was clear when she spat back bravely,

"I am not a whore, and even if I were, I'm not *your* whore! And you've no right to force yourself on any woman, whore or no!"

She tugged her hand free and with both hands to his chest pushed with all her strength. Off his guard and wrong-footed, Westby stumbled but made a quick recover and lunged for her. Before Lisa had taken more than a couple of steps he had her by the upper arm and pulled her into his arms, pinning hers to her side.

"Let's strike a bargain. I'll forget Harry ever rutted Peggy if you go down on your knees for me, over there in those bushes. And if you don't play the whore for me and do what I want, I'll tell Harry you did it anyway. He'll believe a Batoni Brother before he does—*Sweet Mary Mother of God!*" He yelped. "What the—*what the devil!*"

Instantly he staggered back and away, a hand to his ear and swearing profusely. It was obvious he was in considerable pain. Lisa could only stare, wondering what had happened. She breathed a huge sigh of relief

Salvation had arrived in the form of a six-foot four-inch smoking giant.

TWENTY-FIVE

When Henri-Antoine had stepped off the terrace back into the ballroom he found a footman with a drinks tray, absconded with two glasses of champagne, and was almost at the open French doors again when his brother stepped into his path. He blinked at him, wondering what was the matter. Roxton might look to be sailing on a calm sea, smiling serenely, jeweled snuff box in hand, but Henri-Antoine took one look into his eyes, eyes that were so like their mother's, and just like hers, could not hide his innermost feelings. He saw troubled waters. So he immediately thought something must be the matter with one of his nephews or nieces.

"Julian? What is it?"

The Duke took the glasses from his brother and offloaded them on the liveried footman at his elbow, then sent the servant away.

"Stay inside, Harry."

"Wh—why? What's happened?"

"More than enough. Your private performance has fed the fire, when I had almost put it out. Or did you think it would go unnoticed? Half my guests were at the windows."

At the word *performance*, Henri-Antoine's eyes went dull and his jaw tightened. He watched his brother shift his gaze out across the ballroom and smile benignly as he spoke. It was only when he finally looked at him again that Henri-Antoine deigned to reply.

"Keep your concerns to yourself, and stop interfering unnecessarily in my affairs."

"Interfere unnecessarily?" Henri-Antoine had the Duke's full atten-

tion. "Everything is my concern, Harry, most particularly my family—
you, what goes on here at—"

"I'll be gone tomorrow, and she is coming with me. Concern yourself with that!"

Henri-Antoine went to step around his brother, but the Duke
walked into his path again and they bumped chests. Henri-Antoine
stepped back, but he did not step away.

"Out. Of. My. Way."

The Duke moved closer, doing his best to ensure their conversation
was not overheard. He lowered his voice to a hissed whisper.

"You risk making an even greater fool of yoursel—"

"More fool you for not trusting in my judgment."

The Duke huffed his disbelief. "Judgment?" He looked his brother
over. "But it's not your brain that's doing the thinking, is it?"

Henri-Antoine's lip curled. "Envious I got to taste the menu and
choose my favorite dish and you didn't?"

"How dare—*Mon Dieu*, how dare you speak to me—"

"This isn't about you. It is about choice."

"Choice?"

"Mine. To live as I please with whom I please."

"That's not choice. That's being selfish."

"Yes. I am. I can be." Henri-Antoine regarded his brother with
some sympathy. "I'm sorry you didn't get to choose whom you were to
marry, or how you wanted to live your life."

"Have I ever shirked my responsibilities? Have I ever disappointed
Deb, our parents, my children, you? Have I not done the best that I
can with the estate for Frederick, for posterity?"

"You have, Julian. You are an exemplary duke, a wonderful
husband and papa, a good master, and a wise and circumspect politi-
cian. Everything you do is commendable. No one has ever said otherwise; I certainly sing your praises."

"Thank you. Which is why, as your brother, I concern myself in
your aff—"

"Still, if it all went to the bottom of the sea tomorrow—your
marriage, the estate, the respect and esteem in which the family, the
children, *everyone* holds you—as an eldest son you could blame it all
on *mon père*. Seb Westby blames his father for everything. He can. He's
the eldest son. I cannot. My choices are mine to make. So are my
mistakes."

The Duke took another sweeping look about at his guests, saw his
duchess regarding him from across the room, smiled and rolled his eyes
at her, then looked back at his brother. He smiled.

"No one is prouder of you than I, Harry. The inheritance *mon père* left you, you could've squandered the lot. But you haven't. You're putting it to good use. What the Fournier Foundation has already achieved in a few short years could change medical science forever—"

"Yes. It will. You have never meddled in that aspect of my life, so refrain from interfering in my private life."

The Duke opened his mouth to speak, then felt a presence at his elbow and looked about to find his mother had swept up to them with a bright smile, fluttering a painted gouache fan at her *décolletage*.

"Julian, I require your immediate attention to a matter that has been troubling me for quite some time," she announced in French. "And it cannot wait. So please, to come with me." She put her arm through his and did the same with Henri-Antoine. "You too, *mon chou*. This problem that has arisen requires both my sons."

And without a word of protest, she swept her sons off to an anteroom a few feet behind them which had been set aside for guests who wished to rest somewhere away from the noise. Unsurprisingly it was deserted. Antonia had seen to that, and two footmen stood guard at the doorway to make certain no one entered. With the door closed on the noise of orchestra competing with dancers and conversations, the Duke looked to his mother, nonplussed.

"Maman, you certainly know how to pick your moment. What is this problem—"

"You. You are the problem, Julian."

Roxton's face turned brick red. He had the expression of a guilty four-year-old caught with his fingers in the strawberry jam.

"Why am I the problem, when it is Harry who—"

"Do not blame your brother."

"But, Maman!" The Duke wiped a hand over his face, exasperated

Henri-Antoine gave a start. Had His Grace actually whined like a four-year-old? And then he looked at his mother, this tiny woman in heels who glared up in warning at her big, pouting forty-year-old son, that she was not to be trifled with, and his anger evaporated at the absurdity of this scene. The laughter bubbled up within him until his shoulders shook. Now his mother and brother were staring at him.

"It's not—it's not—*all* Julian's fault, Maman," he finally managed to say.

"Thank you, Harry," the Duke conceded, much mollified, by the concession and his brother's good humor.

"Most of it, but not all."

"Harry, if you had not—"

"Enough! Both of you!" Antonia demanded. She looked from one to the other, pointing her fan. "Why is it that these conversations they arise at the most inopportune times? Could this not have waited until tomorrow?"

"It seems not. Harry is leaving in the morning."

Antonia put up her brows in surprise and waited for her younger son to explain.

"To Bath."

"To Martin's house?"

"Yes. Though we should stop calling it that, now it has reverted to me."

"Yes. Of course."

"And more importantly, because Martin is here now, with *mon père*, where he belongs."

"He's taking that girl with him," the Duke stated sullenly.

"Lisa is not *that girl*, just as Martin was never *that servant*," Henri-Antoine corrected.

"You can't compare the two!"

"I can and will," Henri-Antoine stated. "Martin may have been *mon père's* valet, but he was much more than just a servant, wasn't he? He was our parents' life-long friend. He was your godfather and confidant. He was a friend of this family. And most of all he was an estimable and honorable gentleman. An aristocrat in thought, word, and deed, if not in blood. And we all loved him."

"Yes. Yes, he was," Antonia agreed quietly. "And you said it very well, *mon fils chéri*. He was more honorable and noble than many of those born to it by blood. You do not have to look further than our own relatives to find those of noble blood who have not lived up to their potential: My uncle, the grandson of a king, was a scoundrel."

Roxton looked at his brother. "And this girl—this Miss Crisp... What is she to you, Harry?"

Henri-Antoine did not hesitate in his response. "Lisa is priceless."

There was a stunned silence until the Duke found his voice.

"And you, Maman? What is your opinion of this g—of Miss Crisp?"

"Oh? Is someone finally asking me what I think?" Antonia teased, a wink at Henri-Antoine, though the Duke continued to look uncomfortable and anxious. "If my son says she is priceless, then I believe it. So," she added, looking from one son to the other, "what is to be done with Mlle Crisp?"

Jonathon, Duke of Kinross, stuck his cheroot in the side of his mouth and scooped up the discarded fichu from the terrace tiles. He gave it a little shake and inspected it a moment, orientating it to its purpose, and then he smiled at Lisa and held it up, saying jovially,

"Let's tie this back on you and then we can have a little talk."

With her arms crossed over her low bodice, Lisa stared up at him. Here was Elsie's papa, and at the wedding breakfast, when she had been seated beside Elsie, also at her end of the table were the Duke and Duchess of Kinross. She had witnessed how father and daughter adored one another, as did the Duke and Duchess. And for her to be seated in their company was an honor indeed. Though she was thankful she had Elsie to talk to, because she felt out of her depth in such exalted circles. Her de Crespigny cousins would definitely be envious, and possibly not believe her. Then again, there wasn't much she could tell them that they would believe about her stay. And this latest episode—Lord Westby's attempted seduction—made her feel foolish and embarrassed. So much so that she burst into tears of relief when Kinross placed a comforting arm about her and patted her shoulder.

"I'd cry, too, if an oaf like Westby had pawed me! Drunken dolt! Come. Let me arrange your fichu. I'm rather an expert in female attire, particularly those outfits belonging to Mademoiselle Yvette and Signorina Simonetta. Elsie can attest I'm the best personal maid those two have. That's better! You should laugh. You'd laugh even harder if you saw Elsie and her papa having afternoon tea and chattering away with her two dolls in French or Italian or both!"

"I would enjoy such an afternoon tea, Your Grace," Lisa assured him with a watery sniff.

She let him arrange the fichu about her shoulders and turn her this way and that, and finally, when he had tied the bow to his satisfaction she thanked him and would have said more, but he stepped away and disappeared back into the shadows, alerted by a series of moans and muttered threats. And when she heard another yelp, followed by pleas and assurances, she could hardly believe her ears, least of all her eyes, when Lord Westby stumbled out of the darkness and crossed in front of the windows, a silhouette of a man crouched over with a hand to his ear.

Kinross returned to Lisa, puffing on his cheroot and then exhaling smoke up into the night sky.

"He'll not be bothering you or Harry again. That nasty hole to his ear will be a nice reminder. Me threatening to geld him if he ever came near you again was the decider."

Lisa's eyes opened wide. "You burned him with the end of your cheroot?"

"I branded him with a good behavior mark. He'll look at it and he'll behave."

Lisa gasped and then giggled.

Kinross grinned. "That's better. You have a lovely laugh and it suits you. Are you feeling up to having that little talk?"

Lisa nodded. "I'm feeling very much better, Your Grace. So yes. Though…" She looked over at the open French doors. "I had expected His Lordship to have returned by now… He went to fetch refreshment. I wonder what has detained him—or who…"

"Who" was right. Kinross knew. Before his attention was diverted by Westby coming out onto the terrace and bothering Lisa, he had been watching Henri-Antoine through the windows. Saw his brother, and then Antonia sweep up to her sons, before all three disappeared from view. He did not need an imagination to know what was being discussed—this girl standing before him. But he pretended ignorance, his smile just as friendly as before.

"Possibly detained by some fellow or other wanting a word. You know how it is at these types of functions—Come to think on it, you wouldn't know… Lucky you! But trust me. So many people want to bleat in m'ear about something." He lifted his cheroot. "Which is why I came out here. I gave these things up years ago, so don't tell my wife."

Lisa cocked her head. "Somehow I suspect Mme la Duchesse is aware of your ploy, and your habits, Your Grace."

"Ha! I knew you had a good brain the first time I saw you. It's written all over your face, and you have intelligent eyes, just like my wife. Besides, Elsie has taken a shine to you. My daughter may only be eight-and-a-half years old, but she has an old head on her shoulders. Far too grave for a little person, but later that will stand her in good stead, as it has you. Particularly…" His smile turned sentimental. "Particularly when it comes to choosing a mate."

Lisa's smile dropped and so did her gaze. She was thankful they were standing by the balustrade and not by a wall sconce or taper and thus in a blaze of candlelight, for she was sure her face had flushed with color.

"The thing about being loved by an intelligent woman," Kinross continued smoothly as if he were blind to Lisa's sudden awkwardness, "is that I know my wife loves me—for me. She fell in love with a plain-speaking, no-nonsense, bull-headed fellow who doesn't suffer fools, and sets more store by a man's courage and loyalty and friendship than he does the type of coronet he's got stuck on his head. I came late to my ermine, and I don't mind telling you that being a duke is more trouble than it's worth. And mine wasn't worth a groat until I brought to it my merchant fortune.

"But my wife was a duchess when I met her, and her son's a duke, and by all accounts the most powerful peer in the realm, who owns half of England. Which means a lot to their relatives and friends, and the many people who surround them. So I've bought into the family business, if you like. I trot myself out at functions, and play my part. And I let people bow and scrape to my dukedom when it suits me, or when I must. But I never lose sight of who I am, and neither does my wife."

Lisa wondered where he was taking this homily, and could have kicked herself for not realizing at his mention of a mate that his story was leading straight to Henri-Antoine. But she had forgotten her own predicament, fascinated by his story. So when he eventually mentioned Henri-Antoine in the same breath, she should not have been surprised, but she was, and again she felt herself blush. But this time she did not look away.

"And as you're an intelligent girl, you won't take this the wrong way or be missish when I tell you that when we are alone together we are simply Jonathon and Antonia, a man and a woman who love and respect each other and are the best of friends. The ermines and the titles and ancient lineages only mean something on public occasions, and that's where they belong, and where the earwigs and foot-lickers swarm like flies to carrion, feasting on our self-consequence. What's important as a couple is that you live as if those trappings don't exist; that you live honestly, and without the prejudice of family interference and expectation. Do you understand, m'dear?"

"I think that I do, though for me—"

"What am I saying? Of course you understand!" he declared, deliberately interrupting her because he had more to say, and because he was aware time was short. Henri-Antoine would return at any moment. He drew back on his cheroot and exhaled away from her. "Which brings me to the family I married into. I can tell you—I'm certain you'll understand because you're not one of them—it's not easy being part of this lot. You think I'm being flippant. After all I'm a duke. But my wife's first husband was the venerated fifth Duke—You've heard of him?"

"Yes, Your Grace. I have. My aunt was Mme la Duchesse's personal maid for many years—"

"That's right! Gabrielle! How could I forget that?! Wonderful woman. Couldn't have done without her at Elsie's birth. And she was there for the birth of the two boys, too." He smiled slyly. "I'll wager she has a story or ten about her time here—"

"Stories, yes. But nothing inappropriate or any confidences broken. She is—has always been—most circumspect with her storytelling. And she guards her memories."

Kinross nodded as if this was a given, and returned to his line of thought. "The fifth Duke was very much his own man, Miss Crisp. And so am I. People take me as they find me, or not at all. And that pleases my wife, and the family know where I stand."

"I see that you are. And Mme la Duchesse would not have fallen in love with you and married you otherwise. I dare say she would also have been most disappointed had you changed just to please her or her family."

"Precisely! And that brings me to my step-son Henri-Antoine, though except for his mother, we all call him Harry. He's-he's—complicated," Kinross mused, gaze seemingly on his cheroot, but with a heightened awareness of Lisa and her reactions. "He not only looks like his father, but his mother tells me he has his temperament too. He's not one of these fellows who trumpets his feelings about, or easily shows his emotion, even with family. His illness has left him self-absorbed. And I guess with good reason. It's a hell of a disadvantage to live with, not knowing from one day to the next if you'll be struck down with a seizure. Though we—his mother and I—suspect this last episode was of his own making—"

"Your Grace, I—"

"—and said more about his emotional state than it did his health. But apart from his aloofness with his fellows, and oft being inscrutable he is also—"

"—kind, generous, caring, shy, intensely private, and-and—loving," Lisa stated, and having had the courage to speak her mind she added for good measure, "And I-I am in love with him."

"Yes, I rather thought that was the way of things."

She bravely looked up at him with a wan smile. "I'm afraid I have allowed my heart to rule this old head of mine…"

"May I offer you a piece of advice? It's what I've been wanting to say to you from the beginning."

"I welcome any advice you care to offer, Your Grace."

"Be yourself. Always. Don't second-guess. He either loves you as you are, or not at all. And I am confident he does love you, Miss Crisp. No man dances with a woman the way Harry danced with you just now and not be in love! That you love one another is evident. And that's all that matters. Not his family. Not his mother. Most certainly not his brother. And the rest of it—ancient ancestors, this pile of stone, the relatives, society—it's irrelevant when all is said and done, ain't it?"

"To me and how I feel about him, most definitely. But what about my humble circumstances? I see no shame in being poor. It is not something I can alter about myself, other than do my best to find useful employment and try not to be a burden on my family. But I have no family connections, certainly no ancestors worth mentioning, and if we ever did have a pile of stone, there certainly wasn't enough of it to build anything useful. I wonder if that is irrelevant to him…?"

"Ha! I made my fortune on the subcontinent, and all I had when I started out was self-belief, a willingness to work hard, and a good business brain. Some things can't be measured in pounds and pence, or by examining a parchment to see what branch you sit on in the family tree. It is often intangibles that mean the most—they do to me. Things such as honor, integrity, intelligence, love, kindness, faithfulness, generosity, loyalty, I could go on. But I think I've put my case well enough, don't you?"

"Yes, Your Grace. And thank you."

He smiled and patted her shoulder, and at the sound of voices, straightened and stubbed his cheroot on the sole of his shoe. "Just you remember when the time comes what I said about being yourself."

And as he went off across the terrace to return to the ballroom, Lisa wondered what he meant by "when the time comes," but she certainly remembered his words, and they were to be a comfort and a strength when she needed them most. For now, Teddy and Jack had escaped their guests to join her on the terrace, and Henri-Antoine was a few steps behind them, and at his back a footman carrying a tray of drinks.

"Here you are!" Teddy announced, rushing up to Lisa in a whirlwind of silk petticoats and smiles. She gave Lisa a hug. "We were looking for you inside everywhere, were we not, Sir John?"

"Everywhere. Didn't think to look out here," Jack admitted. "Until Harry told us where you were. At least you had Kinross to keep you company." He frowned. "Thought I saw Seb slip out here, but Uncle Charles and I were deep in conversation about his plans once he gets to these new United States of America, so I couldn't get away. Must have been mistaken…"

Henri-Antoine distributed glasses of champagne, and held his up, a wink at Lisa.

"Before I toast the newlyweds, I first must implore your forgiveness for my asinine behavior at the cricket match, the results of which are still starkly evident—"

"No, Harry. No! Not tonight," Jack said firmly. "All's forgiven and forgotten. To point out fact, I'd forgotten all about it until Lady Fittleworth asked how I'd come by my purple eye."

"I was very helpful and said he'd run into a door," Teddy told them with a grin.

"A door! Might as well have said I'd stuck myself in the eye with my viola bow!"

Everyone laughed, except Jack.

Teddy kissed her husband's cheek. "I'll remember that for next time."

"There won't be a next time. I've sworn off hitting best friends."

"So have I, Jack. Never again." Henri-Antoine raised his glass. "To Sir John and Lady Cavendish. Wishing you a long life, a happy marriage, and infants aplenty. The best friends this best friend could have."

The other three raised their glasses in reply and sipped.

"Thank you, Harry. And I should like to toast my best friend," Teddy said, raising her glass again and smiling at Lisa. "To Lisa Crisp. The best friend a girl could possibly have. I am so happy you are in my —our—lives."

They all sipped again.

"But you're not coming to live with us, are you?" Teddy added wistfully, gaze still on Lisa.

Lisa teared up and shook her head. "No, dearest. I am not. But— but I do hope you will allow me to visit you—both of you—"

"Most definitely! Whatever the circumstances," Jack stated emphatically, not a glance at Henri-Antoine. "Would never turn you away. Always welcome. Always. Isn't that so, Theodora?"

"Yes. Whatever the circumstances," Teddy replied forlornly, giving Lisa's arm a squeeze. "Always..."

As she, too, avoided looking at Henri-Antoine, Lisa wondered if Jack had confided in his bride, and precisely what it was he had said to her. It did not bode well that Teddy was regarding her as if she were about to be sentenced to hanging, or her neck was for the chopping block. There followed a moment's awkward silence between the four, until Henri-Antoine coughed into his fist again and said quietly,

"This is your day, Teddy—Jack—so I do not wish to say anything further tonight. But tomorrow... Tomorrow I hope to have something to tell you both."

"We'll still be here tomorrow, won't we, Sir John?" Teddy replied, suddenly bright and eager again. "We aren't departing for Bath until the day after tomorrow. We have all day tomorrow."

Jack looked at Lisa and then at Henri-Antoine and noted they were going out of their way not to look at each other. "Yes. That's right. All day tomorrow, and night. We'll be here tomorrow night, too. And when we leave the day after tomorrow, it won't be until mid-morning. So plenty of time…"

Teddy and Jack hoped that Henri-Antoine's announcement was what they were both secretly wishing for and wanted to hear but had not voiced out loud for fear it might not come true. Lisa had no idea what that announcement could be. When Henri-Antoine enlightened her some hours later, she was speechless. It was not the reaction he had hoped for. He was left mystified. She was left miserable.

TWENTY-SIX

Not long after the toasts on the terrace, Henri-Antoine dismissed his lads for the rest of the evening, and taking Lisa by the hand, slipped away from the ball, to his apartment. He took her through a labyrinth of passageways, ill-lit back stairs, and rooms that seemed to go on forever. Most rooms had some form of lighting, or a fire in the grate, and if there wasn't either, there was always a manservant or a maid just around a corner, going about their duties, and who could offer His Lordship whatever he required. At one stage she asked, "Are we still in the same house or have we trespassed onto another's property? This place goes on forever!"

"If you do not know your way around, it does. I am taking the shortest route possible."

"So your apartment is closer to Paris than it is to London?"

"You may well be right. It is as far from everything as I could possibly make it. And it might as well be in France. It is staffed with my servants. I bring them down with me from the London house, even my cook."

"Of course you do," Lisa muttered and tried to quell her surprise. "Who else is to cook for you in your own kitchen, if not your own cook—"

"Precisely, and—" He frowned and flushed. "Is that your tongue I see planted in your cheek, Miss Crisp?"

"A trick of the light, my lord."

He said nothing further, though he gave her a sidelong glance so she knew he had noted her playful impudence, and then she made him stop again as they were about to pass through one room in particular that made her wonder if they had stumbled upon a smuggler's hoard. The room glittered with gilding and gold metal thread in the furniture tapestries. One wall was covered floor to ceiling in the largest mirrors Lisa had ever seen. But it was what was reflected in the candlelight, as Henri-Antoine walked about with his taper, that opened wide Lisa's eyes: A treasure trove of trinkets, boxes, statues, paintings, furniture, fixtures, and oddments, all piled up and in a jumble, as if these items had been ransacked, not only from other houses, but previous centuries.

This monolith of a building had a surprise around every corner, and each surprise was more surprising than the last.

"This is the room the family calls the Ancestral Guilt Room," Henri-Antoine explained. "My nephew Freddy, who will one day—a day long into the future—be the seventh duke, has dubbed it the *What do we do with this lot because we don't want it, but it's been in the family for generations* room." He ran a finger around the rim of a marble pedestal that supported a cup made from polished sea shell and silver. There was an inscription but he did not read it out. "Some of these pieces date back before Queen Bess's time. Some of it belongs to me. Most of it my brother inherited from our father, who inherited it from his. My mother has a few pieces here, willed to her by her grand-mother, a nasty old witch of a woman. None of us want this-this —*stuff*, but we don't know what to do with it."

"If none of you want it, not even your nephew, then perhaps it could be put to better use?" Lisa suggested, trying to take in as much of the hoard as possible.

"Such as?"

"You could hold an auction—"

"Auction?" Henri-Antoine was surprised but Lisa had all his atten-tion. "Go on."

"There may be other pieces your brother and your mother, and any other relatives, would like to contribute to the auction, and feel they are superfluous to their needs—"

"That would include most of what's stuffed in this house," Henri-Antoine quipped. He smiled. "But go on."

"You could have a catalog printed, like the one advertising the Duchess of Portland's collection, and list all the items here in this room, and whatever else is contributed."

"I know Deb, my sister-in-law, would gladly contribute. She's been wanting to do something with this lot for years. But my brother is a sentimentalist. He would need convincing."

"It seems a waste to have all this sitting here being of no use, particularly when no one in the family wants it, when it could be used to better purpose, and for other's enjoyment. Lots of people bought objects from the Portland collection, and no doubt most of those items had been gathering dust for years."

"Such as Elsie's shell."

"Yes. Just like Elsie's shell. And perhaps your brother would be more agreeable to the idea if it was named the Roxton Catalog?"

"He might indeed."

"And if the proceeds were used for a worthwhile cause…?"

"That would certainly add weight to the argument for him, his duchess, and our mother."

"And what more worthwhile cause could there be than the one closest to your heart: The Fournier Foundation for medical research."

He grinned. "You are a mind reader."

"Oh? I thought I was a witch."

He stuck the taper on the nearest surface, grabbed her and gently took her face in his hands. He kissed her. "You're so clever. No wonder I love you. Come," he said and snatched up the taper, and took her by the hand. "My apartment is through this door and along the passageway."

Lisa followed, mute. She was dazed by his declaration. He had said it before, when they were making love that first time, but later when her mind and body had cooled she wondered if she had misheard him. And now he had said it again, but in such an offhand manner she was left all at sea. So she did not attach great importance to it. And by the time they entered his apartment she was distracted enough not to dwell on it. For there on the carpet by a sofa was her battered trunk, and sitting on the lid was her rosewood writing box in its cloth cover.

"Where's Becky?" she asked, looking about, as if the girl was to be found near her belongings.

"Returning to London with the Strathsays—"

"But—"

"If you want her back, you'll have to write to the Widow Humphreys offering her niece employment."

"Is that what she told you?"

"That is what she told my major domo."

Lisa was suddenly awkward. "Her aunt may not allow her to be employed by the likes of me."

"The likes of you?" Henri-Antoine was puzzled. "She should be so fortunate. Widow Humphreys can advertise to her clientele her niece is seamstress to Her Ladyship. Her business will treble overnight." He pulled her to him, and with her in his arms he untied the bow at her back that held her fichu in place. "You'll need a proper lady's maid," he murmured, dipping to kiss the curve of her throat. "Someone well-versed in the care of silks and satins…"

Lisa stayed his hands, suddenly ill at ease, and took a step away, and glanced about at her opulent surroundings, which she had not done that first time when she had come to speak to his major domo: Velvet curtains, high ceilings, paintings of foreign abodes in heavy frames of gilt, deep carpet underfoot, and everything bathed in a golden glow from the very best beeswax candles. She felt foolish for having a frisson of panic, thinking of what had happened on the terrace with Seb Westby, and quickly banished him from her thoughts. She would not allow that episode or that drunken lecher to intrude into her life again, and drew Henri-Antoine back to her.

He had instantly withdrawn his hands and stepped away, too, and made her a small bow. Now, as she put her arms around his neck, he said with a concerned frown, looking into her eyes, "I should not have presumed… It's been a long night… You must be tired."

Through the open double doors she glimpsed an equally opulent and expansive bedchamber, home to an enormous four-poster bed, and smiled up at him to say cheekily, "I'm not the least tired. But I wonder what His Grace would say to me staying with you under his roof?"

"My apartment; my roof: That's our agreement. And this is where you belong, with me, always. That's all that matters."

"I would very much like His Lordship to show me the rest of his apartment…"

He kissed her palm, and holding her hand led her into the bedchamber and closed the double doors on the world.

SHE WAS WRAPPED IN HIS ARMS AND DRIFTING OFF INTO A blissful sleep when he made enough movement to wake her. And once she was awake and he had plumped the pillows for her, and she was sitting up against the carved headboard, he slid out from under the covers. He crossed the room and disappeared into the next and returned carrying her rosewood writing box, perfectly comfortable in his own skin. But for Lisa something about the scene sent her into a fit of the giggles. It wasn't his tumble of messy hair, which fell into his eyes so that she wondered if he could see at all. Or his nakedness, which was splendid and intriguing. It was the rosewood writing box. She'd had a flash of memory of him presenting it to her in Gerrard

Street, dressed magnificently, and how formal he had been with her upon that occasion. And here he was, not that many weeks later, presenting her with the same box, in all his magnificent nakedness. And what was she supposed to do with it? Write a letter? At this hour? And to whom?

"Does His Lordship require an amanuensis in the middle of the night?"

"I can't sleep until I have your answer," he said as he slipped back under the covers beside her, the writing box on the coverlet between them.

She had curbed her giggling, but the laughter was still in her blue eyes.

"You intend to dictate this answer and I am to write it down?"

He looked at her with one eyebrow raised over his blackened eye.

"Droll. No. There is more to this writing box than meets the eye, isn't there?"

She knew at once. Without further prompting she opened up the writing box, which was unlocked, and folded back the red leather writing surface to expose the compartment below, pressed on the panel that concealed the three little drawers, and removed it. She looked up at Henri-Antoine.

"You have left me a note?"

"Notes."

She gave a little gasp of pleasure.

"When? How? I don't recall you having access to my writing box since Gerrard Street."

He smiled thinly. "His Lordship works in mysterious ways. But I know you won't leave it there, so let me tell you. I wrote the notes. I had Michel conceal them. I was otherwise occupied at a wedding."

"They were put there tonight?"

"Today. Yes."

"And you wrote them—when?"

Henri-Antoine leaned his shoulders against the mountain of feather pillows.

"You're not a witch. You're a grand inquisitor!"

She giggled. The truth was she was excited and apprehensive and these were her first secret notes. She took a deep breath and asked, "Which drawer should I open first?"

He threw up a hand. "It matters not. Only your answer matters."

She gave a tug on the little round horn pull of the left hand drawer, and there inside the tiny compartment was a tiny piece of folded paper. It read: *Try the third drawer along.* She folded the paper and put it back and slid the drawer closed, a look up under her lashes at Henri-Antoine who was grinning at her. So she did as the note instructed, and pulled open the right hand drawer. Inside was another piece of paper, but this paper was wrapped around something. Lisa slowly unwrapped it, and what she saw made her stare at Henri-Antoine in astonishment.

"It's a ring!"

"Wonderful. Michel managed to place it there without it falling out of the paper. That would have required a treasure hunt to find it—"

"It is real? Is it old?"

"Do you mean are those diamonds and sapphires paste? No, they are not paste. Yes, they are real. Yes, the ring is old. It requires a good polish. The last to wear it was my grandmother, Madeleine-Julie Salvan Hesham, Marchioness of Alston, daughter of the Comte de Salvan, and my father's mother."

"Your father's mother?"

"Yes. She died over fifty years ago…"

Lisa held the ring between thumb and forefinger and inspected it closely, turning it this way and that in the candlelight.

"Your grandmother had slim fingers."

He smiled. Trust her to be interested in the anatomy of the wearer rather than the value of the stones, or, surprisingly, the significance of what the ring symbolized.

"She was five-and-forty when she died. Of course, there is the possibility her fingers were even slimmer when she married, and the ring has been altered since. She was just sixteen when she eloped with my grandfather."

"Eloped? How—How did you come by the ring?"

"I see the grand inquisitor has returned," he muttered. "My father left it to me, along with a letter," he explained patiently. "I opened the letter for the first time this morning. That ring was inside the packet."

"A letter from your father?" Lisa was intrigued. "He wrote you a letter to be opened today?"

"Not today precisely. The letter was for me to open when I had come to a particular decision about my life."

"Did he not also leave you a letter to be opened on your twenty-first birthday, too?"

"He did."

"How delightful and farsighted of him! He loved you very much." She frowned and leaned in and kissed his mouth, before looking into his eyes. "I can imagine reading such a letter was very emotional for you..."

He held her gaze. "The entire week has been like that."

She kissed him again, and then lightly pressed her lips to his black eye. She held out the ring shyly. "Will you put it on me?"

"Gladly. First, you should peek in the middle and final drawer, and give me your answer."

"Oh yes! Silly me forgot that drawer. Dazzled by precious stones!"

"Dazzled by the circumference of *grandmère's* ring finger."

Lisa laughed and was still smiling when she pulled open the tiny middle drawer of her writing box. She was not surprised to find tucked inside a third small piece of paper. She quickly pulled it out and unfolded it and was smiling up at Henri-Antoine before she even glanced at the note itself. And then she let her gaze drop to the paper, and she saw drawn a love heart, and inside the heart were two words: Marry me.

She stared at the heart, and at the words, and took a deep breath and thought she might stop breathing from happiness. It lasted but a moment, before she exhaled, folded the note with shaking fingers and then just sat there, head bent, long hair falling about her face and bare arms. And then the tears came and dropped onto the paper, and she could not stop them, nor did she try. She was indescribably happy that he loved her so much he wanted to marry her, and she was unutterably miserable because she loved him so much she had to refuse him.

When she was finally able to articulate her feelings, and she enlightened him that she was crying from happiness, overwhelmed by the occasion and what it meant, but most of all because she could not give him the answer he was expecting, he was stunned. But he was not angry or sad, or even disappointed. He was strangely numb. He believed her when she told him she loved him. He even believed her when she confidently assured him she had every intention of living with him as his mistress, and they would be a couple in every sense. But he did not believe her when she said he could not marry her. It interested him that she did not say she could not marry him, but that he could not marry her. What did that mean, precisely? What doubting bee was buzzing about in her head, and who had put it there? Two and two did not add up to four.

Perhaps a good night's sleep would bring perspective and some answers. With this in mind, he removed the writing box from the bed, set his grandmother's wedding band on the side table next to the silver chamberstick, and found Lisa a clean white handkerchief. He then tucked them both up under the covers and snuffed the candle. Snuggled up, silent and still, yet acutely aware of each other, it took them both a very long time to fall asleep.

LISA WOKE IN THE BIG BED, ALONE. SHE HAD A RECOLLECTION OF being suddenly cold. Henri-Antoine was no longer beside her. It was early morning. There was bird song. Distant whispered conversation was somewhere far off. Then it went quiet. She had not slept well all night. She wondered if she had slept at all. She was exhausted. She fell into a deep sleep...

For a single moment she thought herself back in her narrow bed in Gerrard Street. But she was surrounded by plump pillows filled with the softest down, and covered by sheets of the finest linen, and the bed was enormous, the canopy and bed curtains of velvet. The curtains covering the windows had been drawn back, and light streamed across the carpet. The diamond and sapphire ring once belonging to the Marchioness of Alston was not by the chamberstick, and where her rosewood writing box had been placed at the end of the bed there lay one of Henri-Antoine's banyans, this one of golden yellow silk damask, the sleeves rolled up.

Lisa threw back the covers, and wearing the banyan, arms hugged about her body, she followed the light through to a spacious dressing room, furnished with chaise longue, chair, and curio cabinets. Stacks of books lined the windowseat. A fire smoldered in the grate. And sitting on tiles before the fireplace was a large, linen-lined copper bath. Beside the bath, a pile of towels and a copper pail. Through an open doorway she could see into a closet, and hanging on pegs along the wall were sumptuous frock coats in silks, linens, and cottons, alongside matching waistcoats, and there was a row of mahogany clothes presses.

What surprised her most were the clothes laid out on the chaise longue under the window sill. They were hers. A floral cotton caraco, petticoats to match, a flimsy apron, clean stockings, and a chemise. She was staring at this assortment when a thin-shouldered man dressed in black frock coat and breeches came through from the closet, and introduced himself as Kyte, His Lordship's valet. Two manservants carrying pails of hot water followed, and behind them a maidservant, who kept her eyes lowered to the parquetry.

"Good morning, ma'am," Kyte said cheerfully, as if it was an everyday occurrence for Lisa to be in his master's dressing room. He made her a small bow. "Rose will help you bathe and dress and arrange your hair the way you like it, while I make certain your breakfast has been set out in the alcove of the drawing room. I trust hot chocolate, toast, and an egg meets with your approval? After breakfast the lads will escort you to His Grace's library."

The thought of eating made her queasy. She might sip the hot chocolate. What made her lose her appetite altogether was mention of the library. And any awkwardness she had being in Henri-Antoine's room vanished, replaced with apprehension and dread; she had heard tales of what it meant to be summoned to His Grace's library. But mention of Henri-Antoine's lads made her curious.

"The lads are to take me?"

"M'sieur Gallet is to take you. The lads will be your escort."

"Escort?" Lisa thought the word ominous.

"Yes, ma'am."

When Lisa continued to frown, Kyte thought it best to explain. He dumped a towel, hair brush, and pins on the maid, and sent her across to the bathing area to supervise the placement of a privacy screen, then turned to Lisa with the same noncommital smile.

"His Lordship has assigned two of his lads to you. For your protection—"

"Excuse me, Mr. Kyte—"

"Kyte, ma'am. Just Kyte."

"Oh? Excuse me, Kyte, but I do not understand why I need protection here in His Grace's house."

The valet's fixed smile slipped slightly. The girl might be wrapped in one of his master's banyans and wearing white stockings tied up over her knees, but he would wager that was all she was wearing. With her long hair tumbled about her shoulders and down her back in messy abundance, she looked every inch the lover the morning after the night before. She was young and beautiful and he was not surprised his master was besotted. But there was nothing tawdry about her, or her relationship with his master. Michel Gallet had confided about the little notes, and the ring, left in the rosewood writing box. And as she carried herself with dignity and was devoid of artifice, he treated her with the respect he thought she deserved, and said politely,

"His Lordship considers it necessary for your well-being and his peace of mind that whenever you step outside the confines of his apartment, the lads be with you at all times. In this way you may move about freely, unconcerned at being approached by persons with whom you do not wish to have speech or contact. I assure you, all of His Lordship's servants are most discreet and loyal."

"I would never doubt it, Kyte."

The valet bowed and would have departed but Lisa had one further question, and that was the whereabouts of his master.

"His Lordship rose early with the intention of taking a morning ride. I dressed him for just such an outing. However, he did not inform me of his subsequent movements, but M'sieur Gallet may be able to provide you with the answer after your breakfast."

Later, when the major domo arrived to take her to the library, Lisa asked him the same question. He apologized for not being able to tell her His Lordship's present whereabouts. But he was able to elaborate on his master's early morning activities, and gave Lisa an entertaining account while she finished her hot chocolate.

"His Lordship did indeed go riding," Michel told her. "But first he attended to some unfinished business at the stables. It seems that last night he ordered a carriage to be made ready for departure at first light, and instructed that the trunks and belongings of a number of guests be packed and these guests and their personal servants be aboard the carriage by dawn. Unfortunately, His Lordship's directive was perceived as one of amusing himself at their expense and they were all disbelieving. Thus, while their servants had indeed done as instructed and had themselves and the trunks and belongings of their masters aboard the carriage as ordered, the guests were still abed when they should have been making their way to the stables. Undeterred by this circumstance, His Lordship had the guests rallied, and when they objected to the early hour, and what they considered gross mistreatment and refused to do what was ordered of them, His Lordship took the only option left to him."

"What—what did he do, M'sieur Gallet?" Lisa asked, chocolate cup paused between saucer and her parted lips.

The major domo's mouth twitched.

"His Lordship had the lads manhandle them to the carriage in their nightshirts. And when the females objected most stridently, His Lordship ordered the lads to swing them over a shoulder and carry them, kicking and screaming if need be, to the waiting carriage—"

"There were women involved?" Lisa put aside her chocolate cup, and sat up straight.

"Two gentlemen and two females. A brother and his sister—the Knatchbulls— and Mr. Knatchbull's close friend Lord Westby, and Miss Knatchbull's friend, a Miss Medway. All four were subsequently bundled into the carriage, their various items of clothing thrown in after them, and the carriage, under escort of outriders, was ordered to take them to The Swan—"

"—at Alston?"

Mention of the local inn where she and Becky had been set down by the stagecoach gave Lisa a kernel of an idea as to why Henri-

Antoine had sent the carriage to that particular location, and under escort.

"Yes, ma'am. A number of stagecoaches pass through the town, setting down and picking up passengers, mostly for travelers taking the London to Southampton road."

Lisa set aside her cup and patted her mouth with the linen napkin before asking calmly, "What happened at Alston, M'sieur Gallet?"

"While the Knatchbulls, Lord Westby, and Miss Medway were taking refreshment at The Swan, their carriage left for London without them—"

"To London—*without them?*"

"Yes, ma'am. Their personal servants and belongings were permitted to depart in the carriage provided by His Lordship, while their masters were detained under armed escort until the stagecoach arrived."

"Dear me. I fear they will not enjoy their journey on the common coach."

"They will not. Although, one of the lads confided Mr. Knatchbull was inclined to see the humor in the exploit and confessed that they were all deserving of His Lordship's justifiable ire. He was willing to take the inconvenience on the chin. Lord Westby was not so inclined and had to be restrained from lashing out at his friend, whom he blamed entirely. As for the two females... They burst into howls of self-pity and nothing the gentlemen said or did could silence them."

"I have sympathy for those unfortunate people having to share the carriage with them all the way to London—"

"His Lordship's sympathy was also for the common traveler. He instructed the carriage carrying the servants and belongings to stop five miles up the road and wait for the stagecoach's arrival. Whereupon their masters were permitted to rejoin the carriage for the rest of the journey to their Westminster abodes... If you have finished your chocolate, ma'am, it is time for us to go. We do not want to keep His Grace waiting."

Lisa suddenly looked ill, as if she were about to climb a scaffold. And as she followed Michel Gallet through a warren of passageways and rooms to what seemed the farthest reaches of this palatial collection of buildings, two of the lads at her back, she wondered if they were her escort to make certain she did not escape and dart off to hide. There must be any number of hiding spots, and that was only from what she had seen. She imagined there was a whole other world inhabited by the servants, and lost count of the number of liveried footmen they passed. And as she failed to see any of the guests, she presumed she was being taken to the library via a route that deliberately avoided the public rooms.

Finally they came to a set of inlaid double doors where two footmen stood as sentries. Here, M'sieur Gallet left her with a bow, and the two lads at her back went over to an alcove to wait. One of the sentries disappeared inside, and did not return for over a minute, and then with the unsurprising news His Grace was ready to receive her. Once inside, she was to walk to the other end of the room, and not to dawdle, and in a straight line, and not to deviate. With those instructions, the door was held wide, she entered, and the door closed on her back before she had taken more than four steps.

She did not loiter, but she could not resist looking about her in fascination and awe. She had never been in a room quite like it. It looked to be on the same vast scale as the ballroom, with floor-to-ceiling bookcases divided into two floors, a narrow walkway with an ornate railing running around three sides of the room and accessed via a spiral staircase. The domed ceiling was painted with blue sky and white clouds and colorful scenes, but she did not stop to make out the scenes or the figures, and she feared giving herself a crick in the neck. There were collections of chairs, tables covered in maps and large folios and rolled parchments, world and celestial globes on pedestals, statues and marble busts in alcoves, oriental rugs scattered across the parquetry, and along the entire length of one wall, windows divided by walls hung with paintings, and where the velvet curtains had been pulled on all but two of the windows, to keep out the harsh summer light.

As directed, she kept to the central path that divided the library in two, and made her way to the far end of the room, keeping her back straight, her chin parallel to the carpet, and with her elbows in and her hands clasped under her bosom. And because she could see the Duke seated behind an enormous desk, she concentrated on keeping her gaze straight ahead and did not look left or right, the arrangement of furniture, the shelves of books, and assorted paraphernalia a peripheral blur and of no consequence or interest.

She came right up to the desk, heart beating hard in her chest, and dropped a curtsy as the Duke rose out of his chair to meet her. She was surprised when he came round to her side of the wide desk, and invited her to join him by a fireplace that was to one side of a second spiral staircase, leading up to the narrow walkways and more bookshelves. Here there was a collection of comfortable wing chairs and two high-backed settees back-to-back, one facing the fireplace, the other the spiral staircase. It was on the settee facing the fireplace that the

Duke indicated Lisa sit. She did so, and found the cushion hard. She decided this must be the settee where he put his children when and if he needed to deliver them a stern lecture about their behavior. She wondered why he did not sit opposite her and if he meant to deliver her a similar stern lecture while on his feet. And then she was joined at the sofa, which startled her, for she had failed to notice there was anyone else in the library. This was the reason he remained standing.

The Duchess of Kinross had swept up to stand beside her son. Lisa instantly shot up off the settee and down into a curtsy in one motion, heart beating even harder to think she was to be interrogated not only by Henri-Antoine's brother, but also by his mother. She was sick to her stomach and so nervous she wondered if she was about to be ill.

TWENTY-SEVEN

A LITTLE WHILE EARLIER, WHILE LISA WAS BEING ESCORTED TO the library, the Duke and his mother were already ensconced, grim-faced and concerned.

"If this is to be done properly, then you must do as I ask," the Duke stated, watching his mother pace before him.

Antonia threw up a hand and kept pacing. Roxton was tired and after the previous day, with the wedding celebration and then the ball, he had hoped to enjoy a morning of doing nothing more than sharing it with his wife. And now this... Watching his mother walk back and forth in front of his desk made him even more tired. Did she never weary?

"Maman—"

"Yes. Yes. Naturally we will do it the way you say, Julian. It is just —It is just—"

"—unpleasant. For everyone. But we must think of Harry—"

"He is all I am thinking about." She met her son's gaze. "Be gentle with her. She is young. And this—" She swept an arm in a wide arc. "—all of this it is overwhelming to our friends, so imagine how it must be to a girl from her background. Incomprehensible, yes?"

"I will strive to be as gentle as I can, given the circumstances."

Antonia was unconvinced. "That is what worries me, Julian. The circumstances."

Roxton resisted the urge to roll his eyes. He lifted his buttocks off the edge of his massive desk and stood straight.

"And what worries me, Maman, is that you will attempt to soften the blow. That will not work in this instance. Miss Crisp is not a stray kitten in need of a bowl of cream. She has—by all accounts—a brain, and I will call upon her to use it so that she understands the gravity of her situation. She must. For all our sakes."

Antonia wrung her hands, but when she nodded, Roxton sighed his relief.

"So you must resist interfering—"

"Interfering—?"

"—for Harry's sake. I know you. You are too kind, too emotional. You want everyone to be happy—"

"And there is something wrong with that?"

"Not in the least. I love you for it. But there are times when kindness won't work. Please, leave this to me."

"I do not know how it is you can be so-so—*indifferent*."

Roxton gave a bark of laughter and shook his head.

"And this from a woman who was married to the most inscrutable nobleman of his age!"

Antonia pouted. "But your father he was never like that with me."

"No. He was not. But just like him, it falls upon me as duke to put the planets of our world back into alignment. So. You will play your part and say not a word?"

Antonia nodded again. "I will. For Henri-Antoine. It will be difficult, but me I will do it."

"Good. That is all I ask. Then we are all agreed." Roxton looked over her head towards the fireplace. "I only hope you will thank me in the end…"

"PLEASE SIT, MISS CRISP," THE DUKE STATED. HE WAITED FOR his mother to take her place on the sofa, then flicked out the skirts of his frock coat and sat beside her. His gaze remained on Lisa. "Now that the wedding is over, and so, too, the ball, I wonder at your plans?"

"My plans, Your Grace?"

"I suspect you must be eager to return to Gerrard Street and your duties there. I do not doubt Dr. Warner has missed your assistance. And his patients requiring the services of a scribe must be lining the footpath waiting for your return."

Lisa moved a little on the settee, but kept her back very straight. She glanced at the Duchess, then looked to the Duke in some surprise.

"You know about-about my duties at the dispensary?"

"I do." The Duke smiled. It was not pleasant. "I know everything there is to know about you, Miss Crisp."

Lisa cocked her head in curiosity. "Then… surely… Your Grace does not need to ask about my plans?"

Antonia's fan shot up to her mouth to cover a smile, and she cleared her throat to stop a laugh and quickly lowered her lashes. Roxton ignored her and did his best to ignore Lisa's question, though he did not think her being impudent.

"Indulge me, Miss Crisp."

"Very well, Your Grace," she replied calmly, though her fingers tightened in her lap; her only sign of nervousness. "Upon my arrival here, I had every intention of returning to Gerrard Street to resume my duties but-but my—*circumstances* changed—

"—and so you no longer wish to assist the sick poor or continue writing letters for the poor…?"

"I do, but I hope to help many more than just those who attend Warner's Dispensary by assisting in the work of the Fournier Foundation—"

"—from Bath. To be precise, a manor house on the outskirts of town?"

"Y-yes, Your Grace."

"My brother's house to be precise."

"Yes, Your Grace."

"Where you intend to live and assist in the work of the Fournier Foundation? And how precisely will you do that from Bath?"

"I-I do not know exactly, Your Grace. The-the particulars have yet to be worked through with His Lordship—"

"My brother, with whom you intend to share this manor house on the outskirts of Bath?"

Lisa dared not look at Antonia, but she bravely met the Duke's gaze.

"Yes, Your Grace."

"And you fully intend to live in sin with him."

"Your Grace, I-I… It may look to you as-as—"

The Duke sat forward. "I understand perfectly, Miss Crisp. I am a man of the world. And in the lofty circles in which I live, it is commonplace. You've been made an offer of a far better life, and so you have made the hard-headed decision to change your vocation from dispensary assistant to prostitute."

Lisa could not have been more shocked had he struck her across the face. Her cheeks drained of color and then glowed pink.

"A-a *prostitute*? No! No! No, Your Grace. That is not how—"

"And why not?" the Duke continued smoothly, as if she had not spoken. "You're very pretty. Why would a taking little thing of beauty want to toil away helping the poor, the diseased, and the dying? That must be the fastest route to losing your looks. God knows what diseases you could catch from such a hell hole! And how could you ever hope to escape such a place if not through the—um—patronage of a wealthy gentleman? What luck for you you happened upon my brother—"

"It wasn't like that. I am not like that."

"—whom I hear you tended with your own fine hands. He was grateful for your assistance, and of course when he saw you again, he could not help but notice your beauty. He is a mere male after all. Is that when you formulated your plan to ensnare him? Knowing you would be attending the same wedding? You must have thought all your Christmases had come to you at once."

"Excuse me, Your Grace, but I did no such thing as-as *ensnare* His Lordship. For the longest time I did not even know who he was. I only knew that—that it was—that it was *fate* that had brought us together—"

"Fate?" The Duke scoffed. "Come now, Miss Crisp! That is the stuff of fairy tales."

"Pardon, Your Grace, but Treat is the stuff of fairy tales for someone like me, and yet here I am."

The Duke's features hardened. "Yes. Here you are. How old are you, Miss Crisp?"

Lisa took a deep breath and was inclined to tell him that he knew the answer to that question, as he did all the other questions. But she suspected these questions, indeed this entire interview, was designed to humiliate her into thinking twice about being Henri-Antoine's mistress and make her return to Gerrard Street. What the Duchess thought of this, and her, she could only speculate. But she did not want to do that, because it would only make her sadder than she already felt. Best to answer the questions, and hopefully she would then be able to flee the library as soon as possible.

"I am nineteen years old, Your Grace."

"Nineteen?" The Duke looked genuinely surprised, and then he pulled a face and dared to look her over as if she were a prize filly with an eye to purchase. "Nineteen... Then I'd say you've a few years to enjoy that fine house on the outskirts of Bath. But I wouldn't become complacent. If you want my advice, I'd trot off to town upon occasion, best when my brother is here or in London, so you can scout for potential suitors to replace him when—"

"Replace him? I have no intention of—"

"Your intentions are irrelevant, Miss Crisp. All I care about is my brother. He will tire of you, and he will move on to something younger and fresher, so you had best have your wits about you, and a new lover waiting for you in the wings. For I will not countenance him spending one penny more on you than is necessary." He smiled briefly. "I dare say, a pretty girl like you, who has had a smattering of education, will have no trouble in attracting a new lover—"

Lisa shot to her feet, furious. It was the phrase *smattering of education* that burst the dam of her tolerance and circumspection. She could not defend the indefensible. The Duke could call her prostitute if he so wished, under the circumstances. She was sharing Henri-Antoine's bed and she had agreed to be his mistress. But she was proud of her education, and there had been nothing shoddy in her schooling. Besides, she would not have Blacklands maligned before the one person who had been instrumental in her gaining a good education.

"With respect, Your Grace, I did not have a-a *smattering of education*. I had an excellent education," Lisa stated confidently. "Blacklands was—*is*—a superior educational institution for young ladies, and I took full advantage of what was on offer." She dared to address Antonia. "Please believe me, Mme la Duchesse. I am forever grateful to you. I only wish—I only wish—matters had turned out differently—"

"Sit, Miss Crisp," the Duke demanded wearily. "It is rather late in the day for you to wish for an outcome that will not disappoint my mother, particularly when you have every intention of further wasting your education by becoming a nobleman's whore, regardless it is her son you are bedding—"

"I am not a-a whore," Lisa stated. "I am His Lordship's mistress, and there is a difference."

She resumed her seat on the settee, and returned her hands to her lap. But she could not bring herself to look at the Duke, and she dared not even glance at the Duchess. When the silence stretched she kept her chin tucked in, gaze on the flimsy apron covering her floral petticoats. Finally the Duke spoke, and she detected a note of regret which sent her to the brink of tears.

"And yet, Miss Crisp, you were offered so much more…"

This did bring Lisa's gaze back up to look at the Duke. She knew he was alluding to Henri-Antoine's marriage proposal, and she was surprised he knew about it so soon afterwards. Perhaps it was the Duke with whom Henri-Antoine had gone out riding earlier that morning, and no doubt confided in his brother. Knowing this did bring the tears spilling onto her cheeks. But she was quick to dash them away. Perhaps she had detected regret in his voice, because looking into his eyes she saw it. Or was it wishful thinking on her part that he considered her acceptable as a wife for his brother? That indeed would have surprised her. No doubt it was because the Duke had his mother's eyes, and thus this gave a false sense of the compassion in him which was writ large in hers. She decided to pretend ignorance of his meaning.

"I beg your pardon, Your Grace?"

"You have refused my brother's offer of marriage."

"I have, Your Grace."

"May I—we—know why that is?"

"The offer was made under duress…"

"Duress? You mean he would not have asked you had you not forced his hand?"

"No, Your Grace. I did nothing of the sort. He should not have asked me, that is all."

"And yet, he did… Why do you think that is?"

Lisa shrugged, eyes on the flimsy apron. She plucked at a thread. She swallowed and looked up. "Because he-he is a gentleman. Because he is good and kind and loving and all that is honorable."

"I do not disagree with you. But that does not answer my question as to why you refused him."

Lisa looked from the Duke to the Duchess and back again, and smiled sadly. "Surely you know the answer, as you've known the answers to all the questions you have put to me."

"Ah, but the answer to this question I am not entirely convinced. I must hear you say it."

Lisa stared at him through a film of tears. "Because I love Henri-Antoine—too well—to marry him."

"I see… You refused his offer of marriage for his sake?"

Lisa nodded. She could not speak.

"But—if marriage to you is what he wants…?"

"It is not what he wants!" she said in a rush and sniffed. "He wants for us to live in his house in the country, where we will be husband and wife in all but name. And I am willing to do this because I love him, and it would suit us both, And when we come up to London, I will stay with him at his house. And it is from his house in London where I can be of assistance to him with the Fournier Foundation. I will visit dispensaries under cover of the foundation, and no one need know who I am, or my connection to His Lordship. Foundation trustees are anonymous after all. Besides, who amongst the poor and the sick will care about my morals, when they have larger problems to worry them, such as their next meal, or where to obtain enough pennies for their medications? And the physicians most certainly won't concern them-selves with His Lordship's carnal arrangements—they certainly haven't up to now—I do beg your pardon," she added stiffly when there was a sudden snort of laughter. "I am sincere, Your Grace."

"No one would accuse you of anything less, Miss Crisp."

"I assure you that aside from the work of the Fournier Foundation, I will not be seen in public with him. I will be very discreet and I will do everything I can not to be an embarrassment to him, or to you, or to your family. But I will live with him, support him, love him, and be his wife in every respect."

Finally, Antonia could no longer remain silent. It was her turn to sit forward. Her voice was soft and very gentle.

"You could do all those things and more, *ma petite*, and not ruin yourself, by simply marrying my son."

"Mme la Duchesse, marriage has-has—expectations."

"Surely those expectations can only be to your benefit, Miss Crisp?" said the Duke. "And if you are concerned lest he take a mistress in the future, I can assure you that in my family the males are rather prone to uxoriousness. Once they find a mate, it is for life."

"Oh, I believe you, Your Grace. And I am confident of his fidelity."

"You are?"

"Yes. Because—" She smiled and blushed. "I do believe that he loves me as much as I love him. And I do not say that with conceit or as a wishful thinker. I believe it, with all my heart."

The Duke stared at her with surprise, and then he surprised himself by smiling.

"And I believe you, Miss Crisp. Thus, here is my dilemma. If you love him, and he loves you, and you are willing to live with him as his mistress, in what is essentially a marriage, then why the fickleness?"

"Fickleness?"

"In not allowing my brother to give your union its spiritual and legal due?"

"I told you. I cannot marry him, for his sake."

"So you have said, again."

Lisa looked from mother to son and back to the Duchess, a frown between her brows.

"I thought perhaps Teddy—that Teddy may have confided in-in her mother at the very least, and that Lady Mary may have confided in you, Mme la Duchesse, and that you, Your Grace, would know the answer to this question, too… The simple truth is I cannot be a true wife to Lord Henri-Antoine."

For the first time since Lisa had sat on the settee, mother and son looked at one another, and both were nonplussed. They waited for Lisa to provide further clarification, the Duke confessing, "No one has said a word to either of us. So we must assume Teddy has kept your confidence."

"I did not ask her to do so, nor have we discussed the matter in depth. But it is something she has known about me since we were at school together. She did enquire about it when I came here, which was only natural, because it was something which is not in the common way for most females once they progress past a certain age. And I did tell Teddy nothing has changed in me since we were at school. And since my time at the dispensary, and having consulted Dr. Warner, who would never break my confidence, I do know I am not unique. There are others, but Dr. Warner tells me these women are few."

The Duke tried to make sense of this but was completely baffled.

"Which is what, Miss Crisp?"

There was no other way to say it, so Lisa just came out and said it. She had not openly discussed this quirk about herself except with Dr. Warner, and it surprised her how much it affected her to say it out loud.

"I will not bear children, Your Grace. More correctly, I cannot conceive. I am barren, and will likely remain so for the rest of my life."

The Duke was so shocked that it was as if a great weight had just fallen on his head and fuddled his brain. He stared at Lisa as if he did not believe her, and she stared back at him with resignation and sadness. He was so affected that he felt the emotion well up within him and had to look away. Lisa in turn saw that he was genuinely distressed, and she tried to reassure him, and it wasn't until she looked at the Duchess and saw that she, too, was on the verge of tears, that she faltered and had to resort to her handkerchief.

"You both must see now why I cannot marry Henri-Antoine. Your Grace, you of all men understand that such a defect disqualifies me from being his wife. Marrying your brother is out of the question. I could not do that to him—deny him fatherhood. And I was too overcome to confide in him when he asked me. But I will tell him. I promise you that."

"Are you certain?" asked the Duke. "I do not mean to pry. I just—Dear me. I do not know what to say. I am—"

"Sorry for me? Please, there is no need to be. I have come to terms with my failing, accepted it, almost welcomed it—"

"Welcomed it?"

Lisa glanced at the Duchess, who was smiling in understanding.

"Yes, Your Grace. On those particular days of the month when females have their menses and I do not—"

"Ah! I see! Yes. I understand—"

"Of course you do," Lisa interrupted to save him further embarrassment. "What husband does not? And while there were girls at school who cursed their monthly courses, I was praying for them! But what I want and wish and pray for has not happened and so I fear it may never happen."

It was the Duchess who asked the question.

"Do you not think—as you are only nineteen—that matters they may change for you one day?"

"Perhaps, Mme la Duchesse. I can live in hope. But living in hope is no way for your son to live, for any husband to live, is it? Every husband has a right to expect children of a marriage. A barren marriage is not something I would wish on anyone. Surely that way leads to heartbreak? And you are wrong, Your Grace," she stated, looking back at the Duke. "I do not believe Henri-Antoine will cast me aside without providing for me. But if the day came when he decided he did want children, then I would accept his wishes. It would break my heart to lose him, but because I love him, I will encourage him to marry and have a family. I only hope that he will at least allow me to continue my work for his foundation, for I wholeheartedly believe in his cause. It is only through advances in medicine that people's lives will eventually change for the better." She smiled, remembering the Duke of Kinross's advice that when the time came she should be herself, and so she added, "You may think my words the fanciful expectations of an idealist, but that is what I believe, how I feel, and what I am."

"Your convictions, they are not fanciful in the least, *ma petite*," the Duchess responded, getting up off the sofa, indication that as far as she was concerned, this interview was over.

The Duke stood, and so did Lisa, who smiled and blushed and bobbed a curtsy, before addressing them both.

"I do not know if I will have this opportunity to be in your company again, for I think Henri-Antoine has plans for us to travel on to Bath as soon as it can be arranged. So allow me to thank you both for having me to stay. I hope my presence did not cause you too much embarrassment or social discomfort. At least it will not happen in the future, for I shall, as I assured you earlier, be exceedingly discreet, as I am sure he will be, too."

The Duke looked over his shoulder and nodded to a footman who stood to attention halfway up the library towards the main entrance, and mother and son watched on silently as Lisa was escorted away, and with her back and shoulders as straight as when she had entered the library. They then stood there, not knowing what to say. The interview had not gone as they had expected, and yet it had gone beyond their expectations. And they were still in shock from Lisa's revelation. Both were wondering at Henri-Antoine's reaction to such news. Impatient, the Duke turned to the settee where Lisa had been seated.

"I'm sorry, Harry. I don't know what I can say that will give you any comfort."

Henri-Antoine came lightly down the spiral staircase. He kissed his mother's cheek and then embraced his brother.

"No need for an apology. And thank you both. Miss Crisp has sealed her fate, and mine."

TWENTY-EIGHT

"The view from here is enchanting," Lisa said conversationally when Henri-Antoine joined her on the bench outside the family mausoleum. "You can see all the way to France! Or that's what I'd like to think that blue haze is off in the distance."

"At least you know what you're looking at," he replied in the same conversational tone. "We've had family members think that way lies London, looking for St. Paul's, and arguing about it."

He handed the reins of his mount to one of the two lads who had arrived on horseback with him, and they moved off down the path and disappeared behind the building to join their fellows in the shade. He removed his gloves and shoved them into a pocket of his riding frock coat, all the while an eye on Lisa, who was watching him from under her wide-brimmed straw hat.

This was the first time they had seen each other since Henri-Antoine had left her to go riding earlier that morning. When Lisa had departed the library and returned to his apartment, Michel Gallet gave her the news that His Lordship wished to see her here, at the family mausoleum. A carriage had been fetched, and with two of the lads, she was driven across the stone bridge to the other side of the lake. Where the path divided, going one way towards the Gatehouse Lodge and on to Crecy Hall, the carriage went the other way, on up and around a hill that seemed to climb forever. At its apex was a Palladian mausoleum with a domed roof and a glass oculus.

The door was wide open, but Lisa waited on the bench in the

shade and admired the scenery. And here Henri-Antoine found her fifteen minutes later.

He sat beside her and looked out at a view he had seen so many times since he was a small boy he was certain he could draw a map of it from memory. But as this was the first time he had looked out on this landscape in Lisa's company, he gave the moment its due.

They silently held hands, both wanting to speak about the night before, acutely aware that much still needed to be said, and soon. Yet, they continued to enjoy the summer's day, with its blue sky and haze of heat blanketing the landscape, and to admire the sweep of countryside, with the big house dominating the foreground, and further afield, forests and a meandering river, and the gently undulating patchwork of farming lands. It was such a delight to be still and say and do nothing, fingers entwined. And they were happy in each other's company, despite the undercurrent of unease and uncertainty that still swirled about them.

"Shall I tell you about two of the happiest days of my life, and a third, which I hope will be today?" he said at last.

She nodded and smiled, but instead of saying yes, asked, "Why today?"

"Trust you to choose the more difficult alternative! No. Not that one first."

"Then tell me about the other two days."

He shifted to face her.

"The first happy day was the day my nephew Frederick—Freddy—was born. I was nine years old. It was the happiest day because it meant I was no longer my brother's heir. That if my father died, and so, too, did my brother, it would not be I who would be duke, it would be Freddy. I cannot describe to you my relief."

"Because you felt unworthy of the title? You were, after all, only a little boy."

"There was that, of course. My father was in his middle years when Julian was born, and an old man when I finally arrived. There was a real fear he might not live to see my brother have children, and thus not know if his dukedom would live on after him. And there was I, the second son: Always sickly, always coddled, a constant worry to my parents, and second in line to inherit a dukedom... Then Freddy came along, which was a huge relief to everyone, particularly my father."

"And the second happy day?"

Henri-Antoine grinned. "That day was when Deb presented Julian with twin sons, two years after Freddy's entrance into the world. So with the heir to the dukedom producing three sons in two years, its future was secured beyond doubt, and this second son was set free from all obligation—"

"But you would never have shirked your responsibilities and the obligation had it come your way."

"Thank you. I would not. But with three nephews, I was now free to live my life how I pleased to purpose it, not how others deemed I must, as my brother must. And having slid to the fourth notch on the branch of the family tree, I was able to breathe easier. I cannot prove, but I am certain that the births of my three nephews helped decrease the frequency, if not the severity, of my seizures."

"And the third happy day? Today, did you say...?"

"Ah, that depends on you," he replied as he untied the silk bow holding on her hat. He carefully laid the hat on the seat, stood and held out his hand. "You won't need it inside. I want to show you something—No! First, must come introductions."

They walked hand in hand across to the mausoleum. The iron gates were unlocked and one of the heavy, brass-inlaid double doors was open in invitation. The vestibule was lit by two burning tapers in elaborate sconces, and fresh flowers spilled from urns either side of the entrance. There was a chair in the corner and beside it a mahogany box filled with candles.

Once inside the cavernous space of the main room, Lisa let go of Henri-Antoine's hand and walked on ahead, fascinated, eager to look about. Not only was the Italian marble floor and much of the interior surprisingly well-lit from above by the summer sun streaming through the enormous glass oculus, but so too were the painted walls and marble monuments to long-dead ancestors. Tapers in sconces at intervals around the room had been lit by the caretaker in preparation for His Lordship's visit. That old gent came out of the shadows, bowed and quietly returned to his chair in the vestibule, where he would remain until needed, or until it was time to snuff the candles at sundown, when the doors would be locked and the padlock clamped to the iron gates.

"The mausoleum is opened up each morning while my mother is in residence at Crecy Hall," Henri-Antoine told her. "She visits my father once a week. And there are times during the year when it is open to celebrate anniversaries, and of course on those days when it receives a new resident."

"It is a beautiful place... And welcoming..."

"I thought you would think so. I do. I've been coming here since my teens. At first it was not a happy place, for obvious reasons. But my mother finds great comfort in spending time with my father, who was taken away from her much too early in her life. She brings flowers, and Kinross often accompanies her. And when I'm in residence I will often stop in on one of my rides, to see my father, and now that Martin— now Martin has joined my father, I-I come to-to see him, too…"

"Are all the dukes of Roxton in residence?" Lisa asked conversationally, hearing the break in Henri-Antoine's voice at the mention of Martin, and so she hoped her question would help him make a recover.

She had wandered over to stand directly under the glass oculus, to bathe in the light, and then moved off to study the walls painted with classical figures in white robes and wreaths, and carrying musical instruments and dancing in a never-ending procession that remained unbroken around the interior. The procession weaved in and out of the alcoves set into the walls, each alcove flanked by a burning taper. A few of the alcoves were vacant, awaiting occupation, while others contained a marble statue of its resident, some of a man and a woman, reclining on polished granite platforms carved with names and dates, and under which was the stone casket that held the coffin containing the mortal remains of the ancestor immortalized in stone.

"They are all here," Henri-Antoine said at last, watching Lisa and through her eyes, enjoying this first visit to the last resting place of his ancestors. "Except my grandfather, my father's father. He died before he could become duke, and as he lived in France for most of his life and married a Frenchwoman, is buried along with her in Paris."

"Madeleine Julie Salvan Hesham, the Marchioness of Alston, and whose ring you-you wanted me to have?"

"Yes. And all the duchesses are here," he continued. "And when her time comes my mother will be laid to rest here, too, beside my father. And like him, she will have a seat in the mausoleum—"

"Seat?"

"Come. I'll show you."

"What about the Duke of Kinross?" Lisa asked, staying put. She did not like the idea of Elsie's papa being left out of the family group.

Henri-Antoine came over to her, and smiled down at her frown. He understood at once.

"My father is the love of my mother's life, but in this life, the one she has now without him, Kinross is the love of her life. Fate has favored her with two great loves."

"She deserves nothing less."

"Yes. I think so too."

"And will he—will His Grace of Kinross have a place here with her?"

He heard her hesitancy, and his smile widened into a grin.

"What a romantic you are, Lisa Crisp!"

She pouted. "I am not ashamed to agree with you."

He flicked her cheek. "And I am not ashamed to say that I am glad you are."

She smiled. "So. Tell me. Will he have a place here with your mother?"

"He will. But not all of him."

Lisa gave a start, intrigued, as he knew she would be, by his cryptic reply. She leaned in and whispered. "Not all of him? Oh! Which parts? And what is happening to the rest of him?"

Henri-Antoine laughed out loud and shook his head. His laugh echoed and he put a hand to his mouth. "Dear me! Now look at what you have made me do!"

She pouted again, but could not hold back her smile. "You have no one to blame but yourself for that outburst. You baited me with that reply. Do not deny it! You knew I would ask just such a question. Surely you did not expect me to pretend to be revolted, or squeamish?"

"I am guilty as charged. And my father would be most impressed. Come. I want you to meet him—Ah! But first, Kinross… His heart will be interred here, with my mother. The rest of his earthly remains must be buried on Leven Island, which is in the middle of a loch in Scotland, and is the last resting place of the chiefs of his clan, and the dukes of Kinross."

"How romantic," Lisa said on a sigh, satisfied with this outcome.

"I knew you would think so. Others recoil as soon as they hear the bit about the heart—"

"Why should they? It's not as if he's having it cut out while he is still alive! It is a wonderfully romantic gesture, and I understand why he would leave that part of himself here with your mother. I'm sure your father does not mind in the least, and approves, because His Grace of Kinross loves her just as deeply as he does."

"I'm sure he does, too. Come."

He took her hand and they walked across and sat on a marble bench set back from the wall and directly in front of one monument in particular. Vases of white roses had been placed on the floor and on the monument's lower heavy plinth of red marble, a row of candles burned brightly.

Staring out at the world in white marble was a life-size statue of a nobleman seated on a high-backed chair. He was dressed in frock coat and breeches, had across his chest a ribbon, the Star and Garter, and across his shoulders was draped a ducal robe on which he sat and which pooled at his buckled shoes.

Lisa knew immediately this nobleman's identity, and had no doubts the sculpture was to the life. Henri-Antoine was in this nobleman's image, from high forehead to cheekbones, to strong nose and square chin. The resemblance was uncanny. If there was a point of difference it was in the nobleman's mouth. The Duke possessed a thin-lipped sneer, whereas Henri-Antoine had that oh-so-kissable mouth. She kissed him now, and said with a cheeky smile,

"Your father is an exceedingly handsome man."

Henri-Antoine grabbed her hand and kissed her fingers, too overcome with emotion to speak. She wondered if she had offended him, and thought her bad-mannered for kissing him in front of his father's tomb, which was not giving the fifth duke or the occasion the proper veneration. After all, this was her first visit to a mausoleum, and this was the last resting place of an ancient noble family, and he the son of this duke who stared out at the world as if he owned it.

"Forgive me. I meant no disrespect. I was just so happy to finally meet him, and to see that you are indeed in his image. I've not yet seen the portraits in the Gallery. Teddy says there is one in particular of your parents, not long after they were married. She says the Duke is so like you, or should I say, you are so like him, that the hairs rise on her arms every time she looks at it... I do not doubt he would've been pleased at the resemblance, but he would have been prouder of how you conduct your life and what you have set out to achieve."

"There is no need to apologise," he muttered, still holding her hand. "He would have enjoyed meeting you very much..." He rallied and said in a clearer voice. "That his portrait sets the hairs up on the arms of young ladies he would've found amusing in the extreme. I do." He smiled then surprised Lisa by turning to address his father's effigy, and in French. "*Mon père*, this is Lisa, the girl you told me about in your letter. Is she not just as you described her to me? And more beautiful and more clever than even you could have foreseen..."

Lisa stared up at the fifth duke in awe. Finally she found her voice.

"He told you about-about *me*—in a letter? But—but he has never met me! You were only a boy when he died. He could not have foreseen my existence. So how is it possible?"

"He did not need to meet you. In his letter he described the girl I would marry, and that girl is you."

"Perhaps—perhaps he told you about the girl who loves you and with whom you would share a house in the country. Is that not the same thing?"

"No. He left me a letter to be opened in the event I was contemplating marrying for love. Had I made a dynastic match, one not based on my feelings, then the letter would have remained unopened, and thus unread."

"And you read his letter yesterday before you had M'sieur Gallet put those little notes in my writing box?"

"I did."

"And inside this letter was your grandmother's ring."

"Her wedding band. Yes."

"But if you had never opened the letter, her wedding band would have been lost forever!"

"Not forever. No doubt a descendant would have eventually opened the letter and found the ring. But lost to me, yes."

"He-he must have been confident you would marry for love."

Henri-Antoine again kissed the back of her hand, and smiled. "So now you know. I not only resemble him in looks, but in temperament. He married for love, and for no other reason. And that is the only reason for me to marry. What about you?"

"Me? I-I never thought I would marry… I dreamed about it. What girl doesn't? And of course I dreamed of marrying for love. But I also dreamed of marrying a man who would—who would love me for me, for myself, and-and that is the stuff of dreams, isn't it?"

Henri-Antoine kept his features perfectly composed, though his top lip gave a twitch, when he asked, "Then, surely, last night, all your dreams came true…?"

Lisa nodded, so forlorn she failed to see that twitch, her eyes downcast and shoulders slumped. She sniffed. "I-I never expected they would. I-I was caught off-guard. I was so dull I did not even suspect that ring was a wedding band." She looked up at him through her lashes. "I-I still want to live with you in your house in the country, even if it is in sin, and without a wedding band."

"But I do not want to live with you in sin. I cannot."

"No?" Lisa repeated in a small voice. "Why not? I thought—I thought we had an agreement…" She glanced up at the fifth duke. "Is it because of the letter your father wrote? Would he not approve?"

"No. It is because I love you. There. I have said it again, and I can keep on saying it until you are convinced. And because I love you, I want to marry you, and I have brought you here, before my father, to convince you of my sincerity."

Lisa smiled into his eyes. "I love you, too."

"Yes, you do. And so you have told me, and with sincerity from the first. I am the dull one. It took me a little longer to realize I had—as Jack calls it—fallen off the cliff into love with you."

Lisa looked at their fingers entwined, and then up at him. "If we love one another then surely we can live together in sin—"

"—until such time as I decide to marry someone else…?"

She sat up, hopeful. "Yes. That may never happen, and I hope it won't, but if I were your mistress, you would still be free to marry, and—"

"Don't be an infant, Lisa!" he demanded harshly. "I love you. I want to marry you. I offer you my grandmother's wedding band, and you throw it all back in my face with the notion that one day I will leave you and marry someone else? What type of man—nay, monster —do you think I am? Do you honestly believe me capable of such a despicable act? If you do, then you do not love me at all!"

"I-I do believe you! I know you would never leave me! You are not a monster. It is me! I'm the monster because-because I cannot give you what you have a right to expect as a husband, and for that alone you cannot marry me."

"If you tell me you cannot marry me because you do not love me, then I accept that. But if you are about to tell me you cannot marry me because you believe yourself to be barren, that is not a reason I accept. That makes no difference to me. I love you. I want to marry you—as you are."

Lisa sat up, big blue eyes blinking away tears, and stared at him, shocked. "You-you—*know*?"

"I do now. Such an impediment may have swayed another man, but I am not like other men. And while I am sad for you, I am not greatly troubled that our marriage will remain childless. I believe fate has other plans for us." He smiled. "I have a much grander vision, and with you at my side to help me, I hope to achieve great things, not for a handful of children, but for thousands of children, and their children's children. That by harnessing the power of science we can advance medicine, and in so doing we will improve the health of this country's most vulnerable subjects." He shrugged. "And there is the small detail that if you do not marry me I will not allow you to help me—"

"You are threatening me?"

He put up his chin. "I am. It is the only recourse I have left."

She glanced at the fifth duke's monument and smiled crookedly. "It must be. *He* doesn't scare me."

Henri-Antoine's mouth dropped open, and then he laughed heartily. "*Mon Dieu.* You are the girl for me!"

She giggled, then said seriously, "And your family, what will they think—"

"My mother and brother are at this minute waiting for us to join them for nuncheon so my brother can make a formal announcement to the family."

"*Announcement?* Your brother and-and your *mother?*"

"You've met my brother. How eager do you think he is for us to marry, when the alternative is us living in sin? And when I left them, my mother was having him draft a letter to Moore—he's the Archbishop of Canterbury—requesting a special license. All going well, we'll be married before the week is out."

"Before the end of the week?" Lisa was heady and happy and all at sea at one and the same time. She hardly knew what to say. So when Henri-Antoine dug in a pocket and held up his grandmother's ring she marveled at him. "You brought it with you."

"I did. And now I would like to slip *grandmère's* ring on your finger here, before my august parent, to seal our commitment. We can then toast our engagement with the family, and of course Teddy and Jack, who are also awaiting our news."

Lisa put out her hand, and he slipped the diamond and sapphire band on her finger, then kissed it. She then held up her hand and turned it this way and that, admiring the ring which fit her finger remarkably well.

"Does everyone know we are here, and am I the only one who is surprised by this?"

He leaned in and kissed her. "For someone who is exceedingly clever, and who is perceptive about the needs of others, you have been rather dull-witted about your own, my darling."

"What I need, my lord," she breathed, kissing him again, "is for you to kiss me properly to seal our bargain—and then I will truly believe this is happening to me."

A little while later, when they came up for air, he stood, and helped her to do likewise. He went forward and briefly placed his hand across the bridge of his father's shoe, before stepping back and making him a quaint little bow. He then turned to Lisa with a smile and put out his hand.

"I have one last detail to show you before we return to the house."

They walked not half-a-dozen steps toward the double doors, when he stopped and turned to face an alcove, his back to the light streaming through the oculus. Lisa wondered why this particular alcove because it was empty of monuments and tombs to ancient ancestors.

"Do you remember, at the folly, telling me about guide books—"

"—to grand estates? The ones visitors and travelers use to know something about the families and homes of the nobility? Of course."

"And how you said that if we decided to remain in bed forever we would eventually become skeletons and be written up in a guide book as some sort of curiosity?"

Lisa giggled. "Oh dear. Did I?"

"You did. And you said such a discovery would be worthy of an entry in any guidebook."

"It would."

He indicated the alcove. "This is much better."

Lisa stared at the painted wall and the space, a niche large enough for a sizeable monument, two at a pinch, and she peered at Henri-Antoine with an inkling of an idea, but she could hardly believe it so let him explain further.

"Had you refused me, this was my final ploy—my wonderfully romantic gesture, one you at least would appreciate—to convince you of my sincerity in wanting to marry you. This will be my final resting place. When that time comes, hopefully far, far into the future, I will join the rest of my family here. And when your time comes," he added, drawing her closer and putting an arm around her waist and then kissing her temple, "you will join me. And Lord and Lady Henri-Antoine Hesham, those great medical philanthropists, will be written up in guidebooks, and not only will family come to pay their respects, but hopefully we will have done enough good work in our lifetimes that we'll have the odd visit from a grateful physician or two. In any case, we will be here together, our monument an earthly symbol to our eternal love for one another."

Lisa looked up at him through a film of tears and when he turned to her, she put her arms up around his neck. She was so happy. "That is indeed a wonderfully romantic gesture, and I love you even more, if that is possible. I always thought fairy tales were just that, tales, but you have made my fairy tale come true."

"But of course," he drawled, and winked. "My mother is, after all, a renowned fairy godmother. Come. I cannot wait to introduce my future wife to the family…"

EPILOGUE

THE SMART TOWN CARRIAGE WITH ITS FOUR OUTRIDERS PULLED up in front of Warner's Dispensary and immediately attracted a crowd. Those walking the footpaths stopped to stare. Patients entering the dispensary alerted those inside to the arrival, and soon the ill and the not-so-ill were spilling out onto the street to discover just who was inside such an expensive town chariot. A liveried footman hopped down from his box at the rear of the carriage and after pulling down the steps, opened wide the door. Two of the four outriders dismounted, and such was their height and width that the crowd stepped back without a word and just a look.

A gentleman dressed all in black stepped down from the carriage. He went not to the entrance used by the sick poor, but to the one for the exclusive use of private patients. He did not need to knock. The door was open, and standing on the threshold was the Warners' butler, waiting to welcome the distinguished visitors on behalf of his master.

Inside the consulting room a group of persons had assembled to hear what they knew to be good news. Still, regardless of the funding the dispensary was to receive from the Fournier Foundation, everyone was nervous, and none more so than the dear doctor, who paced back and forth with his hands behind his back. Three of the doctor's assistants loitered in the corridor which connected the consulting room to the dispensary, hoping to catch a glimpse of the visitors, while in the room waiting to welcome them, along with Dr. Warner, were his two consultant physicians, the anatomy instructor, Mrs. Warner, and her sister Mrs. Cobban.

Less than two months had gone by since the dispensary had been visited by the trustees of the Fournier Foundation. And upon that occasion Dr. Warner was warned not to expect any word on the progress of his application until late autumn at the earliest. Yet, here it was the first days of August, and a letter had arrived with news that his application had been successful. Not only that, but the foundation's patrons, normally reticent to divulge their identities, were eager to visit his dispensary at their earliest convenience, due to their imminent departure abroad; the noble couple were setting off on their bridal trip.

Dr. Warner, Minette Warner, her sister Henriette Cobban, the entire de Crespigny family, the dispensary workers, and its regular patients, all knew why Miss Lisa Crisp had not returned from attending her best friend's wedding in the country. She had written to the good doctor and his wife, and also sent a letter to her Aunt de Crespigny, with the news that she and Lord Henri-Antoine Hesham had married by special licence in the Roxton Family Chapel at Treat. It was the most astounding piece of gossip about the nobility any of them had heard since His Lordship's widowed mother had up and married a man ten years her junior, and that was a decade ago. And now this! Who would have thought it possible. Certainly not the de Crespigny sisters. And while they had to grudgingly accept their cousin's turn of fortune, they had done their best to ignore it as if it had not happened. But a visit from the noble couple they could not ignore, and Lord Henri-Antoine was determined that they would pay their respects to his wife.

Michel Gallet returned to the carriage with the news everything was in readiness. And with the lads keeping the crowd back, Lord Henri-Antoine alighted from the carriage, diamond-headed walking stick in hand. He then turned and helped his wife to firm ground. But no sooner had he wrapped her arm around his to make the short walk to the consulting room, than the crowd surged forward to take a better look at the couple. They were particularly interested in the beautiful young lady in her redingote robe of gray, red, and yellow striped satin; a string of pearls about her white throat; and set at a rakish angle over her upswept curls, a black felt hat decorated with plumes and satin ribbons that matched her gown. More than a few could not believe their eyes, but it was true, and they recognized in this fashionable lady their amanuensis from her previous life. A cheer went up in greeting. And then another.

The noble couple paused. Her Ladyship stayed her husband while she thanked the residents of Gerrard Street and the patients to Warner's Dispensary for their good wishes. She smiled at the eager grubby faces of the wide-eyed children and the grinning adults, all happy to wish the couple many years of wedded bliss. A final cheer went up as Henri-Antoine and Lisa disappeared inside the building, the lads at their back staying vigil on the steps.

Inside, Dr. Warner greeted his esteemed guests with a bow and smiles, genuinely happy for the couple but most particularly for Lisa, whom he bashfully complimented as quite the most lovely bride he had ever seen. His Lordship's stare swept the room, and he noted with satisfaction the due acknowledgement of the de Crespigny sisters, Mrs. Warner and Mrs. Cobban, as they lowered themselves into an appropriate curtsy in recognition of their cousin's elevated status as wife of the second son of a duke, and sister-in-law of the Duke of Roxton.

Henri-Antoine smiled, unable to hide his pride, when he announced to one and all, "Allow me to introduce my wife, the Lady Henri-Antoine Hesham, patroness of the Fournier Foundation…"